"WOODWORKING LESSONS"

Marilyn Hayes
Phillips

Marilyn Hayes Phillips

Woodworking
Lessons

Book Three
Peace Ridge Village Series

XULON PRESS

Xulon Press
2301 Lucien Way #415
Maitland, FL 32751
407.339.4217
www.xulonpress.com

The characters in this novel are purely imaginary. Their names and experiences have no relation to those of actual people except by coincidence.

Unless otherwise indicated, scripture quotations are taken from The New International Version (NIV). Copyright © 1973, 1978, 1984, 2011 by Biblica, Inc.™. Used by permission. All rights reserved.

Scripture quotations taken from the King James Version (KJV)–*public domain.*

Printed in the United States of America.

Hamlet "To Be or Not to Be" speech in Chapter 46 is from Shakespeare's play, "Hamlet", Act 111, Scene 1.

ISBN-13: 978-1-54566-611-1

By the same author:

Shattered Peace, Book One in Peace Ridge Village series
Jason's Gift, Book Two in Peace Ridge Village series
A Wild Olive Shoot, personal spiritual memoir
How About A Little Lunch? family history and cookbook

For John B. "Jack" Hayes

Woodworker Extraordinaire

1956-2019

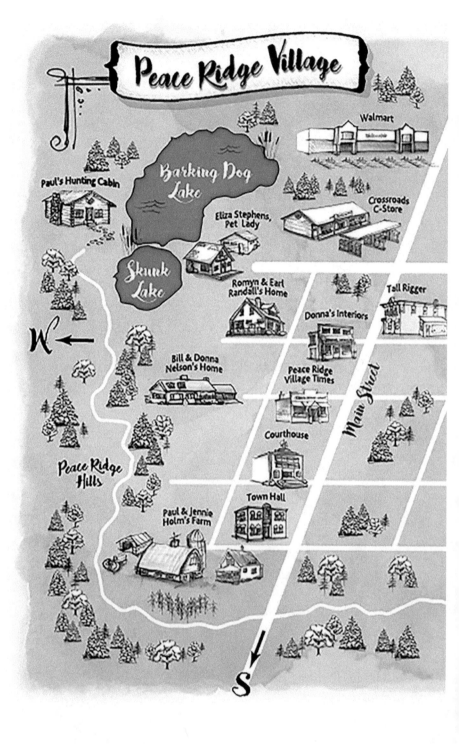

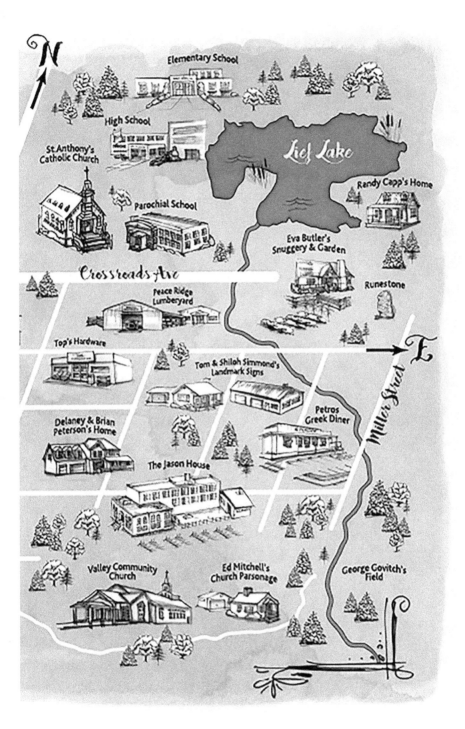

The Good Neighbors of Peace Ridge Village

- Lisa Shapiro, from North Carolina and an occasional visitor to Peace Ridge Village with her kids, Clay, eleven years old, and Sophie, seven years old
- Shiloh Simmonds, ten-year-old neighborhood girl and daughter of Tom Simmonds, artist and sign painter
- Brian Peterson, eight-year-old neighborhood boy, his mother, Delaney Peterson, and his father, Michael Langster
- Romyn and Earl Randall, owners of the Crossroads Convenience store who are building a new assisted living center in Peace Ridge Village called The Jason House
- Randy Capps, handicapped man who lives nearby on Lief Lake
- George Govitch, long-time town resident and "town crier"
- Paul and Jennie Holm, dairy farmers who live south of town with their dog, Thunder
- Eliza Stephens, old English woman who rescues dogs and cats and lives in a ramshackle Victorian home with her dog, Bartholomew
- Bill Nelson, owner of Brady Construction, and his wife, Donna, owner of Donna's Interiors
- Kellie Nelson, Bill and Donna's daughter, estranged from Bill
- Pam Winthrop, manager of the Westin Hotel, Edina, Minnesota, and her son, Bradley, and daughter, Tory

- Ed Mitchell, Pastor of Valley Community Church, and his wife, Jill, and their son, Robby
- Titos and Maria Papadopoulos, new residents in Peace Ridge Village, who are opening the Petros Greek Diner in Peace Ridge Village
- Jeremy and Tafani Hardin, George's nephew and his Afghani wife
- Veronica Marshall, resident on the Ridge, and her father, Archie Meadows
- Steve Banfeld, private investigator and friend of Archie Meadows and Earl and Romyn Randall

A Walk Around
Peace Ridge Village

The late spring sunlight was fading into peaceful dusk in Peace Ridge Village. It was the time in a weekday night when Ben at Tops Hardware was serving his last customer of the day and getting ready to snap off the lights and turn on the security system. When the folks at the Morrison County courthouse were filing their last license plates renewals and tax papers and shutting down their computers, thinking about whether they could get in any yardwork tonight before the light faded completely. The time when the gang of four –middle-schoolers Shiloh, Clay, Sophie, and Brian— finding days of endless hours of sunshine to play and explore, would begin to sense the subliminal pull of home and supper. When dusty pick-ups slowly drove away from their job sites to make their way home, stopping at the Crossroads Convenience store to honor a last-minute request for bread and milk. With a cheerful "Good night!" and smile from the owner, Romyn, thrown in for good measure.

Peace Ridge Village in central Minnesota is a tight-knit small town where 'everybody knows your name,' as a famous television show once claimed about a bar in Boston. People know one another's business pretty good, too. Hard not to with police scanners and the "town crier," George Govitch, walking around town all day, collecting insights he shares around the table at the convenience store. Even if they know one another's business, when one person hurts, everyone hurts. When a Peace Ridge villager needs defending, the whole town comes to the rescue. When secrets are brought out into the open, most villagers look inward at their own sinful nature and are quick to forgive.

Maybe it's because of the presence in town of three churches— Father Brandon's towering St. Anthony's Catholic Church opposite the Crossroads Convenience store, the Good Shepherd ELCA Lutheran Church to the north of town, or Pastor Ed Mitchell's own Valley Community Church south of town— that reminds people of their religious heritage and the importance of God worship, not money, fame, nor success. "That's just not who we are!" someone will say.

Many in the town have generational ties, their families having settled the land long ago, around the turn of the 20th century when the railroad coming to town was the big event. Others have arrived more recently and have been welcomed seamlessly into the community, despite being from out-of-state.

Titos and Maria from upstate New York came just last year and are nearly finished with their Petros Greek Diner. "About time we have a real diner in Peace Ridge."

Tafani Hardin—the tall, exotic beauty so different from Peace Ridge Village women— married Jeremy, George's nephew, when he finished his special forces service in Afghanistan in 2015. Fitting in, while also retaining her own distinctive style.

Lisa Shapiro and her kids, Clay and Sophie, arrived from North Carolina. Lisa just showed up one day and she dazzles with her womanly beauty, bedroom eyes, and languid southern accent.

When will Lisa's lifestyle catch up with her? What she is involved in now can't be good for the kids, Clay and Sophie. "Selling her wares," someone offers darkly. "To all comers."

Even the old English lady, Eliza Stephens. She came from England so long ago that people think of her as one of their own, despite her reclusive ways, her Cockney accent, and the horde of dogs and cats she's collected. Terrible the way her pet shed burnt down last winter, but heartwarming to think of the teenagers from all three churches who came together to rescue all the cats and dogs and help rebuild the shed.

"I sure wish she wasn't so insistent on living alone. What is she? Ninety years old?"

"And Jennie keeps a close eye on her. She's adopted her as her own grandma."

"Yeah, too bad Jennie can't seem to have children of her own. They've been married – what, eight years or more? Bet their kids would be lookers – he's so handsome and she's got that Scandinavian look, blonde hair, high cheekbones..."

Yes, Jennie and Paul—they have the big farm to the south of town. She has big ambitions; he just wants to be a farmer. "Interesting how God brings people together like that."

"Though she is dedicated to him completely; she just wants to be a professional woman," someone will say.

"I don't know how she's going to keep up her pie baking business and run that herbs business, too."

"There are twenty-four hours in the day, aren't there?"

"Aren't we glad that Pastor Ed Mitchell's wife is now serving with him at Valley Community Church after her stay in some kind of hospital in Edina?" one will offer.

"Depression," another adds kindly.

"Still seems rather fragile."

"I heard that their blind son, Robby, still won't come to Peace Ridge to visit them. That has to be heart-breaking."

Will Delaney Peterson, a long-time resident of Peace Ridge, ever settle down and be happy here? "Wouldn't you think that she'd learn a lesson from her father's bankruptcy and suicide?"

"So sad, that. He was a good man and worked hard. Built that Peterson Printing business into a success."

"She needs to stop drinking her wine and begin to focus on her little boy, Brian. She should learn to be satisfied with what she has!"

"Which is a lot."

To that, another will reply, "Well, beauty and wealth aren't what you need for happiness, are they?"

"Too bad Tom Simmonds isn't good enough for her. He's a good man," someone will say, to heads nodding all around. "Steady as he goes."

Romyn and Earl – winning all that money in the Maryland state lottery – luckily wanting to invest in Peace Ridge by building The Jason House, an assisted living facility, in honor of their lost son.

"They are good people," someone offers, "even if they are from out east. She has a heart of gold."

"I still think it's very sad about Earl's accident when the tree fell on him and he lost the use of his legs. When was that? Going on ten years now, isn't it?"

"Cutting down trees can be bad news. Gotta know what you're doing. I always hire it done."

"I'll bet Romyn and Earl will have to move old Eliza Stephens into The Jason House when it's finished."

And Veronica Marshall, tied to Peace Ridge Village since the 1920s when her grandfather built his property on the ridge. Veronica, she of the suicidal depression that nearly claimed her life last winter. She was the one who brought everyone's attention to that shyster, Dane Johnson, the smooth-talking real estate guy from Minneapolis who was working a scam to steal the land of many Peace Ridgers. Just as he had stolen her property in Minneapolis. Trying to kill herself at the parsonage— good thing Pastor Ed was there to save her life.

"Now that was an obvious cry for help," someone says.

"I feel sorry for her," another replies. "Hope she's doing better now. Her father, Archie, sticks pretty close."

"Well, I just hope the lawyers are close to getting the lawsuit over and done with so everyone here can move on. That land grab business – we're not used to that kind of stuff here in Peace Ridge. We do deals on a handshake basis. A man's word is good as gold."

"The one I feel especially sorry for is Bill Nelson. With his wife in a coma now. He's trying to rebuild his construction business and someone told me she was up to some financial hanky-panky before that car ran into her at the hotel in the Cities."

"Hope he gets his business back on track. His daughter, Kellie, is no help, either. Into drugs. Always a bad end."

"Steve Banfeld, that private investigator that Archie knows…"

"Romyn and Earl know him, too. He tried to find their son, Jason, when he was lost in South America. Peru, wasn't it?"

"Steve is working on Bill Nelson's case. Tracking down the people who pulled the scam on Donna."

"He's a good guy. He'll find out all the dope. I'm sure our 'esteemed' senator, Hal Jefferson, is involved in it in some way."

"Some say he and Donna –"

"Now, don't you go spreading gossip."

The people at the table are silent for a few moments. Then finally someone says, "Well, this isn't getting the work done."

"Yeah, I s'pose. Gotta get a get on. Wanted to do a little more in the garden tonight but it can wait until morning."

Then the perennial subject which ends nearly every conversation in Peace Ridge Village. "What's the weatherman promising for tomorrow?"

1

Lisa discreetly tucked her wrapped overblouse, letting the top of her breasts peek out a little more. She gracefully waved an errant wisp of hair back behind her ear and settled back onto the bar stool. She felt like a million bucks tonight and knew she looked like it. She had dressed carefully for this new date. A new pair of gold-flecked black leggings, topped with a sheer lavender-printed overblouse over a matching orchid silk camisole were sexy without being over the top. Worth every penny of the $500 she'd spent on the outfit, and made her look deserving of every dollar a man wanted to spend on her.

She'd had her hair done in the most expensive salon in Kansas City and the bronzed blonde color suited her, making her creamy porcelain skin and warm, large brown eyes even more dramatic. She knew she turned eyes wherever she walked, and if this new man didn't show up soon, she'd find another place to market her wares. That much was certain.

For some time, she'd been aware that she'd been the subject of intense scrutiny from a businessman in the corner booth who was deeply involved in a business deal but not so involved that he couldn't appreciate beauty when he saw it. The bartender brought over another bourbon and water and nodded at the man.

"Compliments of the gentleman in the corner booth."

Lisa turned slowly to gaze languorously at him and lifted her glass in a graceful, but silent, "Thank you." *Fresh pickin's in this city. Maybe I'll stay a while here.*

She had planned to go back to Minnesota this week – and last week, too, if she was honest with herself. But somehow, she felt more comfortable here than in St. Paul. Closer to her southern roots, though she couldn't call Kansas City the South, for goodness sake! They still talked like Yankees here.

Still, St. Paul was where Clay and Sophie were. And she should go back and collect them soon. *I miss their little faces, but I have to make a living so I have to sacrifice for them. I know they are in a safe place. Better than living in the car with me, anyway. I am going to get some money ahead here in Kansas City, and then we'll move into our own apartment and be a real family again.* And how many times had she made that promise? The nagging whisper of her conscience.

"May I join you?" The man's voice was resonating and confident as if saying "No" was unthinkable.

"Of course. For a time." She smiled demurely. "I'm waiting for a friend."

"My name is Andrew."

"And I'm Lisa," she said.

"Lisa. Pretty name. Beautiful name for a beautiful woman." He looked deeply into her eyes.

"Imagine you say that to all the girls," she drawled.

"You're from the south. I can tell from the accent. Where? Let me guess? Birmingham? Savannah?"

"No, North Carolina. 'A better place to be,'" she said, quoting the state slogan. "Have you ever been to Chapel Hill?"

"Oh, a college coed," he flirted.

"Well, honey, long out of college," Lisa replied.

"I bet you were on the cheerleading team. I can just imagine you in a cheerleader's outfit." His eyes darkened and Lisa's emotional antenna quivered.

He's moving fast.

2

"No, athletics weren't my thing," she clarified, "outdoor athletics, that is." *Might as well lay it on the line. Let's see how quick on the uptake he is.* "I just took general studies."

"I bet you were a Home Economics major. All things housewifely."

Lisa had been around the block a few times and she could see where this was going.

"No, not really. I like to cook but it's not my profession."

Andrew signaled the bartender who brought over another drink for Lisa and a boilermaker for Andrew, who quickly drained the glass.

"Lisa, looks as if your date has been delayed. Are you free for dinner if he's stood you up?" He smiled intimately, "though I can't imagine anyone doing that!"

"It was a business deal we were going to discuss," she said opaquely, her meaning deadly clear to someone who could read between the lines.

"Well, my dear, I have a business proposition for you: Have dinner with me and we can talk about Chapel Hill and how you got to Kansas City. I'll bring you back to this hotel bar, and if he's a real man, he would have left word with the bartender here. And you can conduct your business deal later. Deal?"

"Deal." Lisa offered her soft, beautifully manicured hand to Andrew, who raised it to his lips and gave it a sweet, brief kiss.

"Deal, my dear Lisa." Then all business. "I know a lovely small bistro in the suburbs near my home that serves a wonderful Osso Buco. That sound good?"

He works fast, Lisa thought, as they walked out of the bar together. *But that's the story of my life. Fast. At least I'm getting a meal out of it.*

"What say we head to my place for a nightcap?" Andrew placed his hand over Lisa's and looked deeply into her eyes.

Showtime!

"It's not too far away, close to my golf club." He took her elbow decidedly and guided her to his Lexus. They were both silent as Andrew skillfully guided the car out of the bistro parking lot and onto the wide, suburban streets. Lisa felt relaxed and confident in her ability to maneuver this contact into a paying proposition. Time for that later. For now, she'd just enjoy the luxury of an expensive car ride.

Their dinner had been a combination of charm and flirtation on both sides, coupled with a physical urgency that periodically emanated from Andrew, a targeted intensity that led to one conclusion for the evening. Lisa knew exactly how to play out the line and she feinted and thrust with a combination of innocence and seduction. Her usual game of skill. Running through her mind was the thought that this encounter might end differently than they usually did – a *Pretty Woman* kind of ending that she thought might eventually be her reward for this kind of life. But she was also realistic and knew better: the prettier the words, the more likely the simple transactional nature of their relationship. *It's just business,* she thought wearily, feeling the need to dampen the bourbon and wine-fueled emotions that she usually kept hard under lock and key.

She suppressed a slight hiccup as the car turned up into the sweeping, circular drive and smoothly braked to a stop in front of a grandiose Italianate villa. Andrew quickly came around to open her car door and escort her to the entrance. The door opened grandly into a two-story hall with a curved staircase that led to a mezzanine. That exquisitely designed level overlooked a living room that could have been the cover shot for *House & Gardens* magazine.

"Stay here," he commanded, "until I put the car away. I'll be right back." He kissed the top of her head and then escorted her to an overstuffed sofa chair. She looked around carefully while she waited for Andrew to return, wondering if she could play her cards right and perhaps be more than just an escort for an evening. *I wouldn't mind being the mistress of this estate*, she thought. She rose gracefully and walked casually around the room, attempting to discover any cues to a personal life. Photographs. Kids. Wife. Whatever. But the rooms were devoid of personal clutter. It was as if the living room was a set piece for a movie or magazine photo, not the real place where a real person lived.

And was Andrew a real person? He had acted the part of a successful businessman. Had a few quirks she noticed when they had dinner. His contempt for the waiter, but then his obsequious deference to the Maître D. His fussiness over his food, sending the entrée back two times and rejecting two bottles of wine until he was satisfied with the third. His shift from probing, intimate questions about her life to a complete bored indifference to her conversational replies.

I've had difficult men before, she thought, *so I can deal with this. And here I am. In a mansion in Kansas City. Well, I'm a risk-taker,* she thought, as she turned at the sound of his re-entry into the living room. Somehow in the brief time he'd been gone, he'd changed into a deep maroon silk robe and carried a silver wine bucket with an expensive bottle of wine resting in the ice. He smiled at her but didn't say anything. He set the bucket on a table near the antique cherry buffet and opened the doors to retrieve two large Reidel wine glasses. After uncorking the wine and filling their glasses, he walked over to where she sat, and setting the glasses down, lifted her gracefully from her seat.

"A toast to you, Lisa," he said, his smile perfunctory with a hint of mystery. Before he handed the wine to her, he unloosed the wrap tie of her blouse, destroying the trim line of the over-blouse and causing her neckline to plunge even more. "More of this, I'd say," he declared as he determinedly fixed his mouth on hers. From there it was a short step to his hand under her blouse, pulling it off her shoulders with a haste that threatened to tear the fabric. Lisa pulled back quickly and suggested a trip to the bathroom.

"Meet you in the large bedroom at the top of the stairs," Andrew said, carrying the tray with the wine glasses.

She stumbled slightly as she mounted the stairs, but slowed her pace to be more poised and graceful. *The promise,* she thought. *Always the promise. Channel the great courtesans of the past.*

Their lovemaking began in the usual way with long, intimate kisses, but it soon became clear to Lisa that Andrew urgently wanted more from her. His hands pressed painfully hard against her upper arms as he embraced her and she knew she'd be covered with bruises in the morning. In the middle of their encounter he became distracted and quickly got up to open a drawer in the bedside table. Inside was a pile of silk ties and he began to wrap one of them around her wrists, talking lovingly all the while.

"Sweet Lisa, sweet Lisa," he murmured under his breath. "My Lisa, my woman, my slave, my captive."

Those words were a wake-up call for her but her reactions were sluggish and she pulled against the silk ties.

"Andrew," she murmured, "this is not part ..." At that, he put one of the silk ties gently and then harder against her mouth, quickly securing the ends to the bedposts.

"Part of....?" he asked, "part of what, Lisa? Part of what you usually do or don't do?" He looked at her fixedly. "You slut!" he snarled at her in a soft, deadly voice. "You piece of flesh posing as a woman. You think you're a real woman, don't you? You're nothing but trash." His face was demonic. All traces of the sophisticated and understanding businessman disappeared and his gaze was other-worldly, of someone not there.

"Andrew," she pleaded, her voice muffled with the tie stuffed in her mouth.

The weakness in her voice seemed to trigger something uncharted in his personality and he began to slap her face systematically, one side to the other, back and forth, causing her head to whiplash back and forth. Her whimpers seemed to stimulate him more. With an energetic grunt, he lifted himself up off the bed and walked over to the closet. Lisa could hear him make odd noises. He grabbed something from inside the closet that gave off a metallic glitter.

Her fear began to rise in her throat and tears formed in her eyes. She looked at him pleadingly as he returned to the bed where she was helplessly tied to the bedposts.

"Lisa, Lisa, you stupid bitch!" he said. "You think you are so smart. You women. You are nothing but trash, sluts, empty minds. Stupid pieces of crap fit only for a landfill." He put his hand over her mouth and nose and watched as her eyes began to flutter back and forth, struggling with the effects of oxygen starvation on her body.

She was strong and she fought hard to breathe, but he was heavy and he was straddling her, his body weight resting completely on her torso and compressing her chest, making breathing torture.

Faint, faint, Lisa, she told herself. *Pretend he's won. Faint, faint.* She relaxed her body, then, and with a supreme act of will, let her body completely collapse into a melting puddle. She let her eyes roll back into their sockets and deliberately peed herself. From a distant place she heard the sound of metal on metal, but her mind couldn't process it.

And then she fainted for real.

The elderly, homeless street resident pushed her packed shopping cart down the shabby street and stopped at an over-flowing garbage receptacle. Sometimes she could find half-eaten sandwiches from McDonald's. She plowed through the garbage, steadily pushing it to the side with her hands, and then caught a flash of beautiful purple. Something filmy and beautiful. She stood on her tiptoes and nearly toppled into the garbage can as she reached deep into the buried kitchen trash bag.

She pulled out the fabric which was caught on something else, and her breath came out in smelly puffs as she exerted herself to grab the entire bag. It came free all of a sudden and her eyes widened as she looked at her treasure. She couldn't believe her luck. A beautiful new purse! Could there be some money in it? She slumped heavily to the sidewalk alongside the trash can and tore open the clasp with her dirty hands. The purse was empty except for a small zippered pocket. To her disappointment, it was empty except for a tattered snapshot of two small children. She stared at the photo for a long disappointed moment. Then she placed it back in the purse and resumed her digging.

The sound of rush hour traffic on Highway 35, commuters heading south into the city, was like easily forgotten background noise. The fast food restaurants were opening, the senior "regulars" standing before the door waiting for the opening click. A back door would open and a brief snatch of random everyday conversation could be heard before the door slammed and the parking lot was again the province of foraging squirrels and swirling dust. Towards the east across the highway, the roseate glow of the rising sun signaled a warm day. Just another uneventful spring day.

2

Their bike ride out into the woods was a big treat. Clay was surprised; he hadn't been sure he'd be allowed to go. Shiloh and Brian had asked if they could take Clay to the village hills– "not too far; only to the edge of town," they pleaded to Romyn. She reluctantly gave her approval, telling the three kids to be back right at lunchtime or she'd send Chief Baldwin out after them. "And you know what he'll do?" she offered threateningly.

"Yeah, Chief Baldwin. He's a softie," Shiloh said scornfully.

"Is he the police?" Clay asked, trying to camouflage his nervousness.

"He's the chief, but you can talk to him. He's not a bad guy," Brian offered. "He helped me out when Grandpa died."

"Yeah, that was sad. I remember that day," Shiloh said confidently, though in her mind Robert Peterson's funeral and her own beloved Eva's funeral blurred together so all she could remember was a wistful sadness.

"We will only go past Paul and Jennie's farm and go a little way up into the hills," Shiloh reassured Romyn. "There's a stream there that we can explore – but don't worry!" she added when she saw Romyn's expression. "We won't go into it. We'll just look at it."

"And if I see that you come back with wet jeans, you know you'll have to answer to me," Romyn threatened, adding ominously, "or Earl. He might just spank you all."

The kids laughed at that, knowing how unlikely it was that Earl would spank them, even if he could get out of his wheelchair and wield a paddle.

"I'll keep Sophie here," Romyn said. "She and I have been planning to make caramel rolls and I think today is a great day to do it."

"So-o-o," Clay bargained, "when we come back home, there will be warm caramel rolls?" His look was innocent.

"There just might be." Romyn waved her hand at them. "Shoo. Make sure you follow the traffic rules. Bicycles go with the traffic. And you need to signal all your turns. If I find you've been disobeying the laws, I swear I'm taking the bikes away from you. You hear me, Clay?"

It was a beautiful May day. It hadn't been too long since the lingering winter had kept new growth under lock and key, but a few warm, beautiful, late spring days had brought out the green and it was as if the daffodils, bleeding hearts, rhubarb, and Creeping Charlie had all decided on the same day to come to life and shout, "I am here!" On their way down the hill towards the farm, each front lawn showed new growth. The parking lot next to Perkins was filled with bobbing yellow heads of dandelions with a few wisps of dried blossoms that drifted across the children's faces as they biked, bringing an intermittent soft focus to the view. Only a few fluffy clouds in the sky marred the perfect blue of a Minnesota spring. In the distance they heard the sounds of trucks traveling slowly along Main Street and Crossroads Avenue, but mostly the three children concentrated on one another, keeping the right distance. Just enough to allow for slowing down and speeding up without running into one another, yet still within hearing distance.

Shiloh led the convoy, the alpha child despite her gender. Besides, in her saddlebags she had the snacks and the drinks and both Brian and Clay were aware that she could be a savage mistress if they misbehaved. Clay swore he'd become the leader of this pack of three once he knew Peace Ridge Village better.

Their own adventure! Earl and Romyn had insisted that both Sophie and Clay have new bikes from Walmart as soon as they could spend a couple of weeks with them in Peace Ridge Village. The kids' shelter in St. Paul had pegged these two weeks as good ones for an extended visit so Earl and Romyn made a big deal about going to Walmart and having the kids pick out their bikes. Sophie always deferred to Clay on every decision, but with the help of Earl she managed to pick out her own pretty pink bike, a Disney Princess with sparkly streamers on the handlebars. She loved it but was quite shy and clumsy when perched precariously on the seat and her peddling was still wobbly. Both Romyn and Earl thought she would be out of her league with the older kids and encouraged her to stay back home for this first long voyage to the hills.

She also needs to have some independence from Clay, Romyn thought. She knew Clay was Sophie's anchor, her security blanket with the uncertainty of her mother and no father, but Clay needed a little boy freedom, too.

"We need to encourage Sophie to do things on her own away from Clay," Romyn said to Earl. "She is too dependent on him. Following him with her eyes wherever he goes, clinging to him all the time." Romyn looked at Earl with deep concern. "I know that she feels safe when she's around him. But that's too much of a burden on an eleven-year-old. He should not have to take care of a seven-year-old girl at his age. I hope these times in Peace Ridge Village can help him unload some of that responsibility and let him be a little bit more – carefree."

Romyn walked over to Earl and stroked his shoulders. She brushed his hair away from his face and planted a kiss on his forehead. "I know she loves you more than anything in the world and you are her security blanket, too. Let's see if a baking session can't give her a bit of home that is separate from Clay."

"And Brian and Shiloh will give Clay a run for his money," Earl said with a chagrined smile.

"Especially Shiloh! Brian will be composing a poem with every new turn of the bend. Shiloh will want to show off her

11

neighborhood to Clay." He paused. "It will be good for all three of them. Clay is old for his age; Brian is young for his age, and Shiloh... well, Shiloh, she's just one of a kind. We are going to enjoy watching her grow up, aren't we, Romyn?"

"All of them. Watching all of them." A flash of a young Jimmer at eight years old, his fascination with turtles, ants, lizards... She turned resolutely from that thought and went into the kitchen to write out her grocery list. Gooey caramel rolls. Cream. Butter. Brown sugar. Cinnamon. Pecans. She'd show Sophie how to make them right. If that child would only get out of bed! "Sophie!" she called, as she walked towards the bedroom. "Time to get up! We gotta get to Walmart and lay in our baking supplies!"

The pavement ended just beyond Jennie and Paul's farm and the bikes naturally slowed down as the gravel road grabbed their tires. Brian braked to a stop along the fence that enclosed the Holm's cows. There was a glimpse of bucolic beauty in the contrast of white painted fencing that framed the soft black and white rounded mounds of Holsteins who grazed indifferently on lime-green grass under a spacious cerulean sky. A bald eagle swooped above, its graceful flight echoing the slight breeze that wafted through the pale grey-green weeping willow trees softly waving alongside the road.

Peace Ridge hills smudged the horizon in the near distance. It was early enough in the morning that a warm mist still kissed the tops of the tallest pine trees, but the young birch and poplar trees traced the ridgeline with fragile calligraphic beauty.

A three-dimensional poem of nature, Brian thought. But the shouts of Shiloh and Clay, now quite far ahead, disrupted the word melody that was forming in his mind and he reluctantly pulled up his bike and began to catch up. *Click. Click. Click. Mental snapshots so I don't forget,* he reminded himself. *Glad I remembered my Moleskin notebook. Inkblots on suede, placid pondering flat faces, purple drifts of shale and ever-green...soaring eagle, wings like eyebrows.*

Shiloh was very proud of setting a fast pace. Girl or not, she'd been on her bike for weeks now and she could show Clay how it was done in the country. The city kid himself, he was playing around with the different gears on his new bike and trying to find the right gear for the slow incline up to the ridge. He was not going to admit to Shiloh that this was his first-ever bike. His mom, Lisa, never let them have a bike in their city apartment and, of course, it was impossible when they were living in their car.

His inner joy at the bike and freedom was imperfectly hidden though he pretended a protective visage of stern indifference. A slight grin crept unbidden onto his narrow, freckled face as felt his leg muscles hit their stride. He glanced back at Brian – old slowpoke – and then focused on Shiloh's narrow, graceful back as she effortlessly skimmed forward up the hill.

"Wait up! Wait up!" Clay soon called to her, and pulled over to the side of the road to catch his breath. "We need to give Brian a chance to catch up to us," he commanded. Shiloh braked to a stop with a gravelly swoosh and then walked her bike back to Clay.

"He bikes at his own pace," she affirmed, but smiled fondly at Brian as they watched him doggedly bike towards them.

"Where's this stream you've been telling me about?" Clay asked assertively. "Are you sure you know where it is?"

Shiloh looked at him scornfully. "Of course, I do. I grew up here, didn't I? Even Brian knows where it is, don't you, Brian?"

Brian, more interested in the journey than the destination, affirmed, "It's an offshoot of Skunk Creek that ends up in Skunk Lake. I heard some people say that it comes from a spring deep in the hills and that's why it rarely freezes hard in the wintertime. Someday I'd like to walk the creek from the lake up into the hills to the source. That would be a great adventure."

13

"It would take a whole day or more. Maybe we could camp overnight in the woods. I bet you've never camped in the woods overnight, have you, Clay?" Shiloh asked challengingly.

He looked directly at her, meeting the challenge head-on. "I bet you've never ridden a roller-coaster at Six Flags Over Georgia!"

Seeing a doubtful expression, he pressed in, "I bet you've never even been out of Peace Ridge Village in your whole life!"

"Have, too," she averred. "I went with my Dad to Minneapolis..."

"Stop it, you guys," Brian said mildly. "Let's bike some more. I want to see Skunk Creek and see if there are any otters there yet."

The two older kids briefly glowered at one another, striking a temporary truce as they got back on their bikes and headed up into the hills. Their tires made a pleasant percussion on the gravel, the lilting melody joyously sung by a chorus of bird song. Goldfinches hopped determinedly among the dandelion patches and Brian caught a flash of blue as a pair of bluebirds called to one another from an old oak tree riddled with woodpeckers' holes, perfect homes for the bluebirds.

Shiloh rode her bike onto a barely visible footpath that disappeared into the forest, but soon dismounted and pushed her bike deeper into the spring undergrowth. The warm air was fragrant with growing thistles and honeysuckle, delicate high notes over an earthy wet earth scent, the ground giving up its morning wetness in a slow exhalation.

"C'mon, guys. It's just a little way." Her words sounded distant. The forest cooled considerably once they were out of the open fields. The underbrush thickened, reaching out to grab wheel spokes and protruding pedals. "Let's leave our bikes here and hike in. No one will take them."

They noisily walked deeper into the woods, brushing away the undergrowth and small bushes that barred their way.

"Quiet!" Brian said, pausing. "I hear it. Listen." The three children stood still for a few long moments.

"I don't hear anything," Clay said doubtfully.

"It's the creek. Can you hear it? We must be nearby. I hear a sound like the clapping of a thousand tiny birdwings." The barely perceptible rippling sound was punctuated by the song of bullfrogs and distinctive rusty pump-handle screech of the blue jays.

"Yup. It's just over here." Shiloh strode confidently to the left and both Clay and Brian followed. As if by magic, the trees parted to reveal a small clearing in the forest. The nearly circular space was rimmed by towering pine trees and covered with a green carpet of moss and pine needles. It had a complex scent. The smell of fresh pine barely camouflaged the musky scent of dried leaves and rotting soil from the winter. The small space was bordered on the west by Skunk Creek, which gleamed like sun on burnished metal as it made its lazy way down the stream bed of stones and shale. The three kids exultantly threw themselves onto the soft moss and looked up at the trees trellised by beams of sunlight that cast rainbows on their faces. They were quiet for a few minutes, all skirmishes swallowed up in the companionable magic of the special bower.

"This is my all-time *favorite* place," Shiloh said confidently with a gigantic sigh, as she wiggled herself comfortably into the grass.

"Yeah, I bet you've never been here before!" Clay challenged.

"Yes, I have. There are rocks over there, perfect for sitting on." Shiloh sat up quickly and ran to the other side of a big oak tree that leaned over the creek. A jumble of boulders barred their way downstream. Shiloh turned triumphantly towards Clay and Brian. "See! Told ya'!"

The boys clambered after her and perched carefully alongside. They watched the water carefully, searching for frogs and watching the flies and birds. Their rivalry was becalmed for a long time and each were nearly hypnotized by the creek as it made its way forcefully downstream. Then they shifted companionably as Shiloh brought out the treats and carefully doled them out.

Drops from the creek and dew had made the rocks slippery and the children were mindful of Romyn's warnings, so they soon made their way back to the grove, their hind ends wet from the dampness of the stones. Shiloh took over, leading the discovery of insects, interesting pieces of bark, and piles of deer scat. Squirrels and chipmunks scurried away from their footsteps and then paused at the edge of the clearing, turning to sit up and chatter at them. There was the scent of fresh growing things in the air and Brian was excited to discover wild onion plants. Shiloh was all for harvesting them immediately "for our breakfast tomorrow," but Brian held her back.

"Wait until they grow some more. They are still tiny."

Brian was a dutiful pupil but Clay had little interest in the schoolmarm and her finds. He wandered around the edge of the clearing, diligently trying to be interested in the different types of trees and bushes. To tell the truth, he really wanted to go wading in the stream but knew he'd be in a heap of trouble if he even suggested it.

The overhanging trees were a dark green that contrasted sharply with the pale lighter green of emerging buds and grass. There were dark patches on the other side of the clearing and he could smell the rotting of the grasses alongside the fallen oak tree. There were scents he didn't recognize. Give him a city street with its hot asphalt smell, the sickeningly sweet smell of emptied garbage cans, the smell of sun-browned newspaper... then he'd know where he was. But here? The clearing, which had seemed so delightful just a short time ago, now felt oppressive and claustrophobic. Clay was suddenly worried about their path and whether they'd ever be able to find it again. His sense of direction was attuned to city streets and he was off kilter here. Despite the nearness of Shiloh and Brian and their quiet confident discussions of nature, he felt something fearful grip his heart and a small sense of panic caused goosebumps on his forearms.

He felt a coldness then, as if the spring day had turned to winter, and he instinctively rubbed his hands and wrists together in a classic gesture of worry. Despite the warmth of the noontime, he felt his fingers turn cold and he was overtaken with a feeling of fear, of danger and dread. The forest, which had been so benign a moment ago, now felt evil. He flashed on his mother's face for a brief moment.

"Guys," he said, "I gotta..."

Shiloh and Brian looked up and saw the whiteness and fear on Clay's face.

Brian said, "C'mon, Shiloh. Let's go back on our bikes and go home."

She was about to plead, "We just got here!" but saw the look on Brian's face and instinctively obeyed the younger child. They scrambled after Clay who had somehow found the path and was running headlong towards their bikes. All three children had caught some of Clay's fear and they quickly pushed their bikes out of the forest onto the road and energetically hopped on and pedaled as fast as they could down the winding gravel road towards the pavement near the Holm's farm. Only then did they slow to a more normal pace, out of breath and with flushed cheeks.

The sweet-smelling sunlight quickly and magically erased the thrilling fear that had momentarily gripped all three of them. It was a sweaty, happy, tired bunch that soon threw their bikes onto the driveway and swarmed into Romyn's kitchen. And judging by the intoxicating fragrance, just in time for warm caramel rolls.

Shiloh was excitedly recounting their ride to the Ridge, but Clay was quiet. Drinking the cold milk and slowly chewing the sweet, cinnamony links of his caramel roll, Brian puzzled over Clay's flight from the forest. It was perfectly safe there. Things grew in the forest. "Wild onion shoots, harbingers of spring, promise of sustenance..." His mind drifted to his poetry, Clay's unusual fear completely absorbed into art.

3

P am parked her car in the driveway and walked
slowly to her mailbox. Her work at the Westin was neither
better or worse than any other work week, but for some reason,
she felt simply exhausted tonight. Opening and closing the
mailbox door her arms felt leaden, like she'd been lifting fif-
ty-pound sacks all day. She looked around the cul-de-sac, the
houses all cut from the same builder's floor plans and person-
alized with different landscaping and paint colors, but cook-
ie-cutter just the same. Her own taupe house with its maroon
shutters and carefully tended, oversized, pottery flower pots at
the door was welcoming but, in truth, largely indistinct from
her neighbors.

The sky was a perfect blue and the fresh spring leaves in
the birch trees presented a palette of simple beauty, one that
normally lifted her spirits. As she walked into her house she
reviewed the typical Friday night in her neighborhood. There
would have been a bustle around six o'clock as her neighbors
packed their SUVs, loaded up the kids and dogs, and pushed
away from the driveway en route to their weekend places "up
north." She didn't have a cabin on a lake and she usually liked
the quietness of the weekend, sitting on her deck facing her
peaceful backyard and drinking Cokes with Bradley. He was
always goofy, trying to make her laugh and teasing the tiredness and impatience out of her with his unfailing good humor
and his delight in simple things.

Those moments were decompression times for her. Moments set apart for family with no time to ruminate on the "what if?" and "what could have been" events and decisions in her personal life. With Bradley there, and when they were a family of three when Tory was still at home, she felt satisfied with her life.

It was when she was alone and on her own that a blackness could nibble at her consciousness and threaten to inhabit her thoughts. During those times it was simply best to go to bed, indulge in images of ideal marriages on the Hallmark channel, and fall asleep early. *There's always tomorrow,* she'd think. *Who said that? Scarlett O'Hara? 'Tomorrow I'll think of some way... after all, tomorrow is another day'*

Tory had taken Bradley for the weekend. She had planned an outing with her boyfriend and his church youth group and Brad had been talking about it for weeks. Packing his overnight bag over and over and raiding the pantry for snacks; "Tory never has chips," he averred. Pam smiled at that, knowing that Tory was her grandmother all over again, loading the refrigerator and cupboards with more food than an army of teenagers could devour. Still, Bradley loved the anticipation and excitement of the weekend away. His smile filled the car window as they drove away.

And that's what's wrong with me, Pam thought. *There is no anticipation in my life. Nothing to look forward to. It's the sameness in my life that drags me down. I see one day turning into another, the weeks into months, the months into years, my hair getting grayer, more lines in my face, and nothing changing. What was that expression?* "Most men live lives of quiet desperation." *Thoreau —the guy who took himself away from mankind to live in the woods!*

I'm talking to myself again, she rebuked herself. *Thoreau and Scarlett O'Hara. Now if that's not a pair and if that's not a sign of old age...* She flashed then on a memory of her old grandma in the nursing home. *So glad to have company even if she didn't have the slightest idea of who you were. You would be talking and her mouth would be moving along with your words, trying to have a conversation even if it wasn't her own thoughts.*

So sweet. Pam sighed. *Ah yes, another sign of getting old— living in the past and reliving old memories.*

Thinking about the country reminded her of Bill and Donna. The tragedy on her watch at the Westin wasn't her fault but she still felt responsible. The unfathomable grief on Bill's face when he thought of his paralyzed wife. Pam's own recollection of Donna's indiscreet affair with the senator at the Westin. No one was supposed to judge the guests. She knew that. She also could see the pain on Bill's face and felt helpless to alleviate it. There was only so much she could do as the Westin's manager, and even less she could do as a single woman helping a married man.

For a brief moment, she imagined what her life would have been like if she'd had a husband like Bill, one who stood by her through thick and thin. Not abandoning the family because Bradley wasn't a perfect child. Well, he was perfectly made by God's will, even if he did have Down Syndrome.

And this is a dead end. I can't change what happened to us as a family and I can't change Donna's drunkenness and the accident that shattered her skull. And Bill's life.

She sat immobile on the kitchen stool and watched the dusk darken into the deep moody quiet of a summer's night in Bloomington. Suddenly she felt hemmed in and bordered by the four walls of her house. *I wish I could just break free and run away somewhere. In the country. Into a place of hills and green grass and endless sky. A forest with towering pines and needles carpeting the ground that cushioned you when you sank down and looked up into the patterned mosaic of tree branches, leaves, and a shattering prism of sunlight.*

Peace Ridge Village. The name fell into her consciousness like a pearl. A vision of a small, clear stream flowing around flat rocks and mossy hillocks, sending shards of sparkling, clear water that glittered into miniscule rainbows. The perfect

20

quietness of the forest with the soft swoosh of a falling leaf, the scurrying of a chipmunk, the tinkling bells of birdsong.

A slow quiet drive into the country. The balm for city restlessness was the country. A drive up north tomorrow. That would be something to do on a restless Saturday.

And nothing to do with Bill Nelson, she thought. *This is just for me. Something to look forward to.* She quickly checked the weather forecast on her smartphone: A cloudless sunny day. Perfect.

Jennie and Paul slumped tiredly onto the kitchen chairs. They said nothing for several companionable moments, just "resting their old bones for a bit' as Jennie's Finlander grandma used to say.

"I underestimated the time it would take to get all those herbs seeded in," Jennie said with a sigh.

"Yeah," Paul agreed, "on top of all the other farm work. I need to work on the organic acreage. I've been thinking that we need to create a barrier around the five acres to keep it somewhat segregated from the rest of the corn fields. A berm. It's high enough that I don't think the water will leech into it, but I'd like to make sure we're in compliance with all the rules and regulations." He took a long draught of iced tea from his oversized glass. "One of the reasons I have not thought seriously about organic farming, but we'll go slow and work our way into it. We certainly have all the organic fertilizer we need. Those cows of ours…"

Jennie mused, "If we do everything right, we'll be able to use that field for planting next spring. I showed the certification guy proof that we'd never farmed that field and he seemed to accept that. Good thing I kept all those old pictures! In the meantime, I'll just continue to plant by hand in the greenhouse and we'll see how it goes. We don't know anything about the quantities yet, anyway. I think Pastor is thinking small and I don't want to get ahead of him, but it could really take off."

"He's not going to be able to help much. With his wife home. He'll have to take care of her."

"I think he believes that working with the herbs would be a good thing for her. She could get her hands into the dirt and it would help her reconnect to the real world."

"How are you going to run your pie business and do this business, too, d'ya think?" Paul looked at Jennie with a mock stern expression on his face.

"I have been thinking about that. The problem is, the pies need to be baked in the early morning hours and the herbs need to be picked for drying in the early morning hours. And the cows need milking in the early morning hours." Jennie sighed heavily.

Paul said, "You might have to think about giving something up, Jennie. I know that's hard for you."

"You know me too well!" Jennie got up and squeezed her husband's shoulder before going to the refrigerator to refill his iced tea.

"Well, there are so many hours in the day…" Paul looked at her speculatively, "and I know you think you are superwoman and can do everything…"

"I can't do everything, but I can do something. And right now what I need to do is get all the paperwork downloaded for the greenhouse, so we can be sure we're doing everything right. I need to be able to verify that we're in total compliance and then I need to think about the marketing plan and how we're going to take *Peace in the Valley Herbs* to the next level."

"Is that the name you've settled on? *Peace in the Valley Herbs?*"

"Well, what do you think? We're in the valley, we are Peace Ridge Village, we sell herbs."

"Not always peaceful! What does Pastor Ed think?"

"Pastor thinks I am the marketing expert and he's leaving it all up to me. He wants this to be the fundraiser for the church to 'help the hurting and hungry' as he says, and he thinks our blends could generate money. And I do, too." The emphasis with which Jennie spoke undergirded her commitment to the idea and the vision. *Peace in the Valley Herbs*, a product line that would help people to help other people—that was what she wanted to do! Baking pies was great, but she was limited in what she could actually do with the pies. Pies were all home baked and limited to Peace Ridge. Maybe Titos and Maria's new Greek diner could be a potential sales outlet—she'd thought about that.

But creating a line of herb blends took creativity and knowledge, too, and could give her distribution beyond Peace Ridge Village. It might be kinda fun to travel into Minneapolis once in a while and sell to restaurants and independent grocers like Lunds & Byerly's. Or Kowalski's. Maybe even Whole Foods. She remembered Dane Johnson's talk about the "backstory" of selling products. What would be a better backstory than helping people from a little white church in the valley "up north"?

Paul watched the smile play over Jennie's face and he smiled inwardly. *I know exactly what she's thinking,* he thought. *The girl simply has no secrets—I can read her like a book. She's dreaming of being an entrepreneur again. But maybe we can make this one work. Working together. She did all her pies by herself, but with Ed's help we might be able to build this into a nice little sideline business. I like the idea of it, anyway.*

He stood up slowly, his joints creaking a bit. That left leg of his still was stiff if he sat too long. *But if I had to have a farm accident, that one wasn't too bad. Didn't lose my leg anyway.*

"Well, I s'pose, Jennie. This isn't getting the work done. I'd better get in gear. I'm going to go out and take a look at that field and see how much dirt I'll have to push around to create a berm of some sort." He slapped his farm hat on his head, brushing his white blond hair away from his sunburned face. "Wha'd'ya' got on the agenda for the day?"

"I plan to go over and check in on Eliza. She never uses her telephone and now that I've gotten to know her and see just how frail and lonely she is, I worry about her. I'll just have a cuppa with her and see how she is."

"She'll not let you go without greeting each one of the animals!"

"I know, I know! I hope I can escape a visit to the pet shed; maybe I'll take Thunder. That'll please Bartholomew and distract her a bit. I hope she'll let me take a look at her papers again. They are a mess. If she's willing, we should get them all together and take them to see Gerald at the bank. He might be able to find a way to automatically take care of her finances if she would let him. As it is, we discovered the overdue tax bills just in time. The county would have put her on the list for tax arrears and then she would have had a real mess on her hands. I don't think she really understands what's at stake."

"Well, I'll let you to it, Jennie. That's more your bailiwick than mine. You know how I hate paperwork!"

"Yup, you'd take pouring rain on the John Deere over book-work any day!" Jennie stood up and gave her tall husband a kiss on the cheek and a brief hug. "I'll make something nice for lunch, I promise," she smiled.

"BLT?" he asked.

"Bologna and liver on toast?" she teased.

4

The weekend dawned with promise. The sun seemed to get up especially early that Saturday morning and it was already hot when Bill Nelson and Pastor Ed Mitchell shared a booth in the Tall Rigger, glad to get into air-conditioned comfort. They'd finished their hamburgers and fries and both occasionally glanced at the television screens over the bar area, but neither were paying any real attention. They sat quietly over their Cokes. Ed was shocked at Bill's appearance. The big guy who typically overflowed his belt had lost a lot of weight, his blue jeans hanging off his hips. There were drawn lines along his cheekbones that had been camouflaged when he was heavier, but now made him look like a craggier version of his former self. His hair was longish, too; he had forgotten to keep the crew cut he'd had since high school and the longer hair with its visible grey strands made him seem unkempt and unloved. The sadness in his eyes could not be camouflaged by the dim light in the restaurant. Bill had made several attempts at jocularity during their supper, but gave up half-heartedly and fell into long periods of silence.

For his own part, Ed was mostly silent, too. The last few months had been nearly unbearable – Donna's accident, Kellie's meth addiction, a corrupt real estate agent trying to steal their land, Eliza's fire… But there was still so much uncertainty to be faced that it was likely more sorrow than joy was ahead of them. There was a lot of catching up to do, but the collective weight of the recent events seemed to weigh like a ton of cast iron on their minds with no easy words to squeeze out.

Pastor Ed had thought to share his glimmers of joy with Bill, the fact that his wife, Jill, had come out of her catatonia and might even be able to spend time at the parsonage this summer. But he felt uncomfortable with even that little bit of happiness in the presence of the sadness that radiated outward from his friend.

"Tell me about Jill," Bill asked, as if reading Ed's mind. "I've missed out on all the news about you while I've been taken up with taking care of Donna and trying to sort out...the other stuff."

"Glad you asked." Ed took a deep breath, his eyes suddenly bright with unshed tears. "Praise the Lord. Jill came out of her catatonia unexpectedly. I suppose you heard that it had something to do with fresh coffee and my being there with her at the same time. It seemed to trigger a memory that reached deep inside her and she made her way to the surface and recognized me. The people at the care center don't believe any of my theories about coffee, of course. They just explain it as a spontaneous remission of her deep depression but I think it was God's way to restore her to our life. And I can't begin to tell you what it means to me to have hope again."

Bill recoiled as if hit in the face and Ed was aghast. "I am so sorry. That was thoughtless. Forgive me, please?" he beseeched him.

"No, it's all right. I'm all right. It's just that I am overwhelmed with thoughts of my loss of ...us... over the last couple of months. I forgot that you lost Jill for over ten years. I don't know if I will ever feel hopeful again."

"Well, to paraphrase a well-known writer, '...*we glory in our sufferings, because we know that suffering produces perseverance; perseverance character; and character, hope.*'"

"One of your guys, I suppose." Bill raised an eyebrow.

"Yes, one of my guys." Ed laughed lightly. "St. Paul. Romans."

"Well, for me, I was always known as a character. The happy-go-lucky guy. Then things started to go south with Donna and me and we lived like strangers for a couple of years and then the accident happened. I never thought I'd suffer like this, and I still don't see hope at the end of the line. I don't know how you have held on for ten years." He looked down at the table and pensively rubbed his big fingers along the fake wood grain of the laminate tabletop. "But then you're a preacher. You have a way of dealing with it better than I do."

"We're all just fellow travelers," Ed said. "Pain is the human lot and our Jesus comes alongside each one of us. I don't know what will happen with Jill. She seems as if she is making some progress, getting better, more able to cope with real life. But my fear is that she'll slip back and there will be nothing any of us can do. The hope I feel is perilous, as if I am walking a tightrope that could give way at any moment."

"I am sorry I didn't get a chance to meet her at the groundbreaking ceremony of The Jason House."

"Me, too. Though that was pretty overwhelming to her. The drive from Minneapolis to Peace Ridge Village and back again just about did her in. When I visited her a couple of days ago, though, she said she wanted to come and visit again, so I am looking forward to bringing her back home. 'Back home.' I like the sound of that."

"Are you back to preaching on Sundays now?" Bill asked.

"Yup. Took six weeks off but now back in the saddle. Believe it or not, summers are the busiest time of the year at the church. Hope you can make it back to us some Sunday."

"I spend every Sunday with Donna at Sartell. I'm sorry about not making it to church. When we get The Jason House finished and she's moved in here…"

"How's that going?"

Talking about building things was restorative for both men.

"Well, Earl and Romyn are still working through the permitting process, but that's going good. We'll be able to get started soon. Titos and Maria gave me the contract to build their diner on Miller Street in the meantime, so I've got the crew working overtime to get that built. I'd like to get it done before we begin the work on Earl and Romyn's. That's going to take all our days and nights to get finished. The better part of eight or ten months at a minimum, probably a year."

Bill paused. "George's nephew, Jeremy, has joined us and I've never seen anyone get a crew inspired and cranking like he does. That boy has had some really good discipline in the Army. He just blows me away." That brought an involuntary smile to Bill's face. He said softly, "I would have loved to have had a son like him."

It was a small step for Ed to ask about Bill's daughter, Kellie. "What do you hear from your daughter?" he asked kindly.

"She finds her ol' dad someone she just doesn't care about anymore." Bill sighed dejectedly. "You'd think that with Donna in the hospital – she's essentially lost her mom – that she'd want to have some relationship with me."

"Drugs come between family members." Ed said. "And families can have problems even when no drugs are involved. Sometime I'll tell you about my visit from Robby."

It was as if Bill hadn't heard. "I would not have believed it if I hadn't seen it myself." His eyes shone briefly, the wetness conveying his pain. "I hope she'll come back to me. I really do."

Ed didn't respond but said a silent prayer. "Dear Jesus. Please heal this brokenness."

Bill continued. "She's in her apartment with her roommates now. The court is obligated to tell me what's going on because she's still a minor. She doesn't tell me anything. Doesn't call. Doesn't text. Once she's twenty-one in a couple of days she'll be an adult and it will be up to her to get in touch with me.

"If she wants to," he added sadly.

"Well, that's what we'll pray for. We will pray specifically that Kellie sees that she needs her family's support during this struggle. And we'll pray for complete deliverance from addiction. Have you ever heard of Minnesota Teen Challenge? I think it's called Minnesota Adult and Teen Challenge now…"

Bill shook his head, "No."

"Addicts of all ages and types live away from their enablers and fixers, their group, for about thirteen months. It's faith-based and strict, but they offer a great support program. People who've been through it themselves and understand the weakness, temptation, physical pain, and loneliness. They have a pretty good recovery rate – sixty percent or so for people who stick with the thirteen-month program."

"I don't know if she'd even consider something like that. You heard what she said in the hospital. 'As if praying would do any good!'" Bill said sarcastically. "She thinks she's an atheist – doesn't want to have anything to do with God."

"Yes, we'll pray for that, too. But maybe she's seen the bottom of the abyss. Maybe she'll be more receptive, having spent some time in jail. Teen Challenge is in the jails, too."

"She has enough of her mother in her to think that she can con the system," Bill said bitterly. Then he shook his head sadly, "Did I say that? God forgive me."

"Oh, Bill. 'Jesus knows our every weakness. Take it to the Lord in prayer.'"

"I do try to pray." Bill looked directly into Ed's eyes. "I really do, especially since you and I talked…that night." He added softly nearly to himself, "that night I wanted to kill Donna. But I don't seem to connect."

"Do you know that hymn? *What a Friend we Have in Jesus* — and the Irishman who wrote it?" Ed leaned comfortably back into the booth. "Joseph Scriven was Irish, leaned on the Lord totally. Had to. His Irish fiancé drowned the night before their wedding. He moved to Canada and fell in love with another woman who got pneumonia and died shortly before their wedding. *'Oh, what peace we often forfeit, oh, what needless pain we bear…'*

"You can't bear this all this by yourself. We are all here to help. Me, Romyn and Earl, Jennie and Paul. Even ol' George is more comfort than he realizes. And Jesus, of course. The two *paracletes*, one on either side, the two comforters: Jesus and the Holy Spirit. Lean on them."

Tears trickled slowly down Bill's face. He lifted his arm to his face and blotted his eyes with his short sleeve. "Ed, I've cried more in front of you than at any time in my life." He looked around the Tall Rigger. No one was paying any attention to them.

"No worries," Ed said with a smile. "Real men cry."

The two men sat silently for a few minutes. Bill gazed absent-mindedly out the window, as if hoping that the sidewalk held some answers. Suddenly he got up and dashed out the door. Ed sat there puzzled. He thoughtfully took care of the tab, making sure to leave a hefty tip as they'd been sitting there for well over an hour.

Bill walked slowly back into the Tall Rigger and slid silently into the booth. "I thought I saw someone I knew," he said. Ed just looked at him. They arose and embraced chastely as men did.

"'In quietness and confidence is your strength,'" Ed said, quoting Isaiah. "God bless."

"God bless," Bill repeated, his face unreadable.

5

"Howdy. How goes it?" George walked slowly into the Crossroads Convenience store and grabbed his usual chair at the table, making sure of an unimpeded view of the gas pumps and front door. It was quiet in the store that Monday morning and George was pleased to see that he had Romyn's attention all to himself.

"All good, George. All good." Romyn walked to the round oak pedestal table and perched lightly on a nearby stool. "It's coming along, just as we planned."

"Bill able to get to cranking on your project?" George asked sourly. He was tired and grouchy this morning. *Just didn't sleep well last night. Not dead yet, still upright and walking.*

"Yep. He did that little job for the school district and now he's just finishing up the diner for Titos and Maria. He's done except for the cabinet and booth installs in the dining room. Looking for a grand opening in a couple of weeks."

"Well, he'll find a lot of leftovers, things left to do that he thought were done. Things he'll discover on opening day. I know that, for sure."

"Why don't you offer to help out, George? I am sure he could use your advice."

"I'm not sure about that. He's forgotten more than I've ever known about running a diner. But I may just talk to him. Just might...

"You still got those kids with you?" George looked balefully into his empty cup and then stood up stiffly and poured himself a refill. "What do you know about that no-good mother of theirs?"

"A few weeks ago, I would have challenged your description 'No good.' But now, I don't know." Romyn shook her head. "Earl and I took Clay and Sophie back down to the children's home on Friday afternoon. Knew we had a busy weekend ahead of us and couldn't spend much time with them.

"I was sad to learn that there is still no word from their mother—which makes me really angry—it's been weeks! Of course, they both cried and clung to us. I thought Earl was going to fall apart. I reassured them and told them we'd be back for them as soon as we can."

She looked down at the table, ignoring Millie-cat's sinuous weaving around her legs and her silent open-mouth mews for attention. "It's hardest on Earl. I have the store and I get involved in the work here. He's working on the facility plans all the time with Veronica so that keeps him busy. But I suggested he and she take a little break and do a deep dive into the Minnesota rules of fostering and adoption so we can be a little more prepared if...and ...when there might be an opportunity there."

"Seems as if you want them for your own," George said sagely. He'd been to visit Clay and Sophie in the children's home along with Jeremy and Tiff, and the old curmudgeon's heart was touched with thoughts of the youngsters. They needed a real home.

"Why do these women have children if they can't take care of them?" he asked bitterly. "Or take care of them the way she does by selling her wares?"

"I don't know her story. She probably had dreams of a happy marriage and children and a different future when she was first married, too."

"Where's the father?" George's voice was angry and scornful.

"North Carolina. And invisible, as far as I can tell. If he even knows that the kids are here in Minnesota." She got up from the table and walked over to sit behind the cash register, noticing the traffic at the gas pumps. "We only know what we have learned from Clay. Sophie is too young to remember him. Clay said he just left one day and never came home. He, himself, barely remembers his dad."

"The sperm donor, not dad." George's words were savage. He remembered all the years he and Kathy had tried to have children but were left wanting. *Enough to make a man crazy,* he thought. *Not fair. Someday I will have a talk with that little pastor about that. Why children are sometimes wasted on the undeserving.*

"Ah well, Romyn, my dear. Tell Earl that if you guys want to make another trip to St. Paul to see the little bairns, I'll ride shotgun. As much as I hate the Cities..."

"Bairns?" Romyn smiled. "You've been hanging around Eliza too much." But her smile was soft and loving.

Michael and Brian slogged slowly up the sidewalk to the front door. Michael was both sad and afraid for Brian, knowing that Delaney's news would hit him hard. *She probably thought I'd break the news to him,* he thought sadly. *She told me when we were first together that she didn't want to be a mother. Ever. And now she's selfishly acting that out, doing what* she *wants to do* first, *whatever the cost to our son. And that is not going to change. Even if we had married. Even if we lived together. She's just a "me first" kinda person. But because she's beautiful a man overlooks all that.*

"What's on the agenda for tonight, Brian?" he asked his son.

"Mother asked me when I was coming home. Told me she was taking me to the Tall Rigger for dinner and that she had a surprise for me."

"What do you think it is?" Michael said as he rang the doorbell to the Peterson home.

"I don't know…I hope she's planning to go back into the printing business. With those fancy papers she's got stored in the garage. The ones from England." He looked up into his dad's face with a glowing expression. "I'd like to print my poems someday."

Delaney opened the door and looked at the two of them with a sour expression. She turned without a word and walked away into the kitchen.

"I thought you'd bring Brian home earlier," she grouched. "I planned to take him to dinner at the Tall Rigger."

"Yes, I know," Michael said mildly. "We said around six o'clock. It's only six-twenty." He glanced over to the island in the kitchen and saw the wine glass and empty wine bottle.

"It's too late now!" she fussed. "I usually don't like to eat this late in the day. By the time we get there it'll be after seven-thirty and packed with all the regulars."

"It's all right, Mother. I'll just have a piece of string cheese and a cookie. I'm not really hungry anyway," Brian said.

"Did your father feed you?"

"Yes, we had lunch at Culver's so I'm not hungry."

"Delaney, you promised a surprise," Michael said to her in an aside, a reproach in his voice.

"Back off, Michael," she said with deadly venom in her voice as Brian walked sadly to his room.

"When are you going to tell him about England?" he asked quietly. "Or do you want me to break it to him?"

"I am leaving Wednesday, day after tomorrow, Michael. He's yours now, ready or not." She turned away.

"He's always been mine, Delaney. You know he would have liked it if we could have been a family…we could have tried to work it out."

"That was never going to happen, and you know it." Her words were weary. This was well-covered territory.

34

"You need to tell him tonight; don't just spring it on him. But when you do, you can tell him this: I am moving to Peace Ridge Village. I am going to close my company in St. Cloud and move here. I am not about to take him out of his school and away from his friends when his mother takes off for her new adventure. Whatever or whomever it is." The words were quiet and final. *And where did that decision come from?* he thought.

"Oh, well that's great. So, I don't have to worry about him. You can be mom and dad both. That's what you've always wanted anyway. Find yourself a new woman and then he won't even miss me." The expression on her face was unreadable, though he'd known her long enough to know the stubborn implacability that could not be penetrated, even with pleas to her conscience and her love, such as it was, for Brian.

Michael walked over to Brian's bedroom and helped him stow his backpack in the closet. He saw that his son had laid out the treasures they'd collected at the park in their excursion this afternoon, and he sat down on the bed beside him and helped him sort them out in rows. The small rocks and pond shells had dirt and moss clinging to them, which Brian carefully brushed into a pile and dumped in the wastebasket.

Michael sat on the bed near his son. "Brian, I am moving to Peace Ridge Village, maybe even as soon as this week. I am closing my company in St. Cloud— the computer business lets me work from home."

"Are you moving in with Mom and me?" Brian asked hopefully, his eyes betraying his hope but his earnest face showing he already knew the answer.

"No," Michael said, "I will have my own place. But we can spend more time together which is what I really want."

Brian looked down at the treasures and lined them up by size, smallest to largest. "That's great, Dad. Will I have my own room?"

"Yes, of course."

"Can I get a dog?"

That was not unexpected. "What kind of dog would you like?"

"I want to go to a pet shelter and find one that no one wants. It doesn't matter what kind. Little or big. I just want to love on it."

Michael clapped Brian on the shoulder and then kissed the top of his head. "Yes, of course, we'll get a dog. Call me later. I want to talk to you. I want to know what kind of place you think we should look for here in Peace Ridge. Maybe you know a place for sale or rent. We can look around together later this week." He closed the door gently on his son.

And walked out without a backward glance at Delaney, knowing without looking that her face was set in stone. It wasn't always that way. He sighed. *I do remember the early days.* He heard the quiet sound of a popping cork as he softly closed the door.

6

The night admitting staff at Overland Park Medical Center were used to seeing just about everything, especially in the early morning hours after a long weekend. They clicked into a synchronized dispassionate rhythm when the Johnson County police accompanied by EMTs brought in the nude woman, her body blue with hypothermia and distressing signs of trauma across her body. IVs were started immediately to rehydrate and blood samples taken to ascertain the presence of drugs, if any. Melissa, the night RN on call, took one look at the woman and gave an order to the staff to check with her on every intervention.

"What kind of forensic evidence do you have so far?" she asked the friendly sergeant with whom she had become distressingly familiar over her four years in the Emergency Room service.

"I'll check with the lieutenant on what he has. I'm riding shotgun on this one; he was the one who got the call that a body had been dumped in an alley in Grandview behind the hotel. We got her there but I don't know what other tests have been ordered." He looked around wearily, hoping this shift would end without any more drama. *I need a shower and a full breakfast and a nap*, he thought. *Back on at two o'clock tomorrow afternoon.*

"We'll get her rehydrated and get her vitals and then call in the sexual assault nurse examiner."

"Okay, all right. But you know that section of Grandview gets a workout, you know? Too many highway intersections and opportunity for…" His voice trailed off. It had been a long night.

"Where was she found?"

"Near the dumpster outside the hotel. Completely nude and wrapped in a blanket that looked new, like it had just been bought to wrap her in. We are doing forensics on it now. It looks as if she'd been dumped in a shower or bathtub after the assault because there was dampness on the blanket in areas that shadowed her body shape."

"Fingerprints on the blanket?"

"We're running it."

"Any ID?"

"Nothing. Clean sweep."

"Okay, Lennie. We'll take it from here. Thanks, as always. Try to get to bed and get some sleep this morning if you can."

He smiled at her briefly and then turned without a word and walked out of the Emergency Room, his hand on his hip unconsciously cradling his holster. Melissa took a moment and looked at the woman on the gurney. Her breathing was shallow and blue lines and bruises extended from her mouth to her ears, cutting deeply into the perfect skin like gashes in a river gulley. Melissa adjusted the flow of the IV and then took the cloth away from the patient and observed the bruises on the upper arms, the redness and bruises around the neck, the broken veins on the cheeks, the knife slashes across the breasts. It looked as if someone had taken a hammer to her hands which were swollen and bloody. *Hit pretty hard, the scum,* was her silent assessment.

On impulse she called the police lieutenant at the Overland Police Department and asked who was on call. Surprisingly, her call was answered by the Chief of Police himself who rarely worked weekends but had come in to amplify the force, trying to get a better handle on their weekend needs. It wasn't her job to call them, but this case bothered her. This woman was her age and she didn't deserve this, no matter her lifestyle.

"I'll come," was his quick response.

"Thanks," Melissa said, grateful for the partnership of hospitals and police.

They weren't able to get together until early Monday morning as the Emergency Room was thronged with the usual drunken and drug-addled walk-ins and automobile accidents. After grabbing her Diet Mountain Dew from her lunch bag, Melissa walked with Chief Donald Torgersen down to the room to see Patient 124, so noted because of her arrival time.

"No identifying characteristics," Melissa told him.

"Yes, I have Lenny's report here," he replied. "This is not the first time we've run into this, but usually we get some sort of ID from the hotel. She was dumped there. They have no idea who she is and I believe them."

"What do you do now?"

"We need to make sure she gets the care that she needs and then when she recovers, we'll interview her."

Melissa looked at him doubtfully. "I have seen this kind of trauma before. What if she does not regain consciousness? What then?"

"Let's give it twenty-four hours. I'll come back tomorrow night. Do your good work as you always do and we'll see what we have then. She looked pretty healthy other than this mess; we just don't know what trauma she experienced other than what we can observe. We'll just have to wait and see."

Melissa watched the Chief walk out of the room. *I hear him,* she thought. *But in the meantime, she's my patient. Body and soul and mind.* She gazed at the woman in the cold white hospital bed. *Just flesh and blood now,* she thought. *But a focus of love and longing and tenderness for someone.* She turned away and looked at the gauges monitoring the woman's vitals. *All in a day's work, but never easy.*

❀

Tom walked slowly into Delaney's kitchen. She blithely and happily confided, "Oh, thanks for coming over, Tom. I have a favor to ask you. I need a ride to the airport tomorrow. Going to London.

"I'm just going for a month to see if there's a business opportunity there. I'll be back sooner than you think." She turned away before she could see the skepticism on his face.

Tom cocked his head toward the pile of suitcases stacked by the door. The haul signaled a much longer stay than a single month.

"I see a woman running away from home." His words were softly spoken and casual, but also with an underlying tinge of anger.

"I don't know what's going to happen. I just know I need to get away." She turned and practiced a sweet smile upon him. "You know, I've not been myself since Dad died. I can't seem to find...my center ... and I want to change the scenery to see things more clearly." She touched his arm lovingly and didn't notice that he shifted away from her touch in an unconscious gesture.

"You just don't know what you want out of life, Delaney," he said bitterly. He turned her to face him and as he held her arms, he said, "You submerge yourself in your fanciful dreams, in escape, in wine. Too much wine."

She looked sharply up at that and rebelliously yanked free of his grip and grabbed her wine glass, sipping it carefully and trying to lock her eyes onto his. Tom looked over her head to the French doors to the backyard. The evening was winding down and the sunset insistently painted the backyard with muted colors of mauve, lavender, bronze, and a shimmery glow of light.

Yes, this. This beauty, he thought. *We can get all we need here and now in nature. But some of us run away. We run, but we carry it with us. No use to change the channel, the perception is within.*

"And what about Brian? Don't you care that you are abandoning him?"

"I am *not* abandoning him," she snarled at him, unaware of the brief spray of spittle that landed on his face. She walked over to the hallway door and paused at the doorway to her bedroom.

"He's just a little kid! What's he supposed to think? His mother running off halfway across the world to chase another man? He's not stupid." *And neither am I*, he thought.

"I'm not going to worry about Brian. He'll be okay with Michael. They won't even miss me! And who said something about another man?"

"Don't play me for a fool, Delaney. I wasn't born yesterday."

Delaney didn't say anything, but gave a cunning glance as she sauntered to the bedroom and left the door provocatively open. Tom could hear the water running in the bathroom. The invitation was clear. He left the house, listening for the soft click behind him. *Don't look for me when you come crawling back to Peace Ridge Village.* The thought was both savage and regretful.

The small boy stood immobile at the window in his bedroom. He watched as Tom climbed into the cab of the pickup and pulled slowly out of the driveway. He watched the red truck drive slowly down the road and then turned slowly away from the window and sat down carefully at his school desk. He reached for his Moleskin notebook and opened it, but somehow wasn't able to read the words on the last page because his eyes were blurry. Wiping the tears from his eyes on his sleeve, he grabbed his mechanical pencil and wrote,

The empty driveway is the saddest thing,
Abject aloneness cold concrete brings.
Love rolls away; loss and tears seep in
To heart crevices cracked wide open...

Here he stopped and laid down his pencil. He bent down to open a page of a new book he'd recently found in his mom's library. It was a book of illustrations from a man named J.J. Audubon. His attention was captured by an illustration of a ground squirrel family on a moss-covered tree trunk and a large boulder. They were so happy and carefree. The ones on the boulder were bigger — *they had to be the mom and dad*, he thought. The little one perched on the tree trunk looking around was the explorer in the family. 1849. The date was sketched lightly in the corner. So long ago but the chipmunks were still alive on the canvas. *If I stare long enough at this picture, maybe I can really be there. And not be here.*

7

Delaney had arrived at Heathrow Airport exhausted and out of sorts. It didn't help that she and the driver struggled to fit all her luggage into the cab. It would have been much easier to have asked Ten to meet her, but Delaney trusted her instincts. Better to be settled in before she called him so he didn't feel obligated to put her up himself. She had told him she was returning to London but had been vague about the date, opting for a surprise appearance. *Plan the dramatic entry,* she had thought. But tiredness and travel logistics made her tongue sharper than usual and she churlishly apologized to the driver for her nasty mouth.

She'd booked AirBnB and found a small one-bedroom *en suite* in South Hampstead not too far from the London Zoo. Just under a thousand pounds a month. She'd booked it for two months and just hoped the closets were large enough for all her belongings. She had wanted to be prepared for all outings, from walks on the Downs to fancy dinners in a castle somewhere. *Maybe with Ten. We'll have to see.*

I'm going to have to play this one carefully, she thought. *He professes great passion when I'm four thousand miles away, but we've only spent one night together. And text messaging is no way to build a real relationship. If there's really something between us, it will become apparent. In the meantime, I'm in London. Away from my real life. Away from all the stress of Peace Ridge. Dad's dying…and Brian.* Her mind skittered away from her young son. She had become proficient at damping down her guilt at leaving him. *He'll be all right with Michael. He probably won't even miss me.*

The middle-aged woman professor who owned the flat was polite but professional. She raised her eyebrows at the pile of luggage but didn't say anything. Delaney's substantial tip to the cab driver was welcomed after he'd lugged it all to the room. *Just big enough to turn around in,* she thought, as she looked around the plain room. A small three-quarters bed was flanked by two small antique end tables. There was a writing desk in the bay window which overlooked the back garden. An alcove opposite the window could accommodate all her luggage and there was a large Ikea wardrobe and a small chest of drawers. The small bathroom was plain but functional.

"Lovely, just lovely," Delaney whispered to Helen, her new temporary landlady.

"People have been happy here. I think you will, too. The kitchen is communal; you're free to use it anytime, but groceries need to be labeled so there's no filching. House rules are posted on the refrigerator. Mostly cautions about loud music late at night and not sharing one's key with anyone, not even a best friend. If a key is lost, I will replace it the first time, but shared keys are cause for eviction. I am sure you understand."

"I'll be your best guest," Delaney promised, flashing her brightest smile, just wanting to throw herself down on the bed and sleep for a few hours.

"There are guidebooks to Hampstead in the sitting room. Feel free to browse. We're just a short walk to Hampstead Heath. Thank you for your deposit. You can leave the balance due with me anytime in check or cash," she replied, reasserting the host relationship, dispelling any thoughts of friendship.

Okay, then, Delaney thought to herself. *I'm in England now. Gotta get used to English reserve.*

She woke up from her two-hour nap feeling drained and lonely. This trip had seemed like a great idea, but the small, unfamiliar surroundings were depressing. *I need a drink.* She stood at the bay window and looked down into the small back garden which was bordered by Flask Walk. On their way to the house Delaney had tiredly noted the winding pedestrian cobblestone street that featured used bookstores, small pubs, boutiques, and delightful flower shops. *Time to get my act together and explore. Once I have a shower, I'll be back in the game.*

There was no one in the sitting room when she left the house and Delaney wondered if she was the only guest in the house. *Fine by me.* She was glad she'd packed a couple of heavy cardigans. It was quite chilly once the afternoon sun fell below the dense cityscape. Flask Walk was narrow and though most of the buildings were only two or three stories, there were only a few patches of sunlight on the pavement and the empty small tables and chairs outside The Flask pub were completely in shadow. *A little walk and then I'll treat myself*, she thought.

Her spirits began to rise as she gazed into the small shops, making a note to visit the attractive stationery shop and the wine and cheese shop with its enticing array of domestic and imported cheeses. *I just love this city,* she exulted. The small bookshop, Keith Fawkes, promised a rewarding visit. She paused briefly in front of it, exhaling the intoxicating smell of books combined with the smell of roasting coffee from the shop next door. An aphrodisiac. No energy for exploration today, but soon.

Now for that drink! Her footsteps were lively as she made her way back to The Flask. An older gentleman who looked as if he'd just stepped off a Fishermen's Friend package held open the door for her and the scent of pipe tobacco mingling with the familiar tap beer smell wafted towards her. The room was dominated by the semi-circular bar, and comfy maroon leather banquettes by the oversized windows were filled with lively groups of people who totally ignored Delaney as she entered and seated herself at one of the battered, highly scrubbed pine tables. She glanced around with pleasure at the books stacked on the shelves above the radiators, the small simple carafes filled with casual blooms on each table, the highly curved fireplace surround. *Bet this place is cozy in the wintertime.*

A young woman with a freckled Irish face offered the menu with a sweet smile.

At these prices my money will disappear fast. Oh well, I'll splurge tonight, but cut back later. "I'm craving your Ploughman's Board." Delaney smiled. "With a New Zealand Sauvignon Blanc."

The first drink went down quickly and before her meal was over, she'd drunk three glasses of wine and an unfamiliar feeling of utter loneliness came over her. Text messaging to the States was expensive, but she messaged Jennie, and then Brian, and then Tom, hoping for a quick response. Late morning in the States. People out and about, maybe not checking their cell phones. No response. *I must be more tired than I thought.* She felt tears well behind her eyes. *Better make it back to the place and crash.* She stumbled slightly as she left the bar and a man lounging nearby helped her right herself.

"Okay there, luv?" he asked. She smiled wanly and made her way back to the flat, glad that she was still clear-headed enough to find it and get the bulky key into the doorlatch.

The text message dinged as she crawled under the thick blanket.

"Mother, can I have a little bit of those special papers that you found in England? Please? I'm working on a project. Brian."

"Sure," she responded. *Not even an 'I love you' from him. Better go to sleep before my pity party really gets going.*

8

J eremy stretched out on the bed and flipped the remote control through the cable stations, trying to find something interesting. *Not much on.* He'd showered and his hair was still wet which was strangely comfortable. He tucked his now-wet pillow up under his neck and sprawled on the sheets. Felt good after today. The evening was cooling down but the humidity was high and there was no breeze coming through the open windows. Occasionally he'd hear a moth beat its wings against the screen, the coo-coo-cooing sounds of the mourning doves, and the soft hops of the cottontail through the grass. They were comforting, sounds he'd longed to hear when hidden in the rocks of the Hindu Kush, his attention focused on his hidden enemy. *When I get home to Minnesota,* he would think, *I'll never take green nature for granted again.*

As much as he loved construction work, it had really given him a physical workout. *I'm using muscles I had forgotten I had since I came back from Afghanistan.* Just resting in the peace and quiet of their bedroom was pleasant and he looked forward to a night of fooling around with Tiff. If she was up for it.

She was still in the bathroom, lingering as long as possible. He knew it was a woman thing, this fixation with bathing, bath soaps, perfumes, bubbles. He imagined her stretched out in the tub, her glistening, long mocha legs poking out at the end of the tub, her long black hair twisted up in a topknot out of the water, and he smiled. The bathroom, tub especially, was really too small for his six-foot Afghani wife, but there were other spending priorities in line before a home remodel.

That thought brought his mind around to the topic that was never far below the surface for both of them. Getting Tiff's mind psychologically ready for surgery and then getting the money together to get it done. He'd fiercely promised her that he'd do it for her and he didn't abandon his promises. His face hardened suddenly and he felt his muscles tense. *Leave it, Jeremy. Leave it!*

He heard his wife's tuneless singing to herself as she sloshed out of the tub and completed her bath. *Now will come the tinkle,* he thought, as he heard her sit lightly on the commode. At least ten minutes.

This job with Bill Nelson was amazing luck. Looked as if it would last for a while, too, with The Jason House project. His goal was to get in as much overtime as possible so they'd have all the money they needed.

His mind shifted away from Tiff and, once again, he began to go over his mental list. His action steps. The required logistics to complete the mission. The requisite funding and insurance. Their immersion into the various procedures and sequencing of the surgery, research into the best doctors and hospitals, who had the best psychological care, what post-care would be required. And then – he dared hope – his sweet, loving wife, so beautiful on the outside, would be equally beautiful on the inside. Not for him. He loved her wildly just as she was. But for her. A lifting of the shame of over twenty years. Twenty years! His mind shut down and he closed his eyes to the mental pictures that filled his head. Those barbarians! A tradition of over twenty-seven centuries. *We should have bombed them all into the stone age.*

Jeremy walked into the kitchen and grabbed a drink of cold water from the faucet. The shift in setting helped calm his mind and he had a teasing smile on his face when he walked into the bedroom. Tiff had snuck into bed and was, as usual, demurely covered neck-to-toe with the bedsheet. He playfully tugged it away from her as he hopped onto the bed.

"Now, I've got you, my pretty!"

He said that to her every time, and even though she didn't understand the cultural reference, she loved the ritual. And always loved how it ended in Jeremy's smothering kisses. That was the best part.

"I've just been thinking about you!" Romyn gave Titos a warm smile. The older man smiled but didn't say anything, just rested his forearms wearily on her counter.

"Everything okay? Coming along on schedule?" Romyn sensed the exhaustion and frustration in her new neighbor.

"'I grow old always learning many things,'" Titos replied with a familiar Greek aphorism. "I thought New York State was tough to do business in. Minnesota makes New York look like grade school."

"Yes, we say 'if it's not one thing it's another' with the State of Minnesota. They can always find something you're doing wrong. Need to be one step ahead of them. This is the state where nothing is allowed. That's their opening bid."

Titos shook his head wearily. "There are over three hundred and eighty separate rules from the Department of Health. They tell me I can't cook with cast iron unless I also serve the food in it. They tell me my employees should wash their hands. That I should have clean bathrooms. They tell me I should frequently remove dead birds, insects, and other pests. It's common sense," he said forcefully. "If I didn't run a clean establishment, I would be out of business and since it's my money, I am going to be careful." Under his breath he said, "I am not about to invest over $400,000 into a restaurant and then see us closed down or worse yet, someone get sick."

Romyn nodded in sympathy. "I hear some of this from Veronica and Earl. They are going through the hoops now for

The Jason House, too. If you think food service is tough, you should add taking care of the elderly and vulnerable to it. That's where the bureaucrats really get into it." She sighed. "And probably rightfully so, in some ways. But it adds to the cost of doing business.

"Time for a cup of coffee?" she added, nodding to the empty table in the center of the store.

"No, I have got to get back to the store. I left Jeremy in charge for this afternoon. I'm taking Maria into Little Falls to do some shopping. We could get it here at Walmart, but she likes to spend some time talking to Brenda–" his hands signed a conversation unconsciously, "– and I owe her that. She gets lonely."

"Please give her my love," Romyn smiled. "That reminds me. I want to have you two over for a meal, along with George, Jeremy and Tiff. I think I'll invite Pastor, too. He looks as if he could use a good feeding. And Veronica. She's lonely."

Titos nodded slowly. "Nice of you. And Earl."

"Why don't you ask Brenda if she can come, too? Ask her about a Saturday that will be good for her? We'll set a date and then she can be the translator for Maria so she doesn't feel so left out."

"I think Brenda would welcome a chance to come back to Peace Ridge," Titos said meaningfully.

"Are you saying what I am thinking?"

"I don't know if there's any romance there, but there's a connection of some type. Maria tells me she asks a lot of questions about Randy, and if I know women, they always ask a lot of questions when they are interested in a man."

"It does my heart good to see her friendship with him. He's been so isolated for so long. I just don't want him to get hurt— he could lose his heart so easily." Romyn knew she was about to tread on personal territory, but she thought she'd risk it anyway. "Sometime, maybe at dinner, you can tell us how you and Maria met and married? I think we'd all like to know."

"We don't have any secrets, Romyn, but we like to keep things private. New York friends warned us that when we moved to a small town everyone would know everything about us, that our lives would be an open book." He looked at her meaningfully. "I would like to move slowly with our friendships. Maria needs to learn to trust again and we had a bad introduction on the ridge when the rocks were thrown at us. She – we – have gotten over that now and we're starting to feel like we're a part of the town, but it will take time to be accepted. That I know."

Romyn grimaced. "Yes, Earl and I know. We've been here for over ten years now—we're from the East Coast, too — but some people still refer to where we live as the 'old Casey place.' A family named Casey lived there in the 1950s, for heaven's sake! Landmarks reflect the historical storyline of town. Takes a while for new people to become part of the story. Your restaurant will help a lot. We're all looking forward to it." *Time to shift to more neutral territory.* "When's the grand opening?"

"We're targeting three weeks. Should be ready. Still interviewing and hiring staff. Tiff will be the hostess. That will draw them in."

"She is beautiful. All the young women in Peace Ridge Village had set their caps for Jeremy when he went off to Afghanistan, but he comes home with a beautiful bride, leaving a lot of heartbroken women!"

"He's a wonderful young man. Like another son to me." Those last words were choked out. Titos waved a quick goodbye to Romyn, grabbed his receipt for the gas, and hurriedly left the store. Romyn stared out the window as his SUV pulled away from the gas pumps.

Like another son. Those words hit home and Romyn sat down hard on her stool. Millie jumped up on the counter and then onto Romyn's lap, insistently demanding long hand caresses, her green eyes blissfully half-closed and her sweet, perfectly proportioned, heart-shaped face looking at Romyn with love. Romyn blinked absent-mindedly at Millie, her mind on their own JRM, her Jason, Ed's Robby. *We've all lost sons,* she thought, her eyes filling with tears.

Her mind shifted to Delaney who was running away from her young son, Brian. *And some of us leave our sons to fend for themselves,* she thought savagely. But that thought was totally unworthy. Her emotions concerning Delaney were often buried deep in her mind, but for someone like herself, who had wanted and lost children, Delaney's indifference to Brian made her so angry. *Submerge me in Your love, Jesus, that I might spill over and flood Delaney with love. You said 'Love your enemies.' I don't usually think of Delaney as my enemy but I sure get irritated with her.*

Father God, my thoughts toward Delaney are not Your thoughts. Forgive me.

The lines from Brian's tribute to Jason came into her mind, as they often did since dedication day:

Jason, lost soul, young man so alive,
To all the questions simply unanswered.
Your life's promise no man can surmise,
Your legacy played forward, your goodness now transferred.

That's what we're about, she reaffirmed to herself. *Paying it forward. That's the meaning of love.* Romyn felt herself close to an out-and-out bawling session. She took a deep breath and determinedly shifted her mind to the afternoon's "To do" list, good honest work her best coping mechanism for grief. She responded then to the pleading cat and gave her full attention to the sweet little happy face for the next ten minutes, the cat's purr calming her own heartache.

9

Ed drove carefully into the Edina facility and parked the car near the entrance. He had a handicapped permit sticker, but he wasn't going to use it to pick up Jill. He never knew what might trigger something and thought it best to be totally matter-of-fact and normal. He was anxious, though. He had to admit this. Taking Jill home to Peace Ridge from the long-term care facility in Edina was a big risk.

He had reassured the nurses and doctors that he'd be able to cope with whatever happened with their month together in Peace Ridge. It was a trial away from the facility. They didn't believe she'd really recovered from her catatonic depression, but were willing to let Ed take a chance on a normal life for them. Ten years. Ten lost years of marriage, friendship, love, normalcy. Ed grimaced as he walked into the facility. *Sometimes the authorities get in the way of families trying to work things out for themselves. Why don't they just trust me and my love? I'm her husband, for heaven's sake. And a pastor, too. That should count for something.*

Jill was waiting in the lobby for him. A good sign. No wheelchair. A few suitcases. She stood up suddenly as he walked through the revolving door and gave him a welcoming smile. He never failed to be grateful for that simple fact of recognition. Jill had a cup of coffee in a take-out container and as she rose to greet his kiss, she handed him the cup.

"Here's our coffee," she said. "Let's not forget it."

Ed took the cup and sipped from it, then taking her arm said, "Ready or not? Should we head out to Peace Ridge?"

Jill looked at him with a mixture of hope and fear on her face. "Eddy, I want to go home," she said, the words making his heart beat fast.

"Me, too," he responded, his voice thick with emotion. "We're early enough in the day that we won't run into traffic going north. We'll miss the rush hour traffic around Elk River, I think." Those words were meaningless to Jill, but helped Ed make a transition from Edina-equals-Long Term Care to Peace Ridge Village-equals-Home.

"Jill, honey," he said, "are you hungry? Do you want something to eat before we head north?"

She shook her head. "I had a sandwich at lunchtime and I'm okay."

Those simple words warmed Ed's heart. From someone who was immersed in the abyss of depression to be able to mention a sandwich was a gift of God. *Oh, Jesus,* he whispered to himself, *I am so grateful.*

He grabbed her bags and settled her in the car, seat belt fastened. He turned to her, "Ready to go, honey?" he asked.

"Go?" she replied. "Are we going to Chanhassen now?" She saw the confusion on his face.

"No, we've moved. We're going to Peace Ridge Village now where we live. Up north. That's our new church," he said confidently, hoping she'd understand.

"Are Emily and Robby going to be there, too?" she asked. Her face was placid and accepting.

Ed sat in the driver's seat immobile, his eyes fixed on the oak trees that lined the parking lot. There was a slight breeze from the west that ruffled the springtime leaves, turning their colors from pale lime green to pale silver and back to green again. He took a deep breath and turned to her. "Robby is in school now. He doesn't live in Peace Ridge Village; he lives over by the University of Minnesota with other ...students." *I wonder how much she remembers of his self-maiming and*

54

blindness, if anything. Her face remained opaque. In their other life, before the accident, he could read all her thoughts like an open book. But not now. Though she clearly recognized him, he knew there were likely immense gaps in her memory that might never be filled. Probably for her own psychological health. *How to tell her about Emily?*

"I don't know how much you remember about the car accident we had?" Jill looked at him with a puzzled expression. *Please help me, Jesus*, he prayed. "We lost our little girl then — our Emily is with Jesus now."

"In that place? Where we are going?" she asked. "Will we see Emily when we get ...to..." she stumbled, "Peace Ridge Village?"

"We will see Emily when we see Jesus in heaven." He was unsure how direct he should be. It was barely enough that she recognized him. *Would the death of Emily and the loss of Robby push her over the edge and back into blackness? Maybe it's best to just speak the Christian comfort language for now.*

"Do you remember how beautiful Emily was? Her blonde curls, her dancing feet; how she could never stand still when we would play music in children's church?" He struggled with the past tense. Maybe Jill wouldn't notice.

"I remember," Jill said uncertainly. Under her breath she weakly sang, *"Jesus loves me, this I know. For the Bible tells me so. Little ones to him belong...."* She stopped her singing and looked down at her hands, which she had been clutching nervously.

"Take another sip of coffee before we get to the traffic on 169 going north. I don't want it to spill on you." She dutifully complied and Ed shifted the car into gear and began the uncertain drive up north to Peace Ridge Village. *Maybe I underestimated this, Father God. Dear Jesus, help me do and say the right things. Help me to keep her present. In the here and now. Where the three of us are, there is strength for the moment. There'll be a lot of moments in the next month. And so much is riding on it.*

They were quiet and comfortable together when Ed maneuvered the car through the early afternoon traffic out of the city. It took all his concentration to get around the construction on the roads and detours. *Two seasons in Minnesota,* he thought impatiently: *Winter and road construction. This drive really tests my driving competence.*

Finally, they got through the worst of the traffic and were heading up 169 in a straight shot to Peace Ridge Village. He could turn his attention to Jill who had sat unnaturally quiet in the passenger seat, occasionally glancing out the window but looking at the passing scenery as if it was a video travelogue.

"Nearly home now, honey," he said as he reached the outskirts of Peace Ridge Village. It was a glorious late spring day and all the trees lining Main Street were in full "shouting spring" mode. Ed rolled the window down on the car and slowed his speed as he drove into town, calling out the landmarks as they passed. "Here's the Crossroads Convenience store. Romyn and Earl can't wait to be friends with you. Here's the Tall Rigger. They have the best hamburgers in town. Over there is the old Peterson Printing Plant. That's what's going to be the new assisted living place called The Jason House, after Romyn and Earl's son."

Finally, they turned onto Valley Drive and arrived at the church parking lot. Jill looked around, bewildered and uncertain. Ed helped her out of the car and took her along the walk to the parsonage around in back, behind the church. "I'll come out and get your bags later. Let's get settled in first." Jill was compliant, only pausing when they got to the walk to his little garden.

"Let's sit here for a moment, Eddy," she said. "The garden smells so pretty. Can we just sit here for a moment and smell it?"

Ed had an old, cheap, Walmart plastic and aluminum folding chair, and he brought it over and set it on the walk facing the garden. She sank into it gracefully. *Why haven't I invested in real outdoor furniture?* he thought. *Because I never thought to enjoy this space with Jill again.*

"I want to let Biep out. He's my...our cat... and he'll be wanting to go outside." Ed disappeared into the kitchen and soon the tiger cat was sniffing Jill's purse and pants legs and then walked over to Ed who had perched on the side rails of the porch, affectionately nudging his legs. It was a cloudless day and the blues and greens of spring were painted by the Master Painter himself. The bright sun cast the buildings in sharp relief and Ed noticed that he'd need to paint the garage again soon. He could see the faded shadowy colors of the wood behind the paint. *But it will be fun to make this our new home,* he thought exultantly. *A real home, not just the parsonage. Not just a house.* Having Jill here made him realize how incomplete his life had been in this house. He had called it home, but it needed a family to be really home.

"Sit here, hon, and I will go to the car and bring in all the bags. It will take only a moment." He felt enthused, excited about the potential of reclaiming his married life with Jill again. Some things would have to wait. He knew that. But it was sufficient to just be together in their own home for now. When he got back to the parsonage, carrying her over-large suitcase, the travel bag, and a brown grocery bag of toiletries, she wasn't on the porch, but he could see the back door was open, so he set everything down and quietly walked inside.

Jill was sitting on a chair at the dining room table. She had taken a photo from the cherry bureau and was fixedly staring at it. She seemed oblivious to Ed's presence and when he walked over and lightly touched her shoulder it was as if he wasn't there. *Time, time,* he thought. Ed walked into the kitchen and put the kettle on to boil. Tea. The answer for everything. He opened the refrigerator door and took out the chicken noodle soup he had prepared yesterday for their supper and upended it into a pot. *I'll just leave her alone to get familiar with the house,* he reassured himself. He let the Biepster back into the house and opened a can of cat food for him.

"Wanna' cup of tea, Jill?" he asked. No answer. He walked into the dining room. No Jill. *Where'd she go?* He checked the living room and then walked more purposefully into the den, where he found his wife on her knees. She had a photo of the four of them in her hands and she was weeping silent tears that drenched her blouse and the faded velvet sofa upon which she rested.

"Eddy? Eddy?" she cried.

He crouched next to her and tried to take the photo away from her and rest it on a couch cushion, as he put his arms around her, whispering soothing sounds. She clung fervently to the picture.

"Eddy! Eddy!" she repeated. He was without words, at once thrown back into their shared grief and into a state of fearfulness about what was to come about their life together.

"Jill, honey," he said. "Let's lie down, shall we?" He lifted her to her feet and pivoted her down onto the old sofa and then laid down beside her, stroking her hair, her face, her arms, trying in some way to calm the tears that poured out in an unending flow. He dabbed them with his sleeve. There was an old afghan on the back of the sofa and he grabbed it and wrapped the two of them securely in it, the soft pressure of the old wool afghan strangely comforting. Like a Thunder Shirt for scared dogs.

"There, there," he said, the words of his mother whenever anything used to happen to him. "It's okay, Jill. It's okay. We're here. We're a family. This is our family. This is our home. We're together now. We are all okay. We just have our little cat, our Biepster. He's joined our family."

As if hearing his name, the cat jumped up on the sofa and curled up at Jill's and Eddy's feet, washing his face assiduously as if he hadn't bathed in years. Eddy continued to stroke her face and kiss Jill's nose and closed eyes until he heard the sound of deep, shuddering breaths. In the kitchen he could smell the scorched soup, but that was a small matter now. Ed felt the old stirrings and adjusted his body to be more comfortable. He remembered those days before the accident when they would wrap themselves around each other, their faces breath to breath, so close they were nearly unable to focus. *"One flesh... cleaving to one another."* Ten years. Ten long years. He lay quietly next to Jill for a long time, wanting desperately to caress her but knowing now was not yet the time. He shifted his gaze to her face.

Jill had fallen asleep. So beautiful in repose. Serene. Childlike. Untroubled. Without disturbing her, Ed looked at the framed photo in her hand. Their family, of course. He and Jill, Robby and Emily. He had long gazed at it in the dark nights of his soul when in the well of loneliness, those long years without his family. *Times past*, he thought. *I've lived through it. She's just now experiencing it. The loss. The pain. The heartbreak. The loss of Emily. She's never processed it. I don't think she even knows about Robby's blinding himself. How do I— how do we get through this together?*

"Oh, dear Jesus. You are going to have to help us here. I am out of my depth. I thought I could handle this, but I didn't expect this, the need for catching up. Help me. This is my simple plea for right now. I love You, Jesus."

Ed gently lifted himself off the couch and tucked the afghan more tightly around Jill. He briefly scratched the ears of his little cat and then walked stiffly into the kitchen. *The soup is ruined,* he thought, as he turned the fire off under the near-empty teakettle. *Just set it aside. Let her sleep for a while and then we'll go out to the Tall Rigger and maybe meet some of the Peace Ridge Villagers tonight. That'll probably be good for her. A new, fresh start. And maybe give me some breathing room, so I can figure out what I have to do to make our new life, our marriage, work again. I didn't expect this. I thought we could just* resume. *That's not possible. I see that now. It's not to resume. It's a total re-boot.*

On impulse, he called Romyn. "Come for supper on Saturday night," she said. "We're having a little gathering. It'll be a chance to welcome Jill to our special neighbors. In the meantime, I'll be praying, Ed."

"Thank you, Romyn," Ed said. "I need your prayers now."

"I know. Grief for what you've lost and fear for the future plunge us right down into the valley, don't they? 'In quietness and confidence is your strength,' Ed. Be strong, my friend. See you both on Saturday. By then, she'll become more comfortable here in her new home with you by her side. I will pray for you both."

10

It had been a frantically busy day at the family and children shelter. Mary, the center's director, slumped wearily into the faded, overstuffed armchair in the faculty break room and just sat there for a few minutes, her mind blank. She knew the end of the month reports were due in two days and she needed to get started on them but for now she was just going to take her well-deserved break and try to relax. This job was getting both increasingly more difficult and less rewarding every day. After nearly ten years, the revolving door of broken families and homeless children had finally begun to get to her and she felt her natural optimism fade earlier and earlier each day.

I need a vacation, I really do, she thought. *But who would look after the families and kids?*

The break room was empty and she was grateful for the quiet, only the occasional *thunk* of the ice machine breaking the silence. Her staff were busy with their usual mid-morning tasks, with the younger children in the facility pre-school and the older children off to the Maplewood school system. The women victims of domestic abuse were usually in vocational training this time of morning so Mary knew she could steal a half hour. Hope she'd find her energy again.

The *Star Tribune* newspaper was all over the coffee table, the sections scattered as if a tornado had blown through the room. *Really!* She methodically began to gather the paper together, her OCD kicking in as she stacked the paper in proper order, smoothing out the improperly folded newsprint. Maybe she'd find something interesting in it — the Thursday edition usually had features on food and recipes and that could give her some ideas. Her mind was unfocused on the paper. Hard to set the center's problems aside and read about others' problems and challenges. In the national news section a small photograph and paragraph caught her eye. She wondered later how she had even noticed it. A hospital in Kansas City was enlisting the public's help in identifying a woman who had amnesia and no identification. She was about thirty-eight years old, brown eyes, blonde hair, spoke very little but with a southern accent. The hospital staff thought she might be from the south somewhere and hoped someone would recognize her face and help her recover.

Mary stared at the photograph closely. There was something eerily familiar about the woman, but she knew she'd never seen her before. What was it that caught her attention? The eyes? The photo showed a one-time beautiful woman but the sadness in her eyes was overwhelming and compelling. "No memory of who she is or where she's from," the article stated, with a phone number and website address for the Overland Park police department.

Police, Mary thought. *That is not good.* On impulse, she tore out the corner of the newspaper that held the article and stuffed it into her pocket. *Might as well be on the look-out. Never know. Never know.* She walked over to the coffee machine and punched the button for "coffee" on the machine. Instant, but maybe it'd give her a shot of energy. *I'll need it this afternoon.*

Veronica walked wearily to her car and drove unseeing up the ridge to her lodge home in the woods. She was exhausted. She liked working with Earl and Romyn on the plans for The Jason House and checking into foster care regulations, but staring at a computer all day and trying to understand the labyrinth of the State of Minnesota rules for an assisted living facility seemed like an endless, unfruitful walk in a classic maze. *Not Hampton Court,* she thought. *Not a diversion for fun. It's an endless search that is designed to make you throw your hands up in the air and give up.*

Her home in the hills was welcoming and friendly and Veronica sighed in gratitude for this place, even while she busied herself with tasks to try to stave off the nightly depression that always threatened to take over her mind and dominate her lonely evenings. It was the stark contrast of her empty house and the vibrant life and love in the Randall's home that sent her into her nightly downward spiral. Earl was paralyzed, true, but he and Romyn had a rich life together nonetheless. Veronica observed the quiet love and caring intimacy they shared and it was like a dagger to her heart. *Did Gary and I ever have that closeness?* she wondered. *I think we did in the beginning...we were a team, we were building the business. The intensity of those plans may have camouflaged some of the problems in our marriage, problems that led to...* but then she skittered away from the thought of Gary's betrayal and his suicide.

Veronica walked wearily into the kitchen and set her purse on the stool while she walked over to the refrigerator and stared into it unseeing. She was beginning to lose weight again because she had no interest in food, but her fear of falling back into the suicidal madness of last winter caused her to search the freezer for a something substantial. She took out a frozen chicken breast and some frozen peas. *But what is the end? What is the purpose? I feed my body and live for another day, but why?* She knew those thoughts were unworthy and deliberately shut them down, walked over to the TV and switched on the news. *Might as well divert myself with others' issues,* she thought. *Can't handle my own.*

A sudden loud thump rocked the floor-to-ceiling windows. Veronica started and then walked over to the deck to check out the noise. The deck light that came on automatically with any movement revealed the soft feathered body on the deck. A fully-grown grouse had flown full-tilt into the window. It was unmoving. Veronica stared at it for several long moments. Its eyes were open with a stare of surprise, as if it had expected to soar and instead found itself sinking. She knew she needed to do something but she was immobile. A scrap of long-ago Sunday school scripture came into her mind. "Teach us to number our days." Days numbered. Numbered days. The phrase repeated itself in her mind, over and over. She mindlessly walked over to the kitchen and poured herself a glass of wine, her eyes filled with tears.

11

"Ready to head out, Brian?" Michael called into the hallway, knowing that his son had been raring to go since early morning. *It's amazing he's slept at all.* He heard Brian get out of bed at least once in the night to take another look at the pet bed, the kennel, and the ceramic water and food dishes all arranged tidily in the hallway. They'd had long talks the night before as they stared at the dog food section in Walmart and discussed the right food to buy. Michael was totally indifferent but Brian was insistent that it had to be 'just the right kind.' They bought a small bag of dog treats, 'so he'll know I am his friend,' Brian said, as they agreed to buy food after they picked out their dog.

"Different breeds require different diets, Dad," Brian said confidently.

"I see you've been researching this subject," Michael replied with a broad smile.

"And if we get an older dog, he'd need different food than a younger dog or a puppy."

"Are you interested in a puppy, Brian? I thought you wanted an older dog?" Michael began to calculate the commitment of time and training with a puppy.

"I will know him when I see him," Brian replied quietly. "There is a dog just for me there. Just for us," he amended.

The National Adoption Weekend event at PetSmart in St. Cloud would begin at nine o'clock, with time enough for a breakfast stop at McDonald's.

"What do you hear from your mother?" Michael asked casually as they settled into their booth at McDonalds in St. Cloud. Michael had received a cryptic text that simply said she'd arrived in London and would be in touch. Brian carefully unwrapped his sausage burrito and opened his milk carton before he replied in a quiet voice.

"She said she's in her apartment, but it's small." He added in a small voice, "She said she might not come home in two weeks like she planned."

Michael knew Delaney had not been honest with Brian about how long she wanted to stay in London.

"How does that make you feel?" Michael asked.

"I was hoping that I could go there and visit her, but if we get a dog, I won't be able to leave him. I've been thinking that I would like to name him Thor, especially if he's a really strong dog. Thor is the Norse god of strength."

"He might already have a name."

"Yes, but if he's mine, I will give him a name. That's really important, Dad, so he knows I am his person."

"I see," Michael said, camouflaging his amusement with a long drink of coffee.

When they arrived, the PetSmart parking lot was filled and Brian anxiously walked ahead of his father into the store, worried that *his* dog might be already selected by someone else. But most of the customers were busy in other areas of the store and there were only a couple of people in the open kennel area in which a dozen or more dogs romped and played. Brian stood motionless at the edge of the kennel and looked intently at each dog. At a nod from Michael, the attendant invited him in to play with them. Brian sat down at the inside edge of the enclosure and hugged his knees to his chin.

"He's trying to encourage the right dog to come to him," Michael whispered to himself.

"Excuse me?" a stranger said.

Michael turned to the woman who stood a few steps away. "Oh, I was just muttering to myself. That's my son. He's trying to find his new dog by having his new dog find him."

She smiled and her face was illuminated by a sweetness. "Looks to me as if there are a lot of dogs that would like to go home with him."

They watched together in silence as dogs of all sizes and shapes sniffed at Brian and eagerly accepted a pat on the head before resuming their play with the other dogs.

"He's determined that it be a special one, one that no one wants, so he can give him a good home and spoil him with love." Michael smiled at her. "Do you have a dog?"

"No, not now. We used to when the kids were small, but not now. I miss having one though. I sometimes come into PetSmart just to get my dog fix."

She has beautiful, kind eyes, Michael thought, surprising himself.

"You could take one home with you!" he teased.

"I work such long hours, it wouldn't be fair."

"Do you live in St. Cloud?"

"No, I live in Bloomington and work in Edina, but I made a trip to St. Cloud to drop off some stuff at my daughter's house. She lives here."

"I used to work in St. Cloud. My computer business was based here."

"Where do you live now?"

"Peace Ridge Village. About sixty miles northeast of here."

"I know Peace Ridge Village," she said hesitantly.

"It's really just a bend in the road."

"I know. But the hills of Peace Ridge are said to be lovely. Great place to take a dog for a walk. Speaking of which, I think a dog has found your son."

Michael looked over at Brian who was lovingly patting the dirty white Schnauzer mix whose head was lying on the boy's lap. As they watched he looked into Brian's eyes, yawned, gave a big sigh and settled more comfortably into a snooze.

The PetSmart attendant, seeing a likely sale in process, walked over to Michael and said, "I think he's found one he likes."

"It's a Schnauzer, is it?" Michael asked.

"Schnauzer mix, about nine months old. Someone dropped him off in a cardboard kennel box just before we opened about a week ago. He's still got some growing to do and we're trying to get some weight on him. You can see he's a little skinny."

Michael looked at the sleeping dog and could faintly see the outline of his ribs.

"A Schnauzer. Right geography, at least. Germany. Brian wanted a guard dog he could name Thor. Not sure he's quite the guard dog, seems too little."

"They are good watchdogs but make really great pets, too. Loving and loyal."

"Sounds like just what I need!" Michael turned to the woman with a smile.

"They always say, if you want unconditional love, just look down."

"I'm Michael," he said, with an outstretched hand.

"I'm Pam," she replied with a smile.

"Pam from Bloomington."

"Michael from Peace Ridge Village." They smiled at one another as if sharing a secret.

"His name is Whiskers," the PetSmart attendant said as Brian and his dog walked up. "Let me get a leash and you guys can take him around for a walk. We have an open area in the back that's fenced off."

I like her, Michael thought and shot a quick glance at her left hand. *No wedding ring.* "Just a minute, Brian." Pam raised her hand as if to say goodbye and on impulse Michael said, "Would you like to get together for coffee sometime?"

"Not today, Michael. I think you have your hands full here, but yes, sometime would be nice." Her warm smile transformed her face.

He reached into his pocket for a business card and pen. "Here's my card. What's your number? I'll call you next week. We'll get our dog family settled in here and I'll tell you all about it."

"Looking forward to it." There was that smile again.

Brian crouched down to his dog and crooned softly into his ears. The perky feathered ears twitched with happiness as his rear end wriggled back and forth. An exuberant, unexpected cloud of happiness enveloped all three of them, "He's our dog now, isn't he, Dad?" he asked hopefully.

"What did you and Veronica discover?" Romyn set the heavy grocery bags down on the kitchen table and began to unpack them. Earl wheeled his chair over to the table and took the milk and eggs onto his lap and wheeled to the refrigerator. He grunted as he lifted the milk jugs into the refrigerator and then turned back to Romyn with a slight grimace.

"It's more complicated than you can imagine. The good news is that all foster care is administered locally through the counties so we can work it out here."

"And the bad news?"

"The bad news is that the qualification process is lengthy and there is no guarantee that it can be a permanent solution. We need to qualify for a Permanency Resource Family Home, meaning we will take care of Clay and Sophie while we and others try to find Lisa and hope she can take them back someday. And if that doesn't work out, we are qualified to adopt them. It might take months but more likely years." He sighed heavily.

"But if they were here with us in the meantime, it would still be better than where they are!"

"We don't know what would happen if Lisa were to show up unexpectedly in a year or so and want them back. How painful and disruptive that would be for us all."

"But we have to do something for those kids now, Earl. They can't live in limbo there forever, hoping day by day that their mom will show up. They need stability. They need our love. And," she looked at Earl tenderly, "we need them, too. We need to share our love and blessings with these precious kids. You and I both could hardly keep from bawling when we dropped them off in Maplewood last week!"

"I am all for going ahead and starting the paperwork. We have to provide some reason for the jurisdiction of our county as their last living place was Ramsey County."

"In their car! On the streets in St. Paul? How is that their last place?" Romyn's tiredness and frustration caused her voice to be louder than usual and she immediately regretted it when she saw Earl's face. "I'm sorry," she said quickly. "I just want to have them here. Every night I think of little Sophie crying herself to sleep and Clay trying to be the big man and take care of her."

"Veronica had a good idea. Last winter the kids were living in their car on Miller Street and in George's lean-to shed behind the café. She thinks that a case might be made that Miller Street was their last permanent address. If George would agree to it, it would make this county the jurisdiction and add some weight to our claim to fostering rights."

"That makes me feel better right now, Earl. Let me get supper going and let's talk about it."

"Sounds good." Earl wheeled his chair to the buffet and began to collect the placemats and the dinner plates. "There is another wrinkle. If they cannot find Lisa – and they told us at Maplewood that she'd not been once to see the kids in the weeks they've been there – they have to demonstrate that they've exhausted all possibilities to contact her before we can adopt them. And they have to try to find the father and he has to give up his parental rights."

"Ah yes, the missing father. David Shapiro, Richard Shapiro? What is his name? Clay barely knew him and Sophie not at all."

"It's for everyone's protection that kids stay with the biological parents when possible, but in this case it seems to me that both Lisa and this Shapiro guy gave up their rights to be parents a long time ago!" Earl was normally even-tempered and spoke mildly, but there was real anger in his voice. Romyn and Earl's treasured elderly dogs had been peacefully dozing in front of the stove but stirred at the tone in Earl's voice, Sam giving a low rumbling growl.

"It's okay, ol' boy. Just venting. Just venting."

"Let's get it underway, at least. Any little step will help. Is Veronica able to help us or will she be all tied up with The Jason House stuff?"

"She said she could help get the paperwork underway. We'll have to complete most of it." Earl looked pensive. "And I worry about Veronica, too. There's a deep vein of loneliness and maybe even depression there. I see her working hard all day and when we shut down the computer she seems to deflate and retreat into herself. Seems as if her battery runs down every night."

"And she's private, too. Doesn't share much."

"Ashamed of her nervous breakdown and that mess last winter, I think."

"She's among friends here."

"Yes, she knows it but she's alone and has no one to share her life. If I didn't have you, Romyn…" His voice trailed off.

"And if I didn't have you, Earl!" Romyn smiled. Their familiar refrain. 'Praise God from whom all blessings flow.'

"Let's eat."

12

"How's it going, Jen?" Paul slapped his cap down on the kitchen counter and then grabbed orange juice from the fridge. He pushed aside the paperwork cluttering the kitchen table and perched lightly on a chair.

Jennie looked up happily. "Did you see we got the shipment of spice jars?"

"I wondered about that. Must be a pallet's worth stacked in the garage. Where are you going to install your production and packing line, my dear? Have you thought about that yet?"

Jennie pushed her arms away from the laptop and stretched her stiff shoulder muscles. She'd been on the computer since early morning after the chores were done and her concentration had camouflaged her immobility. "Stiff," she declared, as she reached over and downed a swallow from his glass of orange juice.

"First things first, I guess. I know I need to figure that out. I'm sure the organic certification people have rules and regulations there, too. Don't suppose you'd want to give over some of your garage space for a pack house?"

"I was afraid you'd ask that. We need the garage for the farm. That's still the first priority. What about this, though. I was thinking we could throw up a small simple building next to the greenhouse. Wouldn't have to be very big. A couple of windows. Make some long tables. Put in water and a sink. We'd need that. Wouldn't have to be too complicated, but would do for a small start-up. What do you think?"

Jennie's response was to lean over and kiss her husband. "What do you think I think?" she said gratefully.

"I could ask Bill to help out if he has any free time. Though he's swamped with The Jason House. Maybe Jeremy could lend a hand. Menards has all the stuff we'd need. Would have to put in a slab—I can do that — and it would need electricity, too, so we're looking at about $10,000 at least. We'd have to figure out where and how to get that money — I can talk to the bank — but I think we can get it done."

"You always seem to find a way to get money for a new building!" Jennie teased.

"That's what farms are for. More equipment, more buildings."

"And more cows!"

"What's all this paperwork?" He gestured to the papers piled all around the laptop.

"We need to launch the herb company at the Fancy Food Show and I have to be a member of the Specialty Food Association to do that, so there's lots of membership requirements. They need samples and we'll have to develop all the marketing materials. We won't have those for several weeks yet, but I want to know the steps we need."

"Aren't you getting ahead of yourself here, Jennie? That seems a little too big to start out, if you want my opinion."

"Paul, I know how to do this!"

"Why don't you start small? Try to sell to some of the stores in Minneapolis first? Do some farmers' markets around the area. Get a sense of how popular they are ..."

"This is how you create buzz and it doesn't cost very much, about $300 to be a member of the association."

"Plus the cost of the samples themselves and shipping them. The hotel and air fare to the show. The labeling and packaging costs, the brochures..."

Jennie acted as if she didn't hear him. "That reminds me. I need to figure in FDA and Organic approval into the labeling timelines."

"I would sit down and add up the costs. What you've spent so far and what you are projecting to spend. It might get away from you, Jennie."

"Paul!" Jennie's voice was louder than she intended. "You think nothing about $10,000 for a new building, but when it comes to my marketing costs, which are just as important... I feel you are second-guessing me all the time."

"No, I'm not," Paul replied mildly. "I just know how your enthusiasm can get ahead of you." He got up from his chair and walked around to where she sat stubbornly in her chair, her face staring at the laptop screen. "Hey, there. We're in this together. I am not fighting you, Jennie." He touched her shoulder lightly. "I want *Peace in the Valley Herbs* to be a success, just like you do. But we both need to be smart about how we do it. And we shouldn't forget Ed; he's an important partner — he has to weigh in, too. You can't just go ahead and make plans and then, 'Oh, by the way,' tell him. He needs to be a part of the whole thing not just growing herbs in his greenhouse. Keep the mission front and center. It was his mission – to help the hurting and the hungry in the community first. Everything has to fit the mission, Jennie. It's the only way God will bless the work. You know that."

"Otherwise it's only my ego!" she flared sarcastically. "Go ahead and say it. You think it's all my ego that's involved here! Like I need this sermon!"

"I didn't say that, Jennie."

"You don't have to, Paul."

"How did we get here so fast, Jen? Why are you so angry at me?"

"I'm not angry at you. I'm just ... frustrated. I know how to build a business. I know how to do it." She shook her head angrily. "Seems like no one believes in me."

"Here we go again," Paul said softly under his breath.

"And what's that supposed to mean'?" she shouted as she pushed her chair back and walked forcefully out the back door and stood on the porch."

Paul opened the door slowly and at the sound, Jennie marched down the steps and over to the greenhouse. He watched her for a few minutes as she furiously filled one clay pot after another with rich black soil. *That'll drain some of that energy off,* he thought. *Ah well, time for me to get back in the saddle, too. I need to pace off that space south of the greenhouse and figure how big we can make the pack house. Give the bank a call. Take a look at the Menards flyer tonight.* He whistled softly as he went to the pickup and grabbed his measuring tape.

13

Bill jumped into his pickup at the job site. He had just a few minutes to check email to see when the truckload of 2x4s were going to be delivered. The roof trusses had been installed earlier in the week and Jeremy had the crew hard at work putting on the particle board plywood and rubber underlayment. Shingles were due in a few days, but they wanted to get started on some of the interior walls tomorrow. It was coming together nicely. He'd promised Earl and Romyn a walk-through this coming weekend and he wanted to have the two-story residential addition all framed in with interior studs up before then.

Cleaning out the old Peterson Printing Company plant had been quite the challenge. Everyone wanted to preserve as much of the character as possible, so a lot of work was done to carefully remove the old mullioned windows for re-glazing, pull up the century-old wide pine boards, and gently tug off the wainscoting on the office walls. The space was nearly completely empty now, ready for the crew to get in there and get the kitchen, office, dining hall, and chapel built. They'd sent the floor boards and wall paneling off to a refinisher. The fairly new tile that had been placed under the digital print line had been pulled up, but they weren't able to save much of it. *Just as well*, Bill thought. It would be better to have wood floor throughout that large 60x90 space. *Big as a roller rink*. He had been able to nearly match the old floors with newly milled pine. Easier to maintain, easier to keep clean. Romyn and Earl had pretty much accepted all of his suggestions.

"You're the expert," they had said. Veronica had added some good suggestions though she was normally reticent around Bill.

Shiloh and Tom had come by on their bicycles to check on the work earlier in the day. She had a lot of thoughts about the pet shelter and bent Bill's ear about what had to be done until Tom gently drew her away. Bill smiled, remembering the visit. *She is some kid, that Shiloh. I hope she never loses that spunky spirit. It'll help her through life,* he thought. *Wish my Kellie had more of it.* That thought seemed a betrayal and he determinedly put Kellie out of his mind. *Time to think about that later. Gotta concentrate on the job at hand here.*

Bill stared out the window at the building site. From where he was parked, he could see Peace Ridge hills over the top of the building. Large cumulus clouds had formed in the dusky purple late afternoon sky, which could mean a spot of rain. Bill flipped to the Weather Channel app on his phone to check the forecast. Clear for the next couple of days. *Good, that'll help.* Jeremy would get the team cranking putting up studs. *Maybe I can sneak away tomorrow morning and check on Donna for a half hour or so.* Hour there, hour back, take the best part of the morning, but if he left early enough he'd be back to get the crew going on the built-ins for the kitchen and office. Be nice to have that done for Romyn and Earl.

It felt good to be immersed in hard work. That was Bill's natural milieu and those lost weeks spent at Donna's bedside were like a bad dream. Donna was in a safe place; she was looked after by people who knew how to treat coma patients. They'd just have to take each day at a time. No one could tell them the eventual outcome, and Bill knew he was helpless to do anything so he concentrated on what he was good at: building things. The money coming in was essential, too. So much going out. Lawyers, private investigators, endless paperwork to sort out Donna's deceit with her property deals. He wished it would just all go away and life could get back to what it was before.

Although that wasn't so hot, either, with their broken marriage. At least with work, if he couldn't see the end of the tunnel, at least he knew how to build his way through it.

Jeremy walked over to the truck. Unlike most of the crew who slouched and were carelessly dressed, Jeremy's military bearing and crisp appearance gave out an aura of confidence. In fact, Bill trusted him implicitly and hoped that they could work it out so that Jeremy could be more than a foreman, perhaps a partner in Brady Construction. He'd like that. Would be nice to have someone to share that burden.

"Think we're ready to knock it off for the day, Bill," he asserted. "We're at a good stopping point. We could shift over to the main building and start to frame in the cupboards and built-ins, but I think we'd get more out of the boys if we just hit the ground running tomorrow morning with the studs for the residence hall and just crank on that. You and I can shift focus, but these guys are better if they stay with one task until it's completely done. It's hard to get them to shift back and forth."

"You're right. I have a couple of extra men coming in to help with the other work anyway. Let's keep the crew on building the apartments. We can make real progress tomorrow. The load will be here at seven o'clock, they said."

"Let's let them go now and get them back at seven then. Okay, boss?" Jeremy barely waited for Bill's assent before he strode back to the building.

Bill's cell phone rang as he pulled slowly away from the building site and headed home. Time to take a shower, read over the mail, maybe have a beer, watch a little TV. Not a very exciting life but he was okay with that. The last few months had given him all the excitement he needed for a while.

"Hi, Steve." Bill punched the green button for the Bluetooth speaker. "Good to hear from you. What's up?"

"How you doin'?"

"Working on The Jason House. It's coming along well. We've gutted the main building, are ready to build out the interior and have the residence hall framed in, just going to get the

78

interior framing done. Haven't started on the pet shelter yet, but we'll get to that."

"Great to hear. I need to get up there and take a look at it. I'm not good with a hammer but I like to visit building sites. Fun to see them coming along. A kind of genius, I think."

"Well, I don't know about that!"

"I've been working the paper trail on the warehouse loft. Senator Hal Jefferson is in over his head. Not only did he use a false name to buy the properties—it was his mother's maiden name— he also deceived Donna. No surprise there. She put up your $50,000—"

"Yeah, our $50,000 that I knew nothing about."

"—but the controlling interest and all capital gains from the eventual sale of the property would go to him. In plain fact, it looks as if he's *defacto* the sole owner of the place."

Bill swung his pickup into his driveway and turned off the truck, his mind on his conversation with Steve.

"And what happens to our $50,000?"

"Well you actually may be able to recover that through a fraud lawsuit. I think the law is pretty clear on that. Donna had been deceived even though her name is on the title. But here is what's really important: if he is the sole owner, he's actually 100 percent liable for the meth factory in the loft. He could argue that Donna gave Kellie and her friends permission to use the loft and therefore she's responsible, but I don't think that will fly in court."

"Wow." Bill sighed. "Wow. Do you think it's as easy as that? This has been hanging over my head."

"We'll just have to see how it goes. I've got more digging to do."

"What about that business about turning the loft into a gay bar or something?"

"The zoning board had approved it for a private club for gays. That's probably why Jefferson used a fake name. Didn't think it'd fly in conservative Minnesota. I think that issue is secondary to the meth situation, however. It's likely the loft will be unsaleable and perhaps gutted. Those plans are out the window."

"I never liked that guy."

"He keeps getting re-elected. Who knows why?"

Bill reached for the door handle of the truck and froze in place. There was a gaping hole where his back door to the porch had been. Someone had kicked it in completely and the door hung crazily off to the side, barely held onto the frame with its wrenched hinges. Splintered wood and broken glass were everywhere.

"Bill? Bill?"

"Steve, I'm just looking at the back door to my house. Someone has broken the door down. It looks as if I've been robbed."

"Text me your address. I'm coming to Peace Ridge. You need a trained forensic investigator with all that's been going on here. Call the police and tell them I am on the way. Don't you try to solve this yourself."

"Ah, Steve. All this way? Are you sure?"

"I'm sure. There in an hour and a half." He rang off.

14

Bill stood in stupefaction at the porch steps. The back door was concealed from the street and someone could break in without being seen, but by the looks of it the break-in would have made a lot of noise. Wonder if anyone heard anything? Romyn and Earl were the nearest neighbors, but Romyn would be at the store and Earl probably working at the computer with Veronica. Unlikely they would have seen or heard anything.

Chief Baldwin pulled into the yard, the squad car a reassuring presence.

"When it rains it pours, doesn't it, Bill?" The chief briefly laid his hand on Bill's arm. "I'm sorry about this. We'll take a look around and see what we can see."

"A friend of mine, Steve Banfeld from the Cities, the guy that has been helping me with the mess downtown, is on his way here. He's a private investigator and he wants to take a look around before we do anything."

"I know Steve," Chief Baldwin said. "He and Archie Meadows spent time with me last winter on that Dane Johnson runestone mess."

"With all that has been going on there – maybe I should tell you all about it – he thinks this might be more than a simple robbery."

"Can't hurt. Can always use the help. Let's see if we can't take a look around inside. Be careful of that glass, Bill." The chief led the way through the shattered doorway and into the kitchen which was an awful mess. Utensil drawers had been pulled open and emptied onto the floor. A kitchen chair had been dragged over to the counter and dishes from the top shelves had been thrown down onto the counter and the floor.

Looking for hidden stashes, I suppose. Bill thought. *There's nothing there. We didn't have anything hidden away here. There is that quart jar filled with silver dollars in the back of the closet that I've had since I was a kid, but that's not worth a robbery. Though if they were looking for something to sell for drugs, they would be worth something. Why did I think of drugs right away? Times we're living in, I guess. This county is the heart of meth country.*

Bill and Chief Baldwin walked slowly into the living room and looked around. There were drawers open on the buffet and the glass doors to the built-in bookcases were open with several books thrown crazily down on the floor. A basket that held magazines had been emptied and was placed on the table. It held the DVD player and remote control. The men walked down the hallway and into the master bedroom which was untouched. They turned into the home office and paused, aghast. It had been thoroughly ransacked.

"Okay, now," the chief said. "This is where Steve will earn his keep. It's pretty clear this office was the destination for the break-in. The other damage was camouflage. Look at how the locks on all the filing cabinets have been jimmied and the contents emptied. They didn't take the computer. They would have pawned it for cash if money were the object.

"Who would want my bookkeeping records for the construction business?" Bill asked. "Ah, I'm stupid. It's Donna's records they were after. The record of her real estate transactions." He was beginning to feel overwhelmed by the implications of that thought.

"Let's do this. The deputy has the department camera. I'll take a few pictures on my iPhone now but I'll text him to come over and get all the shots, just so we have a comprehensive look.

"While we're waiting, let's take a look at the garage and other buildings. I'd really like to know if anything has been taken. I'm in the middle of this big project and if any of my tools and machines are gone, I swear I will kill someone."

"I didn't hear you say that, Bill!" Chief Baldwin humorously chided. "Do you have your insurance agent's number on your phone? Might as well get him over here, too."

"Well, I think that's everything. I want to do another walk-through," Steve said, "and see if there's anything I've overlooked."

"Then we can head over to the Tall Rigger for a hamburger and talk about it. I'm starving," Bill said.

"I can't join you two," the chief said, "but you go ahead and let's connect tomorrow morning. The force will keep a close eye on your place tonight. I would like to close everything off with police tape for a day or two and we'll help get it all cleaned up tomorrow. Bill, do you have a place to stay tonight?"

"Let me call around. Paul and Jennie will put me up, I'm sure. Or Pastor."

"I'll be staying at the Sleepytime Inn if you need me," Steve said. "Do you mind if I come along with you when you talk to Earl, Romyn, and Veronica?"

"I've told them we'd be by in the morning. That's fine. Eight o'clock too early for you?"

"Let me call Jeremy," Bill said, "and let him know that I have to think about fixing this door tomorrow morning. He'll get the crew going and hopefully I will get there by noon." He looked wiped out, grey with fatigue, anger and despair fighting for expression on his face.

"C'mon, Bill. Let's grab something to eat —- you look as if you could use a beer, too – and you can call Romyn from the Tall Rigger." Steve placed his arm briefly across his shoulder and led him to his car.

Chief Baldwin and the deputy walked slowly toward their squad cars. They stared at one another in silence for a brief moment.

"What do you think?" the deputy asked the chief.

"I think we have a mess on our hands, that's what I think," the chief replied. "There's something going on here. Higher stakes than just drug money. Let's think about assigning a detail to Bill on the QT for a few days. When it comes to politicians and corruption, I trust them just about as far as I can throw them." He shook his head sadly.

Bill laid his head down wearily on the pillow in Pastor Ed's guest bedroom. At the end of a long day he was grateful for Ed's sympathetic presence and no pressing questions. He had shown him the spare upstairs bathroom and with a brief "We're praying, Bill," left him alone with his thoughts. Staying in someone else's house was unfamiliar and Bill lay down on the bed fully dressed, trying to make his body relax. In the house he heard the soft sounds of conversation between Ed and Jill, the creaking of the old house, a branch brushing against the upstairs windows. It took a long time to be able to think clearly about the break-in and what it might mean. Donna, in her coma in the assisted living facility in Sartell, was uppermost in his mind.

She's lost to me now, he thought. *This is the end of us. I need to just move forward. There's no holding out for a miracle and our marriage was broken anyway. She got in over her head with this loft and the Senator, and I'm left to pick up the pieces. I'll never know why. She has no mind left to tell me.*

He sighed deeply and shifted his weight on the bed. Maybe a shower would help. And it did. There were a few books on a shabby old bookshelf next to the bed and he picked out an old Ellery Queen mystery thinking to divert himself but he couldn't concentrate. The AM-clock radio flashed the time – after ten o'clock. He pressed the button to bring in the radio and immediately was transported back to his teenage years. The radio show "Old Times" featured early Beatles music and Bill's mind immediately went to a dusky green late-1980s Chevy Camaro and a petite and beautiful black-haired woman nestled in his arms. The DJ gave a quiet introduction and at the opening familiar chords of "Yesterday" Bill's eyes filled with tears. *Over. Over.* Those were the words that repeated themselves in his mind as he drifted off to sleep. At one point he had a vision of Donna looking up at him with her beautiful blue eyes filled with laughter, but it was a dream. Or maybe a memory. He slept.

15

"Glad you could make it, Bill." Romyn greeted him with a hug, and then turned as Pastor Ed and Jill walked up the front sidewalk. "Hi, Ed and Jill! Welcome to our home." Jill looked at Ed questioningly, and with his slight nod, held out her hand to Romyn. *Still very fragile,* Romyn thought. *It's like holding a birdwing.*

They all stood on the front porch as George made his slow way up the walk. He smiled his greetings to them all but Romyn noticed that his hands were shaking more than usual. Not now, but another time she'd remind him to go to the doctor for a check-up again. He needed nagging, believing that doctors were unnecessary. He wasn't sick, just old and tired.

Titos, Maria, and Brenda had already arrived and were seated around the glass-topped table on the patio. Maria sat closely to Titos as if for protection. *More than one broken person in this gathering,* Ed thought compassionately. But Romyn's gift for hospitality and Earl's genial presence soon made everyone feel at home. All were curious about how The Jason House was coming along and the shocking robbery at Bill's house.

"I'm looking forward to catching up with Veronica," Bill said finally. "Steve said that neither of you heard or saw anything, is that right, Earl?"

Earl nodded slowly. "We're just far enough away from your house, and in my case, getting hard of hearing anyway. The

86

office is on the opposite side of the house and Veronica and I were busy printing out rafts of forms."

"And that's one of the reasons we wanted to have our friends over!" Romyn exclaimed. "Earl and I have great news. The county has preliminarily approved us as foster parents for Clay and Sophie!"

"That's just fantastic," Ed said, as Brenda signed the good news to Maria who smiled radiantly.

"We will be heading down to Maplewood later in the week to bring them home with us."

"Do they know about it yet?"

"The kids? No, not yet. We wanted to keep it as a surprise and we also didn't want to get their hopes up in case something would jinx it. No word from Lisa. They are still trying to find her and have reached out to contact the father, too. They'll still continue to do that, but in the meantime, they'll be here with us and can have some kind of normal life."

"Don't even think they know what normal is," Earl observed.

"'Two sparrows in a hurricane, trying to find their way...'" Bill sang, doing his best Tanya Tucker imitation.

"Don't quit your day job, Bill!" George teased, as Romyn beckoned the group into the dining room.

"How is Veronica these days?" Bill asked Earl as the conversation swirled around them. "Do you think she's getting back on her saddle?"

Earl looked at Bill intently. "Why do you ask? I'm curious."

"Steve interviewed her at her house after the break-in and though she was friendly to him and forthcoming about what she knew about it, he sensed someone in deep depression. He's trained to observe things like that." Bill nodded his head slightly at Jill. "And he was concerned enough to mention it to me. We don't want another ..." He didn't finish the thought.

Earl sighed. "She isn't too forthcoming with me. Very professional when we work together here on the plans for The Jason House or when we were digging into the foster system. Very matter-of-fact. I think she's just a very private person."

"That's probably it, though there is the other thing."

"What other thing?"

"When Steve first arrived at her house, the dining room table was entirely covered with newspaper clippings."

"Oh, that's interesting. Wonder if she's writing a book?"

"Newspaper clippings of obituaries, Earl." Bill replied. "Piles of them."

Earl recoiled slightly in shock and lowered his voice. "I don't like the sound of that."

"How old do you think she is, Earl?" Bill asked. "Late forties?"

"Yes, about that, I think. Don't know for sure. She looks younger now that she's gained some weight after that business last winter. Why do you ask?"

"Steve doesn't miss anything. Before Veronica pushed them over to make room for their coffee cups, he noticed that there were three piles: one pile of children, one pile for people who were very old, late eighties or nineties. And a pile in the middle of people who are Veronica's age."

Romyn glanced over at the two men in conversation and her worry instinct spiked. She caught the name "Veronica," and just then Earl glanced up and caught her eye. *Save this for later,* she thought.

"Bill, you are friends with her dad, Archie, aren't you?" Earl asked.

"He's been a tremendous help to me with the Donna mess. Steve, too. I really trust them."

"Do you think you can give a heads-up to Archie about this? I hate to intervene…don't think she's given me permission to be that personal with her."

"I'm going to visit with Ed about it. He has his hands full with Jill, but he's spent time with both Archie and Veronica and I think he might be the one to broach the subject."

"Did I hear my name?" Ed leaned back over Jill's shoulder and caught Bill's eye.

"Yes, just saying you're the luckiest man in the world to have your wife home," Bill said. "You are the perfect one for something we have in mind. Catch you later on it."

"If I had to guess, I'd bet it has something to do with my profession." Ed smiled.

"Doesn't everything in this world?" Bill rejoined wryly.

"I'd like to see her happy," Earl said. "She's become quite precious to us and an amazing help."

"If I had to guess, Steve might help there. He admitted to me she's his type. Willowy elegant blondes. Don't think he was kidding either!"

"Wouldn't that be a blessing? I don't think she makes friends easily. Romyn invited her here for tonight but she declined, said she was too tired."

"Speaking of tired, you should see Paul these days. He's burning the candle at both ends. Jeremy is helping him with his new shed—the pack house for the herbs business—and they both work late into the night to get it done. Jeremy can do it; he's got twenty years on Paul, and Paul's not as young as he thinks he is."

Earl pushed his wheelchair back from the table. "None of us are! None of us are. Romyn, did you promise strawberry shortcake for dessert? I think I saved room. Hope everyone else did. Romyn makes a mean shortcake."

16

Michael and Tom leaned back into the Adirondack chairs at the end of the lawn and watched the dogs romp. Brian and Shiloh exhausted themselves throwing tennis balls to the dogs who would occasionally break off the chase to wrestle with one another. Dirty brown and dirty white and joyful kids. Happiness emanated from the green playground.

"Not much to look at, but perfect dog for Brian," Michael observed.

"I can see that."

"It's curious. Having a dog has made him more sociable in some way. He has always been quiet and shy…"

"Still waters run deep with that boy," Tom said.

"Yes, but having his dog gives him an object of unconditional love. Not sure he could love his mother unconditionally – sorry, that was a low blow –and until I moved to Peace Ridge, I always felt there was a barrier between us, too. He always felt that I was always going to go away and leave him. So, I think he feels more in control of his love, somehow.

"And dogs just accept it and love in the present moment."

The two men sat silently watching the dogs and children, Shiloh being her usual bossy self, trying to organize the play, but neither Brian nor the dogs were cooperative.

"I suppose you know that I dated Delaney before she went to London?" Tom asked.

"Yes, Brian told me," Michael said briefly. "But I don't own her and we were never married anyway."

"No one owns Delaney. I pity the man who thinks he can!" Tom replied bitterly. Time to shift subjects. "How are you settling in here in Peace Ridge?"

"It's good. My business is thriving. I'm surprised it's really seamless to do all that I do remotely. When I think of all the money I spent on my office in St. Cloud…"

"Once The Jason House is up and running, I don't think you will lack for computer service contracts. Now that broadband is everywhere in the county, everyone and his brother has wireless. Shiloh has been arguing for a cell phone for months, but I want to resist as long as possible. She seems to have a talent for drawing and painting and I don't want her talent compromised with eye candy from a small screen."

"I don't have to worry about Brian. He borrows my cell phone to text Delaney, but the only tech he's really interested in is his mechanical pencil."

"He's quite the writer. Have you read many of his poems?"

"He shows them to me sometimes. He's quite diffident about them and I think he doesn't care one way or another if people like them if he himself is happy with them."

"He gave me a poem about river otters a while ago. I was inspired to make an illustration of the creatures and I had planned to give it to Brian, but I've been reconsidering that." At Michael's sharp look upward, Tom continued, "I think the two of us could publish a book of Brian's poetry with my nature illustrations. You're the first person I've talked to about this and even though my sketching is a bit rusty, I think it captures it."

"I'd love to see it."

Tom walked into the house and was back shortly with a small black folder. Tissue covered the sketch and he handed it to Michael. "Have you seen this one?"

The Sleepy Otter

Reclining 'midst russet willows,
her belly table glistens brown.
The generous river prepares the banquet,
Brown baby tumbles happily 'round.

Eddies and drifts, a peace-filled quiet day,
Noon's green repast is complete,
Sunward she turns and bathes a whiskered face,
And gently tethered to river reed they fall asleep.

Brian Peterson, age 8
For Mr. Simmonds

Michael read it softly to himself and smiled. "That's quite the picture."

"That one was quite easy to illustrate." Tom proffered the sketch. "I was pleased he dedicated it to me. Some of his other poems are more abstract and I have struggled with the right theme and framing, but I think we have something here."

"Wow. I had no idea."

"I still have contacts at the Minneapolis College of Art and Design, even though it's been years since I graduated. I think someone will know how to get this published. Do you think Brian would like that?"

"I don't know..." Michael mused thoughtfully. "He gets some bullying at school because he's quiet and bookish. If this would exacerbate that, I would say we need to hold off. It could go the other way, too. Make him a hero. Let me think about it. In the meantime, I am grateful to you for your encouragement. Has Brian seen this?

"No, he hasn't."

"Let's hold off for a bit," Michael said.

"Yes, I was thinking the same thing. I have been encouraging him to show me his poems as he writes them, and I have quite a few."

"More than I do, I suspect. He's pretty close to the vest with his little Moleskin notebook. I don't want to invade his privacy. We're still working out the father-son relationship a bit now that he's living with me. He had more leeway with Delaney. I have a few more rules and though he never challenges me, he does get quiet and goes to his room. I'm sure there are more than one 'Dad is Bad' poems in his head."

"Try raising a girl. A redhead at that!" Both men sat quietly and reflected on Shiloh. Such a treasure. The two kids were heads down in the garden beyond the lawn and Michael was sure Shiloh was showing bugs or butterflies to Brian as she expostulated wildly, her passion wafting towards the porch.

This scene epitomizes the appeal of the country life, Michael thought. The neat lawn was framed by the white fence to the pasture. Peace Ridge in the distance was a montage of green — pale lime to deep forest green becoming nearly black in the shadows of the old boxelder tree. The white birch trees at the edge of the pasture called attention to themselves by swaying slightly in the summer breeze. Brian and Shiloh turned to laugh at one another in joy as a scruffy white dog gleefully chased an ungainly brown dog. Sunflowers planted alongside Tom's shop turned their golden heads toward the warm western sun.

"This view needs a horse or two grazing along the fence line," Michael observed.

'Talk to me about it! I hear that plea at least once a week, but too much work. The kid can't do it all and neither you nor I have a wife to help out with raising kids and pets."

They fell silent. Tom asked, "Do you think Brian misses Delaney? Do you think he understands why she's gone?"

"I think he understands his mother really well. He sees her restlessness – as we all do. He's such a self-contained little guy. His poems are his outlet—he doesn't say much to me but he writes. I don't snoop, but I found this on his bed one morning when I was making his bed when he was in the shower. I quickly made a copy – probably shouldn't have done it – but I wanted to study it more."

Michael handed the copy to Tom. "He's always reading these nature books...."

The Pelican Dance

What begins the great dance?
Roseate sun tinges Eastern sky.
White wings painted with pearl,
You, spreading wings, eager to fly.

The creature ungainly, unlikely flight.
Graceful spirit amidst earth's whirl.
Distant horizons excitingly beckon,
Rare discoveries to be unfurled.

The pelican gulps deeply,
Seizes life in jowly net
While aloft on powerful wings.
Forsaking home, increasing love's debt.

Soaring high in carefree ride,
Updrafts circle left, circle right.
You long to find yourself free, but
Your flight ends, a battered kite.

"Yes…well…" Tom said thoughtfully.

Both men were silent as the summer evening wound down to dusk and children and dogs finally exhausted their supply of energy. All four plopped themselves on the porch with Tom and Michael and the only sound was deep heavy dog sighs coupled with the unmistakable sound of dogs licking themselves into slumber. 'There is sweet music here that softer falls, than petals from blown roses on the grass…' Michael quoted Tennyson.

Shiloh was the first to break the quietude. "Dad, can we go to the Tall Rigger for pizza?"

17

I'd kill for a cup of strong coffee! was Delaney's first thought upon waking. She stretched languidly and glanced at the bay window to assess the time. It looked to be early morning but the thick fog that blanketed her view was deceptive. She reached for her cell phone: nearly eleven. Wow. Twelve hours. She sat up a little too suddenly for the sharp stab of headache pain that jolted the back of her head.

The sadness of last night had lifted and a quick shower and two Advil completed her revival. She noted her drawn, white face in the smallish bathroom mirror and decided to complete a full-blown make-up session, just in case she ran into someone interesting. She firmly put thoughts of Ten out of her mind, reaffirming her vow to strategize their reunion.

The kitchen was a narrow galley with a small mullioned window at one end overlooking the garden and a larger one open to the outdoors over the porcelain farmhouse sink. There was a large geranium on the window sill, its scent mingling enticingly with the freshly brewed coffee. Opposite the sink was a classic retro Smeg refrigerator in a delightful shade of celadon and a small electric cookstove. A narrow counter held a toaster and caddies of jam and honey, and open washed pine shelves above held an assortment of classic blue and white crockery. Though deep in the heart of London, the room was flooded with light and there was a country farmhouse feel to the place. The small pine trestle table in the dining room adjoining the kitchen was covered with a fringed lemon-yellow pastel cloth. Lounging at the table was a slender man who looked up briefly as she walked in and with a clipped "Good morning," went back to reading *The Guardian.*

He had a lean elegance that intrigued and Delaney cast several discreet glances at him as she examined the contents of the refrigerator and kitchen shelves.

"You can share my coffee if you want," he offered, observing her frown.

"I didn't plan well, I'm afraid," Delaney said ruefully. "I didn't think to stock up on groceries last night. Thank you very much."

"Just arrived in country?" he asked

"Yesterday." She smiled. "I guess finding a local grocery store is the first order of business."

'I'll spot you coffee and you can get me back later in the week," he offered. He didn't sound English nor American, which aroused Delaney's speculation. "There's a Waitrose just down the road a bit. I recommend you shop every day; there's usually no room here for extras nor leftovers."

"Are we the only visitors in the house?" Delaney asked as she sat gracefully at the table, glad she'd made an extra effort to look good.

"I'm not sure. There may be. I keep pretty much to myself. American tourists usually leave the house early to crowd the museums and shops. The kitchen is peaceful this time of day."

"Thank you." Delaney exhaled gratefully after her first sip of coffee. "This is restorative. Got into Heathrow at noon yesterday," she offered. "Exhausting flight. But I'm all chipper now." *Funny, how I pick up the English expressions right away. Tone it down,* she rebuked herself.

He glanced down at his newspaper. *That's a clue.* Delaney took her coffee cup into the sitting room and looked through the basket of guidebooks on the side table. She paged through the books on "London on $25/day," "London by Night," "Mysterious London," and "London for Opera Lovers," with increasing frustration. Not for the first time she realized that her visit this time was ill-defined. It was more than just a tourist trip, but it wasn't an immigration trip either. *Truth told, I expected to be swept off my feet by Ten and my future laid out for me,* she realized. *I wonder if it would be even possible to emigrate here without marrying somebody. And if I want to stay, I need to find a job of some type.*

This is what happens when you do things on impulse. She stared out the bay window at the street below for many moments. *I don't just want to be a tourist; I want a new beginning. Perhaps I should start with finding out what it would take to get a job here.*

"Thanks awfully for the coffee," she said, walking back into the kitchen. "Do you know, by chance, if there's good wireless access here, or do I need to visit an Internet café?"

"I'm Alwyn, by the way," he said, holding out his hand.

"Delaney Peterson," she said, taking his hand.

"There's wireless here—there's wireless everywhere in the UK – but if you want to do a lot of work online, it's best to get a cheap phone and prepaid cards at one of the carriers. British Telcom is widely available."

"I need to research visa processes and applications to work here..."

"You'd be better off taking the underground to one of the immigration centers and asking them all the questions. It's all done through the UK Visa and Citizen Application Services, part of the Home Office. You can get everything you need there, if you can get an appointment. It might be faster than researching online."

"I'm just a visitor now, no specific visa. But I'm thinking about staying for a while longer..."

"American. Looking for work. Wanting to stay in the UK. Challenging. Can be done, but ..." Alwyn looked puzzled. "If you had a patron, an employer, a specific skill, were funded through an investment group – all these things make it easier to get the temporary visas, but the Home Office makes it very difficult for someone to come in and take UK citizens' jobs. Even if they are not qualified, they get first dibs."

"Sounds as if you know the drill."

"I'm not searching for a job. I have a temporary research visa. Six months. And then I'm gone." He leaned back in his chair and smiled. His narrow, lined face gave a cue to his age – *late forties or early fifties* – but the grin was boyish and attractive. Delaney felt the familiar tug of flirtation.

"I am so grateful. Truly."

"Get a good map of the underground and you can pop down to the immigration center near London City Center. It will help clarify things for you. Good luck."

"On the other hand, I might just enjoy myself in London for a couple of months." She dangled the bait, but he was indifferent.

"More than a month? You'll need a visa. I'm heading out in a few minutes. I'll walk you to the nearest news agent or to Waitrose, if you'd like."

"That would be super." *Simply super*, she thought ironically. *Groceries and looking for work. Doesn't sound very glamorous.*

I'm simply too tired today to figure this out. Delaney stood at the news agent and spread out the underground map against a shelf. It was only a short walk to the Hampstead tube station and it wouldn't take too long to transfer to the Circle line and get to the City of London. *The lines are probably fierce,* she thought. *And I'm starving. I'll save this for tomorrow.* She wandered aimlessly in search of a place to eat, finally landing at the Holly Bush pub on Hollymount road where she voraciously ate a classic fish and chips meal. She heard the ding of a cell phone text as she relaxed over her second cup of hot tea. *Why does it always taste better in England?* she asked herself as she reached into her purse for her phone.

"Hallo, friend." Jennie's mock English accent greeting resonated even with texting. Their little joke from years before. "Hope all is well. Wondering if you'd have time to do a bit of research for me? Our pet lady—my new 'best friend,' Eliza Stephens, finally told me she's from Somerset. Wondering if you could hit up the registry office there (born 1929) and trace some relatives...if there are any... and only if you have time. You said Somerset was on your itinerary... if it's not too much trouble...love you, friend. Stay safe...no worries if you are too busy. Luv, J."

Delaney leaned back in the comfortable banquette. *Right-oh. The perfect excuse to find myself in Somerset.* "Bless you, Jennie," she whispered under her breath. She sent a quick text back, "On it!" and felt her excitement begin to rise.

18

Jill and Ed worked side by side in the greenhouse. The day was glorious— sunny, clear blue skies with
the pleasant accompaniment of birdsong in the oak tree near
the house. It was uncomfortably hot in the small structure and
Ed propped the door open and fetched an electric fan from the
garage to set in the doorway so it could pull out some of the
stuffy air. Jill seemed to be enjoying herself, transplanting the
delicate seedlings, pressing the rich black earth down into each
tiny clay pot, and watering each one individually with an old
copper watering can with a long spout. Ed covertly glanced at
her, conscious of the fact that he wanted to be overly protective, yet knowing she needed privacy and independence, too.
So hard to navigate the new normal, he thought.

Jill seemed content to be at the parsonage, allowing Ed to
make the meals, and they shared quiet times in front of the television most evenings. She didn't say much, so unlike the old
Jill who always had something to say on every subject. Perhaps
it was because the house was different and empty without the
kids. He got the sense that she felt like a guest there, as much as
he tried to explain that this was their new home—it just didn't
seem to register.

"When you've finished there, let's visit Paul and Jennie's
and see how she's doing with their greenhouse and the plans."

"I need to change into something else if I am going to
someone else's place."

101

"No, you don't, Jill. You're dressed just fine. Your blue jeans are clean and so's your shirt. That's fine for Peace Ridge. I'll just call Jennie and see if they are home."

"But, Eddy, if we are going to visit someone..." Jill looked upset. Ed flashed back to Sunday morning when Jill had an emotional meltdown over having nothing to wear to church. "I need a dress. I need to be dressed up," she had said.

"It's all right to go to church in jeans and a shirt here in Peace Ridge Village," he had reassured her. "We're just a country church." He finally convinced her it would be okay but she was quiet and uncertain all morning. "I'll take you to St. Cloud to buy some clothes tomorrow," he'd promised, and that seemed to comfort her anxiety. *The old Jill wouldn't have cared a rat's patootie,* he thought, but then felt guilty. *I need to stop thinking of the "Old Jill" and the "New Jill" She's just Jill.* He knew her unreasonable agitation was due to her illness and he reminded himself: *Patience, Ed. Patience.*

"I want to take a picture of you here in the greenhouse so I can show Jennie how our plants are coming along," Ed said. He had begun taking pictures of Jill in various different settings in the house and yard, including selfies of the two of them, he with a big broad smile, Jill with an affectless expression. He had printed them out at Walmart and placed them on the refrigerator, in frames in their bedroom and in the dining room, relegating the old family pictures of the four of them to the guest bedroom. *Maybe this will help her live more in the present,* he had thought.

"Do you feel up for a walk down to the Holm farm?" he asked. "It's only a little over a mile. We could take it slow."

"Whatever you think, Eddy."

He looked down at her feet. "Those shoes were made for walking. I think it will be good exercise."

They headed west down Valley Drive, the sunlight sparkling on the gravel road. Ditches were lined with tall grasses and the blue giant hyssop was in full flower, enticing the honey bees that ponderously circled the blossoms. Field bindweed entangled an old wooden plow that had been abandoned in the ditch decades earlier, and wild white onion plants alongside the prairie lent an intoxicating fragrance to the air. Ed slowed his pace and reached for Jill's hand. "'For the beauty of the earth...'" he sang as he smiled down at her.

She flashed a brief smile in response and then frowned. "Where are we going, Eddy?"

"We're walking over to the Holm farm. To see Jennie and Paul – though I'm not sure Paul will be in the house. He's more likely to be out in the fields."

"Do I know them?"

"You have met them several times, Jill."

"Oh, oh," she said under her breath, "I have such a hard time remembering."

"You'll recognize Jennie when you see her. She's a good friend and she wants to get to know you better."

"She's a friend of mine?" Jill asked doubtfully.

"I got to know them when I first got this church in Peace Ridge, Jill. Ten years ago."

"Ten years ago? Where was I?"

Ed sighed inwardly. This was a familiar conversation. Just at that moment they saw Bill's pickup turn onto Valley Road.

"Oh, here comes Bill." A timely diversion.

Bill pulled alongside the road and rolled down the window. "Where you folks headed? Need a ride?"

"No, Jill and I are just going over to see Jennie and Paul and talk about plants and stuff. Such a nice day; thought we'd walk over."

"When you have a chance, Pastor, I'd like to bend your ear for five minutes or so. It's about Veronica."

"We can change our plans now if you want. We can always do this later."

"No, go ahead and see Jennie and Paul. Give me a call around lunchtime if you can and I'll fill you in. I'm just headed over to Menards now and I'll be back at the job site in for-ty-five minutes or so. It can wait. Just stopped by on the off chance you'd be around. But I see you have a date with a beautiful woman …"

"'…The most beautiful girl in the world?'" Ed sang. Jill looked puzzled while Bill gave a brief laugh. "I'm just going to start calling you Charlie Rich, Pastor!"

The rat-a-tat sound of a nail gun and the whine of a circular saw greeted them as they walked slowly up the Holm's driveway. Paul was bent over the sheet of plywood and frowned in concentration as he marked off the cut line. Ed and Jill paused in the yard until he'd finished the cut and powered down the saw, and then walked over and greeted him.

"Wow, this building is coming along nicely!" Ed exclaimed as he walked around the 20X24 building.

"Yeah, we'll get 'er done in a couple of days. Got the electrician coming next week and the plumber, too, so we'll be up and running in a week or two. Just in time for the harvest. Don't know about your herbs, but ours are coming up like weeds!"

Ed gave a hand as the two men lifted the cut plywood and fitted it around the window opening. At the sound of the nail gun, Jill started and began to back away. Jennie arrived at just that moment and kindly held her arm and guided her towards the house.

"Not used to the noise on the farm?" she asked gently. "I don't even hear it anymore."

Jill looked at her beseechingly. "I can't bear that loud popping sound," she said plaintively. "It reminds me…" She couldn't get the words out and looked helplessly at Jennie and then at Ed, who was at her side.

"Come inside and let's have a cup of coffee. Or iced tea, if you prefer."

"Jennie makes the best pie in the world," Ed said to Jill.

"Well, I don't know about that, but I do have a warm apple pie just cooling on the counter. Must have known I'd have visitors this morning."

"You're spoilin' us, Jennie."

"Paul," she cried out to the yard, "take a break and come inside for pie."

He looked up at that, nodded, and slowly set his carpenter's pencil and level down on the makeshift sawhorse workbench.

"How's it going, Ed?" Jennie asked *sotto voce* as she handed him the coffee cups. She glanced over at Jill, who perched uneasily in the chair, like a bird ready to take flight.

"'Day by day' Jennie," Ed replied. "'And with each passing moment, strength I find to meet my trials here.'"

"How can I help?"

"I'd love for you to show Jill your greenhouse."

"Can do. Wait until I show you the new label design for the herbs, Ed! I think you'll like them. Tom was very helpful. He's such a great illustrator. Paul thinks we should do them in black and white to save printing costs and we're having quite a little discussion about that. Want you to weigh in. I think they need to be in full color."

"Oops, don't want to get in the middle of husband and wife, Jennie!" Ed laughed.

"Why don't you tell Ed how much you think this little venture is going to cost, Jennie?" Paul said, his back to them as he washed his hands at the sink, his smile softening the words.

"Yes, Paul reminds me that you and I are partners in this, Ed. I don't want to get out ahead of you."

"Well, you're the marketing expert," Ed replied mildly. "We just want to have a little profit to spread around the community. Let's do this. You show me what you've done so far, and I'll give you my thoughts about what I think we need to include. We're thinking about eight to ten different herb blends, right? To start?"

"Yes, to start, but I think we could eventually expand into seasoned salts, rub blends, pre-blended dip mixes..." Jennie spoke enthusiastically.

"I agree. In time. I've been thinking about the initial range of products. I know we've got the Faithfulness Blend..."

"Actually, we can have more than one Faithfulness Blend if we want. There are lots of combinations."

"Let's just start with our initial blend. We can always add later if it takes off. I like the coriander, rosemary, and chili pepper blend and it's pretty versatile. Goes with a lot. One thing I've been doing is searching for the right Bible verses to put on each label. Faithfulness is such a big topic and the Bible has so much to say about it. Just want to be sure we pick the verse with the broadest appeal."

Jennie looked pensive. "I hadn't thought about that. We need to leave space on the back label for the verse." She mused, "Maybe we could put it on a hanging tag. Well, we can work that out. I'll show you what we've got so far."

"Proverbs or the Psalms probably have it all, Pastor," Paul said. "They pretty much tell me all I need."

"I have so many favorites; it's hard to pick and choose. 'Trust in the Lord with all your heart and lean not on your own understanding. In all your ways submit to Him and He will make your paths straight.'"

"Yeah, one of my favorite verses, too. Proverbs 3:5-6."

"So many good ones. Micah 6:8: '…what does the Lord require of you? To act justly and to love mercy and to walk humbly with your God.'"

Ed smiled. "When we get to the Love blend, it will be easy. 1 Corinthians 13 has it all! "What is our Love blend, do you think?" Ed asked Jennie.

"Something with basil and thyme, of course," she responded quickly. "Oregano is the herb of Aphrodite, the goddess of love. That would be a classic Italian blend – basil, thyme, and oregano. But I'm thinking we might want to take it in a slightly different direction. There's a lot of folklore around lavender and love and I've planted quite a bit of culinary lavender which is minty. I would like to blend it with perhaps some sage and rosemary. Thinking that it would make pork chops sing or added to a curry…"

"We're going to need a cookbook!"

"I thought about that!"

"You listen to Jennie! She's got big ideas!" Paul said wryly.

"Yeah, Paul thinks I need to dial my ideas back a bit." Jennie's voice held a tinge of bitterness.

"Well, guys, let's just pray over it daily and God will make the plan clear to us all. Let's take a look around that greenhouse and then we'll get out of your hair and let you get back to work.

"And let us know when you're ready to paint the shed. Jill and I will be over in our best painting clothes!"

Jill looked at him with a quizzical expression on her face.

"I will give Archie a call," Ed replied after talking to Bill. "This is worrisome. I think I know what depression looks like after taking care of Jill but there are many different kinds. Veronica is clearly lonely. I wonder if we, if I, have done enough to make her feel welcome, a part of our group here in Peace Ridge?"

"She puts up her own barriers, Ed," Bill said wearily. "I have come to realize that men cannot fix all the problems that women have! There's just no way."

"She told me she was over the madness of last winter. I believed her. But loneliness is hard – and I've been so involved with Jill here that I haven't had the time to reach out like I should have. Jill and I will have her over for a meal."

"Don't feel bad, Pastor. We all have a lot on our plate."

"Any word on your break-in, Bill? It never stops, does it?"

"Yeah, Steve thinks there's more to it than a simple robbery. I'm glad he's on the case along with Chief Baldwin."

"Me, too. Let me know how I can help."

"Will do, Ed. Will do."

"I wonder...." Ed mused.

"You wonder what?"

"I wonder if maybe that because the work on The Jason House is coming to an end – Veronica's part in it, that is – that she does not have anything to replace it with. And that emptiness is driving her depression. She needs a project. I wonder if she'd be interested in helping us out in Sunday School?"

"Talk to her. Might work. Don't know how she'd be with the little kids..."

"I know. Jill isn't comfortable there either, but maybe there's something else she can do in the church. I'll have to talk to her."

"Keep her out of trouble, anyway," was Bill's response. "Something we all need."

"Thank you for being a brother on the battlefield, Bill."

19

"How is Whiskers settling in with you and Brian?" Pam asked as she settled into the booth at Granite City.

"Well, first thing, Brian had to change his name. It's Snow now. Snowdrift actually, Snow for short. He wanted to call him Thor but when he saw him, he thought Snow was his 'soul name.' That's what he told me anyway! I told him he should call him Scruffy because he'll never be clean and white. He's a good dog, though, and the two of them are inseparable."

"I'm glad. Every boy should have a dog." There was that smile again.

"How have you been, Pam? It *is* Pam, not Pamela?"

"I don't mind either one of them though most of my friends call me Pam. And sometimes Pammy. And it's Michael, not Mike, isn't it?" she asked.

"Yeah, I've been called Mikey or Mickey, but never Mike. Even as a kid. My mom insisted on it. Said Michael was a beautiful name and that Mike was the name for a professional wrestler or boxer. She lived in the pages of English history – there were Michaels in Scotland during the 1200s — and I think she fancied that one day I would grow up to make a name for myself. She even bought me a Michael's Coat of Arms as a teenager to encourage me. Trying to get my nose out of my computer and get me to be more heroic. That didn't work. I was the typical ninety-seven-pound weakling."

"Michael, the name of the Archangel. He was pretty powerful."

"Yes, Hebrew origins, too."

"Did you ever do a DNA test to trace your ancestry?"

"I'm sure it's German. My last name, Langster, means farmer or laborer, that much I know. Nothing special in our background, I'm sure. No kings or conquerors. Haven't done the DNA test. Seems a little self-centered, I guess. I'm not one of those people that really gets into genealogy. Don't mind if others do, but I get my kicks researching the tech future. Things are moving so fast that I can barely keep up. How about you? Are you into genealogy? That one of your hobbies?"

Pam glanced gratefully at the server who arrived just then, and waited until she had placed their food in front of them with a cheerful "Enjoy!"

"Well, my work dominates my life pretty much now, and when the kids were younger they were my life with not much left over for hobbies. But now Tory is out on her own and Bradley needs me less and less. I always thought that when I had more time, I'd like to travel."

"Where would you like to go?"

"I'd really love to explore Arizona and the ancient Pueblo Indian civilizations. Visit Sedona... I've heard it's really fabulous. Or a drive along Highway One all the way down the Pacific Coast from Washington to Malibu. I'd just love to drive along the ocean and fill the car with the sounds and smells of the Pacific Ocean."

"You and me both." Michael smiled. Their gazes connected and Pam turned away in confusion, suddenly shy. It had been such a long time since she'd been on a date that she hardly knew how to act. *Take it slow,* Michael thought. *She could scare away easily.*

Granite City was busy, the noontime crowd pushed in the door and clustered together in the entry way to register their names with the hostess. The happy hubbub was coupled with the matter-of-fact orders of the servers and sound of friends

110

greeting friends and exclamations over the food. The patio was open on this beautiful summer day and occasional whiffs of warm air poured into the dining room which turned thoughts to summer weekends on the lake, fishing, cookouts, and outings with friends.

Pam looked up from her salad. "I love long drives. It feels like freedom. Getting away, free from responsibility, wandering wherever an interesting road takes you. Lately I've been too busy to do that much, though."

On impulse Michael said, "Pam, would you like to take a drive down to Lake Pepin some weekend? The bluffs along the river are fantastic. We should be able to see for miles during these clear, early summer days. Can't promise an ocean view, but it's the largest lake in the Mississippi River and it's really pretty. Haven't been there since I was a kid, but I've been promising myself..."

"I'd love it. I work every other weekend at the hotel, but that sounds like fun." *And something to look forward to,* she thought.

Michael saw the brief happiness flash across her face. *Wonder what it would take to make her really laugh.*

"When you come up over the bluffs and see the lake and river, it's quite the surprise. I remember as a kid being awfully impressed, imagining myself as an 18th century explorer of the Mississippi, trying to map it out and being excited about the sheer ...bigness of the river." Michael looked down shyly. "Probably just a frustrated Mark Twain, wanting my little childhood adventures."

Pam looked at him with a sympathetic expression. "We were all young once, and without broken hearts." The silence lengthened between them, each caught up in their own thoughts.

Michael stretched in the booth and smiled at Pam. "Would you mind if we brought Brian along? My boy is quite the nature lover."

"I'd love it. And Snow, too, I suppose?"

"Yes, and Snow, too." Michael smiled. "On a leash. Wouldn't want him to fall off the cliff!"

Pam drove slowly home to her Bloomington house, finding herself humming along with the radio. *Well, that was fun,* she mused. *He seems like a nice guy. A lunch date wasn't as stressful as a dinner might be—only a quick handshake goodbye. Soft hands,* she mused. *Not farmer hands.* She pulled into her yard and sat behind the wheel for a moment, remembering another man in another place, his big calloused hand on her shoulder, his face falling into newly etched lines, his eyes filled with pain and entreaty. She slowly opened the car door and made her way into her house. The inevitable emptiness of the house quickly and completely absorbed her contented mood. *Now what?*

The kids ran to Romyn's side when Romyn and Earl arrived at the children's home in Maplewood. It was clear they'd been hanging out in the reception area anxiously waiting for them to arrive. Sophie quickly ran over to Earl in his wheelchair and leaned over to give him a big kiss on the cheek.

Earl smiled and stroked her hair. "Hi, Sophie. How's my girl today?"

Clay looked at Romyn and said directly, "Mary said to have everything packed up today. We've got our suitcases all packed. Are we going home with you?" His face reflected a mixture of doubt and hope.

"Yes, you're going home to stay with us," Romyn said. Clay threw himself into her arms and she felt his sobbing. She soothed his hair, crooning love sounds, then reached into her pocket for a tissue and handed it to him. She bent down to re-button Sophie's shirt, which was askew. "You're a little off-kilter here."

"Forever and ever?" Sophie asked breathlessly.

"We hope so. We'll see. The people here are still looking for your mom. When they find her, I'm sure she'd like you to be with her. We'll see when the time comes."

"Will we see Shiloh and Brian today?" Clay asked in an easy-to-read diversion from Lisa.

"We'll see. We have some business here to do with the director of the home. You can stay with Earl in the family room while I do that, and then we'll stop for lunch and make our way home. It might not be possible to see them today, but we can call them tomorrow and see if they can come over and play."

"Will we have our own rooms?"

"You'll see. You'll see."

The kids gave out a shout of joy, knowing what that meant.

Mary called for a teenager to load all of Clay and Sophie's belongings in the Randall's SUV, and then she motioned Romyn into the office to sign the release papers for the kids. After confirming that they had all the current contact information, both stood and embraced briefly. "I wish you all the luck with Clay and Sophie. They are good kids and deserve their own family."

Romyn reached into her purse and pulled out a heavily-fingered photograph. It showed a much younger Clay and Sophie with uncertain smiles on their faces as they clung to the beautiful young woman with thick honey blonde hair and brown eyes. She looked into the camera with a wistful smile, the hint of a secret in her eyes.

"This is a photograph of the kids with Lisa, their mother. I think it's the only photo they have. Clay left it in the bedroom when they visited the last time. I halfway hope she never comes back, but on the other hand, if she does show up, she needs to see — and maybe be with — her kids. I made copies of this photo and have it framed in their bedroom at our home. Thought I'd leave this with you in case you ever run across someone who has seen her. Or knows her."

"Thank you," Mary said slowly, as she stared at the faded, tattered photograph. The face looked so familiar. *Where? Who?*

Mary woke with a start in the middle of the night. She snapped on the light and walked over to the desk in her bedroom and opened the center drawer. The newspaper clipping was right where she'd left it. She placed the clipping next to the photograph of Lisa and the kids and stared fixedly at it for a long time.

She shook her head as if her vision was blurry. And looked at the two photos side by side again. *This can wait until morning,* she thought. But morning was long in coming as she tossed and turned in sleepless unrest. Dreams of kids on bicycles being hit by cars, of sirens and ambulances, of fields with landmines exploding every time one made a phone call. A rising feeling of panic and helplessness. The morning light couldn't come soon enough.

20

"About time we got together for a meal." Jeremy escorted Tiff into Titos and Maria's home, then leaned over to give Maria a kiss on the cheek. He submitted to Tito's hearty kiss on both cheeks. "Boy, does it smell good in here!"

"Spanakopita. I can cook, but Maria is the real food genius in our family."

"I know, I know. I remember all those meals in Highland Falls with Petros. The best part of those years for me..." The mention of their son, Petros, lost to Taliban in Afghanistan, caused a brief moment of grief for all four. Maria tugged Jeremy's sleeve and gestured towards the living room of the small house. Titos brought a tray with four glasses, a dish of almonds, and a bottle of retsina. "*Yiamas!* To our health!"

"Are you nearly ready for the Grand Opening, Titos?" Jeremy leaned back into the comfortable sofa, placing his arm over his wife's shoulders.

"We're ready. Just waiting for the final paperwork from the State of Minnesota. We'll be open for business weekend after next and then we'll have the Grand Opening the first of the month. I've invited Father Daniel of the Greek Orthodox church in St. Paul to come and offer a blessing. He's just waiting on the exact date."

"That's great. Are you happy with everything?"

"How could I not be? My second son did all the work!" Titos's smile was proud.

"Well, Bill did it all. I just helped."

"More than that, I think. Well, anyway, I am grateful. Are you busy on The Jason House?"

"Yep, swamped. Bill has more than he can handle now, too." Jeremy took a sip of the retsina. Not his favorite but once they began to eat, it would be delicious.

"I heard about the robbery at his place. Do you think those young gangsters on the ridge had anything to do with it?" Maria shuddered involuntarily as Titos signed the conversation.

"No, not likely. They were after something else. The only things taken were all the papers in his office. That's hit him pretty hard – wondering how he'll ever be able to re-create all those records."

"Who would think to steal business records?" Titos shook his head.

"His wife – she's the one in the coma – did some shady land deals with the State Senator, Jefferson. It was all done without Bill's knowledge. The paper trail there is probably very important. And one of the properties she bought turned into a meth lab, so it's unsaleable. Not to mention the fact that it was their daughter, Kellie, who brought her friends into the place and turned it into a drug den."

"Bill's daughter is into drugs? I didn't know. He always seems so calm."

"He doesn't share much. But I think it's wearing on him. He's essentially lost both his wife and daughter. Kinda hard to take. He just keeps working. That keeps him sane. Just keeps his nose to the grindstone and gets the work done."

Titos stumbled a bit at that idiom.

"I saw a lot of heroin in Afghanistan. People got pretty messed up."

"Not my boy."

"No, never. Petros was a good boy. His father's son." Titos smiled proudly, but Maria's eyes filled with the tears that were always barely below the surface.

"We have our Jeremy and our Tafani here, Maria. We need to be happy," he reproved gently, and his wife gave a wan smile. "Let's get the meal on the table. I'm sure Jeremy is famished." "I think I could eat a horse!" Another idiom to be translated.

Jeremy signed his appreciation to Maria — fingers splayed against the lips and outward with a huge smile. "Thank you," he signed, and then sighed deeply. "No one can cook like our Maria!" Titos signed his compliment to Maria, who blushed and shyly dropped her head. "You'll have to take my Tiff under your wing and show her how to cook Greek. You are amazing."

"How are you doing here in Peace Ridge?" Titos asked Tiff. She looked at him with an unreadable expression on her face before she quietly murmured a soft, "Okay."

"If she goes out by herself – she's not driving yet, so she walks most places unless I drop her off – she is treated pretty well by most people. There are a couple of lowlifes from the Ridge that have harassed her once or twice, but never when I am around. They just slow their truck down behind her and follow slowly and when she yells at them – my girl isn't shy – they just speed up. I think they are up for cheap thrills, but if I ever catch them in the act, they'll get thrills all right." Jeremy's voice had hardened to steel.

"Actually, I am a little worried. I have to go out of town for a couple of days – sometime in the next month — and I'm wondering if I can ask you guys to keep an eye on her? I know this is a terrible time with your restaurant opening and everything, but typical with the military, I didn't get any options. Bill thought he could spare me ... I've been putting them off for months."

"Something to do with your service in Afghanistan?" Titos asked.

"Yeah, the Department of Defense in D.C.—friend of mine there —unofficially asked me if I would be willing to come in and take a look at their post-op training manuals for Afghanistan. Current duty guys have been revising it, but they want it scrubbed. We tried a lot of things that didn't work and they'd like the perspective of an ex-military civilian who's out of the field for a couple of years. And, though I'm over the hill," he grinned, "I never have a shortage of opinions!"

"Happy to, Jeremy. Anything for you. We've been thinking we'd like to put her to work anyway!" Titos smiled broadly at Tafani and said, "Maria had the idea that Tafani would be a perfect hostess for us. If she'd feel comfortable doing it."

Jeremy reached over and place his arm around his wife's shoulders. Tiff said, "Hostess?" in her beautifully accented English.

"Only if you want to have too many customers! They'd come to eat at Petros just to stare at my beautiful wife. They'd think you'd imported a Greek movie star!

"Most people here can't tell the difference between Afghanistan and Greece anyway! Tiff, would that be something you'd like to do? To help out Maria and Titos here?"

"I don't know... how would I know what to do?" she murmured hesitantly. "My English..."

"Your English is fine, *Paidi mou*, my child. Better than you think it is, Tafanitsa. I would show you how to do everything. I expect we won't be very busy during the week; people can seat themselves, but on the weekends, we might have a crowd. You'd have to take names and the size of the group and then just escort them to their tables when one is available. It's not complicated."

Jeremy looked at Tiff searchingly. There was anticipation and excitement on her face. *This might be just what she needs to feel at home here,* he thought. She wasn't shy, but she had difficulty making friends. He had hoped the wives and girlfriends of his Peace Ridge buddies would become her friends but he wasn't seeing much progress there.

"Let's talk it over and we'll call you tomorrow, Titos."

Maria signed something to Titos, who responded, "Yes, *Mana mou*, my mother. Maria says that she can stay with us when you are out of town. Then neither of you have to worry." He smiled. "My Maria's mothering instinct kicks in pretty strongly every now and then."

Maria looked at Titos with an expression of longing on her face. Her hands moved expressively and her meaning needed no translation.

"Soon." Jeremy leaned over and kiss his wife on the cheek. "Soon. We hope."

21

"How's by you, George? Haven't seen you in a while." Romyn walked around the counter and gave the old man a hug. He harrumphed and plopped himself heavily down on the chair.

"Not since yesterday, Romyn. Just yesterday. Don't feel like doing much of anything these days. I look around and see all the young guys building things and I just think… better them than me. What I look forward to is just coming in here, having my friend Romyn pour me a cup of coffee and eating a piece of pie. That's the highlight of my day. What do you have for me?"

"Ah, George. You'll have to wait a bit. Jennie is swamped and running behind. She's got a greenhouse full of plants for that little project with Pastor and it's cutting into her pie baking time. She'll be in, though. She promised."

"Our Jennie always bites off more than she can chew. That I can tell you. She wants to be a successful businesswoman but she's stretched in too many directions. How do you think she is going to do the pie business and the herbs business, too, Romyn?"

"I'm sure they'll work it out, George. They are younger than both of us and have more energy. They'll get it done. Pastor says God will bless it, so none of us should worry."

"Yes, well… Pastor. He has his hands full, too."

"I think Jill is coming along well, George. She's becoming more comfortable here in Peace Ridge."

"Do you think so? I think she is still living in a different world! Like she's still swimming underwater. I don't know how Ed manages it. He's like her babysitter."

"She's his wife, George!" Romyn admonished. "It'll take time, with God's help. 'He heals the brokenhearted and binds up their wounds.'"

"Got your new family settled in, Romyn?"

"Yes, well," she smiled, "the first couple of nights they could hardly sleep. Having their own bedroom with all their stuff around them just didn't seem real. The first couple of nights we found Sophie cuddled up with Clay in his bed in the morning but she seems to have settled in better now."

"I have to give it to you, Romyn. You got your hands full now," George observed.

"Talk about feeling old! Earl and I are in our fifties and we never expected to be parents to young kids at our age. I think they are going to run us ragged when they hit their stride."

"What do you hear about that mother?"

"Nothing. Nowhere to be found. And we're waiting to hear from the county to see if they've had any contact with the so-called father. No word there yet either."

"Well, with any luck, they both have disappeared off the face of this earth."

"Ah, George, we can't go that far. We can't hate them. First of all, we don't know the father at all. And Lisa – well, she found herself in a situation where she needed to do what she did to take care of the kids and herself."

"Mostly herself," George said sourly. "She abandoned those kids more than once. You know that, Romyn."

"Yes." Romyn's face darkened briefly. "I hereby confess that there have been many times that I honestly hated her and had to lay that sin at the feet of our Lord."

"Well, I'll tell you. There are two things I can't forgive: Abuse of little kids and abuse of animals." George pushed his chair out a bit and settled more comfortably in it. "One time I was in downtown Minneapolis and there was a homeless guy on the street. He was begging and I was about to drop some money in his can, but then he started beating on his dog, the little cur that slept beside him. He didn't know what he'd done wrong. He just cringed. I started in on that guy, shouting and yelling, telling him he was a worthless piece of ... well, piece... and doggone it, didn't that little dog start to defend his owner from me! He started growling and yipping at me. I just gave up and walked away. Wanted to report him to the police or ASPCA or something... but... oh, I don't know. He didn't get my five dollars anyway. Screwed himself."

"People like that have usually been abused in their childhood and can never get over it. That's why they live on the streets. Clay and Sophie didn't have any choice, either. At least, Lisa didn't beat them."

"Just neglected them! And left them to fend for themselves. I'll never forget their little hovel in my shed." George's mind went back to his first sight of the pitiful bed made of newspapers and garbage bags on that bitterly cold day last December.

"Yes, you're right there. But Earl and I are going to try to love the sadness out of them. Peace Ridge Village can be a new start for them."

The ding of the gas pump hose signaled the arrival of Paul's truck. Jennie and Paul walked heavily into the store, Jennie carrying a tray with cream pies and Paul lugging a large heavy canvas container filled with fruit pies. He set it carefully down on the floor and went out for another load.

"Hi there," Jennie puffed with exertion and greeted them as she began to unload the pies and place them into the rose-colored pie safe next to the table.

"I'll put the cream pies in the refrigerator," Romyn said. "Set them on the counter. And yes, George, I'll carve out a piece of banana cream. I didn't forget you."

"How'd you get dragged into the livery business?" George greeted Paul as he huffed his way back into the store.

"Well, I had to come to Tops for faucets and drainpipe for the new packhouse and thought I'd give Jennie a hand. She can't carry these heavy canvas bags herself, not with eight pies in them. Just too heavy and bulky. And it's a chance to see you, George! Kinda figured you be here this time of day." Paul sat down and nodded his thanks to the cup of coffee Jennie poured for him.

"How's that building coming along?"

"Great. Nearly done. Got the electric in yesterday – Joe did a nice job – and the plumbing is going in tomorrow if Jeremy can get a few hours away from Bill. The two of us can get it done. He's been a great help."

"That's my boy," George said, a proud smile on his face.

"Jennie and I have been having discussions about the best way to dry the herbs. She thinks we might want to invest in dehydrators, but I think we'll just peg 'em up first. Depending on the volume. We'll see how it goes."

"Eliza wants to help out, too," Jennie said with a smile.

"I was just going to ask you about her," Romyn said.

"Well, she's going strong. As strong as someone eighty-nine years old can be! She finally admitted her age to me when I helped her fill out forms the other day."

"Chasing after all those animals keeps her young," Romyn replied.

"Well, yes. They are her life. Though she's coming out of her shell more now. Staying with us after the fire in her pet shed opened her up to the friendliness of her neighbors in Peace Ridge. She really loves Shiloh. And Shiloh really loves exploring her house! It's all I can do to keep her from snooping in every room and opening every stuffed bureau drawer!"

"Wonder what her story is? That old Victorian pile of hers was once the most expensive house in Peace Ridge. Railroad money. She had to have had a stash to buy it." George looked around at the group expectantly. "Oh, I forget. All you *children* are too young to remember the old days. Well, she just showed up one day and moved in and people never saw hide nor hair of her very much after that."

"Well, Eliza doesn't share much about her early life. She's never married. I got that out of her. And I think she prefers solitude—"

"Except for three dozen cats and at least two dozen dogs!" George said.

"Well, they are her pets and she takes really good care of them."

"Well, she's eccentric, that's what I say," George said definitively.

"I'll have her over to help with picking the herbs in the greenhouse and maybe we can coax her to share a little more. Shiloh wants to help, too, and it will be fun to watch the two of them. I fully expect Shiloh to have a full-blown Cockney accent when it's all said and done!"

"Cracks me up," Paul added. "She's such a character, our Shiloh."

"Say, guess where I am going?" Jennie turned to Romyn.

"Heading over to London to see that young woman?" George guessed.

"Nope. Good guess, though, George. I need to text her and see how she is. No, that's not it." She smiled triumphantly. "Paul has said I can go to New York for a few days!"

"By yourself?"

"Yes, by myself. To check out the Fancy Food Show. It's held there every year and I convinced Paul I needed to go and see how other people were marketing their products, to get some ideas for *Peace in the Valley Herbs.*"

"She wore me down." Paul turned to George with a smile. "Gave into her. Let her see what she's up against, trying to compete with the big boys."

"Will you be okay by yourself in that big city?" George looked at Jennie doubtfully.

"Oh, I can take care of myself, George. Don't worry about me. I've traveled alone quite a bit. New York is easy to figure out and get around. I'll be fine."

Jennie turned to Romyn. "We won't be ready to introduce our herbs until next year, but I want to have all our ducks in a row before we do a big launch. Keep it small this year and do it big next year."

"I suppose I can look forward to savory meat pies once you get underway?" Romyn said. "Use all those herbs you're growing!"

"I've thought about it. You can be sure of that. Though the only thing that would sell in Peace Ridge would be a chicken pot pie that tasted just like Swanson's or Schwan's! Nothing fancy will sell here. The only herbs our good neighbors use is salt and pepper. Though you've given me a great idea – maybe I'll try a quiche or two, see how that goes."

"When are you going to New York?"

"The show is end of June. We'll have gotten in our first harvest for the greenhouse herbs. They'll be drying and I can take off and not miss too much work."

"Are you going to supply pies to Petros Greek Diner, too?" Romyn asked.

"Yes, we are talking about it. Not sure about how many yet. We'll have to play it by ear. We'll have a good variety for the grand opening and then we'll see what sells going forward."

"You're going to be one busy girl," Romyn said drily.

"That's how I like it! Right, Paul?"

"Right. With back-up right here in our backyard."

"You'll be able to get all your crops in, Paul. That's our priority." Jennie spoke firmly. No use sharing their dirty laundry in public.

Paul sighed and stood up. "Yes, well... we need to get back to it. The work on a farm never ends."

"Just like a convenience store," Romyn said, as she held open the door for them. Jennie gave her a brief hug.

She scurried out after Paul, shouting back over her shoulder. "I'll bring you a souvenir from New York!"

Romyn turned back to the table and just looked at George.

He said pointedly, "Just wait until The Jason House is up and operating. You'll be busier than ever. You're going to need more help. Is that crazy woman Veronica still working for you?"

"I am thinking about getting Mary Beth from the high school to help with the kids. And Veronica is not crazy, George. She's just gone through some hard times." Romyn grabbed her cell phone. "Reminds me. I need to call Earl and see if he's talked to Veronica today. She was supposed to stop by with some papers from the State of Minnesota yesterday, but she didn't."

"Speaking of the devil…" George nodded to the gas pumps.

Archie Meadows and Veronica Marshall pulled into the bay and Archie got out to pump the gas. He walked over to the passenger side and said something to Veronica. She hesitated and then reluctantly opened the door and walked slowly into the store.

"Hi there. Just talking about you. Wondering how you are." Romyn noted the deep dark circles under Veronica's eyes and the way her jeans were baggy around her thighs. *She's losing weight. I hadn't noticed.*

"I'm fine," Veronica said briefly. "Dad is up North for a visit. Said he'd like to drop in on Ed and Jill for a little bit. Not sure if Jill will remember me, but …"

"Everything okay at home?" Romyn asked the question levelly, not really expecting an answer. Veronica was always sweetly pleasant to them, but she didn't volunteer much about her life.

"The paperwork for The Jason House is done," she replied, deliberately misunderstanding Romyn's question. "I might go down to the Cities this weekend. See a friend," she said vaguely. Her voice was soft, but leaden, as if the words were dragged out from a deep, dark cistern.

"Come over and spend some time with us, with Clay and Sophie," Romyn said impulsively. "They'd love to show you their new room. And their new clothes closet. I think that's what has impressed them the most. They each have their own special section and you should see how they line up their clothes, their shoes... I really wonder sometime if it's the first closet they've ever had." She shook her head. "What we take for granted."

"I might do that sometime," Veronica replied slowly, looking down.

She doesn't plan to, Romyn thought.

Archie took his change from Romyn and turned to Veronica. "Well, my girl, ready to head out?" She nodded briefly and walked slowly behind Archie to the car.

"And you don't call that crazy?" George asked Romyn. "Something is wrong with that girl. She's like the walking dead. I've never felt anyone with less *there* there than her just now. Archie had better keep an eye on her."

"Hard to do when it's your own grown daughter. And he lives in Minneapolis. Can't supervise long distance. Wouldn't surprise me if they want to see Pastor, and Archie'll get Ed's take on Veronica. He knows a lot about depression."

"And he knows a lot about her, too. After she tried to kill herself in the parsonage last winter. Every time he walks through that back door of his, I bet he thinks about it."

"Pastors are not immune to dark moods, either," Romyn observed. "How he was able to get through that mess last winter, with the reporter accusing him of child abuse..."

"Well, Romyn, as you often tell me, he has a Higher Power to lean on."

"Yes, that's right, as do we all. Changing subjects, George, how would you like to come to a birthday party at my house tomorrow night? Sophie is turning eight years old. I want to have a really special party for her. She doesn't know a lot of kids yet, but that doesn't matter. We'll have us *oldies* in to celebrate and love on her."

"I suppose that means a trip to Walmart for a gift, right, Romyn?" George spoke grumpily, but he had a smile on his face.

"If you want," Romyn said innocently. "Not necessary. We'll have plenty and I'm sure you will love a piece of my chocolate cake with chocolate chip ice cream, chocolate lover that you are!"

"Ah, now you're talkin'."

The church was located in a quiet residential area of south Minneapolis. The parking lot was full and Veronica had to drive around to the next block to find a place to park. The overhanging mature plane trees and pines cast dark shadows on the crooked sidewalks despite the warmth and brightness of the summer day. She walked slowly and carefully, timing her arrival at the church at the beginning of the service, and as she stepped up to the entranceway, she faintly heard the processional piano music begin to play. The family had gathered in the narthex. Holding her head down, she made her way silently past them, nodding briefly at the usher as she took the bulletin and then slid in beside the other mourners in the back row.

The church was small and she could see the bank of flowers and an oversized photo of the deceased on an easel next to the pulpit. She turned her eyes upward to the vaulted ceiling and was surprised to discover that her eyes were wet with tears. Blinking rapidly, she dug in her purse for a tissue as the large group of sobbing family members made their way to the reserved rows in the front and, in a few moments, stood in unison with the others as the casket was silently and slowly brought to the front of the church.

Veronica dutifully opened the bulletin to the obituary as it was read by the pastor. Only thirty-six years old. Attended Gustavus Adolphus College in St. Peter. Biology degree. No children nor wife. Survived by loving parents and three sisters. Interment in the church cemetery.

One of his sisters read from Ecclesiastes 3:

A time to be born and a time to die, a time to plant, and a time to uproot, a time to kill and a time to heal…

Veronica's thoughts were numb to Solomon's wisdom. Her mind had, in fact, shut down completely and she retreated into a white space in her head, coming to only when the congregation rose to honor the casket as it made its solemn way back down the aisle.

"Suicide," she heard one of the others in the pew murmur.

"Such a waste," another affirmed.

Suddenly Veronica felt a panic attack coming on and she bent over as if gripped by stomach pain.

"Are you all right?" she heard someone ask and then an usher quickly took her elbow and escorted her to the church entrance just before the family began to walk down the aisle behind the casket.

"Get some fresh air. That'll help," he said kindly, then watched in puzzlement as she fled down the sidewalk. *Funerals are hard on some people*, he thought, as he quickly turned back to his duties in the church.

21

The Chapel Hill campus bar, The Essex, was a well-known watering hole for generations of university professors and students alike. Originally The Lord of Essex, after Queen Elizabeth the First's unfortunate courtier, it had long lost any royal luster it might have had a century ago when it was built. It had the characteristic smell of gallons of beer drunk and spilled on the worn wooden floors which were also liberally sprinkled with peanut shells from the self-service barrels. The current interior design scheme, if one could call it that, looked as if it had been designed by the sports teams with the distinct baby blue Carolina Tarheels sports memorabilia profusely and randomly scattered on every available wall. The faded red leather bar stools were well-worn as if generations of sports enthusiasts' blue jeans had risen and fallen repeatedly, depending on the scores broadcast on the TV monitors over the bar. There were a few tables in an adjacent room, but the bar area was always packed, the better to shout insults over the heads of the coeds to score points on one's friends.

Richard Shapiro usually made his way into The Essex in the late afternoon. It was just a quick walk from his apartment. He had only one summer class to teach and that was winding down. Meeting with students took up only a few hours a week so he could power through lesson plans and grading and then reward himself every evening with a microbrew and a conversation about college political machinations, hops and mash, and women. Much more fun.

And The Essex was a great place to check out women. It was usually thronged with beautiful young women, "game on" for the men. He and his friend, Randolph, had developed a complicated grading system for the women they ran into at The Essex. The grading system, called the FM dial for "Female Meter," done entirely for their own amusement—neither were really interested, or likely, to score a conquest for the night — evaluated a number of factors: General overall attractiveness, ability to initiate or carry a conversation, "flirtability," a somewhat convoluted measure that measured body language and facial communications especially with eyes and mouth, and depth of intelligence which could be either a plus or a minus and which required the application of a check-list, certain words or concepts having higher value than others. Spinoza or Nietzsche, extra credit; Blaise Pascal or Leo Buscaglia, a negative, anything overtly Christian, double negative points. Extra credit points for a smart quote, Spinoza for example: "All things excellent are as difficult as they are rare." Especially if cleverly applied to a choice microbrew.

Rand was already seated at the bar, his oversized rear-end spilling over the leather seat. Richard clapped his shoulder and eased into the seat beside him. It was early enough in the afternoon that the bartender could quickly focus on them.

"Your usual?" he asked.

"Yes," Richard replied, as the Heineken was placed in front of him. Richard always began his weekly beer marathon with a couple of classic European beers before he began to experiment with the microbrews. Claimed it refined his palate. And got the buzz pleasantly begun. His narrow, saturnine face began to relax. The first beer went down fast and the bartender brought the second without a word.

Rand was a lazy graduate student with a trust fund and was always good company. He didn't have to work for a living, so he was always available, had unlimited cash, and was distinctively prepared for a clever *bon mot*. Richard highly valued clever talk. His standard was the witty repartee of an Englishman who had attended Oxford or Cambridge. The ability to combine pithy observation with a cleverly camouflaged insult wrapped in a literary reference.

Richard didn't consider Rand a particularly great friend. He was useful, decent company on the occasions that he needed it. His own career aspirations required that he cultivate the right people so he could move beyond adjunct professor to assistant professor at the university. Usually he spent his time trying to find the right parties and relationships in the tight social circle of the University of North Carolina- Chapel Hill, but sometimes just hanging out with Rand was a relief. Especially when Rand got snockered and just signed the bill for the both of them. Richard felt superior then when he got him into the taxi and sent him home. *I take care of my friends,* he always thought. *I'm a good person.*

Their conversation was desultory. March Madness was over, so sports were a non-starter. They had already gone over the matter of the resignation of the Vice-Chancellor of the College of Academic Affairs due to "unspecified reasons."

"Everyone knows he was *schtumping* the Senator's daughter," Rand offered drily. "And she's not too bright. It's all around town. She's gone on vacation to an island somewhere."

"Out of sight. Out of mind. In this day and age..." Richard was bored. This was old news.

"I might have something that interests you, Richard." Rand said slyly. "Take a look at this." He handed a newspaper clipping over to Richard and watched as his face darkened slightly.

"Think you might recognize that face?"

"Where'd you find this?"

"In the newspaper, as you can see. They're trying to find out if anyone recognizes her. She has no memory. Seems as if I recall a certain person that closely resembles her..." Rand peered at Richard closely.

Richard's cheek twitched uncontrollably. He stared at the newspaper clipping and his mind briefly flashed on the last time he saw Lisa. Years ago. The woman in the photo had a startling resemblance, but there was something off-kilter about the photo. *Her eyes look dead*, he realized. *That was always her best feature.*

"Well, she'd would rank pretty high on our FM dial," he said. "But only until she opened her mouth. Then we'd know whether she was a high quintile, or not," he said callously.

"Well, I thought it was interesting," Rand said. "There was a time..."

"Forget about that!" Richard warned in an ugly voice.

Rand turned away and signaled the bartender. "Time to experiment with our microbrews!" he commanded. "Dan, bring us your latest flight."

Chief Donald Basich walked into the long-term care facility next to the Overland Park Hospital. He stood at the nurses' station, giving a serious, unsmiling nod to the nurses at their computer stations when they glanced up and noted his presence. The charge nurse finished her quiet conversation with one of the doctors and she turned to him with a faint smile.

"To what do we owe this pleasure?" she asked.

"How're doin', Maggie?" he asked. "Haven't seen you around much these last couple of months."

"Yeah, I'm on rotating twelves. Not at the station very much; pretty busy in the patient rooms. What can I do for you?"

"I need to see your mystery patient, the Room 124 transferred from the hospital a couple of months ago. Do you think you can spare a few minutes and come with me?"

"Marie," Maggie said to another nurse, "can you take over here for a bit? I'll be with the Chief in Room 1212 with Drusilla."

"Drusilla? That's what you call her?"

"Well, we don't know her name and she can't tell us. One of our nurses is a fan of the television show, *Buffy, the Vampire Slayer*, and she gave her that name. Claims it means "dewy-eyed," whatever that means. She does have lovely brown eyes." They walked together into Room 1212. The woman was sitting at the table near the window and looked up with a slight recoil of apprehension when she saw the uniform.

"Hello, Drusilla. How are you today?" Maggie walked slowly over to the table. The woman shifted back into her chair slightly and then gave a wide-eyed, seductive smile to the chief. *Dewy-eyed*, he thought to himself. *So that's what that means.*

"Just wanted to see how you are," Chief Basich said to her. "See if you are okay."

She looked at him and didn't say anything. Maggie turned to the Chief. "Drusilla doesn't talk very much. But she's a very lovely person, aren't you honey?" The nurse stroked the fair, honey-colored hair back from her face. Drusilla reached out with her deformed hands and touched her arm lovingly.

"You don't have to talk. Just wondering if you have all you need here. Are they treating you well?" he asked.

In answer, Drusilla turned her face into the nurse's uniform and gently began to sob. Maggie stroked her head and talked quietly over her head to the Chief. "She has times when she struggles so to remember something, and then there are times when she just retreats into herself, into a world of her own creation and we can't reach her. We are doing emotional and memory therapy to see if we can help her recall some of those times."

"How does she do with that?" he asked.

"Some days good, some days bad. We've tried all kinds of familiar childhood associations – school houses, children, swing sets, lots of flash cards of pets and houses to see if we can trigger some kind of emotional connection, but for now we are coming up empty."

The chief crouched down in front of Drusilla's chair and took her pitiful hands in his. "Drusilla, we are doing everything we can to find your family. We will keep on doing that forever. In the meantime, you are in good hands here with Maggie and her team. They love you like their own family."

Each time the word *family* was said, Drusilla gave a slight jerk as if an electrical impulse went off in her brain. Chief Basich looked at her compassionately and then stood up. As he stood over her, Drusilla shrank back into her chair. Maggie quickly reassured her and then brought a shawl over from the bed and wrapped it around her shoulders. After she kissed her cheek, they slowly walked out of the room together.

"Forgive me, Chief. I should have warned you. Most times, she'll be okay with men in her room. But sometimes, depending on how tall or big they are, she'll become very frightened. I have had to put women only on her detail to give her peace of mind. You must represent a flashback to something. Likely the event that put her here."

"Does she ever say anything about it? It's still an open case. Attempted murder."

"As I said, she doesn't talk very much. Every once in a while, she'll say something like "droo, drool, doo" and we ask her what it means, but she can't tell us."

"And she has no memory of who she is and how she got into this state?"

"No, not to my knowledge. She seems engaged in television shows, especially ones that show beautiful things like the jewelry shopping network and that kind of show, but mostly she lives in her own mind. It's heart-breaking. I lie awake at night thinking that there will be something I will say or do that will unlock her, but it's really a dream."

"Well, her injuries were severe. She's lucky she's alive, even if she doesn't remember who she is. Whoever it was that did that to her didn't care if he killed her or not. He probably thought he did. Loss of blood alone, and certainly brain damage from oxygen starvation."

They stood together at the nurses' station. Chief Basich reached into his breast pocket and brought out a picture and silently handed it to Maggie. She stared at it for a moment and then burst into tears.

135

23

The sound of children's laughter greeted Jill and Ed as they arrived at the Randall house. The kids ran quickly into the kitchen from the backyard, cast an indifferent glance at the new arrivals, and ran over to the pile of presents to check them out before they ran back out of the house again.

"Lots of excitement in your house these days," Ed said as Romyn offered her cheek for a kiss and then turned to Jill for a hug. Jill looked briefly at Romyn and Earl as he wheeled into the kitchen to greet them. Her attention was focused on the children. *She's not been around kids for…ten years*, Ed thought. *Didn't think about how that might make her feel.*

The kitchen was decorated with a "Happy Birthday" banner stretched over the windows and colorful partyware on the table. There was a large basket on the easy chair that held a pile of small colorfully wrapped gifts and the kitchen smelled warm and welcoming.

"Please sit down here in the kitchen. I have a few more things to get done and we can visit," Romyn said. "You're the first ones here. Expect George to wander in at any moment. He strongly suggested that we serve a little lunch, not only cake and ice cream, so I'm making sloppy joes and coleslaw, too. He'll be rubbing his belly…"

"George is a good man. He likes to play the big bad wolf, but he's really a pussycat," Ed said.

136

"He's really turned around on Clay and Sophie. From thinking of them as his little squatters, now he wants to be their Uncle George. Which is nice. A ready-made family for the kiddos." Earl's face darkened briefly. "I think his eyes were opened when we visited the children's home in St. Paul. All those forlorn kids without a home..."

Romyn poured lemonade into frosty glasses and put out a bowl of mixed nuts. "How are you guys doing?" She looked pointedly at Jill, and seeing her hesitation said, "Do you like Peace Ridge, Jill?"

Jill reluctantly swung her attention away from the kids and said slowly in a soft voice, "I'm okay. It's a pretty town."

"We all love our Pastor Ed and are glad you're here, too."

"At first it's hard for me to make my way around. Everything is so unfamiliar."

"It'll take time, Jill. One of these days we should plan a picnic up on the ridge. I know Clay wants to go exploring..."

Jill nodded, but then switched her eyes back to the kids in the backyard. *It's going to be slow going*, Romyn thought.

Ed asked, "I assume we'll see Veronica today?"

Earl replied, "We invited her. Told her we'd love to see her. It's been a week or two. After working together so closely for all those weeks on The Jason House, it seems strange that we don't get together more often with her. We respect her privacy and don't pry, but we had hoped that she'd be a little ...more social. I know Archie is worried about her."

"Yes. The two of them dropped in at the parsonage. He asked me to keep an eye on her. Depression, he thinks. And I don't like that business about the obituaries." They all exchanged worried glances.

"'The Lord is close to the broken-hearted and saves those who are crushed in spirit.'" Ed quoted Psalm 34.

"Well, look who's rolled in? And what do you have there, George?" After a quick knock and a "Hello," George held open the door with his elbow and came into the room bearing a large box. "I know you said you'd made a chocolate cake, but I thought those kids needed an ice cream cake from Dairy Queen, too." He laid it heavily on the table. "Went into St. Cloud. Don't think it's melted. It was hard as a rock when I picked it up." He stood looking down in admiration at the design, which featured the characters from *Snow White* with "Happy Birthday, Sofee" written in a pink lacy cursive.

"A party without an ice cream cake is just a meeting!" Earl said, paraphrasing Julia Child.

"She'll love it," Romyn agreed.

"I'll bet it's her first ice cream cake," George affirmed. "I stopped at Walmart and got her a teddy bear, too."

"You're going to spoil her, George."

"I like to spoil pretty little girls!"

Ed glanced down at his ringing cell phone and recognized the number. It was Archie. He stepped away from the excitement and noise in the living room as Sophie and the kids excitedly played with her gifts amid the general hubbub of conversation.

"How 'ya doing, Archie? We're just over at Romyn and Earl's for Sophie's eighth birthday party. Lots of excitement here."

He listened for a few minutes, "No, she's not here. Romyn invited her and she thought she might stop by but she hasn't shown up. Too bad; we had quite the feast."

Archie's voice was subdued but his concern was palpable. "I talked to her last night and she said she was tired and was going to bed early. Sounded depressed as she has for the last several weeks. I told her I'd call her this morning and when I did, she sounded great. Very cheerful, in fact. Upbeat. That was reassuring. I wanted to ask her something and called her back a few minutes later and the phone went into voicemail. Which it has done repeatedly for the last couple of hours."

"Does she usually call you back right away?" Ed asked, his voice reflecting his rising worry.

"Without fail, unless she's in a meeting or something, but then she usually lets me know what is going on."

"Why don't I run over to her house and check on her?" Ed offered. "I'll give you a quick call back from the house."

Ed walked over to Romyn, who was serving coffee to Paul and Jennie.

"That's not a good sign," was Romyn's worried response when Ed recounted the conversation. "Especially the part about being upbeat. That sometimes means a decision has been reached." She reached for his hands and grabbed both of them in hers. "Let's pray, Pastor. Lord Jesus, we intercede for our Veronica at this very moment. We are worried for her. We ask that You put Your arms of protection and love around her and that she finds the peace for which she is seeking in Your presence. Bless Ed on his journey. In Jesus' name, Amen."

"Amen," Paul echoed. "I'll go with you. Need to get out and stretch a bit anyway."

"Leave Jill here with me," Romyn commanded. "She's happy sitting on the floor with the kids anyway."

Ed glanced over at his wife, who sat close by Sophie as she crooned endearments to her new baby doll. "I'll just tell her I'll be back in a jiff," he agreed.

The two men were quiet on their way to Veronica's lodge in the hills. It was a blissful summer evening. The fading June sunshine cast a golden glow on the fields of growing soybeans near Paul's farm and one could nearly smell the growing corn in the fields if it were not for the dominant note of earthy manure, which a neighbor had just spread on a newly plowed pasture.

"He's been worrying and working that field ever since he bought it," Paul observed. "He won't get anything out of it until he lets it lie completely fallow for a whole year and let it recover. I know the guy he bought it from and he worked it hard. He's got to be patient."

"Lesson for us all, Paul. Patience in recovery," Ed said. He paused thoughtfully. "I don't know what we'll find up here," he gestured towards the road as the Honda made its way up into the hills, "but we might have to break into the house. If her car is still in the yard and the doors are locked..."

"I'm handy with a Swiss Army knife. Farmers are always prepared, Ed. Hope she answers the door and is just fine. Fell asleep or something."

Veronica's car was in the yard. The front door to the house was locked and there was no response to their repeated knocking. The men walked around to the lower level to check on the door to the backyard and it was locked, too.

Paul assessed each of the casement windows on the lower level. "All locked up, tighter than a drum," he said.

Ed got out his cell phone and called Veronica's number, which went immediately into voice mail.

"Does she have any friends who could have picked her up and taken her out to dinner or something?" Paul asked.

Ed looked doubtful. "No, as far as I know, we're her only friends. And that, only as far as she would let us." He flashed back on the dinner he'd spent with her and Archie, and the visit to the Minneapolis Art Institute, realizing that he knew her less well than he had thought.

"Let's check for keys in the car," said Paul.

Ed hurriedly checked the seat pockets and the glove box. Nothing there. Paul examined the front of the house, which faced the driveway, and noticed that the window over the kitchen sink was partially opened.

"Try the door one more time and see if she answers and if not, let's go to Plan B."

His sense of urgency was contagious. Ed knocked loudly on the door and called, "Veronica, Veronica," several times to no avail.

"Quick, Ed. Drive your car over here under the kitchen window. It might get me close enough to that window. If I could get close to it, I could probably squeeze in there and see what's up. What's the church's official position on breaking and entering, Pastor?" Paul asked.

In reply, Ed said, "I have a length of rope in the trunk of the car. We could loop it around the chimney – I think it's long enough – and that would help you scale the side of the house and get to the window." He quickly opened the trunk and threw the rope to Paul as he quickly started the car to maneuver into position beneath the kitchen. It was a good twelve to fifteen feet up, but the roof of the car would give them some advantage. Paul made a long loop in the rope and on the first try, looped the rope around the chimney. He gave it a tug and with a brief smile, hopped onto the roof of the Honda.

"That summer I spent in Colorado calf roping came in handy. Always thought it would," he said.

Even with his bum leg, in just a few minutes he was able to put one knee on the window sill and while holding onto the rope, was able to shift open the kitchen window. Thank goodness it wasn't latched into place. Grabbing ahold of the frame, still tethered by the rope, he brought his other leg up to the sill, and then with skill and grace, shot into the window opening. There was the sound of broken dishes and then Paul's face appeared at the window.

"I'll check on her first, and then open the door."

Ed stood at the door in apprehension. "Oh, Jesus. Oh, Jesus," was all he was able to voice. He heard the sound of running footsteps, then the door opened in haste.

"Call 9-1-1. Call 9-1-1. I've called the chief on my cell phone. She's overdosed in the bedroom. Hurry!"

24

"Don't know if you have the time, Bill, but it might be a good idea to get together in the next couple of days. I've got an update on your property deal. Might be better to talk in person." Steve's voice was matter-of-fact.

"Yup. And it might be better if we meet in Peace Ridge, if you don't mind. I have been planning to call you. Some sad news about Veronica. She overdosed sometime this afternoon." Bill's voice was heavy and he felt as if his face was going to burst with suppressed tears.

At Steve's exclamation of "No!" Bill continued, "She's in the Peace Ridge Hospital here. Alive—"

"Oh, thank goodness for that!"

"—but not out of the woods yet. Pastor and Paul found her – had to break into her house –and she was breathing. Shallow breathing, but they were unable to get her to respond. Paul grabbed the pill bottles—she took the whole bottle of her depression meds and several different pain meds. First responders got there within just a few minutes and began CPR and the ambulance got there quickly, too.

"I am just so sorry. I wish…I had been there. Where is Archie? He's hit pretty hard." Steve's voice was choked.

"He's here. He had called Pastor and asked him to check on her, which was quick thinking and probably saved her life. Got to her soon enough anyway."

"I'm coming to Peace Ridge," Steve said decisively. "I'll go first to the hospital and then give you a call and we can figure out where to meet."

"We'll probably all be at the hospital. Pastor and Paul for sure. I think Jill is staying with Romyn; they were all at Sophie's birthday party. Romyn didn't think a hospital was a good idea for Jill. Meet you there, Steve. I am sorry to be the bringer of this bad news."

"I should have acted on my instincts," Steve said quietly.

"What?"

"Took her in my arms and kissed her. That's what I wanted to do, but I chickened out."

Bill sighed heavily. "I'll tell you what, Steve. Don't leave it too late."

"Well, this is where we all seem to get together," Pastor Ed said quietly to Archie and Paul. Earl sat in his wheelchair in the corner, talking quietly with Jennie. Veronica lay motionless in her bed and she looked like a beautiful waxen blonde angel. She had been intubated when admitted and her stomach pumped, but now the only intervention was an IV in her left arm. She had been sedated to help keep her calm. Archie stood over her bed and looked down at his only daughter, his face working to contain his emotion. Pastor Ed put his arm over Archie's shoulder and quoted Psalm 119: "'My comfort in suffering is this: Your promise preserves my life.'"

"Come and sit down, Archie." He motioned to the folding chair at the side of the window.

"I should have been there. I should have been more observant. I knew she was depressed, but I thought it would go away as it has in the past."

"You can't blame yourself, Archie, and we praise God that she's alive and seems likely to recover."

"But," Archie said sadly, "I don't think she wants to live." He looked up at Ed. "Do you know what I found at her house? A stack of bulletins from funerals she's attended in the last few months."

"Did she have a lot of friends die?" Ed asked.

"Pastor! It wasn't people she knew. It was people she'd read about in the obits! People in her age range. People whose lives seemed fine and then they died."

"How did you...?"

"I have been trying to make sense of this. Even though it doesn't make sense. I went over to the lodge to find her insurance papers and sat down at the table. Those piles of obituaries were staring at me. I just didn't understand it. Then I saw the stack of funeral bulletins on the coffee table. I started to match the obit to the bulletin. In every case, the obit said "died suddenly." Veronica had underlined that phrase in each of the obits. And then she goes to the funerals!" He nearly shouted and turning away, shuddered in grief. "Suicides..." he whispered.

Ed took Archie by the arm and led him to the nearby family room. "Sit here. I'll get a cup of coffee," he said as he handed a tissue to Archie. *This is so hard on him,* Ed thought compassionately. *He's aged ten years since yesterday.*

"Sorry, Pastor. I need to get myself under control." Archie looked up bleakly at Ed. "I thought I'd cried all the tears I had in me in the last couple of hours, but it's not getting any better."

"It will only get better when Veronica is back on her feet and into recovery. I am sure that will happen in God's grace. And I hope, for her sake, that she looks to some kind of therapy to help her sadness. It seems to permeates her life."

Archie snuffled into the tissue and then spoke in a choked voice, "She's never gotten over Gary's suicide and the betrayal of her best friend."

"I have sensed that. It feels as if she needs something else to fill that void and she hasn't found it yet." Ed paused. "Let's pray here and now, Archie. We need God to fill the vacuum here. We ourselves are helpless but He is our very present help in times of trouble."

Paul and Jennie pushing Earl's wheelchair had come into the family room and stood with heads bowed as Ed prayed, "Father God. We are beside ourselves. Helpless. Weak. Fearful.

Uncertain. But You are not any of those things. You know our pain and You are our Comforter. Be with Veronica as she comes back to life—to a happy and fulfilling life — and be with Archie and the rest of us, her friends, as we try to help to move forward with her. Give us the right words, the right 'beingness,' the right lovingness. To help her. Now and in the days to come. We love You, Lord Jesus. Amen."

Pastor Ed looked up as Bill and Steve stood at the door. Jennie walked over to both of them and drew them to the coffeemaker to hand them coffee, the essential lubricant in all circumstances.

Bill sat down heavily on the couch. "Steve met me just as I was leaving the job site; I just need to sit for a minute."

Hospitals are agony for him, Ed thought. Steve greeted everyone, making a special effort to say "Hello" to Earl in his wheelchair, this fresh grief bringing back their shared history over the loss of Jason. He quickly gulped down his coffee and said to Archie, "I'd just like to see her, if you don't mind."

"Room 120." Archie pointed down the hallway and slumped further down into the armchair. Steve walked into Veronica's room and sat down at the bedside next to her. He took her limp hand in his and held it for a long time, gently stroking the back of her hand. *Don't leave it too late.* Bill's words rang in his head.

"Veronica," he began. "Sweetie... He looked at her beautiful face, so peaceful in repose. He reached over and gently stroked her damp hair away from her face. "We want you back with us. I don't know if you can hear me or not, but you are so precious to us. To me. Let us help you, Ronnie. Don't go away. Stay with us. Stay with me."

He felt as if he was babbling. She didn't respond to him, but he didn't care. "Let's plan a time together, just the two of us. We could take a drive up to Lake Superior and see the leaves in the fall. They are fantastic – all the colors of the rainbow. I could take you to New England and we could see what upstate New York looks like in wintertime, the snow falling in pristine clumps on the tall Jack pines. I could drive with you to Monticello to see

Thomas Jefferson's genius. And the northern neck of Virginia to see George Washington's birthplace. We could drive to St. Augustine, Florida, and see the ancient buildings where the Spaniards settled in the 16th century. Go scuba diving in the waters of the warm Atlantic there. We could come home to Minnesota and see the pumpkin patch and the corn maze in Chanhassen. We could get lost and then find one another ...." he fell silent.

The nurse came in and looked at the monitor and said, "Are you family? Her boyfriend?"

"Yes," he said, making the commitment. The nurse left the room and Steve leaned over and kissed Veronica on the cheek. "Bye for now, sweet Ronnie. I'll see you tomorrow. Look for me."

"Did she respond?" Archie asked, as Steve walked back into the family room.

"She's still sleeping. I told her we'd take a trip when she wakes up." He looked at Archie fiercely. "And we'll do that. Together we're going to make her well."

"'We gather together to ask the Lord's blessing...'" Ed said. "I guess I need to get back to Romyn and Earl's and collect my wife."

Paul said, "I drove Earl over in his van. I'll take him home and meet you there."

"Steve, wanna get together at the Tall Rigger for a bite and we can talk about my mess?" Bill said.

"Yes, that sounds like a plan," Steve replied sadly, his mind on the blonde woman in the nearby hospital room

"I'm wiped out," Steve said as he slid into the booth at the Tall Rigger.

"You and me both," Bill confessed. "I can't take hospitals in the best of times. And this isn't the best of times."

"It's hard to talk about this stuff when we're at the hospital, it's life and death."

"I feel so sorry for Archie. He seems beside himself."

"I guess he would be. I am, too." Steve looked at Bill. "I've been divorced for decades. I've never been interested in getting into a serious relationship. But Veronica got under my skin and I was thinking of a way ..." He stopped speaking for several minutes. He looked down and his faced worked. "Somehow. I really hope – pray, really – that she comes back to us and perhaps she and I can..." He didn't finish the thought.

"You know my situation with Donna, Steve. Somehow you never give up hope, even when it seems hopeless."

"Yes. Donna. And the mess with the loft." He looked up at Bill quizzically. "Any word from Kellie?"

"Well, not much. She's just turned twenty-one now and she doesn't have to tell me anything. She is on probation, working through her trial dates and hopefully staying off meth, but I don't know for sure." Bill was discouraged. He looked down at his hamburger and poured a distracted dollop of ketchup on it. "I hate to think of her on her own without anyone in her corner, but that seems to be the way she wants it. She's mad at Donna for having the accident; she's mad at me for turning her in. Who knows who else she is mad at?" he said sadly.

"That's what drugs do. Take away any emotional development. She's stuck. No need to work through the issues we all face when you can just avoid them in addiction. Especially when you are young, in your twenties, and you think you already have all the answers."

"I remember those days. I thought I had it all together. Little did I know."

"Well, you've built a business, Bill. That counts for something."

"I really wonder. Sometimes I think it's all just marking time. The work comes in, we get paid, we pay the bills, another job comes in, we do the work, we get paid..."

"I think the work you're doing on The Jason House is really fantastic. Can't wait to see it, Bill." *Let's shift to practicalities.*

"Yes, it's really coming together." Bill exhaled loudly and drained his Diet Coke with a shake of the ice. "Well, Steve, lay it on me. Might as well get to it."

Steve reached into his shirt pocket and brought out a small notebook. "Let's deal with the robbery first. Think it'll make more sense for you. I've been working with Baldwin here in town and he made inquiries around town to see if anyone had noticed a car or truck out by your place at the time of the robbery. He came up dry at first, but hit a spot of luck with Ben over at Tops Hardware. He told the Chief that he had a strange man come in to buy a set of screwdrivers the other day. But he didn't know if he wanted Phillips head or flathead. He seemed confused. Ended up buying both of them. Ben didn't think too much about it at first, but when your place was broken into ..."

"Did he catch the kind of car he was driving?" Bill asked quickly.

"He didn't pay too much attention but happened to walk to the door to help one of his other customers and thought he saw the guy drive away in a black Chevy sedan, an old one."

"Don't suppose he caught the plates?"

"No, but we had a stroke of luck. The state trooper who works Highway 10 over by Rice stopped a car the day of the robbery because it had a broken taillight. And he was doing slightly over the speed limit. When he pulled him over, he thought there might be drugs involved. Just because of the way the guy was acting. The back of the car was filled with boxes of papers...."

"My papers?" Bill asked angrily. Steve nodded.

Bill thought, nearly to himself. "I wonder if that's why the Chief was trying to get in touch with me last week. He called me and told me that he had an update but I was so busy with The Jason House that it entirely slipped my mind. I guess I wanted to put it on the back burner.

"Baldwin had alerted the Stearns County law enforcement about your robbery and the sheriff there was on the ball. Checked into the perp who happens to have a rap sheet for drugs and DWIs, including an arrest warrant for probation violations. And he had drug paraphernalia in the car. So, they impounded it and held him for Hennepin County. Their jurisdiction. In the meantime, the Chief and I went down to the St. Cloud jail to interview this guy. Name is Mark Slovitsky. About thirty. Complete mess-up. He gave us some interesting information that led to the big fish we're trying to land."

"Our honored Senator," Bill said cynically.

"Yes, Senator Hal Jefferson. Your...Donna's partner in crime."

Bill glanced around for the waiter. "May we have some coffee here, please?" he asked. "Think I'm going to need caffeine."

"Yes, this might be complicated to follow so stay with me. Thanks." He looked up at the waiter who left a carafe on the table.

"This Slovitsky guy is pretty deep into the drug scene in Minneapolis. I think he's a small-time dealer but don't know for sure. A user, that's clear. He told us that he was told he'd get a thousand dollars if he'd do a small-town robbery in Peace Ridge. That the house was unlikely to be locked, but he could jimmy the doors if he needed with a screwdriver. He was told not to steal anything except the papers but to make it look like it was a robbery."

"Did he ask for a lawyer before he talked to you? Seems as if he's giving a confession."

"Honestly, he's not the brightest bulb on the Christmas tree. He had been read his Miranda rights but didn't have a lawyer and wasn't interested in a public defender." Steve shook his head. "What drugs do to the brain ... I think he was hoping if he cooperated with us, we'd put in a good word for him on the other charges. Anyway," Steve gave a big sigh. "his contact was someone he saw only occasionally. Didn't know him really well. They had made plans to meet in the parking lot of Home Depot in St. Louis Park and transfer the boxes there. He was a little anxious – either from missing his appointment or from coming down from his high –and intimated that the guy would 'break his legs or something' if he didn't deliver.'"

"Right."

"In my experience, these guys are paranoid all the time anyway, so who knows what the truth was? I asked him if he looked at the papers if they were so all-fired important. He said he didn't — that they seemed to be 'just stupid bills and stuff' — that he was just interested in getting out of the house and on his way back to Minneapolis to collect."

"Do not pass Go. Do not collect $200. I'm glad the papers are safe, at least. Can I get them back now?"

"Wait for it. We decided to set up a sting operation, convinced him to call his guy and tell him that he would meet him as planned, that he'd been stopped in St. Cloud and was delayed, but would be down in Minneapolis to deliver the goods. That went off without a hitch. We intercepted his *capo,* sent Mark on to Hennepin County with our good wishes after he'd been paid his thousand. Which we confiscated, of course. Then went to phase two, see what we could get out of the other guy."

"Under surveillance, I suppose?"

"Yes, we watched the transfer from Mark's car to the other's car and then tailed him to a small storefront office in the warehouse district. It looked to be a party supplies business. The store windows were filled with dusty party supplies and banners—doubt if they ever have any customers — but the door opened to him easily and he trucked all five boxes into the store with no problem. And that's when we moved in."

"So, my papers are now in a derelict storefront in Minneapolis?" Bill asked with a questioning smile.

"Ah, no." Steve smiled. "We weren't going to hang you up that way, Bill. We swapped out all your stuff for a bunch of used paperwork from a recycling center. Looks authentic. Chief Baldwin has all your stuff."

"That's a big relief," Bill said. "You sure earn your keep."

"This is where the fun comes in," Steve replied.

"We immediately moved in on the thieves. Had the force surround the building front and back and several sergeants moved in quickly and arrested everyone there. Mark's *capo* is a guy named Don Kinley. There were only a few records on him in Minneapolis but they put out the word nationally. Hit pay dirt. He's been working for Senator Hal Jefferson for years, seems to be his enforcer. He's been in the shadows of the Jefferson campaign ever since the Senator ran for office. I asked around and people didn't know what he did specifically, except he seemed to be an ersatz chief of staff. Problem solver, logistics kind of guy. He was known as having a terrible temper and people were wary of him. Arrogant beyond belief. Which is the way we found him in the party store. Full of himself."

"Did he resist arrest?"

"No, he just looked at us and called his lawyer and clammed up tighter than a drum. We took him in for questioning right away, of course. Charge of receiving stolen goods. Potential charge of robbery."

"He must be involved in the loft deal some way, unless you think he's clueless and just doing a favor for Hal?"

"Nah, he's involved. Hal wouldn't do any of the dirty work himself. Just gets others to do it for him."

"The stakes must be pretty high for the loft deal, that he was desperate to get my papers. Think he was trying to build a defense of forged papers, or to destroy records?" Bill asked.

"I think he was trying to build a case that Donna bought the loft in her own name and that he was just co-signing for her, that she was the financier behind the purchase and therefore the primary owner."

"But Donna didn't have that kind of money, Steve!" Bill shook his head, barely registering the fact that he was speaking of his wife in the past tense.

Steve looked down at the table and didn't say anything for a while. "I hate to break this to you, Bill, in this way." He paged through his notebook and opened it at a small tab, spread the page open and handed it to Bill.

"What am I looking at here, Steve?" Bill asked.

"That is the number of a money market fund in the name of Donna Michele Nelson nee Brady. In a small bank in Waconia, Minnesota. You can see the balance there."

"That can't be right."

"Yes, it is right, Bill. $1,256,000."

It took Bill a long time to fall asleep. He knew he was over-tired and had taken a couple of Ibuprofens to see if he could ease the ache in his legs. But it was his racing mind that caused the difficulty. Donna's behavior was simply impossible to figure out. He thought he had reconciled himself to her stealing from the business, but the conversation with Steve flooded his mind with anger, regret, confusion, and sadness. Steve had offered to dig into the source of the money if he had wanted, but Bill didn't want to go there just yet.

"Let's get those papers of yours from Chief Baldwin and maybe there'll be a clue in there," Steve had suggested. "You once told me she had locked stuff away in the office. Did you ever go through it?" he asked. Bill shook his head slowly.

Bill was restless, and after tossing and turning for hours he finally dropped off into anxious dreams. He was running from someone and found himself at the edge of a cliff with nowhere to go. Somehow, he scrambled away narrowly and then was soaring exultantly over the valley on the back of a large eagle that set him carefully down on a quiet spot of ground that was covered with a thick mesh of spider webs. Pushing his way through them, he came to a room with several doors and he stood puzzled before them, knowing that the one door he opened would determine his life.

He shifted in bed and sleepily opened his eyes. Three-twenty. Punching his pillow down, he turned to the left and was startled to see Donna there. She looked young, beautiful, and ethereal.

She looked at him with love in her eyes and said, "Bill, Bill," in such a sweet tone that tears began to well in his eyes. "Donna, you're here," he said in wonderment.

"Yes, and I will always be with you," she said lovingly and reached out her hand. He reached out to touch her and his hand banged hard against the side table of the bed.

He sat up suddenly, his body tingling all over. *What just happened here?* He walked into the kitchen and let the water in the faucet run ice cold and, taking his cold drink walked to the screen door to the backyard, looking out to the dark night. There was a soft light coming in through the door. The full moon had escaped the high clouds and etched every bush in the backyard in high relief. He heard a pair of mourning doves in the trees at the edge of the yard, the sound filling him with a nameless anxiety. *This is loneliness,* he thought. *This.* His mind began to spin with scenes from the past few months. Kellie stoned cold on meth in the loft apartment. Donna immobilized in the hospital ICU, Donna's face as she asked for a divorce, Steve's concerned face at the table last night as Donna's double duplicity was revealed. He groaned involuntarily and then rested his head in his hands, as if by closing his eyes he could block the freight train of his mind. In a daze he walked to the kitchen table and slumped heavily into a chair. The noise of the scrape across the floor was loud and he was startled, his heart racing.

His body was cold and cramped and his rear end felt glued to the hard kitchen chair. He glanced at the clock: *Nearly five.* He stood up and stiffly turned towards the living room where a faint ghost of the sunrise was visible through the trees in the front yard. *Might just as well shower and start the day,* he thought wearily. He made his way to the bathroom when he heard the distant buzz of his cell phone in the bedroom.

"Mr. Nelson?" a woman said when he answered. "This is Adele Thompson from the Sartell Home. I am sorry to tell you in this way." She paused. "Your wife has just passed away in her sleep. I am so very, very sorry."

153

25

Jill was fretful and disoriented when she and Ed arrived home from the birthday party. She wandered around the house forlorn and uncommunicative. This behavior was not unexpected. Ed had suggested many diversions in the past but she displayed no interest in any of them. He would disappear into the library to study or work on his sermon and would return to the living room to find Jill in the same position as when he'd left her, often with Biep on her lap whom she would pet in a distracted way. Sometimes he could entreat her to make a meal with him and she dutifully followed the recipes and seemed to enjoy the good food, but any conversation with her was like pulling words out of a thick vat of tar.

He had suggested therapy but was waiting for her to embrace the idea rather than forcing it on her. She seemed to enjoy playing in the dirt in the greenhouse and she seemed open to his gentle touch, though he was taking it real slow. *How long, dear Jesus?* he would ask himself. Then he would think of St. Peter's exhortation: "Make every effort to add to your faith goodness; and to goodness, knowledge, and to knowledge, self-control, and to self-control, perseverance, and to perseverance, godliness, and to godliness, mutual affection, and to mutual affection, love."

Self-control, mutual affection. Love, he thought. *I guess we'll get there one day. Slowly by slowly.* His thoughts about

154

running over his sermon one more time before ending this long day were interrupted by a phone call.

"Hello, Ed, I am Titos."

"Good to hear from you, Titos. How are you and Maria today?" Ed replied. "I hear the restaurant is just about to open. Jill and I will be there for sure."

"It's coming along and that's why I am calling you, Ed," Titos replied. "I want to ask a big favor of you and I hope it's possible."

"Ask away. I am at your service."

"I would love it if you could give a blessing at the Grand Opening like you did at the ground-breaking for The Jason House?" he asked.

"Happy to do it, Titos. Happy to." Ed replied warmly. "We're glad you are here and know that you will be a success. A big success."

"We hope so. *Aineo*. Praise God." Titos paused. "Ed, I wonder – this is a big request – I wonder if you would mind if we had Father Daniel of the St. Paul Greek Orthodox Church also bless our restaurant. This is really important to me and Maria."

"Yes, of course. Evangelical Christians and Eastern Orthodox Christians have a lot in common, Titos. It would be my privilege to serve alongside him in this event."

"I am so glad. Maria and I have driven down to St. Paul for a few services and have made a great friend in Father Daniel, but I wanted to be sure I wasn't ...twisting someone's nose out of joint, as people say in Peace Ridge."

"We're pretty ecumenical here, Titos. I can ask Father Brandon from St. Anthony's Catholic Church to come, too, if you want. We will cover all the bases!"

"Well, I wouldn't mind. Maria and I really want to fit in. I know that we are outsiders, first as Greeks and then as New Yorkers."

"We take everyone here in Peace Ridge, Titos!"

"Well, except for a few ugly *you-know-whats*, people have been nice."

"We love Jeremy and Tiff, too. I'd love to get them in church someday."

"Yes, I know. That's the ongoing wish, isn't it?" Titos responded.

"Jeremy used to come to Sunday School here when he was a kid. I assume Tiff is a Muslim. Don't know. But we love them both anyway."

"I know. I do, too. It means a lot to us that we live close to them. My Maria thinks that they are our family now." Titos paused. "I have asked Tafani to be our hostess. I think Jeremy has talked her into it. It will be good for her..."

"And good for the restaurant, too. We need to be more global here in Peace Ridge. We have a lot of Germans, Swedes, Danes, and Poles. We need an infusion of southern Europe and Eastern Asia here. Diversity will be good for Peace Ridge!"

"Well, we'll do our part. There won't be better food in the county. I can promise that."

"I know. I love your cooking..."

"...it's all Maria..."

"Say, Titos, do you need a place for Father Daniel to stay? He'd be welcome at the parsonage here, if you want to ask him. He could come and stay with us on Friday night before the opening. I'll just clear it with Jill."

"Are you sure? I'd be happy to ask him."

"We have a couple of extra bedrooms and he'd be welcome here." *And I will have someone to talk to*, Ed thought. *The quiet nights with Jill are just wearing on me. Forgive me, Father God.*

"Hello, Ed." Romyn's voice was cautious, unlike her. "Sorry to call you so early in the morning. I wanted to get you before you headed over to the church.

"No worries. Everything okay?"

"Ed, I want you to consider something that I observed at Sophie's birthday party," she responded.

"I am sorry that we took so long at the hospital," Ed responded.

"No worries. You were where you needed to be," Romyn said heavily. After a moment she continued, "I think we have a problem with Jill." She let that sentence hang heavily in the air.

"Tell me more, Romyn," Ed said quietly.

"She was really resistant to leaving Sophie's side. Was clingy, really. We were able to get her into a chair and Sophie was playing with the other kids, but Jill couldn't take her eyes off her. You may have seen that earlier in the day. In any event, just before you came to collect her after being with Veronica and Archie in the hospital, she was packing up all of Sophie's toys and planning to bring them home with her. With Sophie."

The silence lengthened between them.

"Umm..." Ed said.

"Ed," Romyn said firmly, "I think Jill thinks that Sophie is Emily. I think she's stuck in ten years ago and the accident."

Ed looked over at Jill, who sat unmoving in the armchair facing the fireplace as she had been ever since their early breakfast, her open unread Bible on her lap.

A flash of memories shuffled quickly in his mind. Jill crying over the pictures of the kids...Jill quiet and unengaged in life...Jill focused on the kids at Romyn's backyard...Jill's remoteness...

"Are you there, Ed?"

"Yes, I am here. I am thinking about this. Oh, Romyn, you may be right! I just don't know what to think." Ed turned away to shield his conversation from Jill. "I have been struggling..."

"Yes, I know, Ed. I have seen it," Romyn said compassionately. "Your Jill now is not exactly like she was. She's broken..."

"What...how?" Ed struggled to respond. "What do I do? I'm just not sure how to move forward here.

"She needs to have some kind of counseling, Ed," was Romyn's no-nonsense reply.

"You're right. I just don't know anyone around here and I hate the thought of weekly trips to Minneapolis. Car trips are hard for her in general. She gets pretty anxious, especially in heavy traffic."

"I don't blame here. I hate it, too. We'll just have to figure it out. And Veronica, too. We're hurting here in Peace Ridge these days."

"Did you talk to Archie yet today?" Ed was glad to shift away from the subject of Jill. *Help me, Jesus. I need Your help.*

"I did talk briefly with him late last night. Earl and I will go to the hospital later this afternoon and will spend some time with him. He said Veronica had regained consciousness and she recognized him and said, 'I messed up, didn't I, Dad?'"

"Oh, poor thing."

"I should have acted on my impulses at the time I began to realize that she was struggling. I saw that she was not herself..."

"But you had a lot going on, Romyn, with Clay and Sophie. Don't blame yourself."

"Yes, but we need to trust our impulses and not be afraid to reach out. In love. It's hard with Veronica; she has a pretty strong privacy barrier, and Earl and I didn't want to breach it, but..." Romyn gave a big sigh. "We reap the consequences. Time to do better. Do more."

"Those are my marching orders, too, Romyn," Ed replied. "'Praise to the God of all comfort who comforts us in all our troubles so we can comfort others.'"

Ed was just about to pack up his Bible and notes and head to the church when the phone rang again. Ed could hardly make out the words. A hoarse voice choked out the words, "She's dead, Ed. She's dead."

"Bill?" Ed asked. "Bill, is that you? What did you say?"

There was the noise of a coughing fit and a quiet snuffling sound. A pinched voice said, "Donna is dead, Ed. My wife died in the night."

"Oh, Bill," Ed said, his voice filled with compassion. "I am so sorry. Are you at the hospital or at home?" He glanced at the clock. Not even eight o'clock. *This has been a busy morning.*

"Home. They called me an hour or so ago."

Donna, Donna, Ed thought to himself. *In the arms of God now.* "Let's pray, Bill," he said softly. "Father God, we turn to You. Only You can help us now. We lift our brother, Bill, to You and to Kellie, too, in their loss. Put Your loving arms around them and be their comfort as we walk this walk with them. In Jesus' name." Ed thought quickly. "Church is over at 10:30 this morning, Bill. I won't stay for Sunday School. I'll leave immediately after the sermon and will head over to your house. We can go together to Sartell."

I can't take Jill with me. Hospitals are death for her. Ed quickly called Romyn back and filled her in. "Oh, poor Bill. This is tragic. We have sorrow upon sorrow these days. Bring Jill here to Crossroads, Ed, before you head off to Sartell." was Romyn's immediate response. "I have Beth Ann taking care of the kids for me. Bring her here and she can stay with me at the convenience store. Maybe I'll find some way she can help me. I'm leaving here at noon to go home. Terry has the afternoon shift. Come to our house when you and Bill get back."

Her decisive take-charge orders were just what the doctor ordered. Thus strengthened, Ed collected his Bible and papers and took Jill's hand to walk over to the parsonage. *We'll pray there for all our losses,* he thought. *Go to the source of all comfort.*

26

The car ride was quiet nearly all the way down to Minneapolis. Though Jennie had convinced herself that she and Paul were in agreement about this trip, it was clear, based on last night, that he still had reservations and wanted to rein in her enthusiasm. *Which just makes me mad and he knows it,* she thought stubbornly, staring out the window at the fields and pastures along Interstate 94.

It all started when Jennie began talking about all the retail contacts she'd make at the Fancy Food Show and how she might even explore the PR opportunities with the foodie magazines that were based in New York. She could tell by Paul's expression that his agreement to the Fancy Food Show did not mean he gave assent to all the plans she had for *Peace in the Valley Herbs*. He still wanted to start small and local and her plans were much more expansive and aggressive. Stored away in her mind was the conversation that she and Delaney had last year about Jennie coming into her own, being the face of a rural Minnesota business. A Midwest Martha Stewart perhaps.

Well, not right now, she thought, *but maybe this could become something more.*

A niggling thought came to mind: Pastor Ed's desire for the herbs to become a way to shower blessings on the hungry and hurting in the community, but she pushed that thought away. *If we become really successful, that will mean more profits to share. If we get the publicity and attention we deserve along the way, well, that just means God has blessed us more.*

"Are you going to give me the silent treatment all the way to the airport?" Paul asked mildly.

Jennie slowly turned away from the window and stared straight ahead. "Paul, I want us to be on the same page in this," she said softly, but there was an edge to her voice.

"We've been over this before," he replied. *Until well after midnight last night,* he thought. "I'm not going to rehash the old arguments..."

"It wasn't an argument!" she declared fiercely, her face reflecting the set stubbornness he had come to expect, especially these last few months.

"I agreed to this trip because I think you need it. You need to feel you're a part of something bigger than Peace Ridge. You need to test yourself in another environment. You want significance in this ..."

"Ah yes, the old ego argument. Like *you* are a saint and *never* feel pride in *your* accomplishments!" She threw her shoulder against the window and sat immobile, as far away from Paul as she could in the pickup. "Like I'm just a shallow ego-driven maniac. And you're the good farmer. The one whose motives are always pure. Always better than good."

Paul didn't reply, but she'd dug into a sensitive spot, for his set face and steely eyes were trained on the road for the next fifty miles. She wasn't going to make small talk and she wasn't going to give in. He just didn't understand. And to prove she didn't care, she flipped the radio dial to an oldies station and began scrolling through her iPhone as if she hadn't a care in the world.

I hate it when we fight like this, she admitted. *I know God put us together, but God! We are so different! Did You know what You were doing here?*

"Take care of yourself. Don't get into any trouble. Call me every night. And don't do anything silly." Paul hugged Jennie as they stood at the entrance to the security checkpoint at

Minneapolis-St. Paul Airport. She pulled back and looked at him, longing to touch his face and smother him with goodbye kisses, but she couldn't bring herself to give that little apology.

"See you in a couple of days. Love you, honey," she said. "Thanks for the ride down," she added, the nicety creating just another notch in the distance between them.

Paul walked slowly back to the parking lot, got in his car and mindlessly maneuvered off the parking ramp. He found himself halfway to Maple Grove before he finally was able to be in the present and focus his mind. "I hope she gets her little adventure in the big city," he said savagely under his breath. "And then maybe she'll settle down in Peace Ridge."

If only we had kids... but that thought was a non-starter. He knew that. Earl and Romyn's delight with Clay and Sophie had only made things worse. Jennie picked out children wherever she went and never had one for her own. *These business ideas of hers...*Paul thought, *those are her children. I should be more sympathetic. If we could only adopt...*

The Minnesota night was drawing to a close when he pulled into the yard. He had asked the teenager next door, David, to get the milking started, and he saw that all the cows were in their stanchions and happily munching away. Thunder ran to greet him as he walked stiffly to the barn to help out with the chores. Any drive of one hundred miles or more caused stiffness in his leg that was injured in the farm accident last year, but if he just got cranking on the chores, it'd loosen up.

"Got most of them done," David said. "Took ol' Nickel a long time to get in and get settled but I finally got her into her place. Held a fistful of hay in front of her and she walked in like she was a princess."

"She's a princess, all right," Paul said wryly, slapping Nickel on her hindquarters. She didn't even nod her head, her mind and mouth engaged in the hay trough.

"How was your trip to the Cities?" David asked.

"Fine. Got Jennie off to New York."

"Can't imagine why anyone would want to visit New York," David said, his placid moon face reflecting a deep contentment in the barn and land.

"Well, she wants to create a business and thinks that New York is where she can get some good ideas. Can't get them here in Peace Ridge, I guess," Paul said shortly.

There was a quiet interval when the only sound was the sucking and pumping sound of the milking machines.

"Did you hear about Bill?" David asked, as he walked over to help with Nickel.

"Bill? What?" Paul replied, his mind on the gasket on the milk canister he was eyeing. *Probably need to replace most of these pretty soon.*

"His wife died. That woman in the coma."

Paul straightened and walked slowly over to the side of the barn and braced his arms against the cement blocks and dropped his head. *Bill,* he thought. *Bill and Donna, Poor Bill.*

"Hadn't heard. When?"

"Just this morning, I guess. Pastor Ed went down to Sartell with Bill. I don't think they're back yet. Far as I know."

"I'll call them. When we're done here."

A small kitten, one of the barn cats, wove her tiny legs through Paul's. He picked her up and nuzzled her little black and white face. She pulled back and looked at him as if to say, "Where's my supper?" Paul stroked her head as he put her down and walked over to the refrigerator in the milk house and took out a bottle of cream. He found the crusty stainless-steel pan empty, and as he washed it out the kitten meowed pitifully at his feet all the while. "Take your time. Take your time. I fed you this morning," he reassured her. Finally, placing the pan in front of the kitten who slurped greedily, Paul called out to David, "I've got the rest of this. You can go. I'll see you in the morning, okay?"

When he was finished in the barn, Paul walked slowly to the house and opened the door. Thunder bounded in behind him and immediately walked over to his food dish.

"Yes, you too," Paul said as he went to the cupboard and got out the kibble and filled the pan. He refilled the water dish and then sat wearily at the table and punched in Bill's cell number.

Brian sat cross-legged in the deck chair, his open notebook on his lap, Snow slumbering loudly at his feet. He had laid his pencil down and was intently watching the small chipmunk at the edge of the grass near the large box-elder. Bushy tail flashing, the small creature darted quickly onto the bird feeder, stuffed his capacious cheeks, and then scurried away down the hillside where he disappeared into a pile of rocks. *That's his burrow,* Brian thought. He made a small note in his notebook, his face serious and thoughtful. Words and thoughts were swirling in his head, but this poem was going to be hard to write. He wanted to send it to his mother in London, just to tell her that he was okay and was just waiting for her to come home.

I am the steward of the house, just like little Tamias. I am guarding the home. All will be well when you come home.

He heard his father talking on the phone in his home office. It wasn't a work conversation because his father's voice had changed, becoming slower, softer, and warmer. Brian could always tell the difference and he knew his father would hang up the phone and rise up from his chair with energy and happiness. When it was just work, he only sighed heavily, stretched in the chair, and went back onto his computer.

"How's my Brian today?" The text signed with a heart emoji pinged on his cell phone. Brian stared at the words for a long moment. He missed his mother but with wisdom beyond his years he knew she wanted to be in London for a while and he wouldn't make it hard on her.

"Fine," he texted back to her, unaware of the brief quivering of his chin. "Writing a poem for you, Mother."

"Luvly," she replied quickly. "Will text more later; heading out now. Love you." Another heart emoji.

"Working on another poem?" Michael asked, walking onto the deck and touching his son lightly on the shoulder.

"Yes," said Brian, closing the notebook carefully.

Michael took the cue. "What would you say to a little trip tomorrow? Would you be able to get up really early—it's a long drive?"

"Where are we going, Dad?"

"To Lake Pepin, down in the southeastern part of the state. It's the largest river lake in the Mississippi and it's beautiful with cliffs and bluffs. I think you'll really like it."

"Can we take Snow?"

"Of course," Michael said, and after a brief pause, "I would like to take a friend of mine, too, if that's okay?"

"That lady from the pet store when we got Snow?" Brian asked quietly, to Michael's surprise.

"Yes. Pam is her name. She is able to take a day off of work and come with us."

"I wonder if she ever got a dog. I think she really wanted one," Brian said thoughtfully.

"I don't know—you can ask her herself. We'll pick her up at her house in Bloomington at seven o'clock in the morning. That's early! We'll have pancakes at the Original Pancake House and then drive down alongside the river; it's only a little over an hour. The weather is supposed to be perfect."

"Does she have kids?"

"She has two older children, Brian. They won't be able to go with us on this trip, but maybe we can meet them someday."

"Are they boys or girls?"

"A boy and a girl."

"How old are they?"

"Bradley is about eighteen and Tory is twenty-seven, I think."

Oh, old. Brian lost interest and opened his notebook and picked up his pencil, his eyes focused on the furry steward who was back from his burrow. After a quick, furtive glance around, Tamias gracefully shimmied up the bird feeder.

"Bright-eyed and bushy tailed," Michael said, as he stood next to Brian and watched the chipmunk. "Hey there, get off the feeder!" he shouted to the busy chipmunk, who ignored him.

"Yup," Brian said briefly.

Hold Fast to What's Certain

Chokecherry eyes scout the seed treasure,
Hope-filled harvest for uncertain days.
Tiny rosebud mouth and pink nose aquiver
Soft saddlebag cheeks brim-full of praise.

Quick-footed, he scampers up the oak tree,
Paws like tiny hands, bushy tail held aloft;
Food for today, certain hope for tomorrow,
Packed burrow granary near leafy nest soft.

Tamias's nature within God's grace abiding,
Contentment, the quiet slow waiting begun.
Lavish love richly fills my heart's chambers,
Pending your smile that leaves me undone.

-Brian Peterson, age 9
For Delaney Peterson

British Rail is the best in the world, Delaney thought, *but egad! This trip is endless.* Taunton, the city seat of Somerset County, was about three hours by train from London and she'd started early, but even so, it would be nearly noon by the time she got to the county offices.

And when she got there, it was like a wild goose chase. *Why did I let Jennie talk me into this?* she thought, as she wearily took instructions from the Somerset County Council in Taunton to visit the Somerset Heritage Centre. It was only a few minutes away by car, but a good two-mile walk was still a work-out. And when she got there, she discovered that access to the records was by appointment only and they needed twenty-four hours to pull up the relevant records for her.

The lady was polite but firm.

"But I've just come down from London on the train! Nearly four hours!" Delaney exclaimed. "I can't imagine why you cannot accommodate me. I only have a few hours for this research and this has set me back tremendously. In America..." she began, but stopped abruptly when the clerk looked at her sharply.

"I'm sorry, madame. We have over seven million records here. It would be impossible for us to access your specific records without advance notice and search. It would be our pleasure to do that for you, given notice. Here is our card with all the website addresses. You can make your enquiry on the website and we will schedule an appointment for you."

Well, this was a waste of time, Delaney thought. *Damn Jennie.* Turning to the woman, she charged up her charm offensive and said "I apologize for my shortness a few minutes ago. I am tired from the journey and I should have done more research. I will do as you say and send in my query in a few days from London. In the meantime, I am in desperate need of lunch. Can you recommend a nearby pub for refreshments before I head back on the afternoon train?" She knew her politeness was exaggerated but she thought that acting civil would pay benefits in the long run.

The woman at the desk smiled in relief. *Thought she was going to be one of those difficult American customers,* she thought. "I love the Cross Keys pub just down the way. They are very pleasant. My niece is a server there. Her name is Emily – if you have her, just say Sandra said 'Hello'."

"Much obliged, Sandra. I will and thank you ever so much for your help. And again, I apologize for being so... difficult. It's just a disappointment. I wanted to get the answers quickly and be done with the task."

Americans, Sandra thought to herself. *Always in a hurry. We have records here from the 16th century. They just need a little more perspective."*

"Always, madame. Of course. Looking forward to seeing you again."

The Cross Keys was a friendly pub and Delaney found her equanimity restored after settling into the booth at the window and inhaling a quick glass of wine. The familiar warm relaxation penetrated her body – *I am really wired today,* she thought – and she began to put the day's events in perspective. *Let's get real, the trip down here wasn't to do research; it was to check on Ten and I've gotten nowhere on that.*

She ordered the Chef's Seasonal Garden Bowl and another glass of wine and planned the precise right text to send to Ten. "Just found myself in Somerset...where are you?" Or, "In the Cross Keys in Taunton – may I buy you a drink?" Or, "Drinking in the beauty of Somerset; you, lucky dog, you!" She decided to simply say, "In England. Love to see you," and let the next move be Ten's.

Delaney sat back in the booth and idly observed the other patrons. It was a dull time of day despite the beautiful weather. Housewives had done their shopping on the High Street in the morning and there were few people in for a late lunch after one o'clock. Delaney looked idly out the six-over-six mullioned windows onto the car park. There were a few family groups and singles gathered, talking and laughing. A few businessmen in the typical garb of the rural gentleman, tweeds but perfectly fitted. Delaney's attention was caught by a young couple who were standing very close together against the driver's side of a classic Jaguar. The man was saying something to the woman and she was laughing up at him with delight on her face, her hand brushing her honey blonde hair way from her eyes with a flirtatious expression. He leaned into her and cupped his hands on the side of her head and tenderly kissed her forehead. She laughingly pushed him away. He turned, and grabbing her hand possessively, walked her around to the passenger side of the Jaguar. The way he moved, languidly yet poised with perfect posture, was strangely familiar. The man tossed his head back into the air as he gracefully entered the driver's side of the car.

Delaney sat shock still in her booth at the Cross Keys. Ten. Unmistakably Ten. Yes, she might have expected it. He thought she was 4,000 miles away and she didn't have a claim on him. *Despite all his lovely text messages,* she thought. *Here. In Somerset. Not working, obviously. Had he been in the bar when I came in? I don't think so.* She rapidly glanced at her cell phone, her message not yet delivered. *Oh, too busy, I guess, to check your phone, Ten,* she thought bitterly.

The journey back to London was awful. She slept as well as she could in the uncomfortable seats, clutching her bag, feeling hung-over, out of sorts, and tired beyond belief. She took a taxi from the train station to the BnB and fell into bed, feeling disappointed, forlorn, and angry all at the same time. Checking her text messages before bed; none from Ten, a sweet poem from Brian. *I'll read it in the morning,* she thought, as she punched her pillow and turned over to sleep it off.

27

Richard Shapiro left Randy at The Essex at about midnight, a little too loopy to drive home but he chanced it anyway. He threw his keys on the kitchen table and staggered into the disgusting mess that was his bedroom. He tripped slightly over the dirty clothes on the floor, and emptying his pockets onto the dresser, fell onto the unmade bed, barely able to push his shoes off his feet. He grabbed his computer and booted up one of his favorite X-rated movies. After a night of ogling women, there was nothing better than to dip into deep arousing fantasies. But the beer was too much for him despite the enticement on the small screen and he found himself slipping into a restless sleep, his last thought, *Too much beer again but I can handle it.* The small screen flashed scenes that would make a stevedore blush.

He kept his blinds down year-round, but slivers of sunshine outlined the bedroom windows when he finally groaned and pushed himself upright, his head pounding and his mouth parched. *Oy vey. Overdid it. Why did Randolph talk me into the Bailey's after all that beer?* He slumped upward and sat there for a moment, finally pushing himself off the bed and up into the bathroom.

He wandered into the kitchen and rinsed out a dirty mug, ignoring the faint coffee line that remained. He let the water in the faucet run until it was reasonably hot and then filled his mug, adding a heaping spoonful of instant coffee. His head was fuzzy, as if his mind was in hibernation and filled with cotton wool. He sat wearily onto the kitchen chair and stared vacantly out the window, morosely drinking his coffee.

There was something niggling at the back of his mind. He tried to recall their conversations over the last week—they'd met for beers every night — but the only thing that stuck in his mind was their disagreement over their FM ranking for one of the coeds who arrived close to midnight. Rand always over-scored, perhaps thinking his good thoughts would entice her closer for conversation, but his "39" was way over the top. Richard stuck to his "17."

"You can't get to 39 without talking to her first," Richard had scoffed. "You're giving her a full 10 for looks alone and another 10 for flirtability. I just don't see how you get to 39."

"You're missing it, old man," Rand had said. "Look at her books." The blonde had laid her plastic see-through bookbag on the bar while she signaled the bartender. "*Essential Rumi, Siddhartha,* by Hermann Hesse. Can't see the other one."

"Jelaluddin Rumi and Siddhartha get points but you have to deduct for the Kahlil Gibran book. Every freshman girl gets *The Prophet* and thinks it's simply profound."

"Good eyes, Rich. She's older than a freshman, by the way. But you're missing the key point: Check out her tattoo."

Richard gave a casual look over to the woman, who by this time was completely aware of their interest. She tossed her shiny hair over her shoulder with a quick toss and turned away to talk to her companion, all the while checking them out in the bar mirror. Richard pretended interest in the new arrivals at the bar while trying to sneak a glance at her bare arms. She finally gave a three-quarters view when she turned to talk to her friend, and Richard caught sight of the tattoo just below her throat: the golden ratio, the universal symbol for perfect proportions in architecture and anatomy.

He had turned back to Rand, who had a smug expression on his face. "You're going to have to deduct points for ego, Randolph. Any woman who brands herself with the golden ratio has a pretty high opinion of herself."

"Any woman that confident is worthy of the points," he had pushed back.

Remembering that conversation brought to mind the other woman Rand had goaded him about. *What did I do with that newspaper clipping he gave me last week? Probably lost it.* Richard went back into the bedroom and piled through the pile of coins, flash drives, miscellaneous receipts, and the jumble of trash that covered the top of his dresser. He finally unearthed the faded newspaper clipping and stood at the bureau, studying the paper in the faint light. *It's Lisa, all right,* he thought. *Recognize her anywhere.* He walked into his office and pulled out the chair that caught on the pile of dirty clothes on the floor. Swearing angrily, he threw himself into the chair and clicked on his computer. It didn't take long — *Mystery Woman of Kansas City* popped up on the first page of his Google search.

He arose tired and hungry from his chair about an hour later with a curiously triumphant expression on his face.

Ed and Bill made their slow way back to Peace Ridge from Sartell. Both were quiet, alone in their own thoughts, as Ed maneuvered the heavy Highway 10 traffic. At the Little Falls turn-off, Bill said suddenly, "Let's stop here for lunch. I could eat a horse."

"And to tell the truth, I guess I don't want to walk into that empty house," he said after they'd given the waitress their order. "I didn't realize that I had a little bit of hope that she'd get well and would someday be back home. It was never really final for me until today." His face was white and drawn and new lines around his eyes seemed to have appeared overnight. "We weren't … getting along, Ed," he said, "as you know." Ed nodded compassionately. "But when you spend nearly twenty-five years with someone, you still feel…connected. Even if she's been in a coma for these last few months."

"I understand. Nothing can take away those 25 years. And the bad times of the last few years should not drown out the good memories of your first years together."

"I am not looking forward to calling Kellie," Bill said. "I just can't predict her reaction."

"Do you want me to call her for you?" Ed asked.

"No, I have to do it. She wouldn't answer your call anyway. Hates religion, as you know. No," he sighed heavily, "I will call her when we get home. I hope it sinks in. I hope she's not on drugs. I hope this may help us get back together. Too many 'I hopes' in this." His face worked as he tried to hold back the tears.

"And now I'll probably never get the answers. Her secrets died with her."

Ed thought it might be helpful to veer off to another subject. "Has Steve been helping you any with the loft mess?"

"Yeah, we got together last night and he's told me some stuff and gave me some homework. I need to dig into all the office papers that we got back from the robbery and see if there are any clues to the money." Bill suddenly looked up. "Oh, I didn't tell you, Ed. Donna had money that I didn't know about. When Steve was digging into the financing for the loft, he discovered a bank account in Waconia in Donna's name."

Ed looked up in surprise. "Really? In Waconia? Why Waconia?"

"I guess I really don't know. With all that has been going on today, I haven't been able to even think about that stuff. The only thing I can think of is that her mother was from Waconia. She was not about to use Lakeway Bank in Peace Ridge. She had to keep all her secrets secure." The last was said somewhat bitterly.

That will help out, Ed thought. *He's underwater financially.* "Well, I'm here to help if you need me."

"Just help me get through the funeral," Bill replied sadly. "That's the big thing for now."

"Why don't we do this? When we get home, I'll see if Romyn and I can't lay out the plan for the church service and fellowship." *And maybe Jill can help.* "That will free you up to visit the funeral home and get that started. We can connect later today – why don't you come over for supper? I'll make sandwiches or something, and we can see what's left to do."

"I should probably drive to Minneapolis to tell Kellie about her mom in person," Bill said, as his eyes welled with tears. "If I knew where to find her. I guess I'll call her and see if she wants me to come down."

"If you go, let me drive you, Bill. You don't need to go alone."

"No, I'll be all right. You've done enough."

He's barely had enough time to process this, Ed thought. *Needs some alone time, too.*

"Well, I'm here."

"You got your hands full, too, Pastor." They looked at one another miserably.

Jill was waiting anxiously for Ed when he drove up the Randall's driveway. She had been sitting on the bench at the front door, but she jumped up when she saw his car and walked quickly over to the car door. He got out and gave her a quick embrace.

"Hullo, honey." He kissed her. "Did you miss me?"

"Eddy, I…want to go home."

Romyn came to the door and walked over to the car.

"How are the kids doing?" Ed asked.

Romyn gave him a curiously intense look. "The kids are fine. They are in their room with Beth Ann, reading books and having their quiet time before supper."

"Thank you, Romyn, for being there for us. Really appreciate it."

"Don't mention it. Happy to. How is Bill doing?"

"Well, this is a tough time for him. It's hitting him hard. I think he always thought Donna would have a miraculous recovery and come home."

"Yes, hope. Waiting and hope—those two sentinels of our lost days. It's amazing he's been able to go on, with all that's on his plate. And lots of regrets, too, I'm sure," she replied slowly.

"If you have time, would you be willing to spend an hour with me figuring out the service and the fellowship at the church for Donna? I told Bill that he could focus on the arrangements with the funeral home and that you and I would pow-wow on the rest of it."

"Why don't you let me get supper over with and the kids settled in with Earl and then I'll pop over." She glanced over at Jill, who was fidgeting in the passenger side of the car. "I think you should get Jill home." She looked at him meaningfully.

Ed glanced over at Jill and noticed how she appeared worked up. "Right you are. See you in a bit."

Jill was still upset when they got home. She was fretful and restless and finally gave in to Ed's suggestion that she take a nap before supper. She fell into a deep sleep, not even rousing when Ed suggested she come to the supper table.

Which is just as well, Ed thought. *Likely the emotions of being around young kids; they can tire one out pretty good.*

Romyn was tired, too, when she arrived at the parsonage. "No Bill?" she asked.

"No, he decided to drive to Minneapolis to see if he could find Kellie and tell her about Donna in person. Maybe get her to come home with him for a few days," Ed said.

"He'll get through this and then he'll bounce back to his old self. I see a lot of strength in our Bill—he's one of our rocks here in Peace Ridge. His trunk has been battered and some of his branches and limbs are torn off, but he'll stand strong. I know that." Romyn's smile was bleak.

175

"Pastor, we can talk about the funeral arrangements, but before we do that, I have something to show you." She reached into her purse and brought out a small parcel wrapped in tissue paper. She handed it to him without a word. Ed looked at her quizzically and then unwrapped it. A lovely silver Pandora charm bracelet. Ed sat down heavily on the kitchen chair. The charm bracelet he'd made for Emily over the years. Given to Jill a few weeks ago, hoping to cheer her up.

"I suppose Jill brought this with her to your place, didn't she, Romyn?" His eyes were troubled.

"Yes, she did. And when we got to the house, she took Sophie aside and gave it to her."

Ed looked at her helplessly, a shocked expression on his face.

"Ed, I am totally convinced that Jill thinks that Sophie is Emily. She wanted to bring Sophie home with her. I had a hard time convincing her that she lives with us in our home. She even got a bit angry with me and—believe it or not — was about to argue with me in front of the kids before I had Beth Ann take them to their room. Sophie was confused and upset. I sat with Jill and told her, as gently as I could, that Sophie was our little girl, that she lives with Earl and me, not with you and her. I am not sure I got through to her. She went out and sat on the bench on the front porch for the last hour until you got there." Romyn's eyes filled with tears. "I am sorry, Pastor. I am really sorry."

Ed didn't say anything for a while. He got up from the table and took the plate of sandwiches to the counter top and set it down. He stood with his back to Romyn for a minute and then turned to her, his face wet with tears.

Wiping his eyes with his arm, he said dismally, "You've just confirmed what I've been afraid to face. Jill is not living in the "here and now," she's still in the "there and then." She's not moved beyond the accident. It doesn't matter when I tell her what happened and why we are here, it never sinks in. She's just not processing it."

"I'm sorry, Ed," Romyn said. "I thought when she got to Peace Ridge and settled in with you, that she'd find her way…"

"So did I. In my hubris, I thought that's all it would take."
Ed turned toward the stove and filled the tea kettle. Under his
breath, he said, "'The LORD is my strength and my song, and
he has become my salvation.'" He turned wearily to Romyn
and leaned against the sink as if its strength could penetrate his
spine and hold him up. "Whatever shall I do now?"

"'For the spirit God gave us does not make us timid, but
gives us power, love, and self- discipline.'" Romyn quoted St.
Paul's words to Timothy. "I think this is the time for strength."
She spoke slowly. "It feels to me that Jill needs to face death's
finality by visiting Emily's grave. And she has to come face-to-
face with Robby to see his blinded face and confront that, too."

Ed sat slowly down at the table. "The thought crossed
my mind, but I worried that it would shock her back into her
depressive state and I would lose her for good." The words
were drawn out slowly and sadly.

The teakettle was singing and Romyn got up and filled two
mugs with hot water and teabags. Ed held his head in his hands
and seemed to have no strength in him.

"Drink this," she said.

He looked up at her gratefully and warmed his hands around
the mug, hands cold even on this warm summer evening.

"I'm sorry, Ed, "Romyn said compassionately. "This has
been a tough couple of days for you. Overloaded: Veronica
yesterday, Donna early this morning, Bill's grief today. Now
this. I am thoughtless."

"No, you're just saying what I've been thinking in the dark
nights when I cannot sleep and can't reach for the woman I love."

Jill walked into the kitchen at that moment, silent as a
wraith. She looked at Romyn and her expression shifted from
blankness to a brief glimpse of stony anger. She sat down at
the table with them and Ed got up to get a mug of tea for her.

"Hello, Jill," Romyn offered with a smile. No response.

"Well, Pastor, we'd better finalize these funeral plans. We
can talk later," she added meaningfully. "I have reached out
to the Ladies Aid and they will put on the meal. Lydia Sellers

will coordinate it. She wants to know how many are planning to attend."

"I have no idea and I don't think Bill has either. Probably all of Peace Ridge Village!" A smile briefly flitted across Ed's face. "At least as many as for Eva's funeral – 150 or so."

"Do you think Bill would want the choir to sing?"

"I think he will be happy if we ask them. We can review the suggested song list with him and catch up with him tomorrow."

"I will write up the obituary and funeral notice and drop it by his house later tonight. He can fill in the details and I can run it over to the newspaper tomorrow morning, if he's okay with it."

"And I'll see if Shiloh and Brian will pick flower bouquets to decorate the church."

"Do you think...?" Ed paused. His mind went to two other kids.

"No, not a good idea." *Clay and Sophie here at the parsonage would upset Jill,* Romyn thought.

"I plan to call him in the morning. We'll get more details locked down then. I'll call the cemetery board secretary, too, and get those arrangements made."

Romyn stood up and smiled at both of them. "Well, I'll be off then. We can talk again in the morning, Ed and Jill. Long day for us all." She turned to Ed. "Earl and I will be in constant prayer." Her glance was meaningful.

Her drive home was troubled. Jill's troubled and angry face filled her mind. *Maybe it's a good thing in one way: she's showing emotion, at least. We'll get a prayer group together and have a day of prayer and fasting for them when he – if he – decides to take Jill to Emily's grave.* That thought led her to Bill and his loss. She envisioned that sad face, his round cheeks now narrowed to crevassed angles, his troubled eyes. The fact that he never smiled any more. *I must call him when I get home.* Incongruously, a song ran through her mind as she turned around the corner to her house. *"He stopped loving her today..."*

28

New York! Jennie looked out the window at the expansive cityscape that spread out below her, fully sixty miles or more away from LaGuardia Airport, and felt her excitement rising. *Start spreading the news...* She had planned this trip to allow for enough time to explore the city before she tramped around the Fancy Food Show. This was going to be a long, exhausting few days, but it had been over a decade since she'd been in Manhattan and she was going to make the most of it. She had picked up a cheap guide at the airport and quickly realized how expensive this trip would be. *Well, I won't eat in fancy restaurants. Can probably nibble at the show all day long.* She'd take the express bus into Grand Central Station – just saying the words gave her a feeling of expectation— only $16.00. The Roosevelt Hotel was just around the corner and reasonable. She wanted to buy some souvenirs for Romyn, Eliza, Shiloh, and Paul. The last one would be challenging. Paul resolutely had zero interest in anything big city. She could get him a Big Apple t-shirt at the airport, but it would be fun to find something nice for the girls.

She opened the brochure she'd gotten from the Specialty Food Association and reviewed the agenda of events for the week. Lectures, guided tours, appearances by celebrity chefs and national media personages. The international pavilion for importers. The wine displays which took up nearly an entire floor. Fun! Fun! Fun! She'd poured over the show guide and marked the herbs and spices vendors that she wanted to visit, and looked to see if there were chefs from England participating in the show. She really wanted to check into Stonewall Kitchens from the state of Maine who were great marketers of jams and jellies. She'd admired their labels and presentation for years. So much inspiration! *Can't wait,* she thought.

Some of her excitement had worn off by the time she'd gotten onto the New York Express bus on her way to Grand Central Station. The luggage carousels had been thronged with travelers with the distinctive impatience of New Yorkers, and she found she didn't have the ease of navigation that she had enjoyed when she was younger and traveled lighter. Her carry-on was small and so was her suitcase, but being jostled and pushed in the crowds of people was an unfamiliar experience. *I am so used to the politeness and relative personal space of Minnesota.* She found it disconcerting, wanting to set herself apart without someone pushing next to her, but found that impossible. Finally, she made it onto the bus and sank gratefully into the plush seats in the front row just behind the driver.

"First time to New York, Miss?" he asked.

"No, I was here a long time ago." She gave a friendly Minnesota smile.

"By yourself?" he asked.

"Yes, just for a few days."

"Well, if you need a private guide to the city," he turned and handed her his card. "I do that as an extra service to my customers. Can show you around Manhattan and all the highlights."

"No, I don't think I'll need a guide. I know the Village, Midtown, the Upper East Side – hope to visit the Metropolitan. And anyway, this is a brief business trip. I'll be busy and then back out in a few days."

"Well, think of me if you change your mind," he said, his accent pure Queens.

She could walk to her hotel, the Roosevelt, through the corridors of Grand Central Station. After she got off the bus she walked onto the main concourse and just stood there drinking in the familiar iconic sight. Shafts of light illuminated the expanse which she knew was trampled by hundreds of thousands each day. She walked over to the four-sided clock to orient herself to mid-Manhattan. She knew the Roosevelt Hotel was to the east but she was turned around for a moment. She looked up to the cerulean blue ceiling and looked carefully at the Zodiac outlined in pure gold. "Thank you, Jackie Kennedy," she whispered. The widowed former First Lady had thrown her significant influence behind the restoration of the 1913 Beaux Arts building. *This is why I love New York!* Jennie said to herself. *So much history. Ancient and contemporary. And I feel sorry for Jackie Kennedy. She had a hard life.* But that thought was fleeting. She was determined to get herself settled into the Roosevelt and plan her stay.

She settled into her room which was small but perfect for her and left a message for Paul. She knew he would still be in the barn. Call him later. Perfect time for a little walk on Madison Avenue. She didn't want to go too far; tomorrow would be exhausting, she knew that. She'd save St. Bart's and St. Patrick's for an early morning before the show — they were fairly close. She knew she could get lost in a bookstore if she found one, so she vowed to simply walk a little bit and drink in the spirit of the city. She slipped her hotel card into her money belt and replaced her flats with sturdy walking shoes. Walking out the Madison Avenue door of the Roosevelt, her cell phone pinged. She looked at the number doubtfully.

"Hello, Jennie," a friendly male voice greeted her. "Chris here. Chris Herbain from the Specialty Foods Association. How are you? Arrived in New York okay?"

It took Jennie a moment to recollect the voice and process the words. His words piled out in a nasally New York accent, and he pronounced his last name "herbough," which took some getting used to. They had spoken briefly a few weeks ago when Jennie called the association to find out how many herbs vendors were booked for the show. He had been helpful and pleasant and drew her out about her business and plans, and they had scheduled a follow-up Skype call. He had a pleasant, friendly appearance, but, like all salesmen, was confident and assertive. He had bright curious eyes, deep set with heavy brows, and a strong forehead with lavish curly hair that was beginning to recede at the temples. *Good customer service*, she had thought at the time, *something to consider when we get underway.* But this call to her in New York was a little surprising.

"Yes, I'm here. At the Roosevelt next to Grand Central Station. Arrived about two hours ago. Just ready to go for a little walk."

"Be sure to save your energy for the show. We have over 2,500 booths. You won't want to look at all of them, but prepare to be overwhelmed. Your first Fancy Food show!"

"Yes, I know. I have been looking at the floor plan and trying to outline my action plan for tomorrow."

"Say, I have an idea. I have a brief business meeting near Grand Central Station. If you would like, we could meet at the Oyster Bar at five-thirty, six o'clock and I could go over the guide with you and make some recommendations as to what would be the best booths to visit. The French Farm, for one. You'd love their packaging. I can show you what to focus on in the Incubator Village and that's near the Italian Pavilion, which is always a must-see. But there are at least three dozen herbs and spices booths you can't miss."

Jennie was unsure. This felt quite forward for some reason. She replied hesitantly, "You are really too kind. This must be a very busy weekend for you. Do you have the time?"

"I do, and since you're a potential exhibitor next year, I always make it a point to make the time, Jennie." His voice was confident and unhurried.

"Well, if you're sure. I know the Oyster Bar. I'm wearing –" here she looked down at her slacks and t-shirt "–I'll be wearing a fawn-colored blazer and I'll sit at the bar as near to the entrance as possible.

"Yes, I just look for the beautiful Minnesota blonde Viking. Sounds good. Five-thirty. See you then."

Jennie turned around slowly and pushed the elevator for her room. Better change. What she was wearing was okay for a walk around town, but not for a semi-official meeting. Better throw on a nice blouse, too. *Better call Paul one more time, too,* she thought. *Let him know about the meeting. But that's not necessary,* she reflected. *He won't care. It's just pre-planning. I'll tell him about it later tonight.*

Lake Pepin was glorious on this bright summer day. Shimmery grey-blue water mirrored the clear blue sky and the impressive sandstone and limestone cliffs, undergirded with lush green oak and pine trees, framed the breathtaking expanse. Lake Pepin was dotted with sailing and motor craft and peregrine falcons soared high over the bluffs in a graceful arc. Highway 61 had taken them straight into Lake City and it was a good place to stop and take an energy break. Michael and Pam were all for checking out all the antique shops, but knew that Brian and Snow would be totally bored.

"I've booked the *Pearl of the Lake* paddleboat tour, Brian," Michael said. "It takes off at noon and we can spend a half hour here or so before we go down to the dock and board. That okay?"

Brian nodded slowly, looking longingly at Hok-Si-La Park across the way.

"Let's go over there first and stretch our legs," Michael said. He gave a questioning glance at Pam and she nodded briefly.

The three of them with an over-active small white dog walked into the park. Michael and Pam in quiet rapport watched Snow give Brian the run-around.

"That'll drain some of that energy," Pam observed.

Michael glanced sideways at her. She had on a casual sky-blue fitted cotton shirt over khaki pedal-pushers. She had taken an effort with her get-up for the small opal earrings reflected the blue of her shirt and her eyes.

She smiled at him and said, "I remember raising small children. Both of my kids had energy in excess. It was all I could do to keep up with them." She smiled fondly in remembrance. "Even Bradley. He never wanted to be left behind and so he went crazy when he was around other kids."

"Was that hard?" Michael said kindly. "Raising Bradley on your own?"

"I didn't have a choice," she spoke slowly. "My reward is so much the greater for having the time to be with him more. He's a special kid growing into a very special man. He will grow up to bless others, as he has blessed me just by.... living, by being in my life." She turned to Michael with a luminous smile on her face. "I suppose it's hard for others to understand, how having a handicapped child is more a blessing than a trial."

Michael shook his head slowly.

"The fact is, I have learned much more from Bradley than he ever learned from me. Patience. Uncomplicated love. Willingness to learn and to really put one's heart into figuring it out." She paused and looked down. "Just simple good humor. I confess that I often use Bradley and examples from his life's struggles and triumphs with my team at the Westin. To inspire them." She smiled softly. "They seem to appreciate it. Anyway," she said, as she sat down on the bench. "He's God's gift. I wouldn't have it any other way."

"Tell me about Tory," Michael urged. "What's she like?"

"Oh my! She's going to set the world afire. Already has. She's a store manager at the Walmart in St. Cloud and has already turned down offers to move to Corporate Headquarters in Arkansas. She is in the middle of getting her MBA and is so busy, I hardly ever see her."

"Got her work ethic from her mom, I see," Michael offered.

"Well, I don't know about that. She's much smarter than I will ever be. Going places. I hate the thought of her moving to Bentonville, but if she has to do it for her career, I'm sure she'll go. I'll just have to accept it." She looked down and brushed away a pine needle and an ant that had taken a wrong turn onto her slacks.

They fell silent, sitting side by side on the bench, watching Brian chase Snow around, the dog's happy bark adding to the twitters of the birds and the sounds of laughter from passersby. The park was surprisingly busy on this morning and the sidewalks were thronged with joggers, sauntering couples, and families pushing baby strollers. Michael shifted in his seat and placed his arm casually along the back of the bench.

"He's a sweet boy, isn't he?" Pam nodded her head towards Brian. She shifted comfortably on the bench but didn't pull away.

"I'm grateful that I have him with me – for as long as his mother is in England, anyway. Now that I've moved back to Peace Ridge, I can be with him more. Delaney always wants to control him. And me. I got Brian when she had something she had to do." The words came out more bitter than he intended, and he smiled ruefully at Pam.

"How long will she be in London?"

"We don't know. She told Brian a couple of weeks. Longer, I think. She really wants to move there. She's made no secret about her dislike of Peace Ridge and how she wants to get out of the 'hick town.' Now that her dad has died and the business sold, I guess she thinks there's nothing to hold her in our little town and she can go anywhere, be anyone she wants to be."

"Big cities can be fun. I've never been to London—I am sure it's exciting. But how can she think about moving to London and taking Brian away from his father? That can't be done! I don't think the State of Minnesota or Morrison County will allow it. Aren't there rules?"

"Never underestimate Delaney. I wouldn't put it past her to just leave him here with me and be content with seeing him once a year or so."

Pam's eyes darkened a bit but she didn't say anything. She didn't know the woman, but already she didn't like her.

"He misses her, I think," she said finally. "He's quiet, isn't he?"

"He's unusually thoughtful. Deep thoughts," Michael replied. "He cries sometimes, but he doesn't want me to see. And he pours all his emotions into his little poetry book." He smiled proudly. "He's quite good, actually. Surprising. Don't know where he comes up with some of his words."

"He's a reader, then?"

"Always has his nose in a book."

"I'd love to read his poetry sometimes. I'm not a judge of good poetry, but I like it... if it's not too complicated and intellectual, that is."

"He might share, but you'd have to wait until he offers it; he rarely lets me see them. Has given a couple to our neighbor in Peace Ridge, Tom. His friend, Shiloh's dad. Tom has sketched illustrations for a couple of his nature poems and is thinking about a book."

"Great idea."

"Don't be surprised if he slips off by himself today and starts writing in his notebook." Michael smiled proudly and shook his head." Don't know where he gets it from. Opposite of me. I have no romance or melody in me at all."

Pam laughed. "Oh, you're not just the techy-computer geek that you make yourself out to be! I think I can see beneath *that* surface."

"Well, when I make the effort." He smiled. "And when there's someone worth the effort," he added nearly under his breath. The moment lengthened, his words hanging in the air. *Well, that's torn it,* Michael thought. *Too fast.* Michael stood up and searched for Brian and Snow.

Pam snuck a covert glance at him, the craggy weathered face with the overlong thick blonde hair, streaked with grey. *Brian must look like Delaney,* she thought incongruously. *He's not like Michael at all. Except for their quiet kindness. They both have that.*

"What time are we to be at the dock?"

Pam's practical questioned drained the emotion of the moment and Michael suddenly shouted at the boy and dog. "Brian! Brian! Time to go!"

The paddleboat ride was sublime. As predicted, Brian had opened his notebook and was taking notes on everything the captain said about Lake Pepin: how it got its name, "Lake of Tears," from Father Hennepin in 1680 when he was in custody of the Sioux Indian tribe who were grieving the loss of their chief's son. How Laura Ingalls Wilder wrote her *House in the Big Woods* book about the family's home in Pepin, Wisconsin. How water skiing was invented on Lake Pepin in 1922. There was little wind and the only sound was the water rushing slowly in the waterwheel, the subdued conversations of the passengers, and the intermittent commentary from the captain. Gulls swirled overhead following the wake of the boat and occasionally they saw the peregrine falcons swooping near the shore and then settling in the trees along the shoreline. Their boat made a slow, lazy way downriver and the pace of their travel created a sense of peaceful lassitude.

Pam felt all tension drain from her body. *Didn't realize how tense I was,* she thought. *Legacy of these last few weeks at work. This is nice. I needed this.*

Michael walked over to the snack bar and came back with a couple of Cokes.

"Are you a big fan of Laura Ingalls Wilder?" he asked Pam.

"Well, I loved her books as a child and I read them to Tory, too. She liked them, but not with the same passion I had. I always thought that if I had to make my way as a pioneer, I could really do it. Could do without electricity, could grow my own vegetables, chop my own firewood. As long as one has a family so everyone could work together..." Pam was pensive.

"I think the Ingalls family had to move around a lot to be able to support the family. There are a lot of states that claim her as their own – Minnesota, of course, Wisconsin, South Dakota, Kansas, Missouri…"

Pam nodded her head. "But I think her heart was in Minnesota. That's what I want to think, anyway. When I was in middle school we had an inspired English teacher and she took our class on a day trip to Walnut Grove, Minnesota so we could see her home and museum. I found it fascinating and it created a strong interest in Minnesota history for me. It's one of my hobbies—learning about Minnesota."

"The Sioux and Chippewa, I suppose?" Michael asked.

"Less about the natives and more about the settlers who traveled long distance and began to farm and make their own way. I've always thought it was interesting that the land and the prairies of Minnesota are so like that of Sweden and Norway. I figure the immigrants from those countries got on the train and traveled until they saw what looked like their home country and then told the train conductor, 'Just let us off here.' Malmo, Sweden. Malmo, Minnesota. Upsala, Minnesota. Uppsala, Sweden. The land just looked like home to them."

Michael looked at her for a moment and then pulled out his cell phone. He found the YouTube video and pushed play and handed it over to her. *A Prairie Wedding,* by Mark Knopfler.

Her eyes were bright with tears when she handed it back to him. "It had to be hard on those young people," she said softly. "We really don't have any idea of how good we have it, do we?"

They were quiet for a few moments.

"He sometimes comes to Minneapolis," Michael said. "Mark Knopfler. Would you like to go see him?"

Pam turned to him with a look of wonder on her face. "Finally, someone who loves Mark Knopfler as much as I do." She leaned over and lightly touched his cheek. "Yes, and yes!"

Brian stood at the rail of the paddleboat and intently watched the scenery. He watched the gulls as they swooped over the water, seeking churned up fish, and he and Snow seemed perfectly content to rock with the gentle waves. Michael had a moment of panic when he called to verify that Snow would be able to go on the boat with him – Brian wouldn't go on the boat without his buddy – but *Pearl of the Lake* was friendly and understanding. Brian held his friend's leash carefully as Snow slumped down on the deck, his legs carefully arranged to manage the slow undulation of the boat. Pam and Michael watched Brian in peaceful rapport.

"If we ever do this again, Pam, we should do the Lake Pepin Wine Tour. We couldn't bring Brian, but it might be fun. There are several wineries along this route – not on the boat, of course – but we could drive it." He looked at her with a quizzical smile.

"Might be fun," she said. "Would be beautiful in October with the fall leaves turning color."

"Yeah." *Not the answer I wanted. I was thinking this summer. Oh well, slowly, Michael, slowly.*

They were all languorous, getting their stuff together on the boat and walking over to the car to drive back to Minneapolis. Something about being on the water and in the sunshine took all the intensity out of them. Michael drove through the Dairy Queen drive-through on Highway 61 on the way home and bought them all vanilla cones, including Snow, who delightedly inhaled the icy treat and made them all laugh. The car ride to Bloomington seemed to go fast, and soon Michael and Brian were saying goodbye to Pam and heading back to Peace Ridge.

Well, today was a nice day, she thought as she let herself into her quiet home. *He's a nice man and Brian is a dear little boy. I wonder if he'll ever let me get close to him.* She set her purse down on the kitchen counter and went to the refrigerator to get a cold drink. She turned back to the adjoining dining room and sat down at the empty table, trying to focus her thoughts on the Sunday edition of the *Star Tribune*. And *now this. My real life. The empty house. I wish Bradley was here—he would cheer me up.*

But he wasn't coming home from Tory's until tomorrow. Her cell phone pinged and she glanced at the text message. It was from Bill Nelson. "Pam, can you call me, pls?" She looked up his number and called but it went into voice mail. She tried again a few minutes later, but same thing. "Bill, I'm home. Tried calling. Pls. text me."

Pam slumped into the sofa in the family room, her thoughts churning. Despite the peaceful day with Michael and Brian, it took only one text and all her old worries and fears about the Westin accident with Bill's wife, Donna, swirled to the surface. She didn't feel culpable; it was clearly an accident, but her compassion for Bill and his obvious loss and despair was something with which she had strongly identified. *Bill,* she thought pensively. *Bill. What is wrong?* She stretched out on the couch and looked at her cell phone, willing it to ring. The silence lengthened. The afternoon sun had sunk below the trees in the backyard and the room was darkening. Pam got up and switched on all the table lamps in the house, and switched on the television. *Need more light in here. After a nice day, now this worry and emptiness.*

She went to the kitchen catch-all drawer and found some matches to light the fat vanilla-scented candle on the coffee table. Its comforting scent began to fill the room.

At just that moment her cell phone rang. She had left it on the table and quickly walked over to it and picked it up.

"Pam. Hello. It's Bill." His voice was strained and so tight that Pam could barely recognize it as his.

"Hello, Bill," she said with sincere warmth. "Glad you called."

"Pam. Donna has just died." His own voice sounded dead. "I am sorry to blurt it out like that, but I don't know how else to say it. She died this morning, well, last night really, in her sleep in the place in Sartell."

"Oh, Bill!" Pam sat suddenly down in her dining room chair. "I am so sorry, Bill. I am so sorry. I can hardly believe it. This is such a shock in a way."

"Yes, it is. I guess I knew in my mind that she was never going to recover, but the fact that she's gone is really hard to take in."

"Oh, Bill. I wish I was there to help you out."

It was as if he hadn't heard. "Pastor Ed and I went to Sartell this morning. We did all the necessary things there, came back to Peace Ridge, and started to make the funeral arrangements. I drove down today to Robbinsdale to see if I could tell Kellie in person about her mom, but her roommates tell me she's not living there anymore and she won't answer my texts. So that's that." He sounded defeated.

"Where are you now?"

"I'm in the Panera in Edina near the Westin where you and I had soup a few months ago. I didn't know where to go when I couldn't find Kellie and I needed something to eat, so I came here. And I called you. I've been sitting here for over two hours, trying to get in touch with Kellie with no luck."

"Stay there, Bill. I'll be there in fifteen minutes." Pam's voice was loving but assertive. "And Bill, we'll all be there for you in this."

"I know, Pam," he said unsteadily.

191

29

"Thanks for coming, Ed." Archie waved his arm over to a nearby booth.

"It's not often I get treated to a breakfast out, and I was headed over to see Veronica today too, so it's a good start to the day."

"We can go together. I've spent most of yesterday with her, but she's not very willing to talk. Still weak and probably confused. The doctors tell me those drugs have a lot of side effects and she's still a little groggy and uncertain."

"I have been praying without ceasing for her, Archie," Ed said. "Well, a bit of a clarification: praying without ceasing, but you've probably heard about Donna and so my prayers for Veronica, for Bill…and others… are constant these days. Thank God for Jesus!"

"Yes, Romyn told me about Donna. Sad in a very deep way for Bill. End of a marriage. Lack of closure. Difficult navigation with Kellie. He has his hands full."

"Yes, he does. Romyn and I have been trying to put the funeral together and take some of that burden off of him. He really didn't expect it, as much as we all saw it would end this way.

"Death and denial. I have become way too familiar with that these last couple of days," Archie said, rubbing his forehead absent-mindedly in a repetitive gesture. "I – I guess I am nearly as overwhelmed as Bill. Veronica…" Here he paused and quickly drank a large gulp of orange juice. "Veronica is the most important person in the world to me." He paused and sat silently in the booth, staring down at the placemat. "I knew she was really depressed last winter when she tried to kill herself at your doorstep, but I thought she had really recovered." He shook his head. "I find it incomprehensible in a way. To feel so despairing that death is a better alternative." He looked beseechingly at Ed. "Pastor, tell me, what do I say? What do I do?"

"Oh, Archie! If only I had the right answer to all those questions. Even a Pastor can be overwhelmed amidst the sadness. I do know there's comfort in the Psalms and the Word. The gospel of John 14 is my consolation in the middle of the night. 'Do not let your hearts be troubled...' The practical way forward is to lean on Him and trust that He knows about Veronica and cares for her, loves her. Especially now, in her brokenness. We need to be there for her and be a steady presence. It will take time."

"I thought she was getting better," Archie said sadly. "She seemed happy here in Peace Ridge and loved the work with Earl and Romyn. But then the preoccupation with death, the obituaries, her slow sadness when I talked to her. I felt in my heart that she was slipping away. That's why I asked you to keep an eye on her, Ed. And we nearly lost her!" The last said with a sobbing intake of breath.

Ed reached over and patted Archie's arm and then looked up with a brief smile as the waitress laid down a plate of pancakes, bacon, scrambled eggs, and toast in front of them both.

"Enjoy!" she said brightly as she refilled their coffee cups.

"But, in God's grace, we didn't lose her. We got to her in time, Archie. Cling to that." He reached over and again briefly touched his hand. "That was God's divine providence, too, Archie. God planned that." He looked intently at Archie. "Veronica may have thought she was ending something, but God has other plans. She was beginning something. I really feel that. She was in the abandoned desert cistern with no hope, but now she's in her new Egypt and it will become a new start, a new beginning for her. I think we should focus on that, not on the despair that got her to that place."

"I hope so. I really hope so." Archie poured maple syrup over his pancakes and grabbed a stick of crisp bacon and chewed on it thoughtfully.

"Did she ever go to counseling?" Ed asked.

"I don't know. I don't think so. She never mentioned it. She's private, even with me, her only living relative. What brings people so low?" he asked. "I really want to know."

"It's a vicious mental circle. One goes around and around in one's head and thinks that there's only one inevitable way forward and that no other possibilities can be even thought of. It's a curious mental trick that Satan plays on us."

Archie looked up thoughtfully.

"Satan, our adversary, roams the world seeking whom he can destroy. We can't shy away from discussions about this enemy because he is still at work in the world even though he's been defeated at the cross. PTL!" Ed briefly patted his heart. "Veronica is swirling within that vicious circle. Her losses, her inability to move beyond them, the emptiness in her life when she walks into that beautiful home of hers with no one to share it, the awful feeling that somehow she deserved what she's got..."

"My sweet girl..." Archie's eyes were bright with tears.

"Yes, Veronica has totally dismissed what *she* did for the people of Peace Ridge Village. If she hadn't intervened when she did, so many would have lost their land to fraud. That took bravery. That took courage. She needs to focus on that instead of the losses in her past." His mind flashed on the scene of Veronica on the floor of his parsonage, desperate to kill herself, desperate in her despair.

"I think she feels worthless. Ever since she was a little girl, all she ever wanted to be was a wife and mother. And she failed at that. No fault of her own." He looked at Ed. "Would you talk to her, Ed? Please? Can you see if you can give her some… insights, hope, to move forward?

"Of course, I will, Archie. Would do even if you hadn't asked me. She's precious to all of us here in Peace Ridge. I think it begins with forgiveness…for herself and for others. But I will share with Veronica. Right now, she needs just simple love from all of us."

"I think Steve feels the same way. He's told me he wants to take her on a little trip, just to get away when she gets well."

"That will be good. Steve is a good man. I think he can identify with her pain – don't know what his story is – but I trust him. He's been faithful and a good egg with Bill. That counts for a lot in my book."

"Me, too, Ed. Me, too."

The cultured, deep baritone voice on the phone was unfamiliar. "Hello, Pastor Ed, I am Father Daniel from St. George Greek Orthodox Church in St. Paul. Our mutual friend, Titos Papadopoulos, suggested I give you a call."

"Yes, Father. Happy to meet you on the phone. Titos mentioned you and suggested you might call."

"Titos and Maria are planning the grand opening celebration of the Petros Greek Diner next weekend and I confirmed that I would be happy to give a blessing. Along with you. Titos wanted to make sure of that."

"Yes, I had thought to invite Father Brandon at the Catholic Church, too, but he's on a brief mission trip to Haiti and won't be here. But I am so glad you are coming up. Have you ever been to Peace Ridge before?"

"No, this will be my time going 'up north' as you all call it. I stick pretty close to St. Paul and my parishioners. But I'm looking forward to it."

"And I am looking forward to meeting you. I suppose Titos told you that you could stay with us as our guest in the parsonage. We have a nice guest bedroom and it wouldn't be any trouble at all."

"I plan to come up on Friday evening. Would it be okay to stay with you then? I expect to head back to St. Paul after the dedication because I have services all day Sunday. As do you, probably."

"That would be fine. And plan to come in time for dinner. My wife, Jill, and I will have a meal ready. It will be fun to get to know you. I will see if Titos and Maria want to come, too, though – knowing Titos – he'll be totally involved in all the last-minute preparations for opening day."

"Yes, Titos." Father Daniel said, "He never leaves anything to chance. He'll be up all night going over his check-list. Nothing casual about him."

"Friday night then? About what time do you think you'll be here?"

When the conversation ended, Ed hung up the phone with a frisson of happiness. A fellow traveler.

Jennie was happy to see that the Grand Central Oyster Bar was just a lazy ten-minute walk from her hotel room through the interlinking corridors. Oysters were not her favorite — too much of a Midwesterner for that! But just being in New York and being among New Yorkers was exciting. She had not expected the crowds, thinking she'd slip easily onto a bar stool, but the area was thronged with the mid-town regulars. She stood behind a couple of businessmen eavesdropping on their conversation. One of her favorite things to do: the anonymous listener.

The bartender caught her eye. "For you, miss?" he said and then in a New York minute handed her a glass of white wine. She tried to be inconspicuous and nonchalant but she felt like a Midwestern rube. In the old days, she felt she could fit in anywhere. *I'm not on my game anymore*, she mulled. *And not here long enough to feel at home.*

Her text pinged. It was from Paul: "Heading out after chores to help Titos and Jeremy install Tiff's painting. Back after ten. XX." Jennie nodded slowly. She'd remembered the request, Jeremy asking if Paul could lend a hand with the over-sized oil painting that would be the centerpiece of the Petros Greek Diner. She didn't know Jeremy and Tiff very well, but had no idea that Tiff was an artist – both she and Jeremy were so diffident about it.

Just at that moment a voice said at her shoulder. "Knew I'd easily find you. You'd stand out anywhere."

Jennie turned to greet Chris. "Oh, hi. Just a text from home," she said confusedly. She slipped her phone into her purse. "Hello there."

"Hello, Jennie." He was taller than Jennie expected and standing by his side she felt school-girlish and uncertain. There was a sense of magnetism about him, likely driven by his presence and self-confidence as he quietly signaled the bartender and had a drink in his hand in five minutes. Jennie felt impressed despite herself. Not normally at a loss for words, she took a sip of her wine and stared at the backs of the people crowding around the bar.

"Let's do this. I'll find a table. Stay here," he dictated, as he moved to the hostess table and with a deft gesture came back to guide her to a small table in a nearby alcove.

"Friend of yours? How did you manage that in this crowd?" Jennie tried to keep her voice neutral but she was impressed.

"I come here a lot. They know me," he said. He took her elbow possessively and guided her to the small table. A waiter immediately brought by a basket of sourdough rolls and unsalted butter.

"Oh, I don't want to eat anything," Jennie protested.

"Not to worry. That's just their hospitality. We'll just have a couple of drinks, Jennie." He glanced at his watch. "I have to be back at the Javits Center later," he turned to her, "but I wanted to connect with you and make sure you have all you need to make the show worthwhile." His face lit up with his smile and his eyes lingered on hers for a long, uncomfortable moment.

"I know you went out of your way—" Jennie began.

"I like to make sure that all the exhibitors and potential ones feel that we care about them personally. Want them to have a good and productive show. And I want to be sure that we're ready to help you when you launch next year. Tell me about your plans."

Jennie spoke slowly. "It started with the pastor at our small-town church wanting to find a way to help the community. 'The hungry and the hurting,' as he calls it. We have fantastic land in central Minnesota and growing organic herbs and offering a recipe blend that reflects the herbs' traditional virtues — like love, faithfulness, courage, etc. – could marry food with a mission. We – my husband and I – have set aside a few acres and we are getting organic certification for them. Expect it to come through in a few months, and then we'll be planting and harvesting next spring and summer. It's a non-profit. We just hope we don't go too heavily in the red." She stopped abashed, feeling as if she'd been talking for hours. Chris had been nodding along with her which had encouraged her long explanation.

"Great story, Jennie. Great project. I hope you will be prepared for the ton of orders you'll get after you exhibit at the Fancy Food Show. People can be surprising. You'll be writing orders all day. It's a great idea—the buyers today want a back story, they want niche brands, they want organic, they want meaning." He paused. "It seems as if you have it all," he offered in a warm, personal tone.

"I talked to a potential investor not too long ago and he thought the backstory would be compelling," Jennie said, knowing that Dane Johnson's blather and promises were as empty as a ten-dollar suit picked up a flea market.

Chris glanced at her with an intimate look that made her uncomfortable. "What's the name of your product line?" he asked.

"Peace in the Valley Herbs," Jennie replied, with less confidence than she expected to feel.

"Peace in the Valley Herbs," Chris repeated slowly, looking up at the ceiling.

"Our church is Valley Community and we live in Peace Ridge...we thought it was a...neat combination," she said uncertainly.

"That's part of the story. For sure," he replied. "You may be missing an opportunity to personalize it more. If you want some free marketing advice," he said, touching her hand lightly, "you need to be the face of the product line. You are marketable," he said confidently. "People will love to know the real person, the 'farmer' if you will, behind the products."

Jennie sat silently, remembering the "Jennie brand" discussion that Dane Johnson had talked about last year. Then it was about her pies, now Chris Herbain was talking about their herbs business. *Flattering in a way, but I have to be careful,* she thought. *This is not just my business. It's for the church and it's for Pastor Ed. And Paul, too. It's not just me.*

"Oh, I'm not sure about that," she said with a slight smile. "The products will speak for themselves."

"Oh, no they won't!" he declared, his intimate smile cushioning the disagreeable words. "You need to differentiate. Otherwise you'll be just like all the others. Herbs are a commodity for most people," he said. Seeing her expression, he said, "Oh, Jennie! That was too harsh! What I meant to say is, we need to find a way to stand out. Give people talk value."

Jennie thought, *Moving fast. 'We', he said.*

"What I mean," he confided, "is that we can find ways to promote you and your products here. In ways that are not open to others. Simply because there's a hook. The trade – *Food & Wine, Bon Appetit, Saveur* – the people who write for them are always looking for an angle. You will need that to get any press.

And I can help you with that, knowing this business as well as I do." He smiled confidently and then caught the waiter's eye and ordered another white wine for her and a double scotch on the rocks for himself.

Jennie shifted uncomfortably in her seat. "I really appreciate your interest and your ideas…"

Chris glanced quickly at his watch and then brought out the show catalog. He had put sticky notes in several places in the guide and handed it carefully to her, letting his hand linger on hers for a long moment.

"Let's go through these. I've marked the ones which I think are the best ones for you to see. I've put my cell number on the top of the guide and you can text me if at any time you think you'd like a break or want to see some of the insider booths, the ones that the trade have marked as being exceptionally interesting. Can get some good ideas."

"I expect to hit the ground running tomorrow first thing." Jennie smiled.

"Ah you farmers' wives. Up early all the time, aren't you?" He was teasing, but there was something else. Undefinable. Skepticism or scorn? Jennie wasn't sure, but she was suddenly a bit wary.

"Most productive time of the day," she asserted, lifting her chin. *New Yorkers don't know everything about everything. There is life outside Manhattan.*

"What about you, Chris, "she asked. "What makes you tick? Besides your work, of course."

"Well, that takes up most of my time. But I work out, run in Central Park nearly every day, catch my Giants every once in a while. Hang out with friends."

"You are a native New Yorker?"

"Yes, born and raised in Brooklyn. Moved into Manhattan after college. Rutgers." He smiled dismissively. "Boring stuff. Would rather talk about you." He leaned toward her intimately and clicked his glass against hers before lifting it to his lips, "Here's to Jennie's success." Jennie raised her glass and took a sip as he drained his glass. "Hope you feel that I'm – that the Specialty Foods Association – will play a key role in your success. Which I am sure of. Really sure."

"We're going to try hard to make it work." She spoke stiffly and formally. "It's to benefit others." *What's going on here?*

He glanced at his watch then and said abruptly, "Well, I must be off. Late for the next meeting and it's across town." He signaled the waitress imperiously, making a gesture like signing a tab. "I must run." He pulled out her chair and then leaned into her and kissed her cheek, so close his expensive after shave permeated the space between them, creating a disconcerting sense of familiarity.

"Thanks for all your help," she said.

"That smile is all the thanks I need," he replied quickly. "Can you get back to the hotel okay? It's just across the entrance hall. Just be sure to take the corridor next to the flower shop. Too easy to get lost in the labyrinth."

"I'll be fine." She lingered for a moment in the Grand Central Oyster Bar after he had quickly walked away. *I wasn't born yesterday,* she thought. *He was coming on to me. I guess a wedding ring doesn't mean much to some people.*

She walked slowly past the unobtrusive whispering corner with its cluster of couples and paused at the newsstand and searched for a good magazine to read. She felt disconcerted and knew it was because of her drinks with Chris and his intense focus on her. *New York is really more fun with someone you care about,* she thought. *I thought it would be fun to be here alone, but it's really not the same without Paul.* She quickly purchased the *New York Times* and walked resolutely through the corridor to the Roosevelt Hotel. *I'll just grab a falafel-to-go at the café here and read in the room until Paul gets home and I can call him.*

※

Veronica was sitting up in the recliner in her room at the hospital when Ed and Archie walked in. She looked fragile and pale but managed an unsteady smile for both of them. Archie walked over and kissed her forehead and she accepted Ed's bouquet with a faint smile. "Thank you. For the flowers, but I guess I need to thank you for more than that, Pastor."

"You really gave us a scare. Good to see you up and about." Ed touched her shoulder gently. "Praying for you, Veronica. 'Cast your cares on the LORD and He will sustain you.'"

She looked around anxiously for extra chairs. "Do you feel up to going down to the family room?" Archie asked, noticing her fretfulness. "We could be more comfortable there perhaps."

They walked slowly down the hallway, one on either side. She was as tall as Ed but seemed insubstantial. Isamu Noguchi's thought came into Ed's mind *"It is weight that gives meaning to weightlessness."* Veronica's face was transparent, nearly luminous. Her cheeks showed faint new lines and the pain in her eyes poured out like a smoldering fire.

"Have you thought about when you can go home, Veronica?" Ed asked.

She turned in supplication to Archie. "I have been told I can go home tomorrow, but they don't think it's advisable to be by myself for a while."

Ed had a fleeting thought *—perhaps I should invite her to stay with us –* but rejected it immediately. The parsonage held bad memories and the combination of Jill and Veronica would be untenable.

"She's coming home with me for a week or so," Archie said.

"Do you want me to keep an eye on your place, Veronica?" Ed offered.

"I think it'll be okay for a week. I really want to get home. If I can get well…" She seemed to turn inward and a miasma of depression emanated around her.

Ed tried a distraction. "I hope you can be here for the opening of Petros Greek Diner next weekend. Lots of people. Lots of good food to eat. Father Daniel from the Greek Orthodox

Church will be here from St. Paul, there will be a bluegrass band, some of Jeremy's friends. I think it will be a fun time. You'll be with your friends, Earl and Romyn. The kids. Tom and Shiloh. You'd probably enjoy yourself."

"Sounds like it might be a good idea, right, Veronica?" Archie looked at her intently. It seemed as if she was reluctant to commit to anything, even in the very near future. "Let's plan to drive up on Friday night and I'll stay the weekend."

Ed reached into his pocket. "I was digging in my library the other day, Veronica, and I found that I had two copies of Tennyson's 'In Memoriam,' the long poem he composed over seventeen years for his best friend, Arthur Henry Hallam. It is one of my favorites and I thought you might enjoy parts of it." He opened the book to a section he had marked. "Some of it's slow going—the language of yesterday, and 'the Queen's English' besides. But some parts really nail this 'vale of tears' we walk through." He read softly, the pastor's cadence:

So runs my dream, but what am I?
An infant crying in the night:
An infant crying for the light:
And with no language but a cry.

And this:

Oh many worlds, so much to do,
So little done, such things to be,
How know I what had need of Thee,
For Thou were strong as Thou wert true.

Veronica nodded slowly. "I know I need to start coming to church, Pastor. This...event has made that clear to me. I can't make it on my own." She dropped her head and a single tear fell onto her blouse. She wiped it away distractedly.

"None of us can. We are all dependent on Him and need to fit ourselves within His plan. Our job is to discover that plan,

203

our own customized plan designed for us individually by the Creator of the Universe."

"I've really made a mess of my life...after ..."

"You are forgetting what you did for the people of Peace Ridge, Veronica. Many would have lost everything they had if you hadn't spoken up. That took a lot of courage."

"She's brave, my girl," Archie said fondly.

"You are courageous, Veronica. You've endured a lot. Suffering can break us or it can drive us into the arms of the Great Comforter. Trust that, lean on that."

She nodded slowly, but Ed wasn't sure if she was really taking it in or just being polite. He opened the book again.

> I falter where I firmly trod,
> And falling with my weight of cares
> Upon the great world's altar stairs
> That slope thro' darkness up to God.

> I stretch lame hands of faith, and grope,
> And gather dust and chaff, and call
> To what I feel is Lord of all,
> And faintly trust the larger hope."

"The larger hope," Veronica whispered under her breath.

"The genius of Tennyson," Ed said briefly.

Ed stood up slowly and handed the small book to her. "This is for you. I hope you find it comforting, even if some parts are totally opaque. I'm not educated enough to appreciate it all, but this hit home for me:

> Our wills are ours, we know not how;
> Our wills are ours, to make them Thine.

"Let's say a brief prayer and then I'll get out of your hair." They bowed their heads as Ed spoke softly, "Father God, our dear Savior, the one who calls us, who saves us. We love You,

Lord. Be with Veronica and Archie as they spend some time in Minneapolis together. May it be a time of rest and fellowship and bring them safely back to Veronica's home here in Peace Ridge. Give them – give all of us – your peace. In Jesus' name, Amen."

"I'll walk out with you, Pastor," Archie said. "Be back in a minute, honey. Stay here."

"She's fragile," Ed said as he stood at the door to his car. "I can see why you are worried about her. We are all in deep prayer every day."

"Pastor, if she's open to it, could you do some Christian counseling with her?" Archie's voice was matter-of-fact, but there was a tinge of desperation in it. "I have suggested therapists but she's reluctant. I think she might be open to spending some time with you one-on-one. She trusts you and I think she feels she owes you her life. You and Paul. If you hadn't intervened..." He lifted his shoulders and a shudder shook his body. "Anyway, a few casual get-togethers at the parsonage may help her get back on her feet. We have to do something to prevent her slipping back."

"Happy to, Arch, if you think she's open to it. Suggest it to her. The church is always open to hurting souls —that's what we're there for. And I'd like to think that our friendship can play a role. She's seen my brokenness through her own pain. We are fellow travelers. Suggest it and we can start after the big celebration weekend."

"I love Tennyson," Archie said. "I'm glad you didn't quote the most famous couplet from that classic:

I hold it true, what e're befall;
I feel it when I sorrow most.
'Tis better to have loved and lost
Than never to have loved at all.

"That would have broken her," he said sadly.

Veronica sat at the table in the family room and looked out the window, her face empty of all expression. She felt as if she was made up of thousands of shards of brittle glass and that she would shatter and break apart if she moved at all. She felt the familiar blackness engulf her and it was with an effort she concentrated on the view outside the window – the half-empty bird feeders with the blue jays and grosbeaks feeding happily on the sunflower seeds. The brilliant green grass, newly mown in a geometric crisscross pattern. The lattice shadow of the fencing as the noontime sun insistently poured through the slats. Focusing on the small details brought her mind up from the enlarging darkness and it was with nearly a normal smile that she turned to greet Archie as she heard his footsteps approach her chair.

"A little hungry, honey? he said. "Want to go out for lunch at the Tall Rigger."

She nodded and got up slowly from her chair, her movements a mockery of her usual grace. "That would be nice," she said, willing her voice to sound eager. And normal. *Whatever that was anymore.*

Ed walked into his house and was greeted by a hungry cat. "You haven't been fed yet, have you, boyo?" he said lovingly. Something about the ritual felt eerily like a flashback. With a start, he realized that the house felt empty. *Wonder where Jill is,* he thought, *probably taking a little nap like she usually does this time of day.* He walked over to check the messages on the answering machine, but then thought, *I'd better check on her first.* He walked through the entire house without finding her, and then with concern, hurried out the back door and into the garage, calling "Jill! Jill!" Not in the greenhouse. He ran over to the church, which was always unlocked, and didn't find her there either.

Ed began a fast jog down past the greenhouse onto the Sermon Walk and onto the path that wound its way through George's field before he came to his senses. *She never goes anywhere without me. She wouldn't be down here.* He stopped uncertainly and then returned to the house. He called the Holm farm. *Could she have walked there?* No answer. Jennie was in New York; Paul would be out in the fields. He grabbed his keys and wallet and, with a rising sense of panic, walked quickly to the car. He drove slowly down Valley Road and past the Holm farm and continued on until it began to slope upwards towards the ridge. *She wouldn't have gotten this far.* He made a U-turn and turned onto Main Street, looking right and left carefully until he reached Crossroads. He walked quickly in the door.

"Have you seen Jill, Romyn?" he asked.

She turned to him in disbelief. "Jill?"

"She's gone missing. Not in the house when I returned from the hospital after seeing Veronica with Archie." *Here I was, giving a book of poetry to Veronica while my wife is wandering somewhere*, he thought with a sharp stab of self-reproach.

30

Delaney grabbed a carrier bag from the BnB kitchen and made her way down the steps and out to the shopping area. *I can't continue to cadge coffee from Alwyn,* she thought. She didn't eat in the BnB at all, preferring the local color of the nearby pubs. But she usually ran into Alwyn in the mornings and he always gave her a couple of tea bags. *I really need to do some grocery shopping and replace his stash. Good chance to wander while I plan what to do about Ten.* It was just a brief walk to Flask Walk and she remembered seeing a small grocer. Alwyn said something about Waitrose. *I'll find it.*

It was a spotlessly beautiful morning. She hadn't heard the rain during the night, but the sidewalks were still damp and where the sunshine poured through the break in the trees, she could nearly see the steam rising and the pavement drying to a summertime freshness. Despite her little jaunt down to Somerset yesterday, she felt on top of the world. *Completely over my jet lag. Ready to take on London!* It was early enough in the morning that the shopkeepers were still in the process of setting up. Keith Fawkes, the books and antiques seller, was letting down the green awnings over the sidewalk and a burly assistant was setting up the folding tables that displayed the assortment of smalls, bibelots, and furniture. Mullioned windows in a nearby apothecary sparkled and the oval sign, hanging with black chains, added a subtle swish to the sounds of wheelbarrows, birds, and people greeting one another. A nearby flower seller was setting out lavish displays of flowers that brought a countryside flower garden to the cobblestones of Flask Walk. Messengers on bicycles handed off packages to proprietors and slender sales girls unconsciously adjusted their striped green and white aprons and chatted amiably with one another. Cockney accents, the vernacular of all shop girls across London.

Delaney sauntered slowly, trying to absorb the iconic atmosphere as much as possible. *Imprinting 'ye olde London' on my brain. It would take a lifetime to take it all in. How am I going to find a way to live here?* She leaned against the blue corner of The Flask—*my pub*, she thought — and punched in the address of the Little Waitrose in Hampstead Heath into her cell phone. *Not too far away. Easy to find.* A text from Jennie was in the queue and she opened the text message.

Jennie was in New York but thought Delaney would want to catch up on the Peace Ridge happenings. "You are missing out on the big excitement this coming weekend: the opening of Petros Greek Diner. I'm in New York this week, about to explore the Fancy Food Show. Next time you and I should do this together—would be more fun. Hope you're having a wonderful time. Have you connected with—-?? You won't tell me his name. Did Michael tell you that Donna died in her sleep last Sunday? BTW, Paul and Jeremy installed Tafani's painting in the diner last night (did you know she was an artist?) Paul sent a photo of the install. Take a look. Quite impressive, don't you think? Write back. Stay safe, my friend. xxx, J."

Delaney opened the attachment and studied the painting thoughtfully. It had to be massive. Paul had taken the picture at a distance of about eight feet and the painting loomed over the diner's reception desk and seemed to project into the diner itself. *Must be at least five-by-eight feet.* Delaney thought. It was so richly colored that the painting itself, even on a small four-inch screen, seemed to pop three-dimensionally into view. The scene was of an Afghan village. The background village square was filled with single story mud homes and a fire was tended by children in the middle of the square, their joyous faces laughing at the vivid blue sky. There were three men, dressed in typical Afghani *shalwar kameez* and *karakul* hats, standing in a group by themselves off to the side of a building, the shading and dark colors foreshadowing a sinister threat. Over the hills in the distance there was an indistinct group of men in camouflage with a singular tall young man standing apart from the rest. Hidden, but not so well that the villagers didn't know they were there. An old man, standing by the children, looked at the ridge with a serious and assessing expression. Dominating the foreground was an incandescent young girl. Her lustrous coal-black hair was held in place by a fuchsia and lavender scarf and her blue eyes engaged the viewer with entreaty and challenge. She could have been thirteen; she could have been thirty. Delaney found it hard to withdraw her eyes from the painting. In some ways, it epitomized the historic conflict and generational unrest in Afghanistan. Tafani's artistry was unmistakable and Delaney found her empathy stirred, surprising since Afghanistan had never been on her radar. *Never thought once about those poor people,* she thought.

Jennie had sent along a few other pictures of Paul and Jeremy laughingly hanging the picture with Titos, Maria, and Tafani looking on. There was a single photo of Tafani. She stood by herself next to the cash register. Her height, her elegance and poise, and an undefinable sense of longing made her photo as compelling as her painting. *She's beautiful,* Delaney thought, for the first time. *I really never thought that before. She strode around Peace Ridge like she didn't care about anyone or anything. Who knew she had this—passion – in her? This talent.* But then she dismissed Tafani as she saw the text from Ten. She clicked on it eagerly.

"Terry," Romyn called to her teenage helper. "Can you mind the store for a few minutes? Ed and I need to see if we can track down Jill." Romyn turned to Ed with a warm but sad expression on her face. "She can't have gotten far. And Peace Ridge is small enough that we'll find her soon enough. Just let me make a quick call to Earl and have him keep an eye out."

They walked out to Ed's Honda and both sat silently in their seats for a moment, concern and hope jockeying for position in their minds. Ed started the car and then bowed his head, "Father God, we ask that You keep Jill safe wherever she is. Give us the right direction to find her. Help us to stay calm and keep our wits about us. We love You, Lord Jesus, and we know You have Your eyes on her. Thank you. Amen." Ed turned to look at Romyn helplessly and then turned the car around in the yard, his hands gripping the steering wheel so tightly that his knuckles turned white. They began to slowly drive up and down the streets of Peace Ridge.

"I was just at the hospital with Archie and Veronica for a little less than an hour," Ed explained. "I have left Jill home alone before. Never thought she'd just walk out. She's always been so scared about going anywhere without me."

"You had no reason…" Romyn remonstrated.

"But I wasn't even thinking of Jill. I was preoccupied with Veronica and her pain. And Archie, too. Shame on me."

"You're a Pastor, Ed, and you're a husband. Most often those roles are closely knit together, but with Jill…" She paused for a long moment and then continued, "and Veronica, too, you are called upon to be a psychologist. I worry about you. Worry that the burden is too heavy."

"It's not too heavy. I am just juggling so many things these days," Ed said to divert her. "If you look out the right side of the street, I'll focus on the left-hand side."

"Not to mention Donna's funeral…"

"We'll get through that tomorrow and then I can focus on what I need to do for Jill." He sighed heavily. "And Veronica, too."

Romyn's cell phone rang and she listened intently for quite a while, her face betraying an increasing concern. She slowly

211

put her phone back in her purse. "That was Earl. He wheeled out around the yard but didn't see Jill anywhere. When he got back in the house, the kids came into the kitchen. They had been in the back yard with Beth Ann and Sophie seemed upset. She went over to him and climbed into his lap, something she hasn't done for days. When he asked her what was wrong, she said 'the lady.' He asked her 'What lady?' and she said she didn't know her name, but she was the one that had given her the bracelet. Earl asked Beth Ann if she'd seen anyone and she said she hadn't. Earl asked her to take Sophie out into the yard and ask her to tell her where she saw the lady. When they got back into the house, Beth Ann said that Sophie had pointed out a spot just beyond the gardening shed before the woods begin."

"Let's swing over to your house, Romyn. It had to be Jill and she couldn't have gotten too far."

They turned around to go back up Main Street and then turned slowly onto Crossroads Avenue, hoping to spot Jill along the road. Sophie and Clay ran out to greet them when they pulled into the Randall's yard. Ed quickly walked into the back yard and took a look at the spot near the shed where Jill had stood. There was no evidence that she'd been there, but it gave her a clear view of the kids play area and she may have thought she was unseen. Spying on the kids. Spying on Sophie, who she thought was Emily. Despair and unfamiliar shame began to creep into his mind and he stood silently near the fence, looking into the woods with unseeing eyes. He was oblivious to the wheelchair that had rolled up silently behind him.

"We will find her, Ed," Earl said kindly.

Ed slowly turned to the older man. "It's time to face facts—she's obsessed with Sophie."

"Yes, seems that way," Earl replied briefly. "You got a tough time ahead of you, Pastor." He reached out his hand and patted Ed's arm. "God will show you the way forward."

Ed didn't reply.

"Let's just get her home first and then deal with this later." Earl pointed into the woods and said, "You can't see it from here, but Eliza's house and pet shed is just down the hill on the other edge of the woods. It wouldn't surprise me if Jill made her way down there. Go check it out. Eliza knows you – she won't chase you away."

Detective Young called Mary at the Maplewood children's home near lunchtime and said, "Sorry it's taken me so long to get back to you, Mary. I know you've been waiting to hear. Do you have a minute to talk?"

"Yes, hold on. Let me tell the Assistant Director to spell me at the dining hall." She returned in a few minutes. "Okay, that's taken care of. I'm all ears. What did you find out?"

"Well, the photograph was essential, Mary, and first of all, thank you for realizing its importance. We could not have helped out at all in this situation without it. I scanned the photograph and sent it to the Kansas City Police Department. They took it over to the assisted living facility where the mystery woman is housed temporarily and showed it to the charge nurse who verified that it's a strong probability that she *is* Lisa Shapiro. How she got to Kansas City, how she was so brutally attacked – likely a trick that turned on her – we will probably never know."

"Did she recognize the kids in the picture? Clay and Sophie?"

"When the staff showed her the picture, she seemed indifferent at first, but she wouldn't give it back to them. Later they found that she had put it under her pillow and they just let her keep it. The Kansas City Police think that's a positive ID. They are taking it as such anyway. We sent them the complete files we had on Lisa Shapiro and we are going to work with them to transfer her to Minnesota. Her fingerprints are unreadable. That is probably why her assailant smashed her hands up so bad, so she couldn't be traced. Minnesota has priority custodianship in this case and so we've contacted the Health and Human Services Department and they are working through the admittance procedures for her. As a ward, if you will, of the State of Minnesota."

"Still speaking just gibberish and no memory?" Mary asked.

"Yes and yes," he replied tersely.

"What are the chances of her long-term recovery? Do they know?"

"I think slim to none but miracles can happen. From what they told me, she was nearly killed in the attack and the fact that she's still alive is a miracle."

"Poor Sophie. Poor Clay," Mary said softly. "He so thought of himself as his mom's protector.

"Yes, poor kids. Though from what you've told me – and what I have seen in the files – they are probably in a better place with their foster parents. She is unlikely to be able to ever take care of them, the way she is now."

"Well, it's a sad story. Not that rare, unfortunately. And strange, too. Kansas City."

"And here's something that's equally strange. The Kansas City Police Department told me that just last week, Lisa had a visitor at the assisted living facility. At first, they were wary because they thought it might be a reporter, or even a john that was checking up on her. They alerted the police who were there in plain clothes when the man arrived. He didn't stay long, just gave her a bouquet of flowers and said he hoped she'd get well soon. Sometimes there are weirdos who like to prey on damaged women. The staff thought he might be one of those, but he was dressed okay and seemed normal."

"He knew her?"

"Well, they didn't think so. He didn't act as if he did and he called her Drusilla, which is the name she has been given at the assisted living home. But here is what is strange: when he left – after only a five to ten-minute visit – he said, 'Goodbye, Lisa,' which the staff didn't think much of. Thought maybe he'd forgotten her Drusilla name. Or they misheard it. Only when they got the information from us did they think the guy might have been more involved than they thought. But by that time, he was long-gone."

"Wow. That's strange. Wondering if it could be a trick she'd worked in Kansas City. Or maybe even the guy that assaulted her?"

"I guess we'll never know. It's one of those things. In the police business we hate to see *bad* ends, but sometimes we like to see *something* end, at least. Lisa was well known in St. Paul, and a lot of the force predicted something like this might happen to her. She'd been warned about her lifestyle every time she was taken in, but you can't make someone do something they don't want to do."

"I wonder..." Mary said thoughtfully.

"You wonder what?" Detective Young asked, jerking his head up sharply.

"This is strange. I got a call a couple of days ago from a reporter – said he was a reporter anyway– who wanted to do a public interest piece on children in our facility. Tug at the human heart strings so to speak. I told him that we are private and don't exploit the stories of the children who have had enough going on in their lives and don't need to feel worse. He pushed for success stories and then he suggested that there are foster care and adoption stories that could be inspiring.

"I still told him that we don't talk about our kids, but he said something about he'd heard of two kids who were being adopted by a rich couple in a small town somewhere."

"I told that reporter from the *Star Tribune* not to write the story about that!" Detective Young was irritated. "She'd been pushing and pushing our department to write up the Lisa story and somehow found out about the kids and their fostering in Peace Ridge. She's from there, I guess. Knows all about the town. The story about Lisa and the kids didn't make too much of a splash here, but someone found out about it. Did you give the guy their name?"

"No, I didn't. But the name of the town, Peace Ridge, slipped out before I could stop myself." Mary chastised herself.

"I'm sorry, Detective. I hope I didn't make things worse for those kids."

"We don't know if it was the same guy. Could be totally disconnected. In any event, I wanted to let you know that you were key to solving this case. It won't help Lisa recover, and it won't restore their mother to those poor kids. It might make it easier for the foster parents to adopt, though. The State can rule her incompetent and it seems there's no father to file a claim. So, thanks, Mary. Much obliged."

If it was only so easy, Mary thought. *The police can be happy that they've solved a case, but these kids tear at my heart. It's not just a case to them. It's their mother. I wonder what would happen if they ever saw her. Would break their hearts—even though she abandoned them, they never stopped loving her.*

Mary sat unmoving at her desk for a long while, all energy drained from her body. Then she picked up the phone and began to dial Romyn and Earl's number. At just that moment, the assistant director of the facility rushed into her office and told her that the refrigerator in the kitchen had gone on the blink. Could she find the number for the plumber? Ice had defrosted and there was water all over the floor. *First things first,* Mary thought.

31

Ed and Romyn drove slowly into Eliza's yard. The noise from the pet shed was deafening. If the noise of their car wouldn't bring Eliza out of her house, the noise from the two dozen plus dogs would. But Eliza wasn't in the house. She came out slowly from the pet shed, her skinny figure bent over and seemingly frail, though Ed knew that wasn't the case. She might be in her ninth decade, but she wasn't fragile in any sense of the word. *And she has all her faculties*, Ed thought. They sat in the car for a moment and then slowly emerged and greeted the old English woman.

"Good afternoon, Eliza," Ed said. "How are you today?"

"Searching for your missus, air ye?" Eliza replied, and then turned back into the pet shed. Romyn and Ed followed slowly. It took a moment for their eyes to adjust to the darkness of the shed in dim contrast to the bright sun outdoors. They were received rapturously by the dogs and they made their way slowly into the building surrounded by expectant doggie faces. Eliza was mumbling something but amid the noise and her Cockney accent they couldn't understand a word. But they didn't need to. In the room that housed the pet beds, litter boxes, individual feeding and water bowls for some thirty cats, they saw Jill. She was moving serenely from one sleepy cat to another, crooning over each soft head and tenderly scratching ears and upraised chins.

"Jill?" Ed said.

"She's here to 'elp. Land sakes. Takes me ol' bones 'ours."
Eliza walked confidently into the room and opened a fif-
ty-pound bag of dry cat food and handed the scoop to Jill, who
carefully poured it into three individual cat dishes.

"Oh, hello, Eddy." Jill nodded to Romyn but didn't smile.
"I'm helping Eliza feed her pets."

"Can I help?" Ed moved closer, but felt a sudden barrier
between his wife and him. This was her mission. "Carry on,
honey," he said.

"Eliza, what can I do to help?" Romyn, ever practical, took
the direct approach.

"Me doggies need water." Eliza looked pointedly towards
the large galvanized washtub in the middle of the dog room
and cocked her head towards the hose. Romyn walked over
and lifted the half-filled scummy washtub and carried it outside,
and then came back for the hose. Soon was heard the sound of
fresh water cleaning the tin, a distinctive farm drumming sound.
Even if this farm was only for cats and dogs.

"Oy, there's my boyo," Eliza crooned. A large, old golden
retriever ambled into the pet shed, his open mouth smiling at
the group. Eliza set her scoop down and bent down and hugged
her pet. "Me sweet Barto. Me baby."

"Missing Jennie?" Ed asked. "She's in New York this week."

"I miss me sweet gurl. She helps me every day—she sent
me her." She nodded to Jill, who dreamily looked back at Eliza.
"She's my 'elp today. I am ever so grateful. Jis' walked in."

"I'll make sure she comes every day," Ed said with a smile.
He bent down and scratched the ears and jowls of Bartholomew—
the dog blissed out — his memory filled with the sights and
sounds of the fire in the pet shed last winter. Rebuilt with the
youth group. *Did a nice job, too,* he thought. *Proud of those
kids.* He turned and smiled up to Eliza and even in her dotage,
she was suddenly reserved with the sweetness and beauty of
his smile. She turned away in shyness.

*I'm just glad she's okay. If she wants to be Eliza's helper,
I'm all for it,* he thought. Romyn came back then to ask for

help with the water tub. It was lifted it into place and Ed looked around to find a broom and make himself useful. After the tension and worry of the past couple of hours, these mundane tasks were fulfilling. Solomon's words in Ecclesiastes came into his mind: "I have seen what is best for people here on earth. They should eat and drink and enjoy their work, because the life God has given them on earth is short."

"Eliza," he said suddenly, "would you like to come over to our house for supper tonight? Jill and I were thinking it would be fun to make a roast beef with Yorkshire pudding and there is only one person we'd like to have with our meal and that's you." She turned a delighted face to his and Romyn turned away to hide her smile. *Good thing I took that chuck beef roast out of the freezer earlier today,* Ed thought.

Tuesday morning dawned with temps in the near 90s and no clouds in the sky. George clumped into the Crossroads Convenience store, an irritated expression on his face.

"Why the long face, George" Romyn gave him an encouraging smile. "Are you Mr. Grumpelstiltskin today? On this beautiful morning?"

"Well, for one thing, there's no pie today," he groused. "That girl is still in New York, I suppose. And secondly, I was supposed to meet Tom and Shiloh at Eva's place so we could begin to fix her garden like she had wanted, and after hoisting my tiller onto the trailer and getting it unloaded, I went to start it and the belt snapped. Don't suppose you have any forward drive belts for a John Deere, do you?"

"I'm sorry, I don't think so. I'll take a look. Sit down for a minute and rest while I rummage in hardware and check our belt supply. Do you have the model number?"

George thrust his hand deep into his pocket and pulled out a crumpled piece of paper that had lived a former life as the back page of a car manual. "Here it is."

Romyn poured a cup of coffee and patted his shoulder fondly. *He's lost weight*, she thought, concerned. *I can feel his shoulder bones.*

"If I don't have it, I can order it for you, George. It'll be here in a couple of days."

"Nah. Tops Hardware didn't have it either. I'll go to Menards. Tom and Shiloh showed up at Eva's place and Tom went back to his house to get his tiller. We'll get to work on it sometime this afternoon. I wanted to get going this morning before the sun, but *some people* don't get underway as early as I do."

"Tom has his business to run, too. I suppose he had a project he wanted to finish. I know Shiloh has been nagging to get the garden underway. Ever since she heard Eva's promise at the funeral. She knows Eva gave her that task and she's not going to let it go."

"Well, he has a bigger tiller than I do anyway. He'll probably be able to turn up that soil in only a couple of hours. It would take me all day."

"Nice of you to help out, George."

"Just bein' neighborly. Gotta get to these things before ... while I can still steer the tiller." He leaned back into the chair and said, "Besides, I like that little girl, Shiloh. She's got spunk, that one. Reminds me of my Kathy. What she must have been like when she was a little girl. Kathy wasn't a redhead like Shiloh, but she could unload on me. If I deserved it." He stared deeply into his coffee cup and fell silent.

"And then tomorrow," George said, as if continuing a conversation thread in his head. "Donna's funeral. Suppose the whole town will show up."

"Yes, they will, I'd expect. If not for Donna, for Bill. He is having a hard time. Especially because he hasn't been able to get in touch with Kellie. He drove down to Minneapolis to tell her in person but hasn't been able to find her. She isn't at that place she shared with the other girls and she isn't answering his texts."

"Drugs," George said scathingly. "That girl always thought only of herself anyway."

"No, she did not, George," Romyn said. "She was a good kid in high school here."

"I was talking to Jeremy the other day. He saw a lot of drugs, heroin and stuff, when he was in Afghanistan, and he said it made them totally messed up in the head. Especially the young kids. Their brain isn't developed until they are twenty-five anyway. And some of them never mature emotionally when they are into drugs."

"Maybe Jeremy could talk to Kellie if she ever shows up. Maybe he'd have some advice for her. I just feel for Bill. He's the one that's hurting."

"Heard you and Ed had a bit of fun yesterday chasing after a runaway wife?" There was a faint smile on George's face."

"I wouldn't call it fun. Ed and I were both quite worried."

"She couldn't have gotten far. Where could she go?" George was dismissive.

"We've had enough excitement in Peace Ridge for a while. Donna dying, Jill running away, Veronica trying to kill herself. What's next?" George looked morose. Town gossip usually made him like a cat with its nose in a bowl of cream.

"'Therefore, do not worry about tomorrow, for tomorrow will worry about itself. Each day has enough trouble of its own.'" Romyn quoted Jesus' words from a Galilean hillside.

"There you go, Romyn," George said with finality. "There you go."

George sat silently at the table while Romyn retrieved a stack of cash register receipts and began to make notes on a pad near the cash register. Millie jumped up on the counter with a musical inquiring grunt and Romyn patted her head absently as the cat stretched and yawned repeatedly. This weather made one sleepy, especially this time of day. Sunlight shone brightly on the gas pumps, causing a flash of glare when the intermittent breeze jostled the advertising sign above the pumps. Traffic was typically light for a weekday morning and Romyn's thoughts were occupied with worry about Sophie's scare with Jill, heartache about Bill, and concern about what Ed would do with Jill's grasp on reality.

On top of all this, The Jason House still needed an enormous amount of time and attention. Bill had asked Jeremy to run lead on the building project for a few days and the work was progressing, but Romyn was worried about Earl. They needed to find an administrator for the facility soon and he was fussy and worried about it. They had hoped Veronica might be able to take on more responsibility, but that was now clearly out of the question. It would be more than both Earl and Romyn could do together, even if they didn't have Crossroads to run, and that was another worry: how long would they be able to keep it open with all their other responsibilities? Romyn breathed an unconscious long sigh and turned to stare out the window, her thoughts miles away.

The late model car pulled a little too quickly into the parking lot and stopped abruptly in front of the store. A tall, thin man emerged and stood for a moment by the car door, looking around the parking area with a barely camouflaged look of disdain. He was dressed in tight-fitting blue jeans with his polo shirt tucked in tightly. He looked rather neat but his running shoes were nearly worn out and filthy, a somewhat incongruous sight. He put on sunglasses and walked casually into the store.

"Hello folks." A strange accent. Not Minnesota. A combination of New York and the deep South.

"What can I do for you?" Romyn asked politely.

"Oh, I just stopped in for a Coke," he replied.

"The cooler is on the back wall. We have both Coke and Pepsi."

He nodded to her with a brief smile and slowly walked back into the store, looking around carefully.

"If you need something else – snacks or something, they are over to the right." Romyn pointed at the snack section. He looked at her but didn't say anything. *Not from here,* Romyn thought. *A Minnesotan would be saying "Hot enough for ya'?"* or *"How's the fishin' up here?"*

He took his time in front of the soft drinks and then brought a liter of Coke and set it on the counter. His face was narrow and his lips pursed sullenly. He must have been aware of how he was perceived, for suddenly he pasted a weak smile on his face and said jocularly, "Nice town. Peace Ridge."

"First time here?" Romyn asked politely.

"Yes, just visiting Minneapolis and wanted to see some of the country. Someone told me about this village."

"Are you a fisherman?" George asked from the table. "That's what we're known for. Good fishin' on Barking Dog Lake, if you're interested?"

"Barking Dog Lake? Is that its real name?" he asked, the scorn of city people for rural folks barely concealed. "I suppose there was a dog and no one could shut him up?"

"The original Ojibwe name was '*Anaami-adoopowin-ayaa a'aw – animosh migid*'" Romyn said with a friendly smile. She spoke the name musically and correctly. "But the people here thought that was a little too complicated for the village. It means 'the dog is under the table barking.' So it got shortened to Barking Dog. A long time ago. The twenties."

"I've heard that the natives and the people in Peace Ridge don't get along," he said, a slight smirk coloring the words.

"Where did you hear that?" George harrumphed from his chair. "People telling tales about us somewhere?"

"Oh, just in Minneapolis. Maybe teasing. Linda, a reporter friend, suggested it."

"You friends with Linda Bakry?" George thrust out, his ire coming to the fore.

"I just met her…at a function in Minneapolis," the man said. "Not a friend." He deflected. "She's from here."

"And she can stay away from here," George said sourly.

"Oh, not one of your favorites?" the man replied, his teasing tone an attempt to ingratiate.

"She's moved to Minneapolis to work at the *Star Tribune*," Romyn said. "We don't see much of her anymore since she left last year."

"I see you have a big building going up in the middle of town," he said.

"Bakry tell you about that, too?" George asked.

It was impossible to read him, Romyn thought. *Take off your glasses, sir, when you are inside talking to people. That's the polite thing to do.*

"A new assisted living facility," she replied briefly.

"Wow. That must be expensive. Stretches over a couple of blocks."

"Well, land isn't expensive here, and we have the need."

"Yeah, I hear. Lots of people to take care of."

Where is he going with this? Romyn thought. "It's the aging population," she said. "More and more Baby Boomers needing it."

"Linda told me that it will have a kids and family section, too, for families…"

"She seems to be well-informed," George said. "Strange, because she hasn't been here in months."

"Oh, I'm sure you can read all about it in the Minneapolis papers," the man said.

"Thank you," Romyn said firmly, turning away to her pile of receipts. *Too nosy for my taste.*

"I'm staying at the Sleepytime Inn. Maybe I'll come in for more Coke tomorrow," he promised, and walked out the door.

"See you tomorrow then," Romyn called to his back, walking over to George to pour him another cup of coffee.

"Don't like him. Shyster," George said with venom.

"You seem to have sized him up pretty well, George."

"A man who talks to you like that. Like you're beneath him somehow. I hate those guys. Like 'I'm better than you are' kind of people. Where does he get off?"

"Seems to be pretty well informed. Linda must have filled his ears…"

"That woman!" George expostulated. "Anyone who listens to her…"

"Seems like he was pumping us for information, doesn't it?" Romyn added thoughtfully. She turned to the door as Randy pushed it open slowly. Her smile for him was genuine as always.

"Hi, Randy. How are you?"

Randy looked at her with a smile in his eyes. He didn't speak, but he signed "Good afternoon" to her, and then walked awkwardly over to George and signed "Good afternoon."

"No pie today, Randy. Jennie's gone to New York. Can I buy you a cup of coffee?" he said.

Randy looked at him and didn't say anything. Compared to his usual garb, he was dressed neatly and cleanly. His clothes fit him for a change and his hair had been cut and was brushed back from his forehead, showcasing his angular high cheekbones and beautiful dark eyes.

"Here's a bottle of milk, Randy," Romyn said, "and I want you to have a box of Good & Plenty candy. I know you usually like your Sugar Daddy – got them here," she handed one to him, "but I am starting a new thing. Giving everyone who wants one a box of Good & Plenty. I asked Sysco to send me a few extra cases of twenty-fours so I can preach to my customers."

"What are you talking about, Romyn?" George asked.

"I love Good & Plenty," she said. "Licorice. Black licorice. Love it. And a bit of sweet from the pink and white sugar coating. The other night, Earl and I were talking and I said I wish I had a way to let people know about Jesus and salvation without preaching to them."

"You preach to them just by being yourself," George said.

"Well, I try," Romyn said. "But we were snacking after supper and Earl gave me a little sermon. He said: 'Think of Good & Plenty. That is our God. He is good. He is plenty. If we only trust Him.' He opened a box of Good & Plenty for me and shook a pile of pieces into my hand. Earl said, 'Look at the black inside. That's our sin. But it's covered in pink which represents the blood of Christ and then other pieces are covered in white which represents His grace. And all you have to do is open your hand to receive it.

"It was such a simple lesson in a simple box of candy. I thought if I put a basket out on the counter with a 'Free' sign and a little gospel message, maybe someone would see it, take it and think about it. I need to ask Pastor if I can put the website of Valley Community Church on the tract and his name and telephone number on it, but this can be a way I can be a witness without being a preacher."

"Why 'free', Romyn?" George asked. "You're giving it away. Cutting into your profit margin, aren't you?"

"Because God's grace is free if we only take it," Romyn responded.

George was silent. "Wouldn't have worked for your last customer, Romyn."

"That's up to the Holy Spirit," she said simply.

George got up slowly from the table and walked over to the basket of Good & Plenty. He took a box and then said to Romyn, "Pray for me," as he walked out the door.

32

Valley Community Church was packed to the rafters. There was the normal hubbub of friends greeting friends, the bustle of the Ladies Aid getting the fellowship hall ready for the meal, and small children chasing around in the Sunday School rooms and excitedly pleading with parents to let them go to the playground amid parents' urgent and stern shushing. Small town funerals were always remembrance and grieving occasions, but also social opportunities to connect and gossip. Donna's death announcement was not unexpected and for many long months her physical condition and the prospects of recovery were a *sub rosa* topic of talk. As well as the rumored damage to Brady Construction, Bill being one of the town favorites. Donna was from Peace Ridge Village, too, but according to some of the women of the Ladies Aid making sandwiches in the kitchen, "she always thought she was better than everyone else."

"Shouldn't speak ill of the dead," someone said, and the women all looked down thoughtfully at the trays of ham and cheese sandwiches, the pickle dishes, sweet and dill, the overflowing bowls of cole slaw and potato salad. The president of the Ladies Aid began to make the large urns of coffee and suggested to a fellow Ladies Aid member that she could put out the cream and sugar and see if they had cut all the bars and cakes that had been brought in earlier.

"We should see if we have enough lemonade for the kids," someone said.

"If I had treated my husband like she did, I couldn't live with myself," one woman said to another under her breath.

"He seemed to have forgiven her, though," was the reply.

"Well, what could he do? She had cancer and then that accident..."

"Seeing her boyfriend, I heard," was the tart reply.

"Do you think we'll have enough food?" someone asked.

"We always do," was the reply.

They all quieted down when they saw Bill come into the kitchen with a large ham and salami tray from Walmart, followed by Pastor and Jill carrying an oversized bowl of fruit salad and a pre-made platter of vegetables and dip.

"Hello, Pastor," they sang out in unison. "Hello, Bill."

"Hello, Jill," they added, seeing the quiet, beautiful blonde behind Pastor.

The president of the Ladies Aid went over to Bill and gave him a big hug. "Praying for you, Bill. Know today will be tough for you."

"Thank you, Janice," he said simply, looking around at the women in the kitchen. "Thank you, ladies. What would we do without you?" They preened at that a little bit. Always good to feed the men. They worked so hard.

"Bill, let's go into the office and have some prayer time. Janice, would you mind taking Jill under your wing and giving her something to do to help out?" Ed looked at Janice meaningfully, and she went over to a drawer in the kitchen and pulled out an apron that said, "Valley Community Church. Serving Others" and handed it to Jill.

"Don't want to get that pretty white shirt dirty, Jill," she said kindly.

Bill followed Ed into the nearby pastor's office and they both sighed a big sigh of relief when the door closed on the noise in the sanctuary and the quiet pervaded the little office. Bill slumped in the chair and Pastor Ed walked over behind his desk and brought out his big Bible, the King James Version that was his "go to" for funerals. Nothing else seemed to give him the poetry, the cadence, the familiarity that comforted and consoled.

"Well, Bill. Here we are. The end of a journey and the beginning of another one. A solo journey, Bill," he said quietly. "For now. With the help of Jesus."

Bill sat there silently. Finally, he said, "I have had months to think about this, Ed, but now that it's here, the finality of it is ...kinda...overwhelming. I don't want to think of Donna. There in that casket."

Ed softly quoted Solomon,

The race is not to the swift
or the battle to the strong,
nor does food come to the wise
or wealth to the brilliant
or favor to the learned;
but time and chance happen to them all.

"I know philosophy isn't very helpful at a time like this, Bill," Ed said kindly.

"It's okay. I just want to get through today."

"Did Kellie ever get in contact with you?"

"No. That's what makes this so awful. She should be home."

Through the closed door, they could hear the sound of the piano and they both realized that time was at hand.

Swing low, sweet chariot,
Coming for to carry me home.
Swing low, sweet chariot,
Coming for to carry me home.

"Are you sure you're up to it?" Ed asked.

"Yes." Bill took a folded piece of lined school paper from the pocket of his plaid short sleeved shirt. He looked down at the paper for a long moment. "It's the last thing I can give her," he said finally.

Pastor Ed stood up and walked over to the office door and opened it. There were a few people in the lobby, and at the front of the sanctuary he could see Earl's big wheelchair next to Romyn, Clay, and Sophie in the front pew. He turned to Bill and said, "I asked Romyn and Earl to join you in the front row. Don't like the idea of you sitting there by yourself, Bill." He walked over and put his hand on Bill's shoulder. "Let's pray. Dear Heavenly Father, we come today to put our dear sister, Donna, to rest. Be with Bill and the rest of our church family as we worship You now and praise You for who You are, even through our pain. If we were without the consolation of Your Son, Jesus Christ, we would have nothing. Bless us as we grieve and help us to get through today. In the precious name of Jesus Christ, Amen."

Bill added a soft "Amen" and stood up, his now-lean frame towering over the diminutive pastor. His face was drawn and white and his blue eyes were swimming pools of grief. The congregation all rose as Bill and Pastor walked down the aisle to the front row. Romyn scooched over a bit and patted the seat next to her as Bill nodded his greeting to Earl and sat down. Clay and Sophie were motionless, picking up on the pervading sadness. Sophie had never seen so many beautiful flowers massed together and the scent was intriguing her. It reminded her of something, but she wasn't sure what. Neither child knew Donna nor Bill, but Romyn and Earl thought it time to get the kids used to all the activities of the church, including funerals.

After the choir sang "Turn Your Eyes Upon Jesus" and "Amazing Grace," Ed slowly rose from his chair and stood quietly behind the pulpit.

"'Precious in the sight of the LORD is the death of his faithful servants,'" he began. "We gather here to mourn and to celebrate the life of Donna Brady Nelson. It must seem strange to hear the Musician Warrior King David write these words of Psalm 116 and think that God Himself sees the death of His faithful ones and calls it precious. Precious. We don't think of death that way. We hate death and we grieve when our loved ones are taken away from us like the accident that took Donna's life.

"As Donna's friend, Janice, read her obituary and we recalled the woman, wife, mother, neighbor, and friend and her many accomplishments, we are reminded of the immense emptiness we feel staring at this casket and knowing that we will no longer see that smile, hear that lilting voice, laugh with her, and share life's joys and sorrows.

"I would like to ask you to consider another time and place. A long time ago. A beautiful garden near a beautiful flowing river in a land of the Middle East. An incomparably beautiful garden with trees loaded with ripe, juicy fruit of all kinds – apples, pineapples, oranges. Fresh clean flowing water to drink. Delicious, savory vegetables to enjoy, and the joyous companionship of animals who clustered around the man who gave them their names. But best of all, the fellowship of God Himself with the creatures He had made. The very delight of the Creator of the universe.

"You all know how this story turned out, how the very first ones on earth disobeyed God and were driven from the garden and how ever since that time, mankind has been troubled with sinful instincts. It's deeply embedded within all of us."

One of the parishioners whispered to her neighbor, "You don't think Pastor is going to talk about Donna's catting around, do you?" The other woman shook her head worriedly.

"There is a wonderful ending to this story. The final chapter has not yet been written but in God's gracious plan, over two thousand years ago He sacrificed His only Son – His Son Jesus – so that death could be conquered once and for all and He could have fellowship with all of us again. If we only accept the gift of Jesus on the tree and His death, burial, resurrection, and ascension. This can all be summed up in the one word, forgiveness. Forgiveness. God provided a means to forgive that sin of the garden – and our own daily sins – so that in His holiness

He could once again have fellowship with the creatures He had created for His own pleasure. 'Precious in His sight.'

"That helps us understand His love for us. 'For God so loved the world that he gave his one and only son, that whoever believes in him shall not perish but have eternal life. For God did not send his son into the world to condemn the world, but to save the world through him.'

"Forgiveness is the highest form of love. God showed us the way in Jesus. And Jesus Himself pleaded to His Father to forgive His own tormentors, the Roman soldiers and corrupt religious leaders who placed Him on the tree in Golgotha.

"Forgiveness is the way to extraordinary love, the way to move forward beyond death.

"Bill, himself, found the courage and strength to forgive. Psalm 121 in the King James version says, 'I will lift up mine eyes unto the hills, from when cometh my help. My help cometh from the LORD, which made heaven and earth.'

"In those long months after Donna's cancer diagnosis and then the terrible accident which caused her coma, Bill leaned on the Lord and found the strength to forgive. His heart had begun to shrivel, but in the process of dependence on our Lord and His example of forgiveness, his heart grew in love for Donna and his 'heart of stone' was transformed into a 'heart of flesh' in the Prophet Ezekiel's words. A living, breathing love for the woman he'd made his life with for nearly 25 years. Despite their brokenness and trials — forgiveness and love.

"One of the early church fathers, St. Justin Martyr, was beheaded in A.D. 165 because he refused to give up his Christian faith. He said, 'The greatest grace God can give someone is to send him a trial he cannot bear with his own powers – and then sustain him with His grace so he may endure to the end and be saved.'

"Bill is saved through that sustaining grace. The grace of Jesus Christ that is offered to each one of us. The grace that helps us through our suffering and trials and gives us the ability and the willingness to forgive. And to experience that highest form of love."

The church was quiet and peaceful, sunlight flooding into the sanctuary through the oversized windows on either side, and the colors of the stained-glass window at the front streamed like a rainbow over the small group in the front row and onto Donna's casket. There was the sound of sobbing from the back row. Ed paused and saw that one of his faithful saints, Alma, was cradling the young woman in her arms and stroking her hair. Kellie. Here at last. Ed looked down at the front row and nodded to Bill and then stepped aside as Bill made his tentative way to the pulpit.

He stared out at the congregation and then gripped the sides of the pulpit for strength. He began slowly, "This is an unfamiliar place for me. I am used to being high up but in the cab of a backhoe, not a pulpit. That's where I am more comfortable, for sure." There were a few chuckles and the sound of pews creaking as the tension of the sermon eased into the more familiar stage of remembrance.

"I asked Ed if I could say a few words. I know it isn't typical for the widower – now that's a hard word for me to say – widower— to speak, but Pastor has talked about my journey of the last few months of Donna's illness and I just wanted to share some final thoughts."

Bill straightened out the crumpled paper on the pulpit and smoothed it down repeatedly as he struggled to gain control of his emotions. Romyn quickly opened her purse knowing tissues would be required. Earl brought his arm around her shoulders and Sophie leaned in closer to Romyn's side, offering her little measure of comfort in this strange place.

"Before Donna's accident," Bill began, "we had begun to have real problems in our marriage. We'd go for days without talking to one another and when we did talk, it usually ended up in a fight with one of us storming out. Maybe our nearest neighbors heard the slamming doors. In a town like ours there are no secrets, so you probably all know about this anyway and I don't need to give you the gory details.

"One night I came to Pastor and told him it was too much for me. That our marriage was over and there was no hope. She had made me so mad I wanted her dead. But not this way," he said under his breath. "We talked and prayed and before I left, Pastor told me to just write down all the things about Donna that I loved. He told me it would help me love her more and that would help our marriage. So I began this list. I don't know if I can get through it without breaking down, but I just want to share some things about Donna that I really love. So here goes." Bill took out a big white handkerchief from his pocket and blew his nose loudly.

"Number one. That she married me." There was a small ripple of laughter at that. He looked up. "I was a big country lout and she was beautiful, petite, funny, smart, clever. I didn't deserve her. I thought that every single day of our marriage. Just about.

"Number two. That she gave us Kellie. Our wonderful daughter. Kellie...can't be here today, but she loved her mom, too." He stopped to wipe his nose and looked out bleakly over the congregation with unseeing eyes.

"Number three. I love her drive, her ability to throw herself into everything she does with passion and creativity. Loved, I should say. Donna's Interiors was all hers. I could never have done what she did.

"Number four. I loved Donna's smile, the way she'd say something that was funny and then her lips would curl up and her eyes would soften and become like a little kid's. Laughing eyes. I will never forget that smile."

Janice and several other women in the congregation began to sniffle loudly. Bill looked at them. "Just a couple more, ladies, and then we can...get this over with." Tears were streaming down his cheeks and he made no effort to wipe them away.

"Number five. I loved to watch her with our little dog, Barney, to see how she fussed over him. When he died, an old dog at sixteen years old, I think our marriage began to slip away, and we should have gotten another dog right away. But we didn't.

"Number six. I loved to see her with little kids, especially here at Sunday School. She was so good with them and spent hours creating special projects. Fun for her and fun for them.

"And finally, number seven. That she loved me. In her own way. The only way she could."

Bill stopped then and turned to look to Pastor, who stood up and embraced him briefly before Bill unsteadily returned to his seat.

"Let us end on these timeless words St. Paul wrote to the church at Corinth, 'Love is patient, love is kind. It does not envy, it does not boast, it is not proud. It does not dishonor others, it is not self-seeking, it is not easily angered, it keeps no record of wrongs. Love does not delight in evil but rejoices with the truth. It always protects, always trusts, always hopes, always perseveres.'" Ed closed his Bible and looked over the congregation briefly before walking down to invite Bill to join in the procession behind Donna's casket.

The young tenor from the high school stepped forward from the choir and took his guitar, and with a nod to the audio-visual guy, began the haunting melody.

"Go rest high on that mountain…"

They neared the lobby as a sobbing and visibly pregnant young woman jumped up and threw herself into Bill's arms.

33

The lights, crowds, noise, and banners in the enormous lobby of the Javits Center were overwhelming, and Jennie looked around in momentary confusion, seeking the registration lines. The lines were dozens long and she immediately rued her decision to walk crosstown to the Center. It had felt good at the time. She felt her excitement rise as the tempo of the city filled her heart and lifted her spirits. Though it hadn't been a leisurely walk. She was unused to the density of the sidewalks and was carried along in the wave of the pedestrian traffic, shocked at their blithe disregard for traffic signals, running against the light and lightly dodging the oncoming traffic. Her heart stopped several times watching bicycle delivery guys swerve around taxis and buses, seemingly seconds and inches away from certain death.

I don't think I could live in this city, Jennie thought. *I've become accustomed to our quiet, sleepy little town. I guess I'm a true Peace Ridger at heart.*

That reminded her of the text Paul had sent earlier about Donna's death and funeral on Wednesday. Missing the chance to say a final goodbye to Donna and, more importantly, to give her love and support to Bill. She'd make it up to him when she got home. Make him a special pumpkin pie.

She started off with great excitement and energy but by the time noon rolled around her feet were exhausted and her eyes were dizzy with visual stimuli fatigue. She slumped at the café table, grasping a coffee cup, her eyes unfocused on the surrounding chaos and people. She was surrounded by salesmen and distributors and throngs of reporters dictating stories into their cell phones. She watched idly as a Hollywood celebrity, followed by a camera crew and the press glided by on her way to the Greek pavilion for a feature interview. Jennie had learned the woman was about to launch her own cookbook and she had originally planned to tag along, but right now, all she wanted to do was rest her weary bones and then see if she would be able to even walk when she got up again.

Jennie pulled out some of the brochures she'd gathered at the booths she'd visited. Great examples of packaging designs and some interesting herb combinations that she wanted to think about. *Maybe I'm too traditional and too narrow in my thinking,* she thought. *Maybe we can be more experimental with some of our blends. Seems like there is a lot of interest in dishes made with North African seasoning or for Indian foods.* She had a flashback to a comment that Dane Johnson made last year: 'The Millennials want to explore and find new discoveries.' *Perhaps we could create some unique herb blends that would make it easy to create some of the ethnic foods the Millennials like to eat in restaurants today. And take pictures of and post on Instagram, too.* She took a drink of her Starbucks coffee and got out her cell phone to check her messages. *Funny I haven't heard from Paul. I thought he'd call me this morning.*

"May I join you?" Chris pulled out a chair without waiting for her answer. "How are you, Jennie?"

Jennie gave him a tired smile. "Overwhelmed," she answered. "Taking a break before I plunge back in. Have only seen one fourth of what I came to see."

"It's pretty spectacular, isn't it?" he replied with a confident smile.

"I had no idea…"

"Well, all the products won't get into U.S. distribution. For some of the small international companies, this is a show to build awareness and they can leverage their participation in their home countries. But most of them want to find a distributor so they can get into stores here. That's where the consumers are. That's where the disposable income is."

"It makes me feel that our little herb company won't even get to first base with all this competition."

"Don't give up. You have a vision, you have a smart marketing brain, you can make it work." He leaned over to her and lightly touched her hand. "And there are people here to help you."

Jennie pulled back slightly, but then gave him a bright smile. "What are you up to today?" she asked.

"I came looking for you. I thought I could walk the show with you for an hour or so." He pulled out his show guide. "I don't know if you've gotten to the second floor yet –" Jennie shook her head— but there are some great booths there and I can lead you right to them. Also, since I have *connections*," he smiled deprecatingly, "I can get the show VIP golf cart to ferry us." As if he had supernatural connections, a cart with a sign "Specialty Foods Association Staff" pulled up right next to their table. Chris stood up and with a low bow ushered Jennie to sit in the front seat of the car.

As much as she felt self-conscious, her feet convinced her that this was a good idea. She reached to grab for all her bags and Chris decisively took them from her. Grateful for the relief from twenty pounds of brochures and samples, she sank into the front of the seat while Chris leaned over and told the driver where to go.

The afternoon passed quickly. It was amazing how a chauffeur helped her get around. *I could get used to this,* Jennie thought. Chris left her after an hour and then she was able to see many of the exhibits she'd flagged in her guide. The Greek exhibit was particularly interesting, and with some flattery and talk-time, she scored a sample of some honey from the Taygetos mountainside in Sparta, Greece, a present she wanted to take home to Titos and Maria.

She was intrigued by an exhibit of countertop gardens and made a note to find one. Perhaps part of the project could be a way that others could grow their own herbs. Maybe they could have classes in Peace Ridge Village. She was totally sated by all the samples at the show and was dying for a tall glass of Peace Ridge Village cold water when she was stopped in her tracks by a chef grilling pieces of steak on a large block of pink Himalayan salt. *Never have I seen this before.*

It was a show of firsts and she left the show at five o'clock and went to stand in the taxi stand line along with dozens of other equally frustrated and exhausted show goers. But after thirty-five minutes of no movement, she decided to make her painful, slow way back to the Roosevelt Hotel. A long cross-town walk. *Worth it, yes,* she thought, *but I'm exhausted.* She walked slowly, looking around to find a taxi, but all flags were down and it was only until she was within five minutes of the hotel that a taxi was available. At this point, she was beyond tired and only wanted to get to her hotel room and sink into a tub of hot water.

In the elevator she got a text from Chris. "Missed you; hope I was helpful. Meet me in the bar of the Roosevelt at seven tonight. I'll buy you a drink and help you plan tomorrow."

She looked at it and thought, *All I want to do is take a bath and rest my feet. Maybe order room service.* She stared at it for a long time. *He has been nice to me. Helped me with the golf cart. I should probably have a drink with him.* "K," she texted.

Jennie felt somewhat revived after warm soaking shower and fresh clothes. She wasn't used to wearing much make-up, but she dashed her eyes with some mascara and added some blush to her pale cheeks. The Roosevelt had a free bottle of Kiehl's musk essence oil and she spritzed with that. Nice smell. A last glance at herself in the mirror—pearl earrings, clean white shirt and crisp khaki pants, comfortable Capezio black flats—reassured her that she looked just fine. Good enough for Peace Ridge. Good enough for New York City. It was just a business drink, anyway.

She stood uncertainly at the edge of the door of the Madison Club Lounge. Dark paneled walls and warm discreet lighting made it difficult to pick anyone out, especially with the mass of businessmen with their dark suits clustered three-deep around the bar area. She looked around uncertainly and was about to reach for her cell phone when a tall man snuggled up behind her and placed his arms around her waist. She was startled and turned around abruptly to meet a smiling, cat-swallowed-the-canary Chris, who led her by the arm to two comfortable club chairs in a discreet alcove.

"You're looking extraordinarily lovely, Jennie," he said. "As if you were lounging around a spa all day instead of walking the floors of the Javits Center."

Jennie smiled. "Thank you." She looked up as the waiter delivered their drinks. "And thank you, again, for the cart today. It was a godsend."

"Easy to do, Jen. You don't mind if I call you Jen, do you?" His smile was confident.. *It's what Paul calls me,* she thought, at the same time she said, "No, of course not," with an internal brief twinge of regret.

"I suppose you had a busy day, too," she added conversationally.

"Yes, it was busy all day. Lots of clients and logistics to be seen to. But I had thought about seeing you for a drink and that possibility made the busy day possible. A reward at the end of the day, so to speak."

"Never been thought of as a reward before," she said awkwardly. *I am out of the game. I don't know how to do this repartee.*

"I don't believe that. You've been the blonde everyone wants to be around for all of your life. I know that. Someone as beautiful as you—"

"Now, you're piling it on, Chris. Back where I come from, we'd say 'He just came in from the cow yard and it's flooding his boots.'"

His face reflected momentary confusion and then he quickly recovered and said, "I rarely give women compliments, but this one is deserved. If you had been born and raised in New York City instead of that place in Minnesota, you'd be walking the fashion runways instead of running after the cows. Or planting your herb garden."

"I wasn't born in a barn. I was raised in a fairly upscale suburb of Minneapolis called Maple Grove," she pushed back.

"Ah yes, but there is no place like New York. You must feel that, sense that, when you are here, don't you?" He probed with a secretive smile.

"Well, New York City is unique. That I'll give you. I do love the energy here and—" she gestured around the Madison Club Lounge "–love the atmosphere of places like this. I feel …connected to a different world somehow. It's fascinating."

"Do you think you'd have time to have dinner with me tomorrow night?" Chris shifted gears.

"Oh, I don't know, Chris. I don't know how I'll feel," Jennie parried.

"I am planning to have the golf cart at your disposal all day, so you don't have to wear yourself out." He glanced down at her feet. "You could even wear those cute little ballet slippers and you'd be fine."

Jennie looked at him doubtfully.

"And I have made appointments for you with some of the herb producers and exhibitors at the show." Jennie looked up in surprise. "I know many of them as personal friends. Exhibitors over the years. They will be happy to talk to you and show you some of the ropes." He signaled to the waiter for a drinks refill and then brought out a print-out of the show website. In a yellow marker he had marked out half a dozen herb marketers from Italy, Greece, California, and rural New York. "I've talked to each of these guys. They will spend some time with you talking about how to market your product line. You'll have to work around the customers that walk up to their booth, so I've scheduled only one each hour. That will give you enough time to make your way to all of them. This will really help you," he confided.

"I can't believe you've gone out of your way for me, Chris." Jennie shook her head wonderingly.

"Not out of my way. It's my job," he said simply. "But I am hoping you'll appreciate me even more and have dinner with me tomorrow night?"

Jennie felt boxed into a corner. He was bending over backwards to help her and she knew she needed it, but it felt like he wanted something in return. And she didn't fall off a turnip truck yesterday.

"Chris, call me mid-afternoon and we can plan it. I had thought I might try to catch a plane home tomorrow night instead of my early morning flight so I need to figure that in." She added uncertainly, "See how I feel." He looked at her, a slight hurt expression on his face. She wasn't used to reading the expressions of other men's faces. Paul, on the other hand, she could read in an instant. There was a combination of little boy rejection and assertive male confidence jockeying for primacy on his face. He turned to her earnestly.

"That's fine, Jen. I am looking forward to it. I know a wonderful place in the Village – it's my favorite, go there a lot – Babbo on Waverly Place. I hope you will say 'Yes.' In fact, I'm making a reservation right now for seven o'clock tomorrow night..." he punched in a code in his phone and spoke confidently to someone who answered. "Two, the corner spot. My usual.

"Jennie," Chris reached over and wrapped his manicured hands around hers. "You are so special. I have never..." Here he turned away. A more experienced woman would have recognized the seduction technique. "I have never met anyone as special as you. I want to know you better. I know you are married and this is not what I'm about. I am not about breaking up a marriage. I only want to know you better so that when I find the special one that I want to spend the rest of my life with, I'll know what to look for."

Jennie looked at him with a puzzled expression and gently pulled her hands away, then took a drink of her wine. She wanted to say, "Why don't you date single women and figure that out for yourself?" but she didn't know him well enough to be direct and besides, he was helping her in New York at the show. *Best not be difficult.*

"I'm not the role model for other women," she said modestly. "Goodness knows, others know more than me about just about everything."

"It's not what you know, Jen. It's how you are. How you relate to others. How you relate to me. I feel as if I've known you for most of my life. I rarely feel that with someone else. I feel I can be my 'real self' with you, and that's really what all men – most men – want. To feel that they are accepted as they are. Real."

"Well, that's just the way we are in Peace Ridge Village." *Best to get it back to home.*

"No, I disagree," he said sincerely, his eyes looking deeply into hers. "It's you. There's a quiet core of empathy with you. Overlaid with a passion that comes out when your full emotions are engaged. I saw that today when you were talking to Bona Furtuna, the Sicilian herb company. There was an intensity, but also a unique grace. I could see the team really sparking to you. It's quite amazing."

Jennie watched his face and listened to the soft spoken, seemingly authentic, flattery. Part of her liked it – goodness knew, no one in Peace Ridge talked like this – but it made her restless and uncomfortable. She turned away from his gaze and looked towards the art deco windows, trying to orient herself to the outside. She began to feel somewhat stifled. This bar was just too intimate and she felt the strongest urge to just walk away. She unconsciously twirled her wedding ring around her finger, half registering the stress building in her shoulders.

"Where are you now, Jennie?" Chris leaned toward her. "You've retreated from me. I think you're not used to compliments."

"I think I'm just tired. This was quite the day."

"Forgive me. You're right, of course." He gestured imperiously to the waiter and stood up abruptly. *Dismissed,* Jennie thought. *He's tired of this game.*

But he was solicitous and gentle with her as they walked to the hallway that led to the hotel rooms. "I look forward to our dinner tomorrow night and you'll find that I don't easily take 'No' for an answer." He leaned over and kissed her cheek, coming uncomfortably close to the curve of her mouth. "You'll find some interesting flavor combinations at Babbo, too," he said. "Give you some new ideas for your herb blends. Promise me you'll think about it?"

"Yes, Chris. I promise, and thanks for the drink."

"See you tomorrow, darling." He waved a cheerful goodbye and strode off.

Darling? she thought.

"I'm miles away in Dorset, Delaney," Ten said hurriedly. "Lyme Regis." They had texted back and forth several times and finally Delaney, not waiting for the invite, had called him and asked if he'd like to meet her for a drink at The Flask. "My local," she had said. He continued, "I am in the middle of a big project for a repeat client. We're removing several Regency Carrara marble fireplace surrounds and we will load them later today. Got the transport here and ready to go. Back to London late tonight. Sorry to miss you. I'll ring you up tomorrow, okay?"

So, yet another night in London by herself. Delaney made her now familiar walk down to The Flask and sat at the bar, idly watching the Londoners follow the football matches on television. She had zero interest in it even if she understood the game. She had made friends with the barman and he placed her glass of merlot in front of her before she'd barely sat down.

"All right, luv?" he asked.

"Fine. Fine." She was too abrupt and she smiled her megawatt smile at him to compensate for her rudeness. He was unperturbed and moved away to serve another customer. Delaney tapped her fingers on the bar top restlessly. *I need some company. There's no one here.* She flipped through her messages on her smartphone and saw one from Jennie in New York. She read it quickly and moved on to one from Michael asking if he could take Brian to a soccer camp. Thought he might like it.

"You seem free? May I sit here?" Alwyn gestured to the empty bar stool next to Delaney.

She waved him to sit and said, "Happy to have you. Please. Your research finished for the day?" she asked. She hadn't seen him around the AirBnB very much, just those brief encounters at breakfast over teabags.

"Yes, productive trip down to Totnes yesterday and back just now."

"I always wondered how you pronounced it: TOT-niz. Nice town?"

"Well, I was actually at Dartington." At her confused look, he clarified, "Dartington is a small village near Totnes."

"How did you find such a place?" Delaney asked, taking a long drink of her wine and practicing her seduction glance over the wineglass.

"Dartington is a well-known. Within Britain, at least. The Elmhirsts—she was American – founded the Dartington Hall School there in the 1920s. As a utopian community."

"Hmm. How did that work out?"

"Well, they spent their inherited millions. Elmhirst married Dorothy Paine Whitney, a wealthy American, and they took over a 14th century pile, renovated it, and tried to create a place where people could express their 'multi-faceted personalities,' in their words. The natural world. Environmental protection before it was fashionable. Multi-level schooling before

Montessori. Organic gardening naturally before pesticides. Ahead of their time."

"Sounds interesting. But old news, right? 1920s?"

"Not really. Dartington is a popular venue for conferences, music festivals, and so forth. Scholars come to study at Dartington Hall School and they bring in thought leaders in a wide range of disciplines."

"I figured you for a scholar, Alwyn." Delaney looked at him with a teasing expression on her face. *Let's cast this trout fly.* He was attractive in a scholarly sort of way, dressed in neatly pressed cords, a discreet plaid shirt, and a light windbreaker from Patagonia. His face was narrow and she found him attractive. He seemed peaceful and calm despite the fine lines around his eyes and the light brown hair with threads of gray. There was a kindness in his grey eyes that she hadn't noticed before, and when he smiled, his face took on a boyishness that reminded her of someone. Maybe Brian.

"Do I look like I have my nose in a book all the time?" he asked with a shy smile.

"No, not necessarily. But you have a seriousness about you—" that line was usually guaranteed to make a man proud.

"I wouldn't say I'm a scholar, Delaney. I'm an educator and a writer."

She looked at him, assessing. "So, I suppose you look at everything and think, 'Is this something I can use in my book?'" She smiled ingratiatingly.

"Not really. I don't think of others when I am mulling my own insights." He smiled briefly. "What about you? How have you been spending your time, Delaney?"

"I've been trying to connect with friends. We'll get together soon. In the meantime, I made a trip to Somerset to do some genealogical research and I have decided I am going to visit galleries to represent a new artist I've discovered in the U.S. Think she has quite the potential here." *Where did that come from?* she asked herself,

"Oh, that's interesting," Alwyn said politely.

"Look at this," Delaney commanded, flipping to her smart-phone and sliding her finger over the shots of Tafani's large painting. "This is just one of her canvasses. She's Afghani. Brilliant, really."

Alwyn studied the painting on the small iPhone screen. "It's quite impressive," he said, passing her phone back to her.

"She's got quite the story. Afghani. War zone near Tora Bora. Rescued by Americans and soldier falls in love with her, bringing her to America." *Where did all this come from?* she asked herself. *I'm making it up.*

"So, if you're an artist rep you should be able to easily get a visa. I think you can work with the Immigration Office with those credentials. For a few months, at least."

"Hope so. That's my next step." She looked at him, again assessing. "So, Mr. Alwyn, what's your story? You need to ante up!" Delaney took a long drink of her wine and looked at him with a flirtatious glance.

"There's nothing to tell. I'm just tootling around, following my own interests."

"And what might those be?" she probed.

Alwyn smiled at her and said, "I am here to compare and contrast the different world views of the ancient Christian God-centered world and modern man's 'Environment is God' view. England is a perfect place for it – post-Christian. Writing a piece for a religious journal."

Delaney gave a slight nod, surprised. "Really? I don't think of the two as competing worldviews. More like different shades of the same belief system, aren't they?"

"How do you mean?"

"Well, doesn't the Bible say God created the earth and told man to take care of it?"

"I see."

"But I'm not a biblical scholar. I'm not even particularly religious. More spiritual, you might say. I like to be in the natural world and I think one can find God there. In the warm summer breeze, beautiful waterfalls—that sort of thing." She drained her wine and caught the eye of the barman, who quickly returned with another glass of merlot.

"So, you're more into the latter view, the environment is God, so to speak?"

"Oh, I wouldn't say that, particularly. I was raised in a Christian home, went to church every Sunday. Send my son to Sunday School at the local church every Sunday. That's the small-town life, anyway. You'd be ostracized if you didn't go to church somewhere!"

"I see. I made a little side trip to the Benedictine Abbey in Tavistock while I was in Devon. Just a quick hop from Dartington."

"One of the ruins that are everywhere in England, I suppose," Delaney said.

"Well, yes. An old one. Ruined since 1000 A.D. but still interesting. And it's Benedictine, which is one of my interests."

"I don't know anything about that," Delaney said. "I couldn't tell a Benedictine from a Muscatine! Or chicken Florentine, for that matter."

Alwyn smiled wryly, "Well, one of the oldest sects...they were followers of St. Benedict. He predated the Tavistock Abbey by some 500 years."

"Like I said. They're all old, aren't they? Don't see how they are even relevant to today's life."

"You'd be surprised. There are a lot of people who are interested in the monastic rules for life. It can be...comforting... to live within specific rules. Rules based on ethics and service."

Delaney looked around with a barely camouflaged look of scorn. "I bet you couldn't find a single person in The Flask who would be interested in rules for monasteries."

"Well, there'd be one—me—for example. And I bet if you talked to any one of the people here – no matter how passionate they are about Manchester United beating Arsenal—when they have quiet moments, maybe in their beds at night, don't you think they have more serious thoughts and wonder about the meaning of life? And not in the Monty Python sense."

"Well, that leaves me out. I am here for the here and now. This is all there is – this life. Making one's way as well as one can and finding happiness wherever and whenever one can." She pushed away her half-finished wine glass. "That's what I'm all about." She smiled briefly. "Most people figure that out within five minutes after meeting me."

"Well, I wouldn't say you are a seeker particularly, Delaney." Alwyn spoke slowly and kindly. "You seem to be more like a runner than a seeker. Running from something, I think."

Delaney's eyes suddenly filled with tears.

There was the unmistakable sound of success on the field as several men in the bar yelled and banged their beer mugs on the rough wooden tables in the bar area. The level of noise in the bar ticked up exponentially. Outside the windows, Delaney could see the rain beginning to fall. She signaled the barman for her check and quickly scratched her signature on the tab. She could barely see as she slid down from her bar stool and walked unsteadily out the door with a brief goodbye to Alwyn. Indifferent to the rain and rapidly becoming entirely soaked, she made the short walk to the AirBnB. And also indifferent to the tall thin man in the Patagonia windbreaker who protectively shadowed her brief walk home.

34

The long day was finally over. Kellie had fallen asleep in her old bedroom and Bill sat at the kitchen table, a half-drunk Budweiser in front of him, forgotten and lukewarm. He took another card from the basket in front of him and slowly read the message of his friends from Peace Ridge, commiserating with his loss. Joe, from the towing service. Bart, the owner of the Tall Rigger, with a surprisingly eloquent evocation of scripture and love. Chief Baldwin. Yes, the chief. Her friends from the church, his friends, Romyn and Earl, a brief scribbled note from Paul on notepaper sourced from an implement dealer, Jennie being out of town. Some clients from Donna's business, Donna's Interiors. Each one made him feel his loss more acutely. If the house was empty before, it was even more empty now, knowing that Donna would never come home. The finality was convincing. He dropped his head wearily and sat there in silence. His eyes were cried out, but the pain and loss were just below the surface. How to go on?

As if understanding that loneliness, the phone rang. Bill moved slowly from his chair in the kitchen to the phone in the hallway.

"Bill, it's Steve. I just wanted to say how sorry I am that I couldn't be there today. I wanted to, but was stuck in the Cities. I feel for you, Bill. Today had to be a tough one. I am so sorry."

"Thanks, Steve. I'll get through it. Just now, tonight is the hardest. It will probably get better when tomorrow rolls around. Kellie is here..."

"So that's a comfort, at least. Knowing that she's safe with you, I mean to say," he added.

"Yes, she's here, but whether she'll talk to me in the morning is anyone's guess. I'm just going to let her sleep for now. The scene at the graveside was particularly horrible. I thought I had prepared myself but she was totally beside herself."

And so was I, he thought. The silent walk to the gravesite, the black dirt piled high against the bright green grass, the solemn faces of his friends and Pastor Ed, the silence as they all gathered around the mound. The eerie silence amidst the towering pine trees, hearing the wind rustle the leaves of the nearby bushes. Bill was locked into a place in his head, unused to cemeteries – his parents and Donna's parents' graves were here. Eva, too, but her homegoing was a celebration. The brief ceremony for Donna and then the customary placing of the roses into the grave. That nearly brought him down. And the watery song of his friends clustered around, singing the doxology, "Praise God from Whom all blessings flow. Praise Him all creatures here below. Praise Him above all Heavenly Hosts. Praise Father, Son, and Holy Ghost. Amen."

And his turning to Romyn and Earl and burying his tears into her shoulder as Earl reached out and grabbed his hand and prayed under his breath. The consoling and comforting touch of Pastor Ed, his friend. A glimpse of Kellie being comforted by Jeremy and Tafani. The respectful distance of the funeral people. Paul, standing by himself, looking bereft.

And the vision of Michael Langster ushering Pam away from the grave, his hand resting possessively on the small of her back.

❁

"Jill, honey. We are going for a drive today." Ed looked at Jill who indifferently spooned her Cheerios and then chewed thoughtfully on her whole wheat toast.

"Where are we going, Eddy?" she asked, her voice without emotion.

"We are going to the Cities and we're going to stop at Emily's grave and then we are going to visit Robby in the place where he lives." Might as well lay it on the table.

Jill didn't seem to respond. She looked around the sun-bright kitchen with its homey table and chairs, the smell of the Dunn Brothers coffee filling the air, and the loud purr of Biep, who had moved in onto Ed's chair the minute he vacated it. She looked absently at him and said, "Why are we going there, Ed?"

Ed walked over to where she sat erectly in the chair and kneeled down at her knees. Looking imploringly into her face, he said, "Jill, today is the first day of the rest of our lives. We need to say 'goodbye' to Emily and we need to say 'hello' to Robby so that we can get...past where...we're stuck. We're stuck, Jill. You and me. You are stuck in a place in the past and I am stuck in the present. With you, whom I love beyond life itself. But we need to move forward together and to do that, we need to make this trip."

"Whatever you say, Eddy. Do I need to dress up?"

"No, you're fine with what you're wearing. How about we plan to go in a half hour?" *This fixation with clothing was frustrating. Where did that come from? A throwback to years ago?*

Ed stood at the kitchen sink, looking out the window but not seeing the bright shout of purple of the morning glories, not hearing the twittering of the wrens around the birdhouse next to the garage, the chittering of the squirrels running up the oak trees and scampering out onto the branches and then jumping from one tiny swinging branch to another. Trusting that it would hold. Trusting in Him who holds the outcome of today.

"It will be fun, Jill. We'll stop for lunch and we'll stop at that little jewelry shop in Minnetonka where I get the charms for your bracelet."

252

She looked at him confusedly. Ed walked into their bedroom and returned with the charm bracelet he had been making for Emily these last ten years. "This bracelet, Jill. I've asked the jewelry shop to add an extender and we have a special new charm for you that we will get today. I think you'll really like it." *I hope.*

Jill took the bracelet and laid it over her wrist, fingering the different charms pensively. "I gave this to…" and Ed interrupted her, "You gave this to Sophie, Earl and Romyn's girl. That was inappropriate, Jill," he said somewhat severely.

"It was only a gift," she said in a small voice.

"But, too much—and it's yours. It's a gift to you, to remember Emily. That's what we will be concentrating on today. Do you think you are up to it?"

"Yes, I can do that, Eddy. I can go there — I will get ready." Jill moved off to the bathroom and he could hear her toilette, the running of the water, the sound of the hair spray spritzing her long blonde hair, the closing of the drawers as she tidied up the sink. *My sweet Jill. This is a risk. I will remember these last moments if it doesn't work out, but I pray to God, my Savior, that it does. Help us, Jesus. Be with us.*

The beautiful summer day and the light traffic were blessings on their drive to the western suburbs of Minneapolis. Ed felt his spirits rise in hopefulness as they neared the outskirts of the metropolitan area. Jill was characteristically quiet and would answer his brief questions when asked, but placidly accepted the drive and its purpose. *I don't think she knows what's ahead,* he worried. They had stopped at the jewelry store in Minnetonka and had purchased the new charm and the extender. Jill had seemed delighted with the charm bracelet and the new charm, a small golden apple encircled with a wrapping of silver. *May the words of Proverbs 25:11 inspire me today*

at Emily's grave, Ed thought. *Give me the right words, Jesus, I beg You.*

Jill thoughtfully examined the charm bracelet for several minutes and then looked pensively out the window as they turned onto Highway 5, heading towards the cemetery. Fields of corn and soybeans stretched as far as the eye could see, the view bisected with a towering blue sky. A perfect day. They intersected with Highway 41 and Ed noted Jill's rising agitation with dismay. As they approached the slight hill that was just to the east of Victoria, her body began to shake uncontrollably and she let out a low moan.

"Jill, honey, Jill honey. We'll get past this in just a minute. Hold on, honey. Hold on," he soothed. She looked out the window frantically as if trying to escape and then she slumped down in her seat as far as the seatbelt would let her, hands over her streaming eyes.

"Eddy! Eddy!" she cried. "Take me home. Take me home from here." Sobs began to wrack her body and Ed looked for a safe place to pull over. He quickly pulled into the parking lot of the Dairy Queen, unbuckled his seatbelt and reached over to embrace his sobbing wife.

"We're past it, Jill. We're at the Dairy Queen in Victoria. Let's just sit here for a minute. Let's release your seatbelt, hon, to make you more comfortable."

"I don't want to see it. I can't." Her voice hiccoughed through her tears.

"We won't go back there, Jill. We'll drive home another way."

"Why did you bring me back here, Eddy? Why? I can't stand it. I can't stand to be here," she sobbed in a tiny, muffled voice.

"You're going to have to be strong, Jill. I know you can do it. We have to be strong together so we can go beyond this place—this awful place of ten years ago. Where the accident happened. We will face it together and then we can go on. Until we do, we'll just be living in a kind of limbo. We can face it with God's help. Let's just pray now, can we, sweetheart?" Ed gently took her hands away from her wet eyes and lovingly stroked her forehead, moving her wet hair away from her face and tucking it behind her ears. She shifted in her seat and tried to sit upright, and then she nodded slightly, looking into Ed's wet eyes imploringly.

"Dear Jesus, our Savior. We are two broken people, sitting here and crying out to You. Help us overcome this pain." His voice broke. "Our pain of the awful accident, losing Emily, and losing Robby, too. Though we never give up hope that Robby…" Here Jill's voice shrieked in pain and Ed held her close and just prayed silently. *Help us, Jesus. Help us, Jesus.*

They sat awkwardly together for a long time, seemingly frozen in place as Ed prayed silently and Jill wailed her pain. A red pickup pulled into the parking lot beside them and a burly construction worker looked at them curiously before walking into the DQ. In a few minutes he returned with two bottles of water and handed them to Ed through the open driver-side window.

"Here ya' go, buddy," he said with a brief smile, before jumping back into his truck.

"Let's go and sit at that picnic table, Jill," Ed urged. "It will be good to stretch our legs after that long drive."

She looked at him and pulled up her shirt to blot her eyes, then smiled bleakly as Ed opened the glove compartment and pulled out a small box of tissues. He helped her out of the car and over to the wooden picnic table where she sat down silently, tears still streaming from her eyes. Ed sat with her on the bench, their bodies close together as if for warmth.

"I remember the rain and the noise of the truck. I remember being so cold. Emily was so cold and I couldn't warm her up. We took her to that place and they tried to warm her up, too, but she was too cold. That was a hospital, wasn't it, Eddy?" She looked at him anxiously.

"Yes, we took her to the hospital near here," he replied.

"And we were covered in mud. All of us. We must have fallen into a creek or something, do you think, Eddy? That we were all covered in mud? We were all so filthy."

"The car rolled into the ditch, Jill, and it had been raining so the ground was very wet and muddy."

"That's why Emily was so cold. She couldn't get warm from that – and she left us because she couldn't get warm, didn't she, Eddy? She was just too cold." Tears poured from her eyes and she clutched her water bottle convulsively. "And I couldn't get her warm, Eddy. I tried! I tried to warm her up. I held her close – you remember that, don't you, Eddy? That I tried!"

"Yes, I remember that, Jill," he reassured her, his mind taken back to that desperate scene of Jill clinging to the stretcher where Emily was placed after being lifted from underneath the overturned car. "I remember how hard you tried, honey."

She laid her head on the picnic table and sobbed anew. Ed patted her back, gently stroked the back of her neck, and shifted close to her as if by his firm presence he could push away the memory of that cold day. They sat like that for a long time. In the near distance, Highway 5 traffic passed relentlessly and there was the sound of cars pulling into the Dairy Queen parking lot, the sound of "order up" for take-out orders of hamburgers and Blizzard shakes, the smell of French fries in the air, and the laughter of small children who talked with their parents as they reached for their bags of food. Their excited anticipation was contagious as the parents smiled and gently reproved their manners.

The sound of childish laughter seemed to awaken something in Jill's memory for she slowly raised her head, her face ravaged by memory and said to him, "Do you remember Emily's laugh Ed?" She looked at him, but the expression in her eyes was distant. "Do you remember that giggle – how we couldn't help but laugh, too? I remember you said, it was a – 'chortle.' A chortle, you said, and I laughed at you because that was such a strange word. Funny that word should come back to me now." She shook her head as if to clear her mind.

She's spoken more in the last five minutes than she has in the months since she's been home, he thought.

"What else do you remember, Jill?" he asked. A direct approach but that was a mistake as she seemed to be caught up in a memory from which he was excluded. Ed stretched out his legs under the wooden table and took a long drink from his water bottle.

As if no time had passed, Jill continued, "Funny, I can't remember his face."

"Whose face, Jill?" Ed asked.

"That young man. Robby, you said? He was in our family. I think I knew that. He was part of our family, Ed?"

"He is our son, Jill," he replied.

"Our son." She stared at the grain of the picnic table and began to pick up slivers of wood with her fingernails and pry them apart from the woodgrain until they broke off. "Our son... Robby?" she said. "The one driving?"

"Yes, our only son. He was driving the car when we had the car accident."

"The accident. It was an accident?"

"Yes, a car crash. It wasn't Robby's fault. It wasn't anyone's fault. It just happened."

"Why, Eddy? Why did it happen?" She looked at him earnestly as if her life depended upon his answer.

Ed took her hands in his and said, "We will never know the answer to that question, Jill. That's the one question that has no answers. Why accidents happen and our loved ones are taken from us...our little Emily."

"Is it God's will, Eddy? God's?"

"God does not want anyone to die, Jill. That's not His will. To take our Emily from us. To..." *How do I explain Robby's blindness?* "To have Robby suffer such an injury to his eyes. God wants only the best for us all. Each one of us. But in this world things happen. Awful things. Like what happened to us. Our little family."

"Where is Emily now, Eddy?" she asked.

"She's in Heaven with Jesus now, Jill, but we can take a little visit now to Pleasant View cemetery where she is buried. Do you feel up to it?"

She shuddered convulsively and then said, "I think we need to go back where the accident happened, Ed. It's just – over there, isn't it?" She nodded towards the east.

"Are you sure that's a good idea?"

She nodded slowly. "I think I need to go back there. That place...is like a black hole in my mind. Whenever I approach the black hole it seems as if it will overwhelm me. Like a swirling tornado. And for a long time I let the tornado take me with it. And I was in the swirl, in the darkness. I don't think I can ever get over that unless I go back to that...place. Help me, Eddy. Help me to be there, would you?"

He held her close and said, "Of course, I'll be there. I'm always here. If you can't do it, you just let me know and we'll turn around immediately and go from there."

She gave him the first real smile of the trip, maybe the first real smile of the last few months. "I know you will, Eddy. I know you."

35

The children were busy carrying sheets and blankets out into the backyard. Earl saw the passing parade from his wheelchair and wheeled over to the kitchen bay window to see what they were up to. The nanny, Beth Ann, was in the backyard looking after them so Earl wasn't too concerned about their whereabouts or safety. She was desultorily tossing a stick to Sam who ambled back slowly to her, dropping it at her feet every time and looking up expectantly.

That stick has to be covered in dog drool by now, Earl thought. *He's good at that game for the whole afternoon.*

Sunlight flooded the backyard and the children were busy creating a makeshift teepee, draping their pastel sheets and colorful fleece blankets over some long branches they'd leaned up against a small poplar tree. From the window Earl could hear Shiloh's bossy directions and could tell by the young boy's body language that Clay was resisting the female in the time-honored male prerogative. Earl watched them for a few minutes, seeing a poignant flashback to Jason in Clay's methodical rearrangement of blankets and branches. To Shiloh's dismay he insisted on re-doing one section of the teepee to make it sturdier. Earl smiled at Shiloh's expression, seeing her thwarted frustration.

Sophie and Brian were indifferent to the drama being played out between Shiloh and Clay. Sophie had poured a bucket of water into a small puddle of dirt and was carefully shaping a small mud pie village – a small adobe hut with a blockade and a moat around it. She had a strong stick and was happily creating new water canals and tributaries into her city, her face serene and happy. Brian, as usual, had his notebook and pencil in his hands. He pushed his glasses up on his nose as Earl watched, and studied the distant oak tree.

A bird, no doubt, Earl thought. *Probably a robin or a blue jay. A poem in the making.*

Beth Ann called to the children and told them it was time to come into the house for a lemonade and cookie break. They wandered in and gave a bit of resistance to Beth Ann's strong suggestion that they wash their hands, but then settled at the table and happily scarfed down chocolate chip cookies.

"Here, Daddy," Sophie said, handing Earl a cookie. He took it in his big hand from her delicate one and chomped it down noisily with lots of lip smacking which made her laugh. She leaned against his leg in the wheelchair and delicately nibbled her cookie, sipping occasionally from her lemonade glass. Clay and Shiloh continued their building argument over the kitchen table until Beth Ann told them to "Knock it off, you guys, or I'll make you all take a nap." That quieted them down.

Sophie laid her head down on Earl's upper thigh and he stroked her little blonde head with great tenderness. *These kids. These precious kids.* Not for the first time was he grateful to God for putting Clay and Sophie into their lives. Clay would probably be a handful when he was a teenager – *remember those Jason days well!* – but he and Romyn together would make it work. *Poor Lisa couldn't make it on her own, making her living and raising kids. She was failing at it.* His heart saddened at the thought. *Wonder where she is and what has happened to her?*

"Have you been writing a poem, Brian" he asked.

"Yes, I have been watching the birds in your backyard. There's a lot of different ones, probably because you have the bird feeders. If we weren't in the backyard, they'd come and feed and we could watch them more closely."

"Yes, Sam and I spend a lot of time at this window watching them. But I agree. They'll stay away when there are people in the backyard." He shifted gears. "Do you like the teepee?"

Brian paused for a moment and then carefully replied. "I like the idea of the teepee. But I'd like to see a real one covered in birchbark and hides with pine needles for bedding, a little fire with smoke wisping out the top..."

"We should be able to find a real one, Brian. We should plan a trip to a Native American village sometime. All of us. I bet we'd find an authentic one."

"You can't build a real teepee now, Brian, with real birchbark. You're not supposed to peel the bark off the trees. That kills them," Shiloh informed the group. Brian gave her a measured, thoughtful look.

"I'd like to write a poem about it. How it would be like to live next to the ground and trees like that. Without the barriers of walls and doors and windows."

"You'd freeze to death, Brian," Shiloh said assertively. "We need our houses in Minnesota. It's too cold here for teepees. Summer is okay..."

"But the natives did," he offered quietly. "Before..."

"Yeah, but they had lots of deer hides to keep warm. They made all their clothes from the deer. We learned that in school. Don't you remember?"

"James Fenimore Cooper," Earl said to Brian. "He was a great writer who wrote about the Indian tribes. I might have a book or two here that you can have." At the young boy's breaking smile, Earl said, "Let me look for them and the next time you come over to play..."

"We had Native Americans in North Carolina, too," Clay said derisively.

"Do you remember the tribes, Clay?" Earl asked.

"I don't remember. Cherokee, maybe?"

"We have Sioux and Chippewa here in Minnesota," Shiloh stated, ending the discussion.

There was a knock at the front door and Earl wheeled over and opened the door to the postman. "Certified letter. Need a signature," he said with a smile. "How's your day going, Earl?"

"Fine, just fine." With a broad smile, he nodded back toward the laughter in the kitchen and handed the paper back to the postman, glancing down at the return address. *Minnesota Department of Human Services.* He placed the letter on Romyn's mission oak desk and wheeled back into the kitchen. "Hey kids, who wants to play 'Go Fish'?"

Jennie's last day at the Fancy Food Show filled her with excitement and optimism. Her interviews with the owners of the small organic herb companies that Chris had arranged were educational, thought-provoking, and fun. She found her passion revved the more she talked to them. Her notebook was filled with recipe ideas, packaging thoughts, and distribution and marketing ideas. *Why hadn't I thought of website sales?* she thought, giving herself a virtual slap on the forehead. The golf cart had taken her from one interview to another and she actually found herself feeling full of energy as she made her way crosstown to the Roosevelt. It was only five o'clock. Maybe she would have that dinner with Chris after all. Time to change, call Paul, review her texts.

She stopped at the corner of 8th Avenue and 42nd Street and sent a quick text to Chris. That done, she slackened her pace and began her people-watching in earnest. Yesterday she was too tired to even look at one more thing—today she was able to celebrate the diversity of New York City. All shapes and sizes, colors, and attitudes. Heads bobbing purposefully down the sideway, intent on a mission; others ambling as she was, drinking in the atmosphere. Slender, young fashionistas in their Manolo Blahniks – *how do they walk in those things?* – and frail old white-haired women bundled in shapeless coats and furry hats, even on this warm June day. Tattooed muscular body builders and Hasidic Jews walked side by side, the latter's white shirts, black pants, and wide-brimmed black hats curiously reminding her of the Amish of central Minnesota.

If I had time, I'd duck up to St. Patrick's Cathedral on 51ˢᵗ Street, she thought, *but that would be cutting it short. Funny, I haven't heard from Paul today aside from the 'good morning' text.* She'd connected with him late last night and he talked about the farm activities. She tried to remember what Paul was doing on the farm today, but her mind was so filled with thoughts of the Fancy Food Show that she couldn't shoehorn a Peace Ridge memory into her crammed brain. *I think I'll have some time to write down my thoughts before dinner,* she promised herself.

Babbo! That sounded fun. She'd researched the menu on her iPhone last night and was intrigued by the classic Northern Italian menu. *It's going to be hard to choose – I could take a chance on tripe for once. Probably will be done really well, not stinky like the French do it. Lamb's Tongue is intriguing though I can't even imagine what it'd look like. How do they make it tender? One thing is for sure: I'm saving room for the Affogato, the coffee ice cream dessert. I've been wanting to make that myself ever since I saw the recipe in Marcella Hazen's cookbook.*

These culinary thoughts wafted her all the way to the Roosevelt and she found herself anticipating a fun evening. Chris sent a text regretting that he was not able to personally pick her up because he had a client that was running late, but he had sent a town car for her which would pick her up at 6:30PM. Now that was an unaccustomed luxury. And as the car made its way downtown, she found herself curiously happy to be alone and able to take in New York without having to make conversation. She was rather dreading that, in fact, envisioning a flirtatious and seductive sub-text to everything they talked about over dinner.

But as it turned out Chris was friendly but scrupulously businesslike. He was aware that a beautiful blonde woman on his arm reflected happily on himself and there was a subtle preening that did not go unnoticed by Jennie. There was a welcoming homey feeling to the small, intimate Babbo that encouraged a deeper conversation about families, personal histories, and aspirations. Tables were placed along the wall with its cream-colored wainscoting and interesting scenes of Italy. Double boudoir-type uplights cast a warm glow to the tables and the double thickness of white napery promised a peak culinary experience. The conversation over dinner flowed easily as they shared a passion for Italian food and familiar ingredients cooked in unique and distinctive ways. Chris was skillful in the art of conversation in a way that was interesting and delightful, and without even thinking about it, Jennie made an involuntary comparison to her laconic husband with his direct Norwegian conversational style. *That is unfair to Paul,* she thought regretfully, *but I do enjoy a good conversation.*

She brought her mind back to Chris's soliloquy about his summers spent in the Greek islands with his divorced father and younger brother. "I honestly considered just being a vagabond," he confessed. "It would have been so easy to just bounce around Europe and enjoy life to its fullest."

"Yes, that must have been tempting," she replied, *if you have the money.* "What changed your mind?"

"I saw too many rich Europeans with inherited wealth that just drifted from one fashionable hot spot to another. Cannes during the film festival. Munich for the Octoberfest. Sundance in Utah, South by Southwest in Texas. It seemed like an aimless way to live. And endless travel. My mother and father both worked hard for their money and I didn't want to squander that legacy, that gift of discipline. It felt as if my life was worth more than one party after another. After a while even a glass of vintage champagne seems flat and boring. Speaking of which," he smiled into her eyes, "how about an after-dinner drink in the bar at your hotel?"

"Oh, Chris! You've spoiled me way too much already. I don't know how to thank you for all you've done, but I think I need to head back there and get ready for my trip home tomorrow. Get a good night's sleep – early flight back." *Oops, shouldn't have mentioned sleep; I don't like the gleam in his eye.*

"You'll have time for a small glass of Bailey's, I'm sure?" he teased. "It'll help you sleep better anyway."

"Well, I don't know…"

"I'll take that as a 'Yes,'" he affirmed.

Chris was polite and made no overt moves on Jennie as the Lincoln town car made its way to Midtown. Jennie wanted nothing more than to get to her room and get organized for the flight before falling into a good restful sleep, but she was feeling quite an obligation to Chris. The meal alone was over $200. He had spared no expense on her and she had no illusions that he wanted something from her in return, but wasn't crass enough to demand it. They pulled up to the door of the Roosevelt and the driver came around to open the door for her. Jennie got out as Chris also got out of the car on the other side and came around to take her arm possessively.

"Chris, I am going to say 'goodnight' here, and thanks again for all you've done for me." She held out her hand for a goodbye handshake.

"Jennie, I'm not going to take 'No' for an answer," he replied, pulling her close to him.

"Yes, you are," she said firmly as she gently pushed him away. "Yes, you are. You have been really kind and helpful and I don't know how to thank you for all you've done, but I'm going to take a raincheck on that drink. Maybe next year when I come back for the show." She smiled to soften her refusal.

His look was stony and he abruptly turned on his heel and got into the backseat of the car, slamming the door with unnecessary force. Jennie stood there in shock. *Is that how it works in New York City now? You wine and dine and you get into a woman's bed in return?* She turned to go into the door of the Roosevelt when she heard the ding of a text.

"Forgive me. I don't take rejection well. Chris."

265

Jennie placed her cell phone back into her purse and walked slowly into the lobby of the hotel on her way to the elevator bank. After the emotional intensity of the last fifteen minutes, she was grateful to be back into the welcoming anonymity of the big city hotel. She paused for a moment and re-oriented herself. As she passed the back of an elegant, green satin armchair, she spied the lanky, skinny blue jeans that extended long under the coffee table. Legs she would recognize in her sleep.

Jennie stood in front of the armchair and looked down at her tired, sleeping husband. *He's exhausted* was her fleeting, compassionate thought before he stirred and opened his eyes.

"Some surprise, huh?" he said.

"Oh, Paul, honey, I am so sorry I wasn't here. What time did you arrive?" She crouched down at the arm chair and touched his arm lightly.

He sat up in the chair and brushed his farmer hand over his face, tipping his John Deere hat askew. "Got into LaGuardia about four o'clock, here at the hotel at a little after six, maybe six-thirty."

"Oh, Paul. That's just when I left! I am so sorry! I had dinner in the Village with the director of the association. I...wouldn't have gone if I'd seen you. I am so sorry."

"It was meant to be a surprise. I thought New York would be the last place you'd expect to see me. I kept calling your room but then just thought I'd wait here until you came in. Where'd you say you went?"

"I went to Greenwich Village to have dinner at Babbo. With Chris, the director of the association. We talked about..." *I'm babbling,* she thought. *He's not interested in that.* "Have you eaten anything?"

"Peanut butter crackers on the plane."

"Do you want to eat in the bar here? Or we could go to the room and order room service."

"Yeah, that sounds good. Don't want to sit any longer in this big ol' unfriendly place."

"I am sorry I spoiled your surprise, Paul," she said tenderly, as she took his arm and led him to the elevators. "What do you think of New York City?"

"They can keep it. All these people. The traffic in from the airport just about had me turning around and taking the next plane out."

"How did you manage the tickets, Paul?"

"I wasn't born yesterday. Just ordered them online and checked in," he replied sourly, as if to say, *I may be a farmer but I'm not stupid.*

"Oh, I didn't mean it that way. I just...wondered about the farm...and getting away."

"David has it all under control. I did the morning chores and he will do them tonight. Done by now, I expect. Didn't go out into the fields. And stop apologizing, Jennie," he said, stopping her words in their tracks. "It just didn't work out like I wanted it to."

They entered Jennie's hotel room and Paul walked over and looked out the window at the twinkling lights of midtown Manhattan. Jennie put her purse on the bed and walked over to him, placed her arms around his waist and laid her face on his familiar back. "What do you think of *this* view?" she asked, her voice muffled.

"It's interesting. Bet you can see all the way out to Queens in the daytime." He turned around and hugged her. "Where's my welcome-can't-believe-you-are-here-kiss, Jen?" he asked. Her answering kiss made up for the spat on the way to the airport and the spoiled surprise. "And now let's look at that room service menu," he said, when they broke apart finally, smiling at one another.

It was nearly midnight when he'd finished his hamburger and beer and Jennie finished off his ice cream, talking over what she had learned at the show. She had spread all the brochures out on the bed before she'd left for the show earlier in the day and Paul picked them up thoughtfully and looked at each one.

"So, this is what it takes," he said. "Big undertaking. The 'Big Boys.' That's what you said when you wanted to check it out."

"Yeah. Lots to think about."

"Here's one more thing to think about. I want to spend tomorrow here with you, Jennie. I know this is your dream, the big city, and all. My ticket is good for a return to Minneapolis on Thursday. Let's spend the day tomorrow in New York City and you can show me what it's all about. So, we need to change your ticket."

Jennie gave him a surprised look and then grabbed her room key, noted the wireless code, and then booted up her computer to Delta.com. "Oh, Paul! There's so much to see. Can't wait to show my favorite places to you!"

36

But as it turned out, the large comfortable bed was hard for both of them to leave in the morning and after a leisurely room service breakfast, they made their way down to the hotel lobby well after ten in the morning, their tight arm-in-arm closeness a cue to the warm night spent together. Paul was his usual good-humored self and Jennie was surprisingly giddy with excitement. Paul repeatedly calmed her down and reminded her to save her energy for another surprise tonight. She gave him a puzzled look.

They walked hand in hand to St. Patrick's Cathedral on 51st and 5th Avenue and toured the vestibule and sanctuary in silence, and then Jennie suggested they walk up 5th Avenue along Central Park to see The Frick Collection on 70th Street and its collection of Rembrandt, Ingres, and Renoir. Their conversation was a rambling contrast of the happenings in Peace Ridge Village and Paul's observations of the big city, but he was absolutely stunned into silence at the Frick mansion and its air of refined 20th century elegance and culture.

"I'm not dressed good enough to be here," was his first response, despite his totally respectable khakis and clean plaid shirt.

"Well, no one else is either," Jennie observed, watching the throngs of school children who were barely controlled by exasperated school teachers and volunteers. They wandered around until both of them were stopped in their tracks at Renoir's *La*

Promenade. The young dewy-faced French mother with her exquisite daughters was placed in an alcove under a staircase, as if an afterthought.

Both Paul and Jennie studied it for a long time and then Paul turned to Jennie and said, "Let's go back to the hotel now. I think I've seen all I need to see of New York. It would take a lifetime to see all the beautiful art that this world has to offer, and I can't take it all in. I don't know how to appreciate it. I can tell you soil moisture and chemicals, the right temperature to plant, and the right time to harvest— life from the land— but I can't tell you how to bring life to a canvas like this. It's genius. And it makes me feel ...inadequate, somehow."

Jennie turned to him and kissed him.

In the hotel room as they lay naked and curled together under the sheets, he confessed, "Jennie, this world outside of Peace Ridge, I can see how you long for it. I can see that Peace Ridge represents only a small chapter— maybe even just a paragraph — in the book of life that is this big world. You have had so much more experience than me – you've chosen to live with me in Peace Ridge. It still amazes me!"

To that, she answered with a passionate kiss.

They both slept then and Paul shook her awake in the late afternoon and told her to make herself fashionable for a dinner on the town. He wouldn't say where and she was totally surprised when the taxi dropped them off at Del Posto, the classic Italian restaurant on the newly fashionable west side of Chelsea.

"But Paul, how did you figure this out?" she asked.

"I have my sources," he said mysteriously, and then because he was unrepentantly truthful, said, "Delaney recommended it."

"Oh, Delaney. Still in London, I think, right?"

"Yes, still tilting at windmills."

It was fair to say they didn't think about Delaney once during their delicious meal. Jennie had collected all of Lidia Bastianich's cookbooks and was intrigued by every offering on the menu, but restricted herself to *Branzino con guanciale,* the sea bass with cured pork jowl. She picked out Paul's choice,

270

knowing how much he loved pork chops, and she couldn't wait to see the *maiale in cassoeula Lombarda*, the pork chop tenderloin with trotters and cabbage, wanting to see if it actually arrived with pig's feet. She delighted in Paul's confused expression. The meal was fantastically expensive and fantastically delicious. When Jennie thought about it later, a dinner with a loved one was totally different from a business meal, even if the food itself was comparable. There was an ease, a finishing of one another's sentences, thoughts begun that were completed by the other, lengthy companionable silences.

"There is no one else in the world I'd rather be with than you in New York right now," she declared as the *panna cotta* "to share" was delivered to their table, and shortly afterwards, the $350 check.

"Well, don't make it a once-a-week occasion." Paul laughed, digging out his Mastercard.

Later he whispered to her, "The young French mother, she looked just like you. Long curly blonde hair, sweet rosebud mouth, rosy cheeks..."

"Younger than me," she replied sleepily.

"No, not really. You're both ageless."

And then he added, "She was painted in 1876...you're about 150 years younger than her."

She gently slapped his face.

37

Jill knelt at Emily's gravesite for a long time. Pleasant View Cemetery was quiet as always, an oasis of green amid clumps of pine trees and white birches. Ed was concerned Jill would not be able to manage the visit but she insisted despite her complete emotional breakdown at the accident site.

She had walked up and down the ditch, crying wildly and pounding her shoulders and breasts, throwing off Ed's comforting arms until she had collapsed at a small rise near the ditch, her sobs muffled by the wheatgrass and alfalfa of the nearby field. Ed had perched nearby, crying out to Jesus, until he heard her sobbing ease and then he scooted over to where she had flung herself and handed her his handkerchief.

"I was able to push it away," she said brokenly, her face buried in the grass.

"Push it away?"

"The blackness...the cloud. It wanted to cover me up, but I knew I couldn't let it. I prayed, Eddy, I prayed! I said 'God, please help me, please help me,' over and over. Then just when I feared it might come back again, I saw a bright white light that just filled my mind. It made me feel peaceful, like I could live here again. I wanted to live in that light forever..."

"Thank You, Father God," Ed whispered to himself. Jill pushed herself up wearily, brushing off the dirt and grass from her clothes. She sat lightly with her arms on her knees, looking up and down the ditch. "She was here, Eddy," she said finally.

"We were all here, Jill, then..."

"No, I mean she was here in the light. Just now. Emily was here as part of the light. Just before the peace, I saw her, saw her face filled with joy. That's where she is now, Eddy. She's with the Light."

"With Jesus," Ed confirmed.

"Yes, with Jesus," Jill said, looking into his face searchingly. "Do you believe me, Ed?"

"Yes, I do, Jilly. Yes, I do. I have felt that, too. And we know how much she loved Him. Remember the little kids' Sunday School and how she sang, louder than all the others, 'Jesus loves me, this I know...' her little prayers at night, how she prayed for you and me. For Robby. For her little pre-school friends. For our dog..."

"Our dog, Eddy. I just remembered her. Our Miranda. Do you remember her?"

"Yes, I do," he said tenderly.

"'Now I lay me down to sleep, I pray the Lord my soul to keep. If I should die before I wake, I pray the Lord my soul to take,'" Jill recited. "Do you remember that, Eddy? She said that every night. She'd look up at me and say, 'My soul, my soul loves Jesus.' Do you think she knew what her soul was? What that meant?"

"I don't think we have to worry about it. You saw her in the light, thanks be to God," he said, caressing Jill's shoulders lightly. "She's in the Presence."

They sat there peacefully for a long while. Traffic was busy on Highway 5, but it didn't seem to bother Jill, even when large trucks from Walmart and Home Depot barreled up the highway, their loud engines disrupting the peaceful quietness of the green field where they sat. Ed studied Jill covertly, noticing that there was a blush to her cheeks despite the tear tracks and her red-rimmed eyes.

Ed prayed silently. *I am grateful, Father God, for this deliverance from bondage. You are the one who restores. You are the one who brings Your peace to troubled hearts and minds. I am eternally grateful. I was fearful in my weakness, but You buried my frailty in Your strength. Your unbreakable, inexpressible strength and might. Thank You. Thank You for Jill. For this life.*

Jill said suddenly, "Eddy, I am hungry. Let's go back to that Dairy Queen and get something to eat. And then let's go to the cemetery and see Emily...her grave."

"Are you sure?"

"Yes, I'm sure."

Now Jill bent forward and brushed the gravestone, tenderly tracing the name, Emily Marisa Mitchell, over and over. She was crying freely again but there was a look of peaceful acceptance on her face. Finally she accepted his handkerchief again and loudly blew her nose. Ed looked around the cemetery. They were the only ones there on this midweek day. The cemetery had been mowed recently and several families had placed flower bouquets on the gravesites. The little teddy bear that Ed had left a few months ago was faded and a bit bedraggled, but Jill placed it upright against the stone.

"When we come again, we'll bring flowers and another teddy bear," she said softly. "She loved her little stuffed animals. Remember?"

"Yes, I remember, Jill."

She then turned to him and looked at him with a searching and puzzled expression. "Where have I been, Eddy?"

How to explain? Ed reached over and helped her to her feet and held her tenderly. He whispered in her ear. "Jill, you went away to a safe place where you didn't have to endure hurting. Emily was hurt and you couldn't bear that. So you went to place where you didn't have to feel. But now God has shown you that Emily is not hurting, she's in the light, she's happy. And you can share that happiness with her. Here. And now."

Jill pulled away from him and walked over to the nearby bench and sat down. Ed followed slowly and sat down beside her. Jill fingered the charm bracelet, looking at each charm intently before turning the bracelet to the next one.

"Moonstone. Her birthday stone," she said finally. She counted each charm until she got to thirteen and then she broke down in tears once again. "Thirteen," she choked out. "She would be thirteen. Was I gone that many years, Eddy?"

"Yes, Jill. But you couldn't help it. You were in deep grief and you went where you could feel safe."

"Safe from feelings. Safe from life itself. From losing Emily. From Robby..." She turned to Eddy. "I know there's something wrong about our son. I don't know that I can face it. When I say his name, the blackness starts building in the distance and I feel it barreling towards me like a swirling tornado cloud."

"You don't have to face it today, Jill. *'Each day has enough trouble of its own.'*" He quoted Jesus.

"Thank you, my sweet," she said simply, using an endearment he hadn't heard in ten long years. And that's when Ed's tears fell.

Make a joyful noise to the Lord, all the earth!
Serve the Lord with gladness!
Come into his presence with singing!
Know that the Lord, he is God!
It is he who made us, and we are his;
We are his people, the sheep of his pasture.

Titos and Maria sat down exhausted at the kitchen table in their rented house. Getting this restaurant ready – although all the steps were familiar—was taking the stuffing out of them.

It seems much harder now, Titos mused. *Things that used to be easy to do take much longer now. Maybe it's Minnesota. Maybe it's just us. We're not as young and energetic as we were.*

They had a long conversation over their checklist for the grand opening next weekend. Maria had made a delicious *choriatiki,* the famous Greek salad of fresh tomatoes loaded with olives and feta cheese with the distinctive taste of fresh oregano for their evening meal. They enjoyed her artisanal bread along with a small glass each of retsina but both were preoccupied with the task at hand. Maria was in charge of the bakery and desserts and she had that totally under control as usual, but Titos was worried about the mainstays of the menu. He had confirmed that a local farmer near Little Falls would be able to supply the quantities of lamb required for the menu, but he hadn't had a chance to go over and meet the man in person, something he always did.

"Tomorrow, I need to go to Little Falls and meet Joshua, the farmer who is selling us our lamb. If he can't commit to giving us the amount we need regularly, we'll be hurting. What he sent us for this month is high quality, so I hope he's able to keep it up.

"Don't worry, my Titos. It will work out. Always has," Maria signed.

"Yes, I know. But I still worry. People here in Peace Ridge Village, they like beef. And chicken. I am going to have to convince them that lamb is delicious. That's why I have prepared some special dishes for this weekend. My lamb souvlaki. Kleftiko. Maybe they'll taste them and think 'This is what I have been missing,'" he declared. He flipped his yellow pad and reviewed his "to do" list.

"Remember how it went in New York, Titos?" Maria reminded him. "It didn't take long."

That took both of them down a long trip along Memory Lane and they sat quietly together, lost in thought.

"Have you been in touch with Father Daniel for the *agiasmos*, his blessing?" Maria asked.

"Yes, he'll be here this weekend. We don't need to worry about him."

"I just wish Jeremy could be here," Maria signed sadly.

"Just like the government. Schedule things at their convenience not anyone else's. He has to go – just for a couple of days, but Tiff will be here. She'll be a good help to you, Maria. Count on that."

"Yes, but Jeremy..."

"It'll be okay, Maria. It'll be okay."

"Nearly ready to go, Brian?" Michael paused at the bedroom door. Brian turned at the sound of his father's voice. He took a sticky note and marked a page in his Audubon bird book and then closed his notebook slowly and stashed it in his backpack. Snow had been slumbering on the bed but lifted his head eagerly at the sound of Michael's voice. He stood up and stretched and jumped down to Brian's side, his little dirty white body swinging from side to side with tail-wagging pleasure.

"Can Snow come with us?" Brian asked.

"I'll call Pam. I'm sure it'll be okay. We have to be sure that Bradley isn't allergic. I'll call her."

"Okay, I'm ready." Brian thought about the young man he was about to meet. *He is older but he has Down Syndrome, so maybe he won't have an attitude like most of the teenagers I know.* Brian liked Pam but he mostly liked the way his father whistled and sang when they'd been together or he had talked to her on the phone. He was often lonely himself but it was much harder when he saw loneliness in his dad. His mom was different— she covered up her loneliness with wine and laughter. But it was there. He saw it and he didn't know what to do about it.

"Dad, can I borrow your phone for a minute? Just want to send a text to Mom."

Michael handed him his iPhone as he got their stuff together for the trip to the Cities. Water bottles, leash and food dish for Snow, a bunch of flowers from their little flower garden to give to Pam.

They stopped along the way in Arbor Lakes to pick up some cupcakes at Nadia Cakes and it was nearly noon when they arrived at Pam's house in Bloomington. She had planned a backyard barbeque for them and then they were going to visit

Como Park. Michael kissed Pam's cheek as he handed her the now wilting flowers. She smiled and waved them into the house and called for Bradley. He was a tall, pudgy young man who garbled a greeting with a big toothy smile.

He grabbed Brian's hand right away and shook it enthusiastically. "Bwian, Bwian!" he said. "C'mere, c'mere," he urged. He bent to touch Snow's head lightly.

"Bradley, give him a moment, please. We'll have plenty of time to show him around the house," Pam said. "This is Michael."

Bradley gave a somewhat smaller smile to him and then turned once again to Brian and Snow and beckoned them into the house.

"Brad has been waiting all morning for you guys to come," Pam said.

"Us, too. We've been wanting to meet Bradley – and Tory, too, if she's home?"

"No, she's working. As usual."

"You have a nice place here, Pam," Michael said, looking around in appreciation. He was a stranger to interior decoration, but he could see a designer's touch in the restful palette of blue checked and paisley comfortable armchairs in a warm room lit by sunny yellow walls. A robin's egg blue built-in buffet held pieces of Polish pottery in the same shades of blue and yellow. Light blue linen drapes were open to reveal the bright green of a spacious backyard.

"The flowers fit right in," Pam laughed, placing the stoneware milk jug with the bright yellow daisies and blue-purple bachelor buttons on the coffee table.

"I planned it that way!" Michael said flirtatiously.

"Are you hungry?" Pam deflected.

"I could eat," he replied hopefully. "Brought some Nadia cupcakes."

"Yum," she said. Pam glanced out the window and saw that Bradley was leading Brian around the yard and pointing out each flower planter, his bicycle, the small windmill in the corner with its blades moving lazily in this warm weather, the fire pit, the barbeque, the picnic table.

Snow followed them around, his nose to the ground and indifferent to the chatter over his head. *Nice smells here.* He heard a brief burst of laughter from the big master coming out of the house and he looked up intently to see if there was food in the offing. And in a burst of energy began to run happily around the yard, making Bradley burst out in laughter, an infectious giggle that had both Pam and Michael laughing together.

"Oh, Snow," Brian said delightedly as he ran after him. That caused a small train as Bradley followed.

"Now, kids. Now, kids," Pam remonstrated.

That set the tone for the rest of the afternoon, indulgent adults watching playful children and one small dog. Plans to visit Como Park were postponed to another day. The sun was beginning to fall below the tree-lined fence in the backyard when Michael and Pam finished their barbequed sandwiches, iced tea, and cupcakes, both relaxed and at ease with one another in this gracious home, this peaceful backyard.

Michael slowly gathered Brian and Snow and walked with them to the car, with Bradley and Pam walking down the driveway to see them off to Peace Ridge.

"Thank you for a delicious lunch and a fun afternoon," Michael said. "I really enjoyed myself, and I think Brian did, too, didn't you, Brian?"

"Can Bradley come to Peace Ridge sometime and meet my other friends? I could take him to our special place up on the ridge near Skunk Creek."

"Pam and I will talk about it and see," Michael said, the familiar parental "wait-and-see" response. He turned to Pam. "Pam, would you be open to a day in the country?" he asked, knowing her response. *And maybe we can have some quiet time alone, too*, he thought.

The trip home was quiet with a tuckered-out dog and tuckered-out kid. Michael drove thoughtfully, his mind on the afternoon's cozy intimacy of the little "family" of sorts. Good conversation, ease of being with one another. This felt – *right* somehow — and he felt his heart sing. They'd spent time talking about Peace Ridge and he felt his heart lift when Pam said that someday she'd like to live in a small town. She was guileless, so he knew she wasn't dropping a hint. Just expressing her own sense of loneliness in the big city. Worried about when Bradley would want to have more independence, to live with a roommate, or maybe get married. If that was possible. And then what? For her? For the first time in the month or two they'd been dating, Michael felt that Pam was letting down her guard a bit, showing her vulnerability. He let his mind go on a little fantasy then – but stopped short.

Getting ahead of yourself, aren't you, Michael, my boy?

He turned into his driveway with a little more force than he'd planned and the shift in speed woke up the sleepy boy and yawning dog.

"Home already, Dad?" Brian asked.

After settling in later that evening, Michael handed his iPhone to Brian, who had a text from Delaney. Brian handed it back to his dad with not a word and then went to his bedroom. His little white dog paddled with clicking nails right behind him like his miniature shadow.

Michael read the brief text. "Hi Brian. Plan to stay here for a few weeks. Have possibility to work. Will write. Love you. Miss you. XXX. Mother."

Michael walked around the house and turned off the lights and locked the doors. Brian's door was ajar and he was sound asleep, but the table light on his little desk was still lit. Michael went turn it off and glanced at the poem that Brian had been writing. He picked it up and held it under the light.

The Broken Bird

Red breast shields the fragile heart,
Keen eyes see all, bright sparks.
Flitting gaily nest to nest,

Never-ending search for rest.

Startling plumage, thief of flame.
Conquest completed; just a game.
Omnivorous feeder, life inhaled,
Fermented berries, reason impaled.

Turdus migratorius, thrush, go – go!
Seldom victorious, it's all for show.
Crouching despair, the dark night brings,
But lo', dawn appearing, first to sing.

Robin redbreast, sing your song
Sing your heart out, all day long.
Your rich life of song, of sleep,
Finds love's brief moment short and sweet.

Brian Peterson
Observing bird life, age 9

Michael turned out the light and walked over to look at his young son. His young hurting son, the pain mostly buried but apparent in his poetry. *He sees. He feels.* Michael walked into the kitchen and furiously slammed his right fist into the palm of his left hand over and over, as if by so doing he could pound sense into the head of a literally care-less woman 4,000 miles away.

38

"Pastor, Ed, may I come over to see you some night?" The call came in as Jill and Ed returned from their emotionally exhausting trip to the Cities. Veronica had left the message on his machine. Ed knew that she had been released from the hospital and that Archie was staying with her in the house on the Ridge for a while, to take care of her and to 'keep watch,' as he said.

Everyone who loved the two of them was concerned about her and that she might relapse. Archie replied 'that it wasn't going to happen if he had any say in the matter' and that settled it for most of their friends. Romyn put Veronica on the prayer chain at church, knowing that most of the ladies and men of Valley Community were concerned but also curious. How to divulge but hold back on details that might pass as gossip. At the end of the day, she just said that they all needed to pray for people who were so despairing that they would choose death and annihilation over living. That should sober them up.

Romyn left a message, too, saying, "Please call me when you have a chance. We have a situation and I need your prayers."

Both he and Jill were tired and hungry from their trip to Minneapolis. Jill and Ed went into the kitchen where a hungry Biep argued that he needed attention first.

Jill turned to Ed and said, "I will feed Biep and you can check the messages. I heard the answering machine beeping."

Ed turned away to hide the sudden surge of feeling. *The first time! Biep! She called Biep's name!*

He picked up the messages and called both back immediately. Romyn suggested that they could come by tomorrow but Veronica picked up immediately as he was leaving the message and the despair and unhappiness in her voice made him instantly offer, "Please come here for a quick supper with us. We've just gotten home but the two of you are welcome at our kitchen table."

He heard her say to Archie, "Ed wants to know if we can come over for a quick bite," and then she came back on the phone and said, "We'd love it. And I am so grateful, Pastor. I am brought low and I need help."

Well, that's also a first, Ed thought. "I will tell Jill to put two more place settings on our kitchen table. You are both welcome. Say, in an hour?"

Ed stood in front of the open refrigerator. Eggs, cheese. Yup. Enough for a quiche. Even some broccoli. He wondered if there was enough to make a nice salad, too. He began to bring out the lettuce and vegetables from the crisper when Jill said, "If you want to make the quiche, I'll put the salad together."

Hiding his surprise, Ed said, "Do you remember Archie and Veronica, Jill? Veronica sat next to Romyn at the groundbreaking ceremony for The Jason House." At her slow nod, he continued, "Archie is her father. I don't think you've met him. Nice guy. Easy to get to know."

Despite the outsized emotions of the day, both of them had relaxed completely when they got home and that pleasant rapport between them continued through the dinner hour. Ed watched Jill closely, halfway expecting her to retreat from their visitors. Though she became quiet and observant at their conversation, she didn't seem to shut down and lock herself away as she had in the past. She mostly listened, looking from one face to another as if trying to fix her memory on them.

"Coffee?" Ed asked after the meal.

"Better not. A little too late in the day for me, Ed," Archie replied with a smile. "At *that* age, you know? Veronica will probably want some, right?" He turned to his daughter with a smile.

"Yes, I need the caffeine. It helps me keep my spirits up. As has this meal. Thank you, Jill – and Ed." She gave each a wobbly smile.

"Ed, I know Veronica wants to spend some time with you. I thought I'd take off for a couple of hours. I need to make a run to Tops Hardware — couple of small jobs around the house to be done and I need the right equipment. Let me help with the dishes, Jill, and then I'll just pop back here later. Sound like a plan?"

Jill smiled. "You don't need to help with the dishes. It's one of my little pleasures. The hot soapy water, tidying up the kitchen. Homey stuff."

Ed turned his head away from his guests to hide the tears that suddenly filled his eyes. That behavior was a definite throwback. *True to her nature. Pure Jill. That. Right there.*

"Veronica, how are you?" he asked, when the three of them had settled into his den, Biep sneaking in at the last minute and plopping himself down on Ed's leather office chair, extending and retracting his claws in post-supper relaxation. Ed shifted the visitor chairs to face one another and gestured Veronica to sit down. "How are you? Really?"

"Well, not too good, if you want the truth." Veronica looked around until she spotted the box of tissues on the desk. Reaching over, she grabbed a handful.

"Why don't you just tell me?" Ed said simply.

There was a long silence while Veronica stared down into her lap, twisting the tissues into shreds. "I tried to kill myself... and you helped save me. I couldn't be grateful about that at the time. I really wanted to die, Ed — Pastor — and I was not happy to find myself in that hospital bed." She sighed heavily and then sat quietly for a long time.

Help her, Jesus, Ed prayed silently.

"Dad has been staying with me because he thinks I'll finish it off for good the next time and after I was released from the hospital, I continually thought about how I could evade him." She shifted in her seat to stare out the window. "And make good on the promise I'd made to myself."

It was a perfect summer evening, the shadows lengthening over the white garage cast a purple light that gave a subtle pastel contrast to the warm sunlight as it retreated to the west. Veronica stared fixedly at the tall ficus tree with the hanging solar lanterns. Just as Ed was about to suggest they should move outside to the back garden to talk, she turned once again and looked him in the eyes.

"I need to learn how to forgive," she said slowly. "I won't get well until I can." She looked down at her hands pensively. "Yesterday I sat in the church at Donna's funeral and listened to what you said about forgiveness. At first, I thought it was all about Bill and how he forgave Donna. I was halfway paying attention but then you started to talk about forgiveness being the highest form of love and I realized that I couldn't ever … love again…even live again, unless I could do that. Forgiveness. I don't know how." She looked up at him with tears streaming down her face.

"Why don't you start at the beginning, Veronica?"

She again stared out the window but he knew she wasn't seeing the back yard of the parsonage. "I drove him to Susan," she said cryptically. "I destroyed all of them."

Ed nodded his head, a compassionate expression on his face.

"We wanted to start a family but Gary wanted us to be financially secure before…we had a child. But as these things happen, I got pregnant and I was really happy about it. Though I was worried and fearful about what Gary would say. He was concerned, unhappy with me, and ultimately furious because of *my* lack of protection. Finally, he began to nag me to have

an abortion. I resisted and resisted but he wore me down."
Veronica slumped down in her seat as if to retreat from her
thoughts. "I gave in but that was the beginning of my mental
problems. I didn't think I could live with...what I'd done."

"Father God, we lift our Veronica up to You now as she
relives the horror of this sin. Help her to forgive herself and
understand that even this has been covered by the blood of
Jesus. Give her Your strength now, we pray," Ed softly whispered the prayer.

Veronica stared into the distance, not acknowledging Ed's
prayerful words. "But in consequence, I withdrew from Gary. I
didn't want to take the risk of...intimacy...again and I wouldn't
let him touch me. Naturally, as these things go, he turned to
someone else. I don't think he thought of it as more than just
a fling – I suspected, of course – strange phone calls, secretive text messages, but I blamed myself for it anyway. I was...
depriving him...so I was the cause of his infidelity.

"I didn't expect that Susan would fall in love with him. And
he with her. And then the mess with Dane Johnson happened
and we lost everything. And I lost Gary...and so did Susan. I
lost my husband and our business and Susan lost someone she
loved." She added, under her breath, "And our friendship from
childhood."

She looked up at Ed in desolation. "All these years I've
been trying to forget all of this and get well but I don't get well.
I get worse. To the point of wanting to die. Every day I want
to die. I realized at the funeral, Pastor, that I need to forgive
to get well."

"Yourself, Veronica. For the baby. Then Gary, and then
Susan." He said the hard words kindly.

"Yes, and which will be hardest?"

"They'll all be hard. Forgiveness is hard work. I won't
sugarcoat it and tell you that it's easy. If it was easy, it wouldn't
have this power when we withhold it. It will take time. Are you
in touch with Susan at all?"

"No, not since…that time. She came to Gary's funeral and tried to seek my forgiveness and to…offer comfort in her own way, but I couldn't deal with it at the time and haven't been able to face any of it since then. I don't want to go back there, Pastor. Forgiveness means I have to go back there…"

"Yes, you will, Veronica, I am sorry to say. That is part of the healing process. But you don't have to do it all at once. You can do it in stages and you don't have to do it alone. There are people – psychotherapists – who specialize in forgiveness and there are lots of resources for you to dip into."

Veronica nodded her head slowly and wiped her eyes. Ed continued, "Most importantly, you can lean on Jesus. He is loving and here to help you. Abortion and the grief and guilt that goes along with it is …His specialty, so to speak. At its heart it's a sin against God, not only against your body, your future, your marriage," he said softly, "and the child himself. That is an important part of the healing process. Knowing that the sin is not unforgiveable. It's not. I know you know that," he said gently. "I'm preaching here…"

"I have buried it for so long…"

"That's natural, but the kind of chemicals that go along with that repression are awful – leading to depression, making you feel helpless and victimized. I think that's the cycle you've been in since Gary's death. How long ago was that—?"

"Three years."

"…for three years. Too long a time for it to continue without terrible physical and mental effects which you're experiencing."

"But I don't know how to start!" The statement was nearly a wail.

"Let's start with a prayer and then I have some thoughts and contacts that I'll pass along." They both bowed their heads and sat together quietly. The house was silent, kitchen sounds had faded long ago. Only a loud throaty purr from the chairman in the office chair could be heard in the silence, nearly drowning Veronica's sobbing. "Dear Jesus. We need You more than ever. Each day. Especially now when we consider the difficult journey of forgiveness and healing ahead of Veronica. But we know You are a loving and forgiving God and we feel confident of Your presence with her along this journey. Help her to take the first step. Give her a very real sense of Your love. Beginning tonight. All day tomorrow and the day after. Next week. And always. We love You, Lord. In Jesus' name. Amen.

"He knows the best and the worst in each of us, Veronica. And He is the lover of our souls. Lean on that." Ed got up from the chair and walked over to his filing cabinet. He slowly and thoughtfully searched into his files until he pulled out a list of family therapists. "I will start calling these people tomorrow and find out their availability for regular counseling sessions. I will let you know what I find out.

"And I think you and I should meet regularly – say, once or twice a week – here at the parsonage. I will help you to seek forgiveness for the sin against your own body. Your abortion. And the sin against the child, too. That has to be dealt with spiritually before the other work on forgiveness can begin.

"Why don't you do this: Begin tomorrow by making two separate lists. A list of all the rational and emotional reasons *for* the abortion. That may be painful to recollect because it means you have to go back to that time and revisit your feelings. The second list is the effects of the abortion on you both emotionally and rationally. The impact on you and its impact on the others around you. That will bring you up to the present and will include both thoughts and actions. This will also be hard. It will mean you will have to uncover your thoughts leading up to the suicide attempts.

"And I want you to be really sensitive to what you're feeling. I don't want you to plunge into guilt and despair. If you start feeling like that, Veronica, come over here immediately. You can sit by yourself – or with me, as you prefer – and we can talk about it and with God's help, turn it over to Him for His forgiveness. All the details. All the thoughts, emotions, feelings. 'If we confess our sins, he is faithful and just and will forgive us our sins and purify us from all unrighteousness.' All sins, Veronica. We will pray over each item on the list and give it to Him.

"This will be a healing journey for you. I promise you that. He is faithful."

Veronica had sat immobile in the chair, listening to Pastor Ed for the last few minutes. She was beginning to realize the work she had to do. *I've been burying it all. For all these years,* she thought. *And the drugs didn't help. They just buried it deeper.*

As if reading her mind, Ed said, "I don't know what meds you are on. I can't give you any advice about that, but you could talk to your doctor and see what he or she says. Usually anti-depressants work by inhibiting certain chemicals. You need to find out how they will work in combination with psychotherapy and your commendable desire to do the hard work on forgiveness. It may require an adjustment, but don't take my word for it. I am a doctor of divinity, not a medical doctor."

She smiled at that. "I know, I know. I'm not sure how it will go, but I am sure I have to start." She stood up wearily. "Thank you, Ed. Pastor."

"Will you promise me that you'll call me if you feel overwhelmed or sad or you can't go on?"

"Yes, I will."

"Your state of depression is the devil's playground, Veronica. Saint Paul said 'Put on the full armor of God, so that you can take your stand against the devil's schemes.' He wants you; he nearly had you with your suicide attempts.

"Spend lots of time in prayer and know that we'll be praying non-stop for you, too. And I'm here twenty-four seven. Put my number on speed dial. I don't want to break into your house again."

That elicited a sad smile.

She held out her hand. "Bet my dad is here by now. He doesn't let me out of his sight. I could still be a three-year-old."

39

E d and Jill strolled into the Crossroads Convenience store later the next morning. The store was empty and Romyn sat at the large round oak table reading the *Star Tribune*.

"Sitting down on the job, huh?" Ed teased.

"Quiet for once. No Jennie pies because she's still in New York, so that is cramping George's style a little bit. Though I expect him in later anyway. Gossip central—he needs his fix. You guys are looking good." Romyn pushed her readers up on her head and smiled at Jill who gave her an answering smile. A real one.

"Maybe I should take baking lessons from Jennie and then I could be her back-up," Jill offered.

"Your husband is a pretty good baker. I know because I've sampled his raisin tart!"

"His raisin tart..." Jill was thoughtful.

"We had a really good visit to the Cities yesterday, Romyn," Ed said, his direct look full of meaning. "Will fill you in later. But I am more concerned about you."

"Earl and I wanted to sit down and fill you—and Jill— in, but let me give you the Cliff Notes version." Romyn's face reddened and she cleared her throat, trying to gain control of her emotions. "It seems that the father has shown up. And wants Clay and Sophie."

"Oh, no! How is that possible? After all these years."

"We got a letter from Minnesota Department of Human Services and he has found a lawyer and filed a motion to stop the fostering and the adoption process completely."

"Oh, Romyn." Jill got up from where she was sitting and walked around to place her arm on Romyn's shoulders as the slight woman sobbed, her head in her hands. Jill rubbed her shoulders tenderly and said, "It'll work out. It'll work out. God will make a way."

Romyn halfway turned in the chair and hugged Jill around the waist and leaned in and sobbed as Jill stroked her hair in the time-honored gesture of comfort.

Ed came around the table and said, "Let's pray. Dear Jesus, we come to You with our heartbreak. We know You have all things in your control and we lift this family to You. You know Romyn and Earl's loving hearts. You know Clay and Sophie's longing for their own family. Love does not return unanswered. That is Your promise. We know that You see this anguish and Your own heart is broken. So, we ask You to help us to go on and lean on Your wisdom. Help us solve this problem. In Your will and in Jesus name. Amen.

"How did he find them, if you know?" Ed's direct question helped Romyn calm her emotions and she stood up unsteadily and reached for a tissue before responding.

"That's a whole 'nother story, which will break your heart. I got a call yesterday from the director of the children's home where the kids were for those lost weeks. Lisa has been found." Ed sat back in surprise as Jill glanced at him quizzically. "But it's not good news. She has amnesia and is in a nursing home in Kansas City."

"Poor thing," Ed murmured.

"Yes, apparently beaten and cut up and left for dead. She was found near a dumpster behind a hotel outside Kansas City."

"Oh, my Lord, protect her. How awful."

"Yes, and because the assault left her with no memory, there were articles about her in the national newspapers, trying to see if there was someone who recognized her. Long story short,

Richard Shapiro, the dad, found out about the 'Mystery Woman' and visited her. He must have recognized her and came from North Carolina to check it out in person.

"And somehow got in touch with our famous local reporter, Linda Bakry, who works for the *Star Tribune* now, and who has it in for Peace Ridge Village and seemingly all of us here. She traced the kids to us. To Crossroads. To The Jason House and the foundation.

"So, what he wants to do is uproot the kids from the only normal home they've ever had and take him with them wherever he lives. North Carolina, I guess." Her voice sagged with discouragement.

"I can't believe that we can't fight this, Romyn. This is a fight worth having."

"Children are everything," Jill added in a soft voice.

"Our next step..." Romyn's voice broke, "our next step is to get our own adoption lawyer. I talked to the Department of Human Services at the capitol and nothing will be done immediately. But I am so fearful. I see what Clay and Sophie mean to Earl and to me, too, but then I think about them and I despair. It's not a life, living with a man they don't know. Who never even once tried to get in touch with them in all these years."

"I doubt that even Clay remembers him," Ed said thoughtfully.

"Clay told us – a long time ago—that he can't remember his dad very well, and who knows if this is even the right man? It could be a scoundrel who thinks he can come in and stir up trouble for us. For The Jason Foundation."

"I think you've hit on it, Romyn. He may only want money or some kind of payoff."

Romyn looked bleakly at them both and then involuntarily turned in the direction of The Jason House, past the gas pumps, the familiar view of most of her days. In the distance she could see HVAC unit on top of the old Peterson Printing Company, and if she was outdoors, she could nearly hear the construction work. The sound of backhoes, air hammers, and circular saws penetrated the quiet Main Street of Peace Ridge Village. The building, their life work. The Jason House. And their other life work. Clay and Sophie.

"Well, I'll tell you this," she said fiercely. "He won't get them without a fight. And we have the resources to fight harder than he does. He has no idea of what he's up against. Mama *will* fight. Mama will *fight.*" She said that last to Jill who looked at her in dismay and then broke into tears.

Randy entered the store, a welcome distraction at that emotion-filled moment.

"Sit down, Randy. Have a little visit with us. You remember Jill, don't you?" Ed asked kindly. Randy gave a very brief smile and signed, "Hello, how are you?" to each one in turn.

He looks good today, Ed thought. He was wearing clean blue jeans and his plaid short-sleeved shirt was faded but clean. His hair was cut short, too, and the long lock of hair that typically fell over his forehead and into his eyes was brushed back, showcasing his luminous eyes. Eyes that had lost some of their wariness over the last few months.

"Kinda quiet in here today, Randy. And no pie either. But I can offer you some chocolate milk," Romyn said, as she walked over to the cooler and retrieved the offering, then set the cold bottle in front of him.

After the intensity of the conversation with both Jill and Romyn's voices choked and tear-filled, it fell to Ed to talk about normal everyday Peace Ridge Village goings-on. He chatted with Randy about his gardening and how he was trying to grow some of Eva's lavender alongside his garage. He recognized Randy's hunger for human connection and that he understood more than his lack of talk indicated. At the mention of lavender, Randy pinched his thumb and fingers together and waved them in front of his nostrils.

"Flowers," Ed replied, mimicking Randy's sign language. Randy made the sign for garden and in a moment, after several repetitions, Ed said, "Garden?" and that brought a big smile to his neighbor's face.

Romyn brushed her hair back from her forehead and said tiredly, "What's our word for the day, Randy? Do you have a good word for us? Please?"

He looked at her with the compassion of Christ on his face.

"Kith and kin. Family and friends – to be well known and understood. Old English, originally Germanic. 1300s A.D. Anno domini. Kith and kin." He signed the words for family, making a circle with his thumb and forefinger and then bringing hands close to his chest. There was such tenderness on his face that Romyn turned away, her tears renewed.

"I'm so glad you have a chance to come and visit us, Father," Ed said, greeting the surprisingly young priest from the Greek Orthodox Church in St. Paul.

Father Daniel gave an attractive smile that lit up his entire face and replied, "Me, too. It's a great chance to get up into the country. And I am so grateful to stay here with you two." He walked into the parsonage at Pastor Ed's invitation and handed her Jill a box of cookies. "Just some Greek biscotti. *Paximadia.* Hope you like them. They go over big at our annual church fundraisers." He was dressed casually in blue jeans topped with a black cotton shirt, the small white collar the cue to his vocation.

"Jill has made just a simple meal for tonight. Hope you don't mind. We'll all over-indulge at the Petros Greek Diner tomorrow."

"Oh, no worries. I am simply grateful for a home away from home for tonight. Looking forward to getting to know the both of you better. Titos has told me that Peace Ridge Village has made them feel welcome and that you are a big part of it."

"Well, I don't know about that. We're happy they're here." He led Father Daniel into the den and said, "For one thing, the culinary inspiration of Peace Ridge Village is just about to climb up a big notch. We got a taste at The Jason House dedication..." He quickly added, "I'll fill you in later about our new building project in town that Titos and Maria catered. Most of us are rooting for their success. Come in and sit down. Tea or coffee?"

"Tea, please. Green, if you have it."

"I wish I knew Titos and Maria better," Ed confided after Jill brought in their cups. "He's been so busy with the diner and we've had a full plate here at the church, too. So, time slips by and we don't get a chance to get to know one another like we should. Hopefully that will change."

"I've gotten to know them pretty well over the last few months. Hope to find a way to get them more involved in the church, but the distance and their commitments here make that a bit of a problem. Regardless, I'm just glad to be here for this occasion and wish them success. They need a bit of it now."

"How much has Titos shared with you about how he came to Peace Ridge Village?"

"He told me about Jeremy and Petros being best friends."

"Have you had a chance to meet Jeremy and Tafani?" Ed asked.

"Yes, they came to church one time with Titos and Maria. Striking couple. She's Muslim, of course, so no chance of becoming members. Every priest's wish—conversion of every visitor to a regular parishioner! But they make a bit of a ready-made family for Titos and Maria here in Minnesota. It's hard for them to make friends with Maria deafness."

"Yes, I wondered about that. I don't know them well enough to inquire how it happened. She wasn't born deaf so it must be quite a hardship. To think of not hearing Mozart, for example." Ed stood up. "That reminds me. Let's have some music." He selected a CD from the shelf and placed it in the CD player. Both men silently listened to Mozart's last symphony, No. 41, in pleasant company.

"I think I can share what Titos told me," Father Daniel said. "He was born here but Maria was born in Greece during the time of the Civil War there, right after the end of World War Two when the Communists were trying to take over after the exiled king had been restored to power.

"Maria's family – she was just a small child then – lived in the mountains and they got caught in the fighting. It was horrific. Some estimates say that 50,000 people were killed and about a half a million were displaced. Maria's family was loyal to the king and her father was one of the leaders that fought the Communists in the mountains and in the valleys of rural Greece. Titos told me that they survived on roots and berries for many months. It was a terrible time for the family. In fact, Maria has kidney problems since that time from sleeping on frozen ground. In addition to being deaf.

"As these things happen, her father was betrayed by a friend and while they were in hiding in a makeshift mountain hut in fear for their lives, he was captured and killed in front of his family. If that horror wasn't enough, they threw a grenade into the hut where the family – Maria, her mother, her little brother and a cousin – were hiding. The explosion killed everyone but Maria and left her deaf. She wasn't found for several days and she was nearly out of her mind with fear and hunger."

"I am so sorry! How awful. How did Titos find her? How did they meet?"

"Her father and his father were brothers, so they are first cousins. His dad had emigrated to America and had done pretty well for himself. Began a Greek diner on the Lower East Side of Manhattan and had sent money home for them to emigrate. But the war intervened. After the family tragedy Titos and his father went to Greece to find Maria and bring her here. She had been staying in a home for displaced children and when she saw Titos's father, so like seeing her own father, she collapsed completely. It touched Titos's heart. He was eighteen then to her eight years old but he made a vow to himself that he would never let her feel that kind of hurt again. He and his father brought her to the U.S. and Titos waited until she was eighteen and could marry him. That was the 'happily ever after' story of their lives there in the Hudson River Valley. Titos taught himself sign language so they could talk."

"This gives me a completely new understanding of them. She looks older than she is – I would never have thought that he's older. But that kind of tragedy… I am so glad Titos rescued her."

"Yes, and then they had their precious son, Petros. Making their life complete until he was killed in Afghanistan."

"How do people bear up? Can you tell me that, Father Daniel? How do people survive?"

There was quiet in the den as the two men listed to the finale of the Mozart symphony, their quiet interlude interrupted by Jill who invited them to the table.

"Father, will you offer the blessing, please?" Ed asked.

"In the name of the Father, and of the Son, and of the Holy Spirit. Amen. Our Father, Who art in Heaven, hallowed be Thy name. Thy Kingdom come, Thy will be done, on earth as it is in Heaven. Give us this day our daily bread; and forgive us our trespasses, as we forgive those who trespass against us; and lead us not into temptation, but deliver us from evil. Glory to the Father, and to the Son, and to the Holy Spirit, now and ever and unto ages of ages. Amen. Lord, have mercy. O Christ our God, bless the food, drink, and fellowship of Thy servants, for Thou art holy always, now and ever and unto the ages. Amen."

Jill had prepared a dish that she had made countless times in the old days. Ed had asked her if she was up to it, but she gave a blithe glance and began to get the ingredients ready for chicken breasts in a homemade concoction she'd contrived from maple syrup, rice vinegar, Worcestershire sauce, Dijon mustard and something else she called her "secret ingredient. Ed had run to Walmart to get the ingredients for a Greek salad and that, with Pillsbury dinner rolls in the blue tube, made a simple supper that all enjoyed. Jill seemed to blossom under the laudatory comments of the men at her table and when she brought out an apricot tart with an orange marmalade glaze the satisfied smiles and compliments brought the first real broad smile to her face that Ed had seen in—forever. Ten years.

She's enjoying this. Being a hostess and wife again. Thank You, God. I am so grateful, Ed thought. *Is our crisis over? Let me trust You and You only.*

Jill waved the men back to the den as she gathered the dishes and began to clean up the kitchen. Father Daniel and Pastor Ed were pleasantly sated and slouched comfortably in their chairs.

"What are the big challenges you face here in Peace Ridge Village? With your church, that is?" Father Daniel asked.

"Ones common to your parish, I imagine. Broken, hurting people. Depression, addiction, broken families. Loss of faith. Untimely deaths and the resultant sadness and desperation of the families left behind."

"Ah yes. The problems of the ages. Spiritual darkness. Chasing after the wind of the culture. That meaninglessness." Father Daniel's voice was sad and resigned. "Do you have seekers here in Peace Ridge?" he asked. "Small town…"

"Many of our congregation are perfectly comfortable in their faith. The old people, that is. Those who helped build this church fifty years ago. The young people are seekers but experimental and want to blend our Christian faith in Jesus with other ideas from secular humanity, from New Age religions, from the prosperity gospels. A little dab of this and a little dab of that to make their own personal religion. Our Sunday School classes try to teach doctrine, but we have to go gently. Slip in a little doctrine in stories and personal references. Strict theology may be too strong a dose for most of them, but I keep hoping."

Pastor Ed stretched in his chair and reached over to the stack of books alongside the recliner. "I've been reading John Piper." He saw Father Daniel's nod. "One of his older ones, *Think: The Life of the Mind and the Love of God.* At the same time, I've been reading Malcolm Gladwell's *Blink* – it was a popular best-seller a few years ago. Nothing seems to exemplify the divide in our culture more than these two books. People today want the instant fix. *Blink: The Power of Thinking without Thinking,* is about how we make instantaneous assessments of people and situations, but at its core, I think, is a mental preference for instant solutions, too. *Give me the recipe for life. The formula for success. And give it to me now.*

"John Piper, on the other hand, is all about expositive thinking, digging deep into God's word and trying to figure out how devout Christians can think deeply about God's plan for their life and to meditate deeply – the use of the mind, our intellectual capacity, to better know the mind of God. Blink and Think. The polar opposites of today's culture."

"It's an ongoing challenge," Father Daniel replied with a long sigh. "I see this, too, with our church family. I actually think our formal liturgies and insistence on doctrine in every service helps us. From the time the kids are little they get exposed to it and maybe it's helpful when they're grown. Of course, we have our own problems with people walking away from their own faith, especially when they are teenagers or young college students. That's the most vulnerable time."

"One of the things I like is your emphasis on service as part of your church mission. It's an obligation for all of your parishioners and I think it's helpful." Ed added thoughtfully. "We try to make it voluntary and optional, but usually it's just the same faithful few who participate."

"When someone is struggling, it *is* helpful to find someone else who is in worse shape. That has been the best lesson for some of our people. A teenager who is being bullied who sees a young man who took that bullying and then acted out and is now in prison, well, that's a wake-up call, and it brings up feelings of compassion that they didn't know they had."

"We had a situation here in our town where an old lady had a pet shed burn down. I have never seen more excitement with the young kids — the teenagers from the church — when they helped build a new shed for her pets. I am going to call it a pet palace; you should see it! Anyway, service to others does break down some of the selfishness we are born with."

"Did you ever think about Orthodox Christianity, Ed, when you were studying theology in school?"

300

The direct question took Ed by surprise. "I studied it, of course. In depth." He was thoughtful.

"I know we have a more formal emphasis. We have a great emphasis on liturgy, believing that we can attain a more mystical union with God in the process." Father Daniel added, "It's why we use incense and icons in our worship. To help us use all our senses to feel God in our midst."

"I think if we were to introduce incense into Valley Community, the people would think I had lost it! As for icons — you wouldn't believe the disagreements we have over decorating the church at Christmas. Some people want it gussied up; others want it simple, with only a manger scene. I've been able to stay out of the interior decoration issues of the church, but, believe me, the Ladies Aid have—let us just say — *robust* conversations!"

"Our icons are important to us and I can see how evangelicals can see those as idols, a violation of God's commandment. We don't see them that way, of course. We believe our icons point our way back to God and to the saints who preceded us in our worship. They are our family scrapbook — we find their trials inspiring. But we do believe that holiness can reside in physical places and things. That's a big difference between you and us."

"The big difference is probably Mary and that is an area where we and the Roman Catholics have a different perspective."

"We look at Mary as representing the human characteristics of Jesus Christ. She gave birth to God in the flesh. Fully human. Fully God."

"We are in agreement on that, Father. Fully human. Fully God." Ed smiled. "Hard to imagine, isn't it?" The two of them sat in silence for a long moment.

"Where does your church stand on election, Ed?" Father Daniel's voice was simply curious, not challenging.

"Oh, now you're getting into it! This is a subject where we could talk for hours and still not come to an agreement. Our church is in the Reformed tradition, believing in election. But we also believe in God's grace for all who will believe. Could one argue that was God's plan? Yes, but our church is here to make the Jesus Christ worldview – His immaculate conception, death, burial, resurrection – so compelling—and convicting — that people will want to live within that grace. Thus fulfilling election in God's plan.

"Oh, we don't have any disagreements with that last point, Ed. In fact, we believe that salvation is a long-term engagement with God, to become more like Him in this earthly life and beyond. What we call *theosis*."

"*Solo scriptura* is another defining difference, I think. We evangelicals believe in the inerrancy of the Bible and as the sole authority for our worldview. Doesn't Orthodox Christianity believe in other sources, as well?"

"Well, Ed, like you, we believe that the Bible is the canon which must be applied to all other source documents. And we believe there are others, but—importantly — they do not contradict the Bible. We call it the *Deuterocanonical*. It's because the Orthodox Church produced the Bible and they lived that Christian life fully before the canon of the New Testament church was recognized in Constantinople in the fourth century. The Bible, the inspired scriptures, were always a part of that church. Not apart from it."

"Calvin and the other objectors didn't reject tradition as a help to wisdom," Ed offered mildly, "but it wasn't elevated to the same status as scripture. Ah, Father Daniel, we should get Father Brandon from the Catholic Church in town to come over! We could have a really great discussion.

"I do think," Ed went on," that we could do with a little more formal worship in our services. We are sometimes very casual about our relationship with God, thinking Him our friend – which He is, of course, through Jesus Christ – but neglecting His holiness. We try to imbue that in our prayers and in my sermons, but when one is *friend with friend*, it's sometimes harder to remember that God is *holy, holy, holy*. The majesty and mystery of God. I do think your services keep that relationship of love and profound worship and respect in balance. In perspective. That's a good thing."

302

"That's one of the most important things," Father Daniel said soberly. "There are other important differences. I'm sure we could have a good conversation about infant baptism, for example. But we'll save it for another time. And," he added with some humor, "after this good meal, we could talk about how fasting is a really important part of our tradition, too!"

"Well," Ed said, drawing the talk to its natural conclusion, "let's affirm the maxim: 'In essentials, unity; In nonessentials, liberty; in all things, charity.'" He pushed himself up from his seat. "How about a walk around my little garden, Father? Want to see God's other book of truth? In his revealed natural beauty of nature? We'll have no problems agreeing on that!"

As it turned out, both men wanted to stretch their legs and they took a leisurely saunter along the Sermon Walk behind the garage that led out through George's pasture to the little creek that bordered the property. The pleasant scent of newly mown hay permeated the air.

Father Daniel inhaled deeply with pleasure and said, "We should find a way to bottle that smell for our incense."

Ed had seen Paul's equipment in there a couple of days ago but it hadn't been baled yet. *They should be home from New York soon,* Ed thought. That led naturally to a discussion of his neighbors and a description of who would be at the grand opening of the Petros Greek Diner tomorrow.

"And there'll be a lot of kids running around," he said, "especially two of my favorites, Clay and Sophie."

"I'll pray for them," Father Daniel offered, after Ed had shared the story. "It's a heart-breaker. I remember reading an article in the *Star Tribune* about their mother, the mystery woman. We have a special women's prison ministry in Shakopee south of the Cities, and run into a lot of ladies of the night. I wondered about Lisa, whether one of us had ever encountered her at some time. It's pretty clear from the circumstances of her assault that her lifestyle played a big role."

"So much sadness. Romyn and Earl are doing what they can to flood Clay and Sophie with love and break that cycle."

"That's the most important thing, isn't it? I am so grateful for my wife and children. I couldn't do this priesthood without them."

"Bring your wife and kids to Peace Ridge sometime, Father. They'd enjoy our little mountain and our lakes."

After he'd checked into the Sleepytime Inn, Richard Shapiro headed out for a walk around Peace Ridge Village. *Two-bit, drink-water town,* he thought, after his half hour amble around Crossroads and Main had shown him nothing of interest. *I want to take a look at The Jason House,* he thought. *Linda made a big deal about it; it's where they're putting their money.*

He walked down Main until he spotted the large construction site. It was impossible to miss, the three-story apartment unit under construction rivaling some of the highest silos in the farmyards that dotted landscape in the surrounding country-side. The unit was large, about thirty apartments he estimated. Across a lawn dotted with construction equipment he saw a small building that was nearly completed with several pallets of chain link fencing stacked nearby. The pet center —he had shaken his head when Linda told him about that. The show-case building was the restored printing plant. It was massive, quite a bit bigger than he had imagined. Impressive oversized windows lined the facade, the mullioned windows reflecting the setting sunlight in beautiful multiple shades of yellows and golds. A more poetic man might have been moved by the sight but Richard had a secret pride in his lack of sentimentality and so he missed the beauty.

This project is in the millions, he thought. *But if the stories are true, they can afford it. Some people get all the luck.*

There were a few workmen around the site and he didn't want to call attention to himself so he continued his walk until he found himself at the intersection of Miller Street and came across another new construction site, this one in a more finished state. A diner by the looks of it. Wooden half-barrels filled with petunias and impatiens were placed attractively alongside the west side of the diner and flanked the entranceway. There was a children's playground with a swing set and teeter-totter off to the side. The brown shake mansard roof over the plain white siding was friendly and attractive and there was a banner across the windows proclaiming "Grand Opening" and "Welcome Friends." As Richard walked past the diner, a beautiful, tall woman came out the door, calling her goodbyes back over her shoulder to someone. She was dressed casually, her sleeveless top revealing toned brown skin and skinny blue jeans that accentuated her height. Richard caught a brief glimpse of the beautiful face and something flipped within him. An ugly thought passed through his mind and he casually turned to follow her as she walked rapidly down the street in the dusk.

Just curious. Just curious to see where she's going.

Peace Ridge Village streets were relatively quiet this time of night. Most people were home with their families and there were children riding their bicycles on sidewalks and calling out to one another. The dusky cooling smell of the Minnesota summer evening was in the air, so different from the oppressive heat of North Carolina. The woman's stride was long and fast and Richard found himself having to increase his pace to keep her in view. She finally ended up at a small house on a side street on the west side of town, quickly entering it and closing the door with a decided snap. He felt conspicuous and turned around, slackening his pace as he retraced his steps back to Main Street. Just out for a stroll. But her unforgettable face and that long body occupied his thoughts and were the main visual in his mind when he booted up his computer in bed that night and indulged in a movie from his private stash.

40

"When are we going to the diner, Dad?" Brian asked.

"Nearly done with your poem?" Michael replied

"Yes," he said briefly. "Are Pam and Brandon coming with us today, Dad?"

"She said they were going to try to make it. It's her weekend to work, but she was going to see if she could take the morning off and drive up."

Brian was quiet. Michael knew that his son often got broody when he was poem-working. He walked over to the back door and looked over the yard. Should have time to get it mowed before they arrived. Looking a bit shabby. *Should make more of an effort,* he thought. *I think Pam does all her own yard work. It would do me good to be a little more conscientious. At least, make an effort.* The phone rang just as he was about to go out the door and see if he could get the lawn mower started.

"Michael, we have a bit of a technical problem here at the diner, "Titos said wearily. "For some reason, we've got a glitch in our POS system and it's continually defaulting to the home setting and not uploading to the cloud. It was working yesterday when we gave it a test run."

"Why don't I come over and see what I can find?" Michael offered. "I'll just grab Brian and we'll be there in a few."

"Just what we need. Today of all days. Thanks, Michael." Titos rang off without a goodbye. *Typical Titos. All business.*

"Brian, we have to go over to the Petros Greek Diner for a few minutes." He looked at the concerned face of his son. "You can write over there. I think Titos will find a place for you."

"Okay, Dad," Brian said reluctantly.

All reluctance, however, was subsumed in the friendliness and beauty of the elegant woman who greeted them at the door and ushered Michael to the small office off the kitchen. She came back to Brian sitting at the booth.

"Would you like a Coke, Brian?" she asked, her voice soft and musical, the familiar words like lyrics to a haunting, ancient melody, like a dance amplified by her flowing Afghani dress. It was brightly colored with intricate patchwork patterns integrated into a vivid deep blue background. She wore a beaded silver Kuchi headdress that held back her lustrous flowing hair, and Brian found himself suddenly shy. He gave her a manly, "Thank you," when she returned with the fountain drink. He sat and looked out the window, his mind forming new words and new images. All centered around a beautiful woman with compassionate blue eyes that held the promise of an exotic journey to a new place. An uncharted place.

He was busy thinking up words and writing them down in his notebook when his dad returned. They walked out the diner together just as Bill and one of his crew came in the front door on their way to the kitchen to take a look at a dangling electrical wire in the storage room that had somehow come disconnected. The two men gave them a quick "hello" but Michael sensed an unexpected distance and a surprising dislike coming from Bill.

"Nice job here, Bill," he said. "This place is really something."

"Thanks," he said curtly, walking in towards the kitchen. "Sorry. Can't talk. Need to check this problem out."

I didn't get a chance to tell him how sorry I was about Donna, Michael thought. *Suppose he's miffed.* But then all thoughts of Bill were erased when his phone dinged and he saw a text from Pam, "On our way." And his heart lifted.

✿

George limped into the Crossroads Convenience store and greeted Romyn with a grimace.

"How are you this morning, George?" Romyn asked quietly.

"Well, I'm a little sad, to tell the truth," he confessed. "I am glad I sold Kathy's Kafe to Titos, but today makes it really final. I just drove over there and it's all wiped out completely. Kathy. Us. Our place. It's the Petros Greek Diner now."

"I know, George. I'm sorry for you. But think of it this way: You are passing along something you loved to someone else who can love it now."

"Yeah," he said, sitting down heavily in the chair. It creaked as Romyn brought his coffee over to him. "No pie, I suppose?" he asked hopefully.

"Nope. They're back later today."

"I heard that Paul went to New York to bring her back home. Probably thought she was having too much fun in the big city," he said sourly.

"No, that's not it, George. He wanted to surprise her. Be with her in a place she loves. Looking forward to hearing how it went."

"Well, these women that think they have to be wives and business women, too. In my day the man ran the home and the woman did his bidding." At Romyn's raised eyebrow, he quickly added, "Not that I told my Kathy what to do. She and I would talk it over and we'd make the decisions together. But if there was a disagreement, she'd see it my way." He smiled and stretched out in his chair. "That's just the way women were raised in those days."

"Well, you'd be surprised. I think many women think the same way that your Kathy did. We love and respect our husbands. Respect is the most important thing. I heard someone say that a woman wants love from her husband and a man wants respect. She gets his love when she gives him her respect. That just about wraps it up for me."

"Doesn't mean that they can't do things together. Like the cafe. Kathy made as many of the important decisions as I did.

But we were together as a team. I feel like I am half a man without her, Romyn, I'll tell you that. That's what it feels like."

"I know, George. I know."

They both sighed in unison. The store was busy with people paying at the pump and steady traffic in for bags of minnows, snacks, and drinks.

"How are your brats, Romyn?" George asked.

"My kids. Clay and Sophie, you mean?" Romyn's rebuke was gentle. "We've got a bit of a problem, George." She turned to a customer who wanted a fishing license and it was a good ten minutes before she was able to finish her thought. "And we need your prayers, George. The father wants them back and we are going to fight it with all we have."

"The father? The guy with – Lisa?" George was sputtering. "Him? How does he think—?

"He found out somehow that they are with Earl and me and he has put in a claim against the adoption. Wants to stop the fostering, too. Which is devastating to all of us. How can those two little kids cope with that? Someone they don't even know?"

"I can't believe it. Romyn, if you need help, if you need a lawyer. I have a little saved by…I will do what I can…"

"Thank you, George. We don't need your money—"

"Oh, that's right…"

"—but we do need your prayers. We need to adopt these kids. That's what we're focused on."

"And their mother?"

"Well, this is really sad. She was beat up pretty bad and now she has no memory. Has amnesia."

"Well, when you sell your body the buyers aren't the cream of the crop, if you get my drift."

"George," Romyn was firm, "I don't condone her lifestyle. I hate it and especially for what it did to those precious kids. But maybe no one ever talked to her about how Jesus loves her anyway and could help her to overcome it. She probably thought that's what she needed to do to support them."

"Well, you are more generous than I am. I'm sorry she's lost her mind. Where is she?"

"She's in an assisted living facility in Kansas City. That's where she was found. But she'll be brought here when The Jason House is finished. That's one thing we can do at least." Under her breath, Romyn said, "I need to get in touch with them." and she made a note on a piece of paper by her cash register.

"What do the kids think?"

"They don't know anything. As far as they are concerned, we are their forever home. Little Sophie is so in love with Earl that I have a rival for my affections."

Just then Steve and Veronica came into the store. Veronica looked frail but Steve had a vitality about him that filled the whole store with energy and optimism. Romyn discreetly noticed the way he looked at Veronica. *He is a man in love.* George sat up a bit straighter as Romyn asked them both to sit down and have a coffee. Veronica seemed tentative but Steve accepted with a bear hug to Romyn and a clap on the shoulder for George.

"How's it goin', Steve? Sorting out the Bill and Donna mess?" George asked, in his usual direct manner.

"Well, lots of things to be looked into. I think we're getting to a good place." Steve smiled.

"Well, he needs all the help he can get. That Donna..." George left the rest of the thought unsaid.

"I think she was more a victim than a villain," Steve replied mildly.

"How are you doing today, Veronica?" Romyn thought it best to shift the subject.

"I'm doing well. Steve and I are planning a trip to the North Shore and I am really looking forward to it. I've never been north of Duluth, if you can believe it," she said, as she looked down shyly.

"Are you going to be around for the grand opening of the Petros Greek Diner?"

"Oh yeah, we'll be there. Told Veronica that she didn't know what she was missing. Greek food!" Steve said.

"Steve tells me I just haven't lived," Veronica said. "Your kids going to be there, Romyn?"

"Yup. 'As long as Shiloh and Brian are coming,' Clay said. It really looks nice, doesn't it, George?"

"Yeah. He did a nice job," George said grudgingly.

"Well, look who just showed up."

They all turned toward the door as Paul and Jennie came in with big smiles of greeting for everyone.

"Back from New York all right, I see," Romyn said.

"Yes, it was fantastic!" Jennie enthused.

"Does Paul feel the same way?"

"I'll tell you the truth. You can keep your big cities. I couldn't wait to get home and hug my dog, check out my cows, and smell the cow manure in the air. Home!" Paul walked over to the coffee pot and filled a large mug.

"You'll have to fill us in, Jennie. How was the Fancy Food Show?"

"I got a lot of ideas, but it's a bigger proposition than I had thought. Lots to think about. Need to connect with Pastor Ed and kick it around some more. As it is we're behind on our work already. You should see my greenhouse."

"Farmers can't leave home for very long," Paul said. "It just piles up. Can't wait to get back at it," he added meaningfully to Jennie.

"And I can't do without banana cream pie for more than a few days, you catch my drift, Jennie?" George said.

"Yes, George. Yes, I do. Back at it Monday morning. I'll make a special pie for you." Jennie turned to Romyn, "I didn't bake anything for the grand opening and we'll just have to see what the demand will be there. See how it goes. Depending on how much time I'll have. Right now, I'm feeling like I'm over my head. Just tired from the trip, I think. And I need to get an apple pie over to Eliza."

"Take a vacation day once in a while, Jennie. Do you good," George said.

"I hear you, George. Missed you, too. New York is a great place but there's no place like home." She turned to Romyn. "Everything fine at home? With everyone?"

"Not completely, Jennie. Jill seems to have had an emotional breakthrough – that's a praise."

"How are the kids?"

Romyn fought for control as her eyes filled with tears. "I'll call you later, Jennie," she choked out.

41

"Hello, Bill," Pam said, holding out her hand. "How are you doing?" There was the same compassion in her voice that he'd come to expect from her, but Bill found himself unable to respond. He just stared at her not saying anything. Pam's smile faded and she turned away in confusion as Michael walked up to them.

"Hi, Bill," he said.

"Hello again. Got the computer working?" He managed a brief smile that defaulted to a grimace.

"I didn't get a chance to say how sorry I was about Donna's... loss," Michael offered. Bill shrugged dismissively as if to say, "Don't worry about it."

"Bill," Pam began, "I wonder – well no, this is not the time nor the place."

"For what?" he challenged, his chin up and a stubborn look on his face.

"I wondered if we'd have some time to talk Westin business," she added, "while I'm here."

"I suppose your lawyers are on my case, right?"

"No, not necessarily. Just wanted to fill you in on where they are."

"At your convenience, Pam." His voice was cool and Pam felt rebuked and rejected.

"Bill," she said, "I brought Bradley to Peace Ridge today, too. I'd like you to meet him."

Bill looked over at the large tent that had been erected on the grassy lawn next to the diner. He stared at the children running around and laughing and picked out the big young man with the goofy smile on his face. He slowly walked over to the tent with Pam and Michael following behind him. Pam called to Bradley and he ambled over to the small group.

"Bradley, this is Bill. You remember I've talked about him?" she said.

He put out a big meaty hand and shook Bill's hand with enthusiasm. "My mom, my mom, she always talking about you," he offered. "Happy to meet you. Happy to meet you. Brian is my friend," he said happily, nodding his head over to where Brian listened patiently to an argument between Clay and Shiloh. "My best friend."

Bill softened a bit and said to Michael and Pam, "My Kellie is here, too. Would you like to meet her?" He led them over to a corner of the tent where a skinny, forlorn young woman sat on a folding chair, alternately chewing her fingernails and fiddling with her stringy hair.

"Kellie, here's Pam and —Michael. And Pam's son, Bradley," he said simply.

She looked up at them quickly and then down at her ragged hands again. "Hi," she said, her voice so low it was barely perceptible.

Pam noticed the pregnancy and turned to Bill with a loving, compassionate expression that nearly did him in. They stared at one another for a long moment.

Michael grasped her arm in a proprietary way and said, "Pam, let's fill our plates with some of this delicious food."

Bill looked at her retreating back. *So that's the way it is,* he thought.

"Shiloh, you don't know everything!" Clay pushed back on Shiloh's argument that the Greeks conquered the whole world.

"Well, they did," she said stubbornly, swinging herself higher on the swing set. "The whole world. Alexander the Great did. And he was only a teenager when he did it." She added, "He had a favorite horse. Bucephalus." *Bucephalus. Bucephalus.* She liked that word!

"I don't care, Shiloh. I just don't care. What did he know about America anyway? Nothing, right?" he pushed back. He swung up higher than Shiloh in a burst of show-off male strength. He could see Sophie and Earl near the tent entrance. Sophie was balancing her plate on Earl's lap and they were engaged in a deep conversation. Romyn was around somewhere, too. He had spotted her bright pink shirt in the crowd.

He sensed the man's presence before he actually saw him – a tall, thin man dressed in a rumpled polo shirt and blue jeans. He was watching the kids playing and Clay felt his eyes on him. It was spooky and made him uncomfortable. He wasn't from Peace Ridge Village, that was for sure.

Shiloh was continuing her chatter about ancient Greek when Clay put up his hand in a commanding gesture. "Shiloh," he said, "see that man over there. The skinny dude – not from around here?"

She looked obediently at his subtle head gesture. "Yeah, I see him."

"I have a job for you, Shiloh. I want you to scope him out. Follow him around and report back to me and tell me what you've found out about him. Play private investigator. He makes my skin crawl. See what's up with him."

Shiloh was always up for a mystery and she quickly scooted her shoes into the dirt and came to an abrupt halt in the swing. She swung her right hand up in a smart salute. "At your service, my Captain," she said.

"I will give my finger whistle," Clay said, "and you come back to me when you hear it."

Shiloh nodded as she quickly left the play area and began her innocuous surveillance.

They all heard the bell ring as Titos and Maria asked the group to come together for the blessing on the building. Clay saw that Shiloh had edged close to the man and he turned his attention to the group gathering around the man with the strange black gown and the funny skull-cap. He wasn't very old but he sure looked odd in that get-up.

Maybe the two men are together, Clay speculated, but then rejected that idea. He didn't get any bad feelings from the priest-guy, and when everyone quieted down and he started talking, Clay felt a ray of peace in his heart. His voice was quiet and loving and the words were a blessing on the diner and on Titos and Maria. Romyn had told him that was going to happen.

He lost sight of Shiloh and the man as the crowd broke into applause. Titos and Maria brought a seemingly reluctant George to the front of the crowd and asked him to say a few words. He tried to make a joke but it ended up in tears and then the whole crowd broke into sustained applause. They'd all loved Kathy, too.

The beautiful woman in the colorful Afghan dressed glided gracefully through the crowd carrying a pitcher of lemonade and graciously refilling glasses. The strange man with his little shadow followed a few steps behind. Clay watched for a few long minutes and then gave his distinctive finger whistle. He saw Shiloh look up at him carefully, mark the position of the man, and then walk rapidly back to Clay in the playground.

"What did you find out, Lieutenant?" he demanded.

"Sir, the man is a foreigner. He is not from around Minnesota. His voice is from the South, but he's not a native southerner. There are traces of the North. Sir!"

"What else, Lieutenant? Tell me more."

"He is wearing dirty tennis shoes. And no socks. Ugh. And I could smell him, even though I stayed my distance so he wouldn't know he was tailed."

"Smell him?"

"Yes, like he hadn't used any deodorant or hadn't washed his clothes in a few days."

"Thank you, Lieutenant. What other behavior did you observe?"

"He walked around aimlessly for a while until Tafani came out of the diner and then he perked up and he began to shadow her." Shiloh got a puzzled look on her face. "He had a strange look on his face when he saw her, like he was thinking bad thoughts or something. Made me uncomfortable." She had a fleeting memory of another man at a different time but she didn't want to think about that.

"Lieutenant, your next assignment is to see where Jeremy is and see if he can amplify your forces with his presence. Find him, tell him that a strange man is following Tafani around, enlist his help," he commanded. "Boy, would I like to see Jeremy take the stranger on. That would be fun to see. SEAL Team Peace Ridge to the rescue. Report back to me in five minutes."

"Yes, sir! Right away, sir!" Shiloh was off.

And back right away.

"I asked George where Jeremy was and he said he was on a mission to Washington, D.C., for the military. Back tomorrow."

"Back tomorrow, what?"

"Back tomorrow, Sir!

"Okay, Lieutenant, it's up to us. We are going to have to be Special Forces to protect Tafani. We will split up. I will tail the mark from the front of the diner side, and you tail the mark from the side of the tent. We are not to talk to one another while on this mission. We will reconnoiter back here in ten minutes. If either one feels that Tafani is in any danger we must elevate the command. Immediately find Steve. He's a private investigator. He'll give us our new mission in that situation. Got it, Lieutenant?"

"Got it, Sir!"

The two children walked off the playground together but at the edge and with imperceptible nods to one another split forces. It was easy to find the tall Tafani in her colorful dress and Shiloh began her discreet surveillance a few steps behind her. She didn't spot the mark right away until she looked over to the side of the tent and saw him watching Earl and Sophie. From where he stood he could keep both them and Tafani in his sights. Shiloh paused and watched carefully. Out of the corner of her eye she could see Clay edging closer to the man. She glanced back at Tafani for a moment, and when she shifted her eyes back to the mark, she saw that he'd shifted his attention to Clay and there was a strange look in his eyes, like he was the hunter and Clay was a deer. His eyes narrowed and he carefully watched the unaware Clay who sidled closer and closer.

Suddenly the man reached into his shirt pocket and brought out his iPhone. He stood unmoving and watched Clay, who must have felt something for he stopped suddenly and turned away to walk over to Earl and Sophie. Clay stood there for a moment and then turned back to the man. Who stared directly into his eyes.

Clay felt pinned, like a butterfly on a board. *I know who that man is*, he thought. *I've seen him before. But where? And when?* Random thoughts whirled briefly through his mind, scenes of his mom, Lisa, with someone like him, an upraised hand, a sharp pain on the side of his head. He felt a rising sense of panic and looked at Earl with a silent plea for help.

"Feeling all right, Clay?" Earl asked kindly. "Let's find Romyn and let's get something to eat. You're probably starving, right?"

Shiloh ran up to them just then. "Captain, reporting in. Ready to give my report."

Clay looked at Shiloh and said, "Dad said we have to eat now. At rest, Lieutenant, Report later."

"Yes, Sir!"

Richard put his iPhone back into his pocket with a slight smile of satisfaction. *A couple of good photos. Good proof. Looked just like me when I was a kid. Separated at birth.*

※

318

"Did you enjoy yourself today, Jill," Ed asked when they got home in the late afternoon.

"It was fun," she replied. "Better than the last time when I was just overwhelmed with everyone. All the people. But now I know some of them..."

"They're our people, Jill. Some come to our church, some are just neighbors."

"Those little kids. Clay and Sophie. They have to stay with Romyn and Earl!" she said fiercely. "And Kellie. My heart is breaking for that poor girl. What has happened to her, Eddy?"

"Drugs, Jill. Meth destroys lives."

"And what will happen to her baby? How will... It's just awful to even think about."

"We need to have Bill over for a meal, Jill. He's so alone now and he needs friends more than ever."

"Yes, we'll do that. But not today. I feel the need for a little nap. After the busyness of the last couple of days, it's good to be here with just the two of us. Just you and me, Eddy."

"Good idea, Jill."

They walked to the bedroom together, followed by a tiger cat who liked nothing better than warm bodies under comfy quilts. The bedroom faced east and at this time of day there was a pleasant lulling quietness to the room, an endless place of peace. They took off their shoes and both lay down together, plumping the pillows to make a cushion for their heads. Ed held Jill's hand lightly as she rested quietly next to him. He felt her breathing deepen but when he turned towards her he saw Jill's eyes were open and there was a slight smile on her face.

"This feels right, doesn't it...lover?" she said softly.

Ed turned toward her with a sweet smile. "Yes. It is right, my Jilly. My love. My light for an anxious heart."

The bed had quieted down enough so Biep could jump once more up on the covers and nestle in. His people were sleeping now and they'd be quiet for quite a while, letting him snooze in peace. The tick-tock of the bedside clock added a pleasant rhythm to the soft snore and occasional yawn of the tiger cat. All three dreamed together in peaceful slumber.

Tafani reached for her cell phone to call Jeremy as she walked slowly home from the diner. It had been an exhausting day. Started early. Making conversation with all the customers at the diner. Wearing her traditional dress with her high heeled boots. *I wish Jeremy had been here*, she thought, as she speed-dialed his number. *He would have been proud of me. I was able to remember all the right English phrases. People seemed very happy to meet me.*

And Titos and Maria were happy with how the day went. They would be a success. She was sure of it. She looked down at her phone as her call went into Jeremy's voice mail. She turned up onto her walk, not noticing the car at the curb nor the man who silently and quickly got out from behind the wheel and walked up behind her as she opened the door to their home. She turned to challenge him as he pushed her inside the door and slammed it closed behind her.

42

Tafani was as tall as Richard and with surprising strength she twisted her body and her arms away from him and backed away down the hallway.

"Get out of this house! Get out of here right now!" she shouted, her voice breaking.

In response he moved closer to her and with a surprising fast move grabbed her outstretched arm and twisted it behind her. The sudden pain made her legs collapse and they fell together onto the wooden floor in the hallway. She was like a woman possessed and fought him valiantly until he began slapping her face and tearing at her clothes. She twisted her body right and left to get out from under him but he was surprisingly strong. Acrid sweat poured off him and there was a crazy look in his eyes as he grunted and struggled with her, throwing her voluminous skirt over her head and pulling feverishly at her underwear. His foul breath panted frantically at her and she could feel his fingernails scratching her thighs, reaching for her underwear. Under his breath he was whispering filthy words that she didn't understand but feared with a deep dread.

"Jeremy, Jeremy," she called and then raised her voice to yell but he put his smelly hand over her mouth and pulled even harder at her clothes until her legs were tangled in clothing and she was exposed. She felt the breeze of his moving body above her and tried to twist her thighs to cover herself up but he straddled her, his knees pinning hers to the floor, and began to unzip his pants. He pushed his own jeans down over his thighs and lifted her up with a grunt. With an ugly expression on his face he looked down at her and then paused, an unreadable look on his face. With a short expletive and an ugly expression, he lifted himself off her and pulled up his pants and then scrambled for the door and went out of the house, yelling, "Bitch" as he slammed the door.

Tafani lay on the floor, sobbing. There was a faint sound from underneath her and she rolled over to find her cell phone and the voice of her husband, "Tiff! Tiff! Are you all right? Tell me you're okay! Tiff, talk to me!"

"Oh, Jeremy," she wailed. "Come home. Come home as soon as you can!"

"Mornin', Steve," Romyn said as he walked into the Crossroads Convenience store. "Time to sit down and have a cup of coffee with us?"

"No, I'd better not. I'm on my way over to Bill's house. We're trying to finish up on his case and get the lawsuit in the works."

Romyn looked up in surprise.

"Can't tell you anything about it, of course," Steve said, "but I think Bill will be okay in the end." His face fell into a stubbornness that Romyn remembered well from their early days in their fruitless search for Jason. No one had worked harder to try to find him.

The police cruiser pulled into the parking lot and Chief Baldwin slowly emerged from the car and walked into the store.

"Mornin', Romyn. Mornin', Steve." The chief doffed his hat.

"Here on business, Chief?" Romyn asked.

"Yes, I have someone on a rampage and someone who's fled the county. Need to know if you know anything."

"Well, we'll need a little more to go on."

"Jeremy is on his way home; should be here from D.C. in a few hours. His wife, Tafani, was assaulted in their home late last night after the grand opening at Titos' place. Jeremy is on the warpath. The man who assaulted her is a stranger who was at the diner and had been stalking her. For more than a few days. He's fled the county but we think we have a good I.D. on him."

"Did you ever see this guy?" Chief Baldwin handed a photo from the security cameras at the Sleepytime Inn over to Romyn. Steve leaned over her shoulder to take a look.

"Mr. Filthy Running Shoes." Romyn turned toward the police chief. "He stopped in last week. Do you think it was a random assault or was there a specific target or motive?"

"There's no question that he targeted Tafani. He was seen following her home the night before the opening at the diner, and he was at the grand opening. People saw him there."

"What does the manager of the Sleepytime Inn say?"

"He had checked in under a clearly fake name, Ricardo Spiro. Unfortunately they had a new trainee clerk on the desk when he checked in and she forgot to ask for validating I.D. He paid in cash and made a sweet story of that fact and she was overwhelmed and confused. So, no lead there. Not even a license plate.

"We don't know why he's here in Peace Ridge, how he found our village." The chief looked at both of them directly. "We'll track 'em down. Can't get too far these days."

"Asked a lot of questions when he came in here. Neither George nor I thought much of him.

"And rampage? I can guess that it's Jeremy, right?" Romyn asked.

"Right. She had called him just before she got home and her phone captured some of the assault. He had called her back and her cell phone was under her and opened the line when the guy was attacking Tafani. We will be able to transcribe this and convict him with it when he comes to trial."

"How is Tafani?" Romyn asked. "Has anyone been over to comfort her?"

"I don't know."

"Okay, this is where we come in. Steve, is Veronica home? She and I need to go over to Tiff and give her our love and support until Jeremy gets home. I will call Titos and Maria, too. Maybe Maria can slip away." Under her breath she whispered, "That poor girl, all alone last night."

Steve punched in some numbers into his cell phone. His face transformed with light when Veronica answered. He said a few words and then turned to Romyn. "Veronica will be right over and you can go together."

"Did you get any evidence that needs to be preserved, Chief?"

Chief Baldwin took a long time in answering. "He tried to assault her but ran away when he saw her...deformity."

"Deformity?" Steve asked.

"Her ...female parts," the chief said compassionately. "Messed up. Part of that culture."

"We don't know, do we? We just don't know." Romyn looked down and tears began to fill her eyes. "Poor little Tiff...

"Let us know what we can do to help, Chief. We stand at the ready."

"Yes, I know. That's why I came here first thing. Thank you, Romyn. What would we do without the good neighbors of Peace Ridge?"

"That's a rhetorical question, Chief. We'd be lost and alone. I will call Maria, we will head over to Tiff's house." Romyn punched in Terry's number and asked her teenage helper to come to the store as an emergency fill in.

The phone rang then. It was Tom. "Hi, I heard that the chief might be at your place. May I speak to him, please?"

Romyn handed the phone over to Chief Baldwin with a quizzical look. He listened for a long moment and then hung up the phone and handed it back to Romyn.

"Seems as if we have a couple of amateur sleuths to add to the mix," he said cryptically. "Clay and Shiloh spotted this guy and decided to shadow him. Tom just called to tell me that Shiloh has a story to tell."

Romyn, Veronica, Maria, and Titos knocked gently at Tafani and Jeremy's home. There was a long silence and then they heard the lock slip back and the door was opened. The beautiful young woman looked drawn and bereft. Romyn walked into the house and embraced her with a wide-open hug that brought violent sobbing and wailing. Titos and Maria hugged her and Titos half lifted her in his arms and laid her gently on the sofa. Veronica walked into the kitchen where she found the Keurig coffee machine and began to make some coffee.

"How are you, honey?" Romyn held Tafani back at arm's length and wiped the tears from her face. "I am so sad that this happened to you. It's awful—that mean, awful man. Our police will find him and he'll be put behind bars, but my sweet, to have this happen to you, my heart is broken."

At that, Tafani sobbed all the harder and Romyn hugged her close and said the soothing words that transcended culture. She cushioned her with an afghan that was laid casually on the arm of the sofa. Veronica came into the living room with a tray filled with three mugs of coffee and they sat together drinking the elixir that binds women together. Titos was seething and he punched his cell phone with explosive gestures. Texting with Jeremy before he made a quick exit to get back to the diner.

"When will Jeremy make it home?" Romyn asked.

"He should be here in a few hours. He left Washington as soon as he could get a flight but unfortunately, it wasn't until this morning." Tafani choked it out.

"I think we know who he is. We will find him and he will be in jail and the key thrown away. Chief Baldwin has promised me that."

"Awful. I was so afraid. Maria told me the people in Peace Ridge Village were awful but I didn't believe her."

"He's not from Peace Ridge, Tafani. He's an outsider. We have the evidence that he used a fake name when he checked in to the Sleepytime Inn."

"I felt so afraid. He was stronger than me. I couldn't defend myself. He…" She broke down in tears.

"I know, my dear. I know. It's just awful. Dear God, we lift our Tafani, our sweet Tiff, to You. Give her Your comfort now and in the days to come. Please bring Jeremy home safe – and soon. We love You. Amen."

43

B ill slumped wearily in the kitchen chair and stared out the window with unseeing eyes. He felt exhausted. *I don't know if I have it in me anymore*, he thought. He walked out onto the back porch and looked around the yard at the oversized equipment shed and the two-car garage with its workshop, his preferred refuge. The flower beds seemed to have taken care of themselves over the last few months. The rose bushes were massed in glorious profusion and a faint scent permeated the warm nighttime air. Despite being tired and out-of-sorts, he began to note the projects that needed attention – the step and railing that had come loose when the porch door had been replaced after the break-in. The ladder leaning against the shop door that hadn't been put away. The tilt of the bird feeder that had slumped over like the leaning tower of Pisa during the spring rains and hadn't been righted.

Kellie wasn't home. She had pulled herself together and walked over to her high school friend's house, telling Bill she'd be back later after they'd gone shopping at Walmart. Bill knew Eunie and trusted her — she wasn't into drugs, was a good kid.

I think Kellie's been clean since she she's been home, Bill mused. *George thinks there aren't drugs in Peace Ridge. People can find them if they want them. Even here.*

He and Kellie had been to Minnesota Adult & Teen Challenge to see if she could be accepted into the program. She had seemed indifferent and would walk away without saying anything when Bill asked her about going there.

Can't make *her do it,* he thought, for the umpteenth time.

Endless details. Endless things to do. Stuff left undone. Might as well throw in a pizza and get to work on those papers. I've postponed it long enough. Bill dug through the freezer and found a Heggie's pizza that had been in there for several months but still looked good. He went into the office and grabbed the stack of boxes that had been retrieved from the robbery and brought them into the kitchen. The office itself was still a mess and he couldn't bear to look at the shattered locks and mess left behind when the thief broke in. *Another thing to do one of these days.*

Some of the papers were easy to deal with. He recognized a lot of files from Brady Construction with which he was already familiar. Donna had been in the habit of filing all that away when they were done with it, organizing it for tax purposes. Bill set those files aside in a large stack that filled one box completely. There were a lot of papers for Donna's Interiors, but nothing there seemed interesting.

Bill took time out to inhale his pizza. Paperwork was not his favorite thing and if he didn't have to do it at all that would be his preference. *She always did it for the business and did it well,* he thought sadly. *All the things of our life, the partnership when we worked together, even if we were at cross-purposes sometimes... all this is now over with. I'm going to have to learn how to live differently. How do I do that?* His mind flashed on Pam briefly but he pushed that thought away angrily. *She was just the PR person for the Westin. Her kindness to me was just what she had to do for the corporation. And how did she hook up with Michael, anyway?* Bill's heart seemed to thump harder when he recalled the sight of the two of them together.

Aw heck! Forget this! Bill pushed the other papers aside and pushed his chair back and walked into the living room and stood in the middle of the room suddenly at a loss. *What am I doing here? Oh, yeah. I was going to see if there was anything on TV.* He heard his cell phone ring in the kitchen and he walked back and grabbed it wearily.

"Hi Bill. It's Steve. I wanted to call you yesterday, but the time got away from me. I have another box here from the Sheriff that didn't get delivered to Chief Baldwin with the other boxes. It was taken in the robbery and they called me a couple of days ago and said they had it. I went down to St. Cloud to get it but I hadn't gotten it over to you."

"Come over. I'm just sitting here feeling sorry for myself anyway. I went through some of the stuff already but it's not very interesting. I could use the company."

"I'm on my way."

Steve was whistling happily when he walked up the porch steps with a large bankers' box. Bill pulled a couple of Buds out of the refrigerator and the men sat together at the kitchen table, the box looming importantly like a third guest. Bill got up and emphatically placed it on the floor. "Get to this later, Steve. Hate paperwork."

"Yeah, I know the feeling. I am a private investigator so paperwork is my bread and butter. That's how I solve cases. But my own personal stuff – oh boy, I hate it. When tax time comes around, I postpone that until the last minute. Always getting an extension to file. The government insisting on our compliance. Ugh."

"Didn't get a chance to talk to you and Veronica yesterday at the Grand Opening. Still planning a little trip to the North Shore?"

"Yes, though I think the North Shore is more my thing than it is Veronica's. She's a little bit more delicate than I am" – both men smiled at one another – "and I'd like to rough it and camp out, but she's used to the amenities. Planning it for next month."

"Do you think she's over her episode?" Bill couldn't fathom someone thinking about suicide. It wasn't possible that people would give up life…

"Well, she's coming along. She met with Pastor Ed and he's putting her in touch with some counselors. He's meeting with her every few days or so. Probably a good thing. She has to come to grips with why she doesn't want to live and, of course, I care desperately about that so I can't imagine why *I* can't be enough. To help her see the future. But she has to work it out for herself. And she's willing to do the hard work of introspection. That's the first thing. But I talk to her every day, sometimes several times a day, and I think the connection is really important to her." He smiled wryly. "Don't know if I can make her fall in love with me, but…"

"Who knows how that happens anyway, Steve?" Bill said. "Women…can't live with them, can't live without them."

"Did you hear about Clay and Sophie's mom, Lisa?" Steve asked. "Now that was a woman that walked close to the edge and finally fell off the cliff."

"Poor Earl. Poor Romyn," was Bill's response when Steve recounted the sad story.

"And then there's this." Steve drained his Budweiser and Bill got up and retrieved a couple more bottles for the two of them. "Romyn has asked me to do another investigation for her. I told her that I was finishing up yours but might be able to squeeze in a few weeks for her. They want to adopt the two kids, of course, but now the father – from North Carolina, as far as we know – has put in a stop adoption order. He found out about Romyn and Earl's millions, I think, and wants a cut. Don't think he really wants the kids. Made no effort to be a part of their lives for years."

"That would break their hearts. I can't even see how Earl would stand it. He'd fall apart."

"Yeah. Anyway, I'm going to go to North Carolina for a week or so and see what I can find out. Lisa is in Kansas City. She's been in Minnesota for a couple of years, but she was born in North Carolina in a small town. I need to check the birth and marriage records and see if I can't suss this dude out. I told Romyn I'd help her. She's frantic and falling apart, though she covers it up well."

"Maybe if you figure out how they can keep Clay and Sophie, it might help compensate for not being able to find Jason," Bill said compassionately. "I'm sorry to mention that." "That's the big regret of my life," Steve said sadly. Both men fell silent.

Steve stretched in the chair, drained the last of his beer and pushed his chair back. "I gotta get going. I told Veronica I'd spend a few minutes with her tonight before I head back to the Cities. I'm meeting tomorrow with the lawyers on the loft situation, Bill, and maybe I'll have some answers for you soon about that."

"It's a mess," Bill said.

"It is complicated," Steve agreed. "But we'll sort it out. The whole group of them are a sitcom – the corrupt politician, the innocent, naive small- town woman, the drug culture, the gay culture, real estate that always wants to score the big deals... but this I know for sure: Truth always prevails. You can't hide it, Bill. It always pushes through. That's what I'm after for you and that's what I'm after for Romyn and Earl. And those little kids. That Clay!" He had a big smile on his face. "Did you hear about how he and Shiloh were tracking the guy that attacked Tafani? Now that's a story. He has big potential in the force. I gotta hand it to him."

"Attacked Tiff? Fill me in. I was in such a funk at the diner that I didn't notice anything," Bill said.

"Are you going over there tonight?" Paul asked. He and Jennie had no sooner gotten home when Jennie had laid out her baking equipment and was getting ready to make an apple pie to take over to Eliza.

"She will have missed me. There aren't too many people in her life. I need to let her know that she is loved. And she loves apple pie!" Jennie said.

"I hope you'll make two pies so I can have one when I get the chores done, Jennie girl. Don't forget about your loving husband," he teased.

"I can't forget about that," she replied, wiping the flour from her hands as she walked over and gave her sweet Norwegian husband a sugary kiss.

44

J ennie carried the warm apple pie up to Eliza's
door. She heard the scrabbling noise of Bartholomew before
she heard the "Who's there?" in Eliza's faint voice.

"Jennie here, Eliza," Jennie replied. "Just got back from New
York City today and have a warm apple pie for you and Barto."

The door was unlatched and a little wrinkled apple face
with a beaming smile beckoned her into the house which was
messier than ever. Eliza chortled to herself as she walked over
to the kitchen stove and put on the teakettle. "So luvly, Jennie,
my sweet. I just missed you so!"

Bartholomew nudged Jennie's leg, insisting on equal time
and attention.

She's moving more slowly than ever, Jennie thought. She
took a pile of papers from one of the kitchen chairs and placed
it atop another messy stack.

"I missed you, too, Eliza. I don't think you'd like New York
City, though. Too many people, too many cars. People running
around like chickens with their heads cut off. You'd find yourself lost in the crowds and wanting to be back in Peace Ridge,
that's for sure."

"Was a time. Oy, those days. Me just a slip of a thing. And
livin' east of First Avenue. Fourth floor walk-up, it was. Bathtub
in the kitchen…" Her voice faded away as she turned to the
cupboards to get the teacups.

"I didn't know you lived in New York, Eliza."

"Old times, m'dear. Gone from my ol' brain, now they are."

"Just a young girl? Came over from England?"

"Sent, I was. Sent away from the family. Disgrace, they called it." She turned to Jennie and said fiercely, "T'was no disgrace. A baby! The master's baby. But sent away I was and here am I."

"That had to be terribly hard on you, Eliza." Jennie reached out and kindly patted her friend's hand.

Eliza sat down suddenly and it seemed as if all the air had gone out of her. She stared at the teacups and though her chin quivered she did not cry. Bartholomew nosed his head into her lap, offering the required comfort that pets know by instinct. Eliza was lost in thought and Jennie knew enough to let the moment linger.

"The young master. Oy, handsome he was! Tall, black eyes that saw into my heart, dashing on a horse. Oh, if you had had a gander at 'im, luv. Loved me, he did! Yes, he did! And he 'ad my heart, aye, that he did." She had a faint smile on her face and was lost in reverie, periodically slurping from her teacup. "We was arse over tip, we was. They thought it was just palaver; it was luv." She shook her head. "Lovin' him was easy as kiss yer hand. Luv'ly, he was."

Jennie got up and went over to the cupboard to find plates and forks for the pie. She heard Eliza talking to herself as she rummaged in the drawer for a long knife.

"My lauds, we 'ad fun, didn't we, lad? Those mornings in the Mendips, it was. Along the four wents... You told me all was well and then..." Sobs overtook her and her shoulders shook as she placed her head in her hands, tears flooding through her fingers.

"Oh, my sweet Eliza. Still tender memories after all these years. I am so sorry, my dear."

"Leave me mum, me dad, me little brother, Willie, only seven years old. Beggin' for a chance for jis' one more look at 'im, my young master, but him sent away to the north, too. Those...shysters...tellin' me a vacation, it was. And then on

334

a ship to New York! Oh, Jennie!" she wailed. "Totally skiff-wiff. No idee."

"Oh, my darling, my darling. Eliza, honey, here's a handkerchief." Jennie handed her the cloth and then hugged her little friend, realizing how frail the shoulders, how fragile the little body. "Eliza, my little dear grandma." And then the impulsive offer. "Why don't you come and live with Paul and me? Let's leave this big ol' house. Bring Barto and all the pets. We can find room for everyone. I hate that you are alone here, my dear."

Eliza raised her head and looked at Jennie directly. She wiped her eyes with the handkerchief and blew her nose loudly and then pocketed the damp rag in her pocket. She looked directly into Jennie's eyes.

"Preggers, I was, Jennie. And then, just the little bairn and me. I thought I would go loopy—like a fart in a colander — but we made it. And then here. Praise God. I will make me old bones here in this house."

"I don't want to take you away from your home, Eliza," Jennie said hurriedly. "I just want you to be comfortable … and safe."

"I'll eddy forth here, Jen. Rest your mind about me. Jis' be my pretty friend."

"I am here," Jennie said, giving the little face a warm kiss on the cheek. Bartholomew whimpered then and Jennie was reminded that the outside pets needed feeding. "Can I help you with the pets?" she asked.

"You're to hand, Jennie. 'Preciate it." She stood up slowly then and moved towards the door.

Jennie walked with her and then hugged her impulsively. "I love you, Grandma. You are my sweet grandma."

That brought tears.

Delaney had texted Jennie to get Tafani's number so she could get more photos of her paintings. Tiff had been slow to respond, but ultimately Jennie sent through a number of paint-ings that Delaney could use to begin the dialogue.

I need to talk to Tafani directly, Delaney thought. *I need a portfolio. But this will be good enough for the visa people.*

"Ah, Delaney. Here on the home turf." Ten's voice on the phone was casual.

"Yes, I've been busy for the last couple of days, meeting with galleries and artist reps. Getting appointment is like pulling teeth."

"Tell me about it. I've got just a few before the shipment arrives, but I told the crew I needed some time," Ten said reas-suringly. "Longing to see you," he added softly.

"Me, too," she purred. "Though I'll be taken up for a few days. I have made several appointments in London and will be tied up 'til the weekend."

"That's perfect. Come to Somerset if you can. The house will be full. The parents have invited the whole ensemble and we'll have a full house but I'd love to see you. I'll text you the details. Have you a car?"

"No, but no worries. I can make my way."

"I'll send a car around. It's six-ish on Saturday night. Informal. Throngs of people, mostly mother's friends and father's golf foursome. You'll find someone to talk to, I'm sure. Must ring off now. The lorry is here," Ten said. "Looking for-ward to seeing you."

"Me, too." Delaney punched the red disconnect button in anger and disappointment. *He didn't want to see me immedi-ately, that was clear. Well, screw him. I'm going to the pub.*

Bill finally decided to open the box that loomed like a malign presence at the end of the table. He had gone through all the other boxes but there was nothing that raised a red flag. *I don't even know why I need to keep all this stuff,* he thought. *Once the taxes are filed...* It gave him a repeated pang when he noted Donna's neat cursive on the bills, noting the check number, the date of payment. Every little thing would remind him of her going forward. Even the arrangement of the things on the counter in the kitchen – the retro bread box was allowed but not the modern mixer, the Sur la Table brushed metal canister set, but not the messy butter dish, the porcelain dishwashing liquid dispenser, but not the box of Cascade. Bill looked around the kitchen and missed every little single thing about their life together. *She made this into a home. She is everywhere.*

He heard a noise then and went to the porch to see that Eunie had dropped Kellie off in the yard and had left with a goodbye wave.

"Good time?" he asked.

Kellie walked into the kitchen and sat down wearily at the kitchen table.

"She and I don't have anything in common anymore. Small town friend. Nice girl, but..." She left the thought unspoken.

"Want some supper? Are you hungry?"

"Nah, we ate at the McDonald's at Walmart. I'll take a Diet Coke if you have it." She walked in an unsteady manner to the refrigerator and rummaged around until she found the red and silver can. Bill watched her carefully. Kellie walked very carefully over to the sink and flipped open the can and threw the tab into the wastebasket under the sink. She stared out the window over the sink, her reflection clearly visible to Bill. He was startled at how hollow were her eyes and cadaverous her face. Her pregnant belly protruded painfully; she had told him she was only a few months pregnant and he was no expert, but she looked further along than that. There was a look of despair on her face but she rearranged her visage when she returned to sit down opposite her father at the table.

"Whatcha' doin' here, Dad?" she asked.

"Papers from your mom. Her business. Our business. Gotta go through them and sort them out and then get the office desk fixed."

"Yeah, the robbery..."

"Not a big deal. Got everything back. Just gotta get it all sorted out."

"I want to go back to the loft, Dad, in case you don't know. Peace Ridge is fine for a little time," she said scornfully, "but I need to get back to the city."

"You can't go back there, Kellie. It's a meth lab. For one thing, the police have it blocked out. For the other thing, why do you want to get back into that lifestyle? You need to get straight, Kellie." He looked at her directly but she wouldn't meet his gaze.

"I need to be on my own," she deflected. "I'm over twenty-one. I should be in my own apartment. Mom told me there would be plenty of money for that. Even if I wanted to go to college."

"Tell me more about your mom," Bill said sadly. "I miss her. What was the last thing you talked about?"

"Well, she was going to take me to Mall of America and we were going to shop for clothes. I don't have any real fall clothes. Abercrombie was having a sale…she said we'd go. She had a discount coupon." Kellie fell silent at the table. Outside the wind was picking up. They were about to have a rare summer downpour and Bill worried briefly about the open windows in the house, but made no move to leave the table.

"I'm glad Mom and you had a good relationship," Bill said. "It helps…to know how much she loved you. I know she still cares…"

"Well, I don't know, Dad. I am not sure of anything anymore. I don't believe in anything. Once you're gone, you're gone. That's the end," she said flatly.

"Kells, you're in grief, too. You can't bury it forever. If you want to talk to Pastor Ed…he has helped me…"

"Don't push him on me, Dad! That's not where I'm at! I get by with a little help from my friends. You may have heard that in a song somewhere," she said sarcastically.

"Kellie, why are you so angry? We need to be together now."

"Yeah. Right. You and Mom made a mess of your lives and now you want to tell me how to live," she shot back. "That's not working for me, if you want to know the truth. I can make my own way."

"Don't seem to be doing too good a job about it right now, are you?" Bill thought straight talk was called for, given her pregnancy. But that wasn't the right approach. Kellie shot up from the table and walked purposefully out of the kitchen, shouting as she left the room, "As if you're some kind of hero? Someone who has all the answers. Mom kept the business going — you know she did – and so now you're worried about how to go on. Well, don't rope me into your schemes. I heard enough from her!" was her parting shot as she left the room.

Bill sat in stunned silence. The room echoed with the shouted insult, "Mom kept the business going, Mom kept the business going." His mind went around and around, trying to escape the harsh indictment, but he could only see the ugliness on Kellie's face as she said the words and a mirror image of Donna's face twisted in hatred as she said, "I've always hated you, Bill." *Always hated, always hated,* the words were like a record that was stuck in its groove.

I need a dog, Bill thought incongruously at that moment. *I need a wet nose pushing into my hand and the wide-open panting smile of love.* He sat in his chair, thinking about their last dog and a slight smile that was really a grimace played around his mouth. *He was the one,* he thought. *Only wanted to play. To eat. To be loved on. The basics of happiness.*

Well, we make a mess of it, don't we, God? he said in silent entreaty. There was about half of the last box left and he wearily emptied it on the table and began to sort through the papers and letters.

There was a small bundle of letters that looked important. "Official business" it said on the envelope. He didn't recognize the return address – somewhere in Washington, D.C. He opened the first one at random. Handwritten with the salutation, "My

339

darling..." Bill turned the letter over. "Love always, Harold."
Why did he somehow expect this day would come?

45

Bill didn't have the heart to read the letters. After scanning the first one he opened he laid them all out on the table and sorted them by date. The first one was written three years ago but most of them were in the past year just before Donna's accident. And then nothing. Three years ago – that was before the Dane Johnson mess. Just when Donna's Interiors was taking off.

I remember she talked about a big commission, but I didn't pay attention. I trusted her. Fool that I am.

Bill pushed his chair back from the table and swept all the papers back into the box. *I'll show these to Steve later,* he thought. *He'll probably make sense of them. What's done is done and Donna is dead. I just need to find a way to go on.* He walked into the living room. In the room upstairs he could hear Kellie talking in a dead monotone on her cell phone. He turned on the remote and flipped through the channels without paying attention. After a commercial for Cosequin followed by Otezla and then one for a male enhancement pill whatever that was, he switched to the outdoor channel and blindly watched the show of two men tracking an elk in Montana. Their hushed voices tried to create an atmosphere of anticipation but the distant view of the elk just made him feel sad. He was about to switch the channel to *How It's Made* when the phone rang.

"Hello, Bill. Am I calling at a good time?" Pam's voice was tentative.

"There aren't any good times any more, Pam," he said honestly.

"I'm sorry, Bill. Really I am." There was a long pause. "How is Kellie?"

"Well, she's just stalked upstairs because I told her she's making a mess of her life," he said simply.

"Bill, I ... saw her pregnancy." Pam didn't know how to proceed. "I see a young girl that is hurting and could need a friend. Do you think she'd let me be her friend?"

"I don't know. I don't know that she *wants* friends. She doesn't want me, that's for sure!"

"Bill, you are a wonderful person. I suppose she's hurting and doesn't know where to turn."

"It's the drugs," Bill said flatly. "They've changed her."

"Is she still using? In Peace Ridge?"

"I don't know. I don't know my own daughter anymore."

"I'm sorry, Bill. I hate that you are going through this. If there was only something I could do..."

"'Help me make it through the night,'" he half whisper-sang it.

"Oh Bill, I know how hard this is for you. And I'm so sorry. The accident and the waiting at the hospital— that was awful. I could see how it drained you. But this is somehow worse, the ending of a life together. I've been there in a little different way with the end of my marriage. One that I thought would last forever. I've found it just takes time. It does get better with time, Bill. I can say that, at least."

There was a long silence. Bill knew he should say something, but what? There were no words anymore. And when he tried to speak his throat was filled with a lump as big as his garage.

"Just keep talking to me, Pam. Say anything, just keep talking."

"Brandon and I went shopping at Cub Foods today and then I decided to treat him a lunch out at Chick-Fil-A. He loves their dipping sauces and their mini chicken. He still makes a bit of mess but he's so good-natured, the staff just laugh and help him out. When he was a little boy he loved McDonald's and their inside playground but he's outgrown that now. My sweet big boy."

"Donna and I took Kellie to McDonald's often. She wouldn't touch it now, of course, because she claims she's into 'eating healthy,' though the way she looks I don't think she's eating anything at all."

Pam listened to the thickness in his voice change to something more normal.

"Anyway, I can't get her to eat anything here at home. Misses her mom's cooking, she says, though Donna didn't cook very much these last few years."

"She's grieving in the only way she can, Bill," Pam said. 'I wish there was some way I could help."

"You could say it again, Pam,"

"Say what again?"

"Tell me that I'm a wonderful person. No one has said that to me in...forever."

"Bill," Pam's voice was soft and compassionate. "Anyone who spends five minutes with you sees your big heart. They see someone who would give his last dollar to a beggar on the street. Someone who would drop what he was doing, even if it was very important, to help out someone else. Someone who feels deeply but may not be able to express it eloquently but then..." she paused, "anyone who heard you speak at the funeral, Bill, would have come away thinking '*That's* the way I'd like to be remembered by someone *I* love.'"

There was a long silence on the line. Finally, Bill cleared his throat and said, "Will you call me again tomorrow night, Pam? That would give me something to look forward to."

"Yes, I will. Of course," she said gently.

Her writing pad was smudged and tear-stained. Veronica had tried to be faithful to Pastor Ed's request that she write out her two lists – her emotional and rational reasons why she wanted the abortion and then coping with it after the fact. But facing up to it was hard and she found that she was restless and couldn't sit in the chair. She walked to the large window overlooking the backyard and stared out at the mosaic of trees, now darkening in the night air to the deep forest green of the Black Forest. Peace. Green. Greenpeace. That silly noddle brought a grimace to her face and she sighed heavily and walked back to the table and faced the task. In just a minute, she popped up again and walked to the cupboard and took down the bottle of vodka.

Maybe that will help me focus, she thought. *Or put me to sleep so I don't have to think about this. I'm such a coward. Just do it, Veronica!*

It wasn't the rational reasons for the abortion that were making her hands shake and her sorrow mount.

'Everyone does it, most common surgery for women in the U.S.,' they said.

'Government pays for it, so it must be okay.'

'Less expensive than childbirth, so better economically for us.'

'There's always another more convenient time to have a baby—we need to build the business.'

She looked at her list of so-called rational reasons and tried to remember how she felt emotionally at the time. It always came down to losing Gary if she didn't have the abortion. Losing her marriage. Avoiding the fight and keeping peace between them. That was her selfish reason at the time. Thinking back on it now, she reflected on how far she'd been willing to go to preserve her relationship at the extent of her sanity. She didn't know. Didn't realize.

For when she began to make the second list, all rational reasons disappeared.

"I did the right thing for us," she said aloud. "That was my thought at the time. That I was the one who'd made the sacrifice to save our marriage."

But her list of psychological consequences was lengthy... self-loathing, guilt, shame, shattered self-confidence, feeling dirty and alone, feeling like an empty shell of herself, grief for the baby.

"Oh, the baby, the baby!" she grieved, alone in her house, doubling over in great honking sobs. The house was empty. There was no one there to comfort and console and even if there had been no other person could fill the emptiness inside. "I sold my soul," she whispered to herself through her tears. "I cannot be forgiven."

Veronica staggered up from the table and walked over to grab a kitchen towel to blot her eyes. She felt faint and dizzy though she'd barely sipped from her cocktail glass. *I can't do this. I just can't do this.*

She walked into the bedroom and stared at her empty bed for a long moment and then made her way slowly into the adjoining bathroom and slowly opened the medicine cabinet and took out the bottles of aspirin, Tylenol, an old prescription for a pain killer, and the bottle of oxycodone that she'd hidden from her father when he had demanded all her prescriptions. Her hands reached for the prescriptions automatically and she avoided looking at herself in the oversized mirrors, something she'd done every day since her abortion. She poured the pills into a water glass by the sink. They nearly filled the eight-ounce tumbler.

I'll need to get a bottle of water to get these down, she thought despairingly.

Veronica slowly turned toward the bedroom. The young slender woman sat lightly on the bed. She had long wavy brown hair, was completely beautiful with perfect features and an incredibly sweet smile on her face. She was dressed simply in blue jeans, sandals, and a sleeveless salmon colored t-shirt.

345

But it was her eyes that caught and held Veronica's as she stood there with the water glass filled with death.

"Veronica," she said lovingly, as she slowly stood up from the bed and took a step towards her. She held out her arms then and Veronica fell into them, her tears flooding the both of them. The woman was slight and her hands patting Veronica's back were like the touch of an angel. She pulled out a hand-kerchief and gently and lovingly patted Veronica's face, wiping away the tears. "Jesus loves you very much," she said, "so very much." In the distance Veronica could hear the sound of her cell phone ringing but she didn't want to pull away from that tender embrace. She took a step backward then and looked down as she heard the sound of her feet crunching the spilled pills. There was a slight, barely perceptible movement of air in the room and when Veronica looked back to the bed the room was completely empty, only a slight mussing of the bedspread showing that someone had been there.

"Hello, Veronica," Steve said when Veronica picked up the insistent phone call. "All right, my love?"

"Steve..." Veronica didn't know where to begin, how to describe the last five minutes. "Steve, I need help," she said finally. "I need someone."

"I'm calling Pastor Ed right now," he nearly shouted, "and then I'm calling you back in five minutes and if you don't answer the phone right away, I'm sending the chief over to see you. Don't move. Stay right where you are with your phone in your hand. Do you hear me, my darling?"

"Yes," Veronica said submissively. "Yes, dear."

46

"Pastor, Steve here. I need you to go to Veronica's right away," Steve pleaded peremptorily when Ed answered his phone with a soft "Hello?"

"Right away, Steve," Ed said obediently. "What—"

"I think she's vulnerable right now, Pastor. I wish I was there! I wish I was there!" he said passionately. "I just called her and she said 'I need help.' That is unlike her. Something has happened. Can you go over? I'll call Archie, too, but he's in the Cities. Someone needs to be there fast."

"On my way." Ed hung up the phone and grabbed his car keys in the same seamless gesture. "Father God, protect Veronica. Be with her now, I beg of You, please."

Ed drove as fast as his little Honda would go and was relieved to find that Veronica herself opened the door to his push on the doorbell. She looked white and drawn but she was there in the flesh. She had her cell phone in her hand and as they walked in together towards the living room, she said, "I have to call Steve right away, Pastor."

"He's here, Steve." She listened for a moment and then passed the phone over to Ed.

"Pastor, can you stay with her for a while? I have called Archie and he's on his way north but she can't be left alone. I think she got overwhelmed again."

Ed passed the phone back to Veronica. "Got any coffee here?" he asked with a friendly smile.

At that everyday request she turned toward the kitchen and began the homely familiar gestures of hospitality. "Don't have any cookies, Pastor, I'm sorry."

"No worries, Veronica. Don't need 'em. Jill is making a big meal for supper."

"How is Jill doing?" Veronica's question was flat. Making conversation.

Ed could see she was disassociating from her actions and from him. He got up from his chair and walked over to the counter where she was standing with the filter and coffee grounds in her hands seemingly at a loss. He took them from her and led her by the hand over to the sofa in the great room.

"Veronica, we need to pray right now. We need to have another guest in this house. We need Jesus to make His presence known to us right now." He bowed his head. "Jesus. Our dear Heavenly friend and Savior. Please come into Veronica's home and bless us with Your love and Your kind concern for all of Your fallen creatures. We've asked Veronica to do some hard work and she's overwhelmed. Help us, we pray. We love You, in Jesus' name, Amen."

"Amen," was Veronica's whispered response and then she put her head in her hands and sobbed, tears dribbling through her fingers onto the floor. Ed remembered the last time he'd been in this room with Paul after they'd rescued her from her prior overdose. The atmosphere felt the same – of desperation, despair, of deadness.

"I'm sorry about this, Veronica. Maybe it was too hard for you right now." He had seen the list on the table and knew that had caused this crisis.

"No," she sobbed. "I need to do it. But I can't do it alone. I am so ugly, such a shameful person. I feel such guilt. I wanted to be able to forgive, but my—murder – of my own child, how can I be forgiven?

"There is no sin that won't be forgiven, Veronica, in God's grace. For believers in Jesus who took it all on Himself and showed Himself capable to bear all—our sins."

"I don't know how to go on," she said in a muffled voice. "I'm afraid…"

"We can face it together and Steve will help you, too. And your dad. We're all with you on this and not a single one of us judges you, Veronica. Be sure of that."

"I haven't been able to live a single day without waking up in the morning and seeing the face of a baby, a small child. He would be nearly five years old now, a child I can't hold, can't love. People say they can't live with themselves. I feel as if I should be in solitary confinement on death row myself. In a way I am, confined to my head without a way out."

"Veronica, I want you to sit right here and I'm going to get our coffee going." Ed got up from the sofa and patted her shoulder gently. He watched her covertly as he placed the coffee filter in the pot and measured the coffee. Filling the coffee pot with water at the sink he looked out the window and saw that Romyn had driven into the yard. *Oh good. Romyn. Just in time, as always.*

He walked over to the door and opened it before Romyn had a chance to even knock.

"Hello there. Glad you're here," he said simply as he led the way into the house. Romyn immediately walked over to the sofa and sat down next to Veronica and gave her a tight hug around her frail shoulders. The two women clung to one another as Ed fetched the coffee cups and brought them over to the table. The room was flooded with an unearthly fresh sunlight that cast rainbows of light onto the three clustered together in the living room. There appeared to be a light scent floating in the air and the air itself felt still, pregnant with unspoken activity and words.

There were no sounds in the house except for Veronica's faint sobbing and, not for the first time, Ed thought, *there needs to be a dog or a cat roaming this big beautiful place. She needs that comfort.* He found the remote for the TV and snapped it on, switching the channels until he found the one that featured calming sights and sounds of nature. The crackling of leaves underfoot, rippling brooks, the wind rushing through the trees and the distinctive *chee-chee-chee-chee* of the American robin provided a calming sense to the room and the anguish of the poor human. And the coffee. Veronica's hand was shaking when she reached for the coffee cup but Romyn handed it to her and moved closer to her on the sofa, thigh to thigh. The calming pressure of presence.

"Veronica, let's put aside those lists for a while. We don't need to do them now. I've been researching these issues and I think we should put you in touch with Project Rachel. They do post-abortion counseling— it's a ministry of the Catholic Church. There is an office in St. Cloud and I think what you need most right now is to talk to others who have traveled this journey with you. And to know that you are not alone."

"They never tell you that you won't be able to live with yourself, that there isn't a single day that you don't wake up and remember what you did..." Veronica said.

"There is forgiveness," Romyn said gently, bringing her face around to her own and cupping her worn hands on Veronica's soft cheeks. "Jesus is a loving and compassionate God and He forgives this. Even this. So, you need to follow His lead and forgive *yourself*. That's how you heal. It isn't that He doesn't hate the sin of abortion—He does. But He knows we are fallen creatures and we sin. Not only this, but all the other sins that 'flesh is heir to,' as someone said."

Ed smiled and quoted softly,

To be, or not to be – that is the question:
Whether 'tis nobler in the mind to suffer
The slings and arrows of outrageous fortune
Or to take arms against a sea of troubles,
And by opposing end them. To die—to sleep –
No more; and by a sleep to say we end
The heartache, and the thousand natural shocks
That flesh is heir to. 'Tis a consummation
Devoutly to be wish'd. to die- to sleep.

To sleep – perchance to dream; ay, there's the rub!
For in that sleep of death what dreams may come
When we have shuffled off this mortal coil,
Must give us pause. There's the respect
That makes calamity of so long life."

The three were quiet in the room, a quietness that felt like the calm after a storm. Ed's soft evocation of Hamlet had brought them to both the present crisis but also helped them feel anchored in the trials of humans over the generations. It was curiously comforting.

Shakespeare, Romyn thought. *The genius Shakespeare.*

"I've come to take you back to our house for a meal tonight, Veronica. Earl told me that he was making something special that would be completely wasted unless we had a treasured guest. We both thought of you immediately. It's his Chicken Florentine which he loves to make. I just walk away and let him take over the kitchen. We want you and won't take 'no' for an answer. Pastor, you have plans? You're welcome."

"No, my Jilly is making supper for us. Archie is on his way. Should I send him your way?"

"Yes, please. Earl will like that. Archie is always good for stories about the old times in Peace Ridge and Earl is now digging deep into the history of the village. He will be taking notes as Archie speaks. And Veronica and I can just watch and shake our heads." She gave her friend's hand a comforting squeeze.

"Sounds like a plan. Veronica, should I send you the stuff on Project Rachel? Better yet, why don't you come over tomorrow morning to the church and we'll sit down together and call them?" Ed said.

Veronica gave a weak smile and a brief nod.

"In the meantime," he said, "I think you should listen to this quotation from a man who lived about 2,700 years ago."

Both looked at him with quizzical expressions.

"'I, even I, am he who blots out your transgressions, for my own sake, And remembers your sins no more.'" He smiled. "No more. Isaiah, chapter 43."

"To the heart," Veronica said after a moment, "and from my heart, thank you."

"He wastes nothing, Veronica," Ed said softly.

Romyn hugged her friend around her waist. "You are our precious friend and we love you." She looked around for Veronica's purse, and spying it, said, "Grab your purse; I'll drive you to our place and Archie can bring you back home after supper."

"There's a dog out there that needs a loving home, Veronica, and I think you have just the right fireplace rug for him to lie on," Ed said fondly as he walked out the door.

47

"Father, I wonder if you would have a few minutes for me to pop over and visit?" Ed and Father Brandon and several of the other ministers in Peace Ridge Village got together every once in a while for coffee and conversations and they knew one another quite well. "I want to get some information about Project Rachel for a member of our congregation and I thought you might have the name of the local coordinator. I went online and they have a St. Cloud office..."

"Happy to help out, Pastor. We have referred several to them already. Come on over. I'll put the pot on."

Ed drove over to St. Anthony's Catholic Church and was greeted with an exuberant "Hello!" by Father Brandon. Ed always thought that he needed to be wearing a monk's robe with a rope belt, as he was rotund and always smiling, a Father Brown type of character complete with the discerning eyes and quick intellect.

"Been too long. We always promised that we would get together and review some of the church manuscripts we've got here in our archives but we never seem to have the time. My fault, not yours, Pastor," he hastened to add.

"Well, my life has changed, Father," Ed said as he settled into the comfortable but shabby rectory. "For the better," he hastened to add. "My wife, Jill, is home in Peace Ridge with me now and things are working out." He looked down with a slight secret smile.

"I've been praying, Ed, praying for that. I'm so glad. Your pilgrimage has been a long one."

"I think we're going to regain much of our former relationship but it will take work. She's lost ten years since...the accident...and bringing back some of the touchstones of her old personality will take time. But I'm seeing signs and I praise the Lord!"

"Yes, thanks be to God, Ed."

Father Brandon leaned back in his overstuffed shabby armchair. 'Happy to share what I can about Project Rachel but I might put you in touch with the parish's women's coordinator. She is our first line of defense when it comes to women in trouble, as they used to call it. I only know that we've been able to help several young girls in Peace Ridge Village and we praise the Lord for that."

"The woman I'm thinking about is not a young woman and it's not a current pregnancy. She's struggling and suicidal over an abortion of about five years ago. She came to me to ask me to help her with forgiveness. She knew she needed to forgive others, her cheating husband, for example, and her best friend who was involved in the affair. But we needed to start with her abortion – seeking God's forgiveness and forgiving herself – and that has taken her into a terrible spiral of depression and thoughts of suicide."

"We find that's the usual pattern," Father Brandon said. "The despair and shame. And especially in our church which is so black and white about abortion, it seems the guilt is nearly overwhelming. Other more liberal denominations are more wishy-washy if you'll excuse me."

"No, I know. I know. We Protestants don't completely have our act together. We have progressive denominations that support abortion rights as part of their advocacy for women's right to choose. Along with supporting LGBTQ, social justice, gender equity issues..."

There was an expression of sadness on Ed's face and Father Brandon observed it quietly. Finally, he said, "You can't take it all on, Pastor. Not by yourself. Not in Valley Community Church. All these issues – these theological divides, these weakened doctrines, this..."

"Walking away from the true teachings of Jesus and the Bible," Ed said.

"This tendency in our world today to conform our conscience and beliefs to the culture of the day. I won't say the Catholic Church hasn't fallen into some deep potholes along the way, especially in the last generation. We are not perfect. But I think we really do try hard to be firm on the issues which are truly fundamental. The right to life, for example. Enshrined in our Constitution, but more importantly, enshrined in God's word. And His plan. We will never stop fighting that battle."

Those last words were spoken quietly with a fervent intensity. The room was quiet and both men were silent. The well-worn rectory had seen better times. There was faded wallpaper on the walls and well-filled bookshelves that needed dusting. Ed noticed the faded carpet and threadbare footstool at his feet. In the distance he could hear the sound of shouting children from the parish playground next door. Summertime and the children were without a care in the world.

"That's the sound that keeps me going," Father Brandon said finally. "Those sweet laughing sounds of carefree children. Children who could be cast aside or never born but are here and now adding their joyful sounds to our lives in Peace Ridge. I treasure each one and to think that any one of them may not have deserved to be born – well, that makes me angry, it makes me sick to my stomach, it makes me weep for us all, Ed. We are doomed if we don't think God will eventually judge our sin in this American culture today. Someone once said, 'God sees all and waits.' That will be an awful day of reckoning in all senses of the word."

"Oh my, yes," Ed said slowly. "And you and I are charged to be the traffic lights, the signposts, the warning labels, the counselor and confidantes.

"Other than that, it's a cushy job!"

Both men laughed.

Father Brandon scrolled through his iPhone. "Here are the numbers you want, Ed. The Project Rachel coordinator in St. Cloud and our women's leader here at the parish. Karen. She'll help you. Start with her."

Earl had outdone himself as far as Clay and Sophie were concerned. Schwan's chicken nuggets with Tater Tots followed by ice cream bars flanked Earl's disdained Chicken Florentine. Spinach, ugh!

Easy conversation and cheerful laughter and teasing characterized the conversation. There was absolutely nothing serious discussed. Earl would interrupt his conversation with Archie to tell the kids a few stories from the old days of Peace Ridge but neither was really interested, only wanting to see if Romyn would allow them to play outside in the backyard for another hour. They knew it was nearly time for baths, prayers, and bedtime, but the sun was barely lingering in the sky – its last gasp for the night – and nothing was more fun than swinging on the swing set in the darkness, swooping up to catch a glimpse of stars as the night air cooled and darkened to full night. Clay never missed nighttime play to give thrills to Sophie with his talk of night animals coming to get her.

"Romyn, let's indulge them tonight. Only a half hour, kids!" Earl said sternly. "I'm going to take Veronica and Archie out to my workshop and show them what I'm working on."

"Yay! Yay! Yay!" Clay said and Sophie echoed, "Yay," in a soft voice.

"When we come in, can we have hot chocolate before we go to sleep?" Clay asked in a pleading voice.

"Depends on how good you are and Mom is the judge. Remember that," Earl said in a mock stern voice. "Let's go out to the shop for a few minutes, Archie and Veronica," he urged.

They followed Earl as he wheeled his chair out to his workshop. There was the fragrant smell of wood, turpentine, mechanics oil, and an indefinable scent of—*maleness,* Veronica thought. The scent of a man's domain. For a brief moment she was back in Gary's garage and an image of her rage and his indifference filled her mind. Funny how smell could bring back a memory like that. She gathered her thoughts and walked slowly behind Earl as he made his way to his lathe and band saw.

"I want to show you what I'm working on," he said as he wheeled his chair over to his lathe. The table held a large piece of wood and over to the side of his workshop was a pile of similar clumps of wood, cut off on one side so they could lay down flat, their pebbled bulge protruding with knobs and erratic bumps. The piece on his lathe had been screwed to a flat plate and above it, hovering over the large wooden lump like a flimsy paper saucer, was a round plate. Earl had been working the piece to shape the wood into a rough circular shape.

"It's spalted maple, isn't it?" asked Archie.

"I don't know wood," Veronica replied.

"Yup. Maple. Well, it's sort of a science, wood is," Earl said. "It's not as easy as it looks to people who don't work it. I'm working this burl into a bowl. Thought you might find it interesting."

"Burls, those bulges on some trees you find in the woods, aren't they?" Veronica asked.

"Yes, they happen because there is something that has gotten into the tree, a virus, a fungus, something interrupts the tree's growth and it creates this deformity. The normal grain of the tree gets contaminated by the sickness and creates the burl, which is a swirl of erratic grain, of crazy patterns. Woodworkers like to find burls, especially big ones, because they provide completely unique and distinctive patterns and if one is careful it's possible to make something really beautiful out of them."

He wheeled over to his band saw. "I'm working on this piece now. Ben at Tops Hardware has been going out into my woods and he's finding my burls for us to work. Maple.

Boxelder. From that stand of white oak I have over the hill. He harvests the trees – I give him the wood – and he cuts the burls for me. He cuts the flat side so I can put it on the lathe and then I can shape it into the bowl."

"Ben's a good man," Archie offered.

"The wood is beautiful," Veronica said. She reached out and stroked the rough bark. She didn't know what else to say. It was pleasant to be in the workshop with its pleasant smell and quiet peacefulness. For a fleeting moment she thought about the irony of Earl loving to work with wood when it was wood, the falling tree, that caused his paralysis.

"Let me show you this latest piece, Veronica," Earl commanded, as he wheeled back to his lathe. The maple burl had been carved into a rough bowl shape. He picked up his special wood turning tools and talked about the ones that were used for carving, for shaping.

"You have to be careful when you're doing this. Burl wood is a harder wood than the normal grain of the tree but because the grain is twisted and swirled you never know where there might be a weakness so when you are turning it you have to work slowly and carefully.

"I love seeing the grain emerge. Sometimes you will find a seam of brilliant red or orange, or a chevron pattern. You just never know. The wood holds its secrets and it's up to the wood turner to uncover them."

"It's fascinating, Earl."

"Would you like to see me power up the lathe and see how it works? Just for a little demonstration?"

"I always wished I had a lathe. I'm jealous of your workshop, Earl," Archie said.

Earl's lathe was specially designed at waist height to accommodate his wheelchair and his gouges, round points, and the rest of his carving tools were laid out carefully on a wheeled table nearby. The burl had been already carved into a rough bowl shape and was mounted to a chuck on the headstock.

358

"I'm going to do more rough rounding with this roughing gouge," he said, "and that will get us closer to the right bowl shape." He connected the tailstock to a point opposite the head-stock and adjusted the chuck.

"How do you know what shape to make it?" Veronica asked. "I mean, I know bowls are round, but..." She nodded her head at the shelf over his workbench that held finished bowls of different sizes and shapes with naturally formed edges that evoked the wildness of the forest.

"The burl tells you what it needs to be. This piece is roughly spherical and I imagine it'll be pretty symmetrical when all is said and done but we won't know until we begin to hollow her out and see what she wants to be. The beauty of working with burls is their uniqueness. It's likely this one will finish up uneven. For me that's the beauty of the piece, capturing the essence of the natural wood."

He put on his safety glasses and motioned Veronica and Archie to stand back a short distance. He started the lathe and the workshop was soon filled with the low hum of the machine, the scraping sound of the gouge, and the inimitable scent of woodchips. Veronica was suddenly filled with a strong nostalgia and the vision of her grandpa working wood in his shop when she was a child. Earl's face was one of concentration and she could see how his upper body strength compensated for his paralysis. A fine hand was the essential tool. He powered down the machine and brushed the loose sawdust from the burl.

"Now we'll reposition the burl and use my rounding gouge to continue turning the outer face." He made the adjustments and began turning again and didn't say anything for several minutes.

"You can see the beauty of the grain. I have to work with a gentle hand to work with the grain and not gouge it, because it's compact and a harder grain to work with. Out of the disease of the wood, the fungus or bacteria or whatever got into the tree, we discover a unique design. Someone called it 'the fingerprints of God.'"

Veronica nodded slowly.

"When I work with burl wood—something that was corrupted — I always think that God takes something meant to destroy the fine upright tree and creates something of incomparable beauty." He smoothed the wood and unscrewed the chuck and lifted the blank up, grunting softly as he did so.

"We'll have to cut a recess, a hole if you will, into the bottom here so we can reattach it to the headstock with a chuck and then we can begin to hollow it out. That's the most exciting part of the process for me – seeing the unique pattern – what woodworkers call the figure—emerge from the burl. Emptying, hollowing is also the most challenging and dangerous in the sense that it's easy to make a mistake and gouge it. I have to work slowly and carefully, especially as I work the lip of the piece." He set the wood down carefully and blocked it on the lathe so it rested securely, and then wheeled his chair over to the workbench and retrieved a small can of Danish oil.

"I'll put a little Danish oil on the bottom of the piece so you guys can see the grain and pattern."

Veronica moved closer and peered at the patch of wood.

"Amazing," she breathed. "It's like a winter landscape with fallen leaves, mosses, and patches of snow. The colors are subdued but the abstract design is like that of a fine landscape painter."

"Like Bev Doolittle paintings," Archie offered.

Earl nodded. He set the piece back on the lathe and wheeled back to his workbench. With a great heave, he pulled himself up to lean on the bench and reached up in a jerk to grab a beautiful finished bowl. Sitting back down heavily in his chair, he stared at the bowl for a moment and then brushed the fine dust from it with his work rag.

"This is for you, Veronica," he said, handing it to her. At her soft protest, he said, "I made it for you. Made it from an old boxelder that had been taken down on your land a long time ago. Ben had harvested the tree but the burl was just lying there in his shed. We both had the idea that you needed a burl bowl from your own land and so a couple of months ago he hauled it up here and I made it for you."

She stroked the deep recess, which tapered to a fine symmetrical lip. Her eyes were shining with unshed tears. "You knew I needed this, didn't you, Earl?" she said. "I will treasure it. Pride of place on my fireplace mantle."

"Fine woodworking, Earl," Archie said with a sad and serious expression on his face. "And a fine lesson."

48

The driver was a youngish, taciturn redhead who briefly doffed his cap in Delaney's direction and held open the door to the late-model Mercedes-Benz. She sank into the soft leather seats and thought, *Now, this is my style. I could get used to this.* The mid-afternoon London traffic at Hampstead was heavy and she mused that it was going to be a long journey to Frome in Somerset but she was going to enjoy every single minute of it. Ten's invite had lingered in her mind for the past week and she was excited to think of a cocktail party at his parent's place.

She'd dressed carefully for her reunion with Ten, wearing an outfit she'd bought at an extravagant price at the Galleria in Edina. Creamy, low-cut silk blouse with balloon sleeves and tight cuffs over gold and black silk hibiscus-print straight leg pants. Her Manolo Blahnik buckle slide satin sandals completed the refined but casual look. This morning she'd treated herself to a manicure and pedicure at a small shop on Flask Walk, and with her carefully applied makeup she felt completely on top of her game. She had no idea who'd be at the party – Ten had been vague – but she felt she was ready for anyone or anything. *'Country house in Frome, Somerset.'* That could mean anything.

Especially ready for Ten, who had been elusive in the last couple of weeks. They'd texted several times and talked briefly on the telephone, but he didn't seem too anxious to get together with her. Flashing through her mind was a scene in a car park outside a restaurant in Taunton. The slender blonde woman and an unmistakable intimacy between her and Ten. Delaney had often hardened her heart against men and their inevitable betrayals. She knew she was chasing Ten by coming to England. *But so be it!* That thought ran through her mind as she idly watched London pass by as the Mercedes powerfully made its way through the western suburbs and onto the M25.

"Two hours or so?" she asked the driver.

"Yes, mum," he replied, as he looked over his right shoulder and then moved over into the passing lane, increasing his speed.

"Do you often drive for Ten?" she asked casually. Might as well see if she could learn something about the family.

"Mum?" he asked.

"Ten Sellwood?" she replied.

"I drive for the Lady Sellwood," he said. *He is close-mouthed,* Delaney thought. *Won't get anything out of him.* "Do you like it? Is she nice?" she pursued.

"She's a right proper lady," he said, fiddling with the air conditioner. "Comfortable, mum?" he asked.

"Yes, fine." Delaney turned her attention off the driver. Nothing happening here. She grabbed her cell phone and put Frome in the GPS app to track their journey. *Might as well learn a little geography if I am going to live here*, she thought. That thought had crept into her mind more and more often in the last couple of weeks. She hadn't really planned to move to England, but in the back of her mind she had left open the possibility. At first it had all hinged on Ten and how that relationship went, but as she pursued her occupational visa as an artists' rep, the probability that she could swing a longer stay became increasingly possible. With or without Ten.

Brian's face popped into her mind – he would love this scenery, she thought – as they sped west on the M4 past the North Wessex Downs. He would be in his glory walking these green hills. *Can't see any of the Bronze Age white horses carved into the chalk hills from here, but he would find so many subjects for his poetry.* That thought gave her a momentary sense of desolating loneliness but she crammed that thought back down deeply in her mind. *Cross that bridge when we come to it. Don't need to plan ahead now.*

After turning south at Bath onto the A36, they began a more leisurely drive because of the hills and twists and turns of the road. They made a turn at Brassknuckle Hill and Delaney retrieved her notebook from her purse and wrote down the name. That was a good one to add to the English name collection she was making for Brian. Nearing Frome, they turned off onto an unmarked road which quickly ran out of macadam and became a single lane gravel road. Tall hedges on either side of the road blocked the view at first but soon opened up onto a vista of rolling hills and neat paddocks with grazing sheep. She saw a crooked road sign alongside a small trail intersection: Sellwood Lane. *So we're getting close.*

They turned onto a gravel driveway shaded by mature trees that had been carefully trimmed and mathematically placed at discrete intervals. Each had been carefully mulched and the row of trees was bordered with bricks, interrupted intermittently with large plaster urns with flowering plants. *Professionally landscaped.* After the rural bucolic drive, Delaney was unprepared for the size and imposing presence of the house. It was a large two-story granite-faced building with at least six chimneys and large oversized windows that blinked at the setting sun. The circular drive led to the car park which was already filled with Jaguars and Range Rovers. The driver slowed smoothly to a stop in front of the covered arched doorway and quickly came around to open the door for Delaney.

"Thank you lots," she said.

"My pleasure, mum,"

She stood in the door but only for a moment for a maid quickly appeared at the entrance hall and greeted her. "Welcome to Sellwood Place," she said, smiling.

"I'm here to meet Ten," Delaney said confidently. The woman smiled but looked a bit uncertain. The ancient appearance of the building from the outside was contradicted totally by the modernity and classic proportions and design of the interior entrance hall. She noted the marble floors, creamy white walls, a polished mahogany staircase leading to the mezzanine off the entrance hall, and impressive modern art sculpture as the maid led her down the hallway towards the open bi-fold glass doors out to the backyard.

The coolness and sophistication of the entrance hall was warmed by the welcoming hospitality of the large patio terrace filled with sounds of the laughter of the milling guests. Several round tables covered with white linen napery had been set up with garden chairs scattered around. A muslin drape interwoven with twinkling lights was affixed to a long rod which was placed over a long table featuring an impressive array of appetizers. Nearby was a drinks table with a young barman and a fresh-faced young girl who smilingly retrieved chilled bottles from nearby ice buckets.

Delaney stood at the threshold of the patio terrace for a long moment assessing the view and reasserting her poise. Several people glanced at her quickly but then turned back to their conversations. She didn't spot Ten in the crowd and she gave a discreet look at her watch. *Am I early?* No, fashionably on time at twenty past six. At the end of the garden she noticed a gazebo-like brick structure in which several people were lounging. *He's probably there.*

She walked gracefully over to the drinks table and requested a white wine. The barman smiled and handed it to her. "Welcome," he said. "Good to have you here."

"Thank you." *This feels like it's a special occasion.* These people all seemed to know one another. She stood to the side and watched the people grouped in twos and threes having animated conversations about horses, drinks, Tories, soccer, Brexit, zoning restrictions, and tourists flooding Frome. The conversation swirled around her and she found it challenging.

I'll pick up the lingo one of these days and I'll be able to hold my own with the slang, she thought. At that moment an older man who had just ordered a whiskey with soda came to her side and looked at the crowd with her.

"The ruling class at play," he said, turning to her with a smile.

She liked the way his eyes lit up when he made a small joke. It reminded her of someone.

"The weekend and beautiful. A perfect time to let off steam," she replied, with a grateful smile.

"Let it fly. The weekend is here."

They stood there in companionable silence observing the scene. Near the entrance to the house was a swinging patio settee piled high with exotic pillows. Resting comfortably in the corner was an elegant older woman who was engaged in an animated conversation with a younger woman dressed in an Indian sari, arms were covered with silver bangles. The greying blonde hair gave her away as a not a native Indian, but her loving intensity with the older woman was compelling.

He saw Delaney's glance. "My wife," he said.

"She's beautiful," Delaney whispered.

"Yes, she can be bamboozled by others, but she always retains her 'to the manor born' presence." He looked at her closely. "I am Sellwood," he said.

"I'm Delaney Peterson," she replied with a smile. "From America."

"You didn't need to add that," he said with a smile.

"That obvious?"

"The clothes – to a certain extent –" he began to say, "not that they—and you—aren't beautiful...but it's the openness that we see immediately. Americans are raw when they come here. They want all the seasoning that England can give them."

"I've never been described as raw before." She smiled.

"I don't mean it dismissively. I mean only that we admire the Americans for their embrace of everything new. With passion. Intensity. Curiosity. We English like to think that we've seen it all, that there's nothing new."

"Been there. Done that." Delaney said with a smile.

He turned to the barman and said, "Please?" and the man came around with a refreshed drink for him and a fresh glass of wine for her.

"One of his?" he asked, after taking a long drink of his fresh glass.

Delaney paused. She was skilled at reading between the lines. "Yes," she said simply. "Met him on Delta over the Atlantic and we connected over wood and artifacts."

"Wouldn't say 'wood' in front of him in this group. He's likely to go off on a tangent on what he's working on and people will flee in droves."

"I love his passion," she said simply.

"My son thinks he's found his calling," he said. "He loves nothing more than finding an old piece that is about to be tossed into the skip and retrofitting it to a two-million-pound mansion in Mayfair. 'Upcycling' he calls it," he said wryly. "We didn't use those terms in my day."

"He's an entrepreneur," she said.

They stood together in silence for a few moments. "Would you like to meet her?" he asked, nodding towards the older woman on the settee.

"I'd love to."

"Angela, darling, one of Ten's friends. This is –" he turned to Delaney who quickly supplied, "Delaney Peterson."

"Pleased to meet you," the older woman said, holding out her hand but not standing up. "This is my friend, Nikkola," she said, nodding her head to the younger woman who had been monopolizing her.

"I'm Delaney Peterson," she smiled. "Friend of Ten's."

"Friend of Ten's. Friend of Ten's. We have a lot of them here," his mother said, her sweet smile softening the harsh words. "From America, given your accent," she stated.

"Yes, here on a short visa," Delaney explained.

"He's around here somewhere. I saw him earlier." She looked around at the group and then put on her glasses, which were dangling on a lanyard around her neck and stared at the annex. "I think he's out there. He needs to come and greet his guests but he gets involved in a story. Bad boy," she said fondly. "With his mates."

"I'm not bothered. Grateful to be here. This is a lovely place," Delaney said, looking around with an expansive gesture.

"This old pile," Angela Sellwood said dismissively.

"How old is your home?" Delaney said.

"We've been here – how long, Freddy?" She turned to her husband.

"Thirty years but the family, over two hundred."

"You've done an amazing job modernizing it," Delaney said. "Love the foyer."

"We work hard at it. It's constant. Thank you." She turned to Nikkola, "Darling, get me another G&T, would you, please? The younger woman got up from the settee and walked slowly over to the drinks table. "Freddy, darling, go find Ten. Make him mind his manners for once, please? Not leave this beautiful woman stranded."

Ten's father nodded with a smile at his wife and walked over to the annex.

Nikkola walked back to Mrs. Sellwood and Delaney. "Your aura is a beautiful shade of purple, nearly violet," she said to Delaney.

"You can see that in this light?" Delaney said with a slight smile.

"You're lovely. Surrounded by a rainbow of light. I can see why Ten was attracted to you."

"You can see all that in five minutes?" Delaney asked, but her smile softened the words.

"That and more. You are in love with him, aren't you?" Nikkola's voice was friendly and certain. "You feel that Ten and you are soul mates. I see that. But the path won't be smooth." She placed a confiding hand on Delaney's arm. "Love will prevail." She turned towards Mrs. Sellwood and handed her the drink. "Here, my sweet," she said, and she sat down closely next to her hostess.

Delaney heard Ten's drawling voice before she saw him. He was with a group of people who were talking and laughing as they congregated at the drinks table. Ten turned and walked slowly over to Delaney. "Hello Delaney," he said. "Pleased you've arrived."

"Happy to be here," she said. "Thanks for the invite."

"See you've made acquaintance with the Sellwood clan already." He nodded towards his mother who was deep in conversation with Nikkola. "Come with me. I'll introduce you to my mates." He took her arm and walked over to the table where several attractive young men were standing around talking about soccer.

She put on her brightest smile when introduced to the men, but didn't respond when one mimicked her American accent with a "How ya' doin?' in a heavy Brooklyn accent. She just smiled at him.

"Delaney is from Minnesota. Central U.S.," Ten explained.

"Snow!" They all laughed dismissively.

One of the men assessed her. He had the splotchy red cheeks of a redhead who drank too much. He sized her up frankly. "How did you meet up with this bounder?" he asked not unkindly, tipping his glass toward Ten.

"Our secret," she said mysteriously. She could play this game.

"Let me guess: at the Merlin Theatre. Our Ten really likes his pretty actresses."

"Be kind, George," Ten said warningly. "She's my guest."

"Nothing unkind meant," he replied and turned away, signaling to the barman for another drink.

Don't like him, Delaney thought. *Typical priggish English male, full of himself.*

Ten was engaged in brief repartee with one of his friends and Delaney studied him covertly. She noted the resemblance to his father in the narrow, high-cheek-boned face and the lean frame. There were lines around his eyes and she thought he looked tired. He sensed her studying him and he punched his friend lightly on the shoulder and turned to her.

"Come with me," he urged, and led her to a pair of teak ottomans at the edge of the patio. Gesturing her to sit on the woven wicker seat, he sat down opposite and placed his wineglass on the table next to it. He grasped her hands in his and said, "I am glad you could make it here, Delaney. I've been wanting to see you. These last two weeks have been just – frenzied."

"I understand. Able to take a brief breather now?"

"Well, we're back at it on Monday. A salvage auction in Wales that is promising. My crew has been scouting and it's worth the gander down there." He gave Delaney an apologetic look. "How have you been keeping yourself?"

"I've been good. Working on several projects..."

"I'm sorry about your father, Delaney. That must have been a blow..."

"Yes."

"And Brian? All okay at home?"

"Yes, he's fine." *This is a conversation between strangers*, she thought. The silence lengthened between them.

"Excuse me." He stood up suddenly and walked over to greet a willowy blonde. Delaney was instantly offended but mollified when she saw him urge her to come and join them. "Delaney, this is Catherine."

Delaney stood up to greet the tall young woman who offered a languid hand and a bored, "Hello."

"My cousin, Catherine Foxworthy-Kent. This is Delaney Peterson from the States. You two may share interests. Delaney, Catherine is an artist and owner of a gallery here in Frome."

His cousin. "I am an artists' rep in the States," Delaney said, making conversation, casually skipping over the untruth.

"Oh, how interesting," Catherine said drily, clearly meaning the opposite.

Delaney got out her iPhone and scrolled to the Tafani photos that Jennie had sent. "Here is my latest. Realistic portraiture but compelling use of color."

Catherine took the phone and slowly scrolled through the photos. She handed the phone back to Delaney. "Awfully hard to appraise talent from a small screen but the work looks promising."

"She's Afghani. Caught in the war and rescued by an American soldier. Beautiful girl." Delaney found the picture of Tafani in front of the large canvas in the Petros diner and handed the phone back to Catherine.

"Striking," she said, exhibiting slightly more interest. "Does she exhibit here?"

"No, not yet."

"Dropbox good quality jpgs and I'll nose around. The back-story is a good angle. Here's my card," she said, handing it over. She seemed a little friendlier. "How do you find Frome?" she asked. Her upper-class accent made it sound like Frume.

"Haven't had a chance to explore. Just down for the day," Delaney said with an apologetic smile.

"Know Ten long?"

"We met the last time I was in London. Met on the plane over, actually."

"Dazzled you with his story, did he?"

"No, we talked a lot about his architectural salvage business."

"Oh that! That's just a hobby for him. Gives him something to do when he's not playing the horses and chasing women."

"You're joking, I'm sure?" Delaney looked her squarely in the face.

Catherine looked away, her face an impenetrable mask. "My dear, sweet cousin Ten. Heir to this pile—" she gestured contemptuously at the lavish house and grounds –" *and* the title." She turned and looked directly at Delaney. "You can play out the line but you'll never land the fish."

49

North Carolina was sweltering with temperatures in the high nineties and suffocating high humidity. Steve had put on the air conditioning in the rental car but switched it off and opened the windows and let in the hot breeze. Liked the smell of the pine woods. He'd picked up the rental car in Raleigh and found it an easy drive to Hillsborough but was glad once he found himself on the outskirts of the metro area and could see some of the country, even if he was traveling on an interstate. In the distance he saw the green farmland, cut now and then by irregular burnt umber clay ditches and an occasional derelict tobacco drying shed tumbling into ruins. He was headed to Hillsborough, the county seat of Orange County, North Carolina. From official records he'd unearthed in Minnesota he had learned that Lisa Shapiro, formerly Lisa Jean Jamps, had been born in a small town near Chapel Hill. He'd start with the courthouse to see what he could find.

His flight from Minneapolis-St. Paul airport had landed late in the day and it was nearing evening when he parked at the Days Inn and walked into the refreshingly cool lobby to register. He'd hit the courthouse the next morning.

First thing: Call Veronica. Their conversation was casual and basic. She seemed relatively cheerful and interested in his description of his travels so far. He had wanted her to come with him on this trip but she seemed reluctant. "Need to work on myself," she had said resignedly. He had set up a group text with Pastor Ed, Archie, and Romyn, taking no chances while he was out of state.

Might as well check out Chapel Hill, he thought. This Richard Shapiro fellow lived there. The one who claimed he was Clay and Sophie's father. Romyn and Earl had shared the lawyer's letter filed with the Minnesota Department of Human Services which stated he was an adjunct professor at the University of North Carolina at Chapel Hill. Sociology. Should be pretty easy to uncover something about him.

He was hungry after his long flight from Minnesota and the trip to Hillsborough and then into Chapel Hill. He pulled into the parking lot of the first restaurant he saw— The Essex— and wandered into the dark interior and sat at the bar. It was early and relatively quiet this time of night. Summer, so most of the students were away from campus and he and the bartender had a quick but friendly exchange about sports and the weather as Steve ordered a catfish sandwich, hush puppies – they only make them great in the south — and sweet tea. *When in Rome...*

"Suppose you're busy when school's in session?" he asked.

"Yes, there are about 19,000 students at the school. The population of Chapel Hill is only about 60,000, so you do the math. They like their beer, especially the micros. Quieter these days, but it'll still be packed on Friday night. You sound as if you're from the North somewhere."

"Minnesota. Just here on a quick business trip."

"Y'all's welcome. We serve Yankees here," he said humorously, as he moved to another customer. "Your money's good."

Steve looked at the sports memorabilia on the wall and slowly drank his sweet tea while waiting for his meal. Lots of Tarheel fans—to be expected. Alongside the wall leading to the restrooms he saw a series of old paintings of bearded men in military uniforms. Hanging above them all was a Confederate flag and an old saber that looked as if it couldn't slice bread. *Civil war,* he mused. *Memories die hard.*

He had a copy of the security camera photo of Ricardo Spiro on his cell phone and he studied it as he ate his delicious fried catfish sandwich. It was a side view and from a top down angle as he had been standing at the reception desk at the Sleepytime Inn so it wasn't a clear picture. No one in the restaurant looked remotely like him. His main purpose in Hillsborough was to track down Clay and Sophie's birth certificates but he had an intuition he needed to track down. The man that attacked Tafani was not from Minnesota. He had a southern accent.

When Chief Baldwin talked to Shiloh, she told him to talk to Clay, who was 'the Captain,' she said. He made a quick visit to the Randall's home, but Clay was didn't speak, unusual for him.

Not going to get much out of him, the chief thought.

Just as he was leaving the home, Clay said, "I seen him before."

The chief had turned toward Clay with empathy and said, "Tell me, Clay," and choking it out, Clay said, "He was with Mom," and then he ran toward the bedroom and closed the door with a sharp *thunk.*

Clay knows something, Steve thought. *The slime bag, ol' dirty tennis shoes, is involved in this mess somehow.* Need to get a better picture of him. He had done a quick Facebook search on his iPhone but came up empty. His mind was spinning. *Wouldn't put it past Richard Shapiro to take a visit to Peace Ridge and scope out Clay and Sophie. And Romyn and Earl while he's at it. Could he have been the one to attack Tafani? Just circumstantial evidence. But since I'm here... The security photo from the Sleepytime Inn isn't any good. But I bet I can get a better one. There has to be a photo somewhere at the university since he's on staff there. I'll spend some time on the laptop later tonight.*

Steve decided he had the time to drive up to Morrisville. Clay had told Jennie that they'd sometimes stayed at their grandparents' farm in Morrisville. *Check off that box.* He expected to find a run-down rural town, but Morristown was prosperous.

Close to the university, headquarters for large multi-national corporations and expensive developments with over-sized red brick mansions.

Researching on Ancestry.com had provided information on a family of Jamps that lived on Holly Springs Road. He was curiously reassured that he was on the right track as he left the highways and began to travel secondary roads that led increasingly to poorer run-down houses and empty gas stations, tumbling farm buildings, and a general air of desolation. He found the last known address of Frederick and Tweetie Jamps and pulled up in front of a derelict white clapboard farmhouse. He could see past the sagging back porch into the fields and saw what looked to be the remains of an old barn and a small outbuilding. Overgrown and untended bushes shadowed the front of the house.

Steve pulled to a stop in front of a cockeyed mailbox upon which he could read the faint letters '_am_s'. *I'm here,* he thought, feeling both sadness and the innate jubilation when a piece of the puzzle fell into place. There was a "For Sale" sign on the property and he leaned against his car and called the agent's number. A cheery southern answering machine voice promised to return the call as soon as possible. 'Have a great day, y'all."

The nearest neighbors were a small group of low-end trailer houses, and Steve thought he'd be able to walk around without being seen. No use raising any questions. At the least he could take pictures for Clay and Sophie—that would be a great excuse, if challenged. The house was likely to be torn down soon anyway. Residential developments were only a few miles away and it was only a matter of time before this land would be parceled and sold. He tripped over an old piece of iron that was buried in the long grass. Part of a small shovel. There was little traffic on the road and there was an eerie quiet about the place. Above his head he saw an occasional crow that flew to the only remaining tree in the yard and bossily chastised the intruder, 'caw-caw-caw.'

Steve walked carefully around the foundation of the old barn, watching carefully for camouflaged holes. He stopped and turned to look back at the house. *Probably good memories made here at some time,* he thought, as he gazed at the forlorn house. The sun was behind him and sinking fast, and he thought it was about time to head back to Hillsborough. At that moment his phone rang with an unfamiliar number.

"Hello there. This is Becky Reliant, agent for the property on Holly Springs Road. You called me a little while ago and I wanted to get back to you," a woman said.

"Hello, Becky. Thanks for calling back. Yes, I would like more details on the property, if you don't mind.

"I don't mind. It's a lovely piece – it's forty acres of undeveloped land real close to Morrisville. Easy commuting distance to the university and businesses. You can see that the house is in rather poor shape. Most people would want the parcel for the land and tear down the house. What are you interested in?"

Steve walked over to a corner of the foundation of the old barn and sat down. The lie came easily. "I have a new teaching job at the UNC-CH and will be relocating here from California. I have an interest in land as I don't want close neighbors. Thought this might be an option."

"Yes!" she said enthusiastically. "A new build is certainly possible. You'll find that the zoning in this area is really accommodating. Not like California – I understand there are a lot of restrictions there. I'd love to meet with you and walk around the property with you. A new build could be relocated back from the highway and you'd have more privacy."

Steve casually rubbed his shoe into the dirt and scraped away a small square of clay dirt. "I don't think that will be necessary right away; I need to bring my wife out and have her take a look around this area with me." Another lie. "Can you tell me anything about the history of the place? My wife always loves the backstory."

"Interesting story. This farm has been in the Jamps family for a long time. Since 1923. Before that it was part of a larger farm holding of the General Joseph E. Johnston family. The famous Confederate general. So, it does have an historic association."

"I'm sure my wife would be more interested in the Jamps family," Steve said drily. The inference was not wasted on the agent.

"They were a simple rural couple. He was a farmer, she was a farm wife. Really small family, which was unusual for the times and may be the reason why he wasn't very successful at farming. Not enough farm labor. One child, a girl."

"What happened to them?"

"They both died in Riverdale—it's a nursing home here in town—just a year ago. Up in years. The girl had left home quite a while before and no one has been able to find her. She didn't stay in touch with her parents as far as anyone knows. The State will own the property now by default and will realize the sale proceeds. Help pay for the nursing home care for the old people."

"Sad end." Steve's voice was heartfelt. He knew the truth and she didn't. The 'rest of the story,' in Paul Harvey's iconic phrase, was even sadder.

"I have your name and number. If you want to give me your email address, I'll send you the particulars on this property and I have a few more that you and your wife might find interesting, if this one doesn't work out for you."

"That's great," Steve said. "Thanks. Talk later." His shoe unearthed something metal from the patch of land he'd been working unconsciously. He bent down and scraped the earth away from the piece. An old beer can opener from the looks of it. The lettering on the metal was covered with red clay dirt and he rubbed it with his thumb. "Gunther's Premium Dry Beer." He rubbed the small opener against his jeans and spat on it to clean it up. *Something for Clay. Something from his grandparents.*

Maybe a small family wasn't the only reason grandpa was a poor farmer, he thought.

Steve strolled into the Register of Deeds office on Churlton Street. The pretty young girl at the desk gave him a big welcoming smile when he walked up. *Southern hospitality. Never fails.* He explained his purpose and she got a puzzled expression on her face when he explained his legal authority for copies of the records. Minnesota Department of Human Services...advocate for the children...need original birth records to finalize the adoption.

"Let me check with my supervisor," she said. An older woman came to the desk and gave Steve a pleasant greeting. She examined his business card and the official paperwork for the adoption which he'd hoped would pass muster as he repeated his request.

"This is strange," she said. "Kathy," she turned to the young girl, "wasn't there someone else in here asking for the Jamps records just a few weeks ago?"

"I'm not sure," she replied.

"Could it be that our office at the Minnesota Department of Human Services mailed in a request? My colleagues had asked me to follow up since I was in North Carolina in person..."

"No, I don't think so," she said slowly. "I remember the day distinctly. He was pushy and wouldn't take "no" for an answer. Told me he had a Ph.D. in health and human services. And that we were just...clerks. I sent him away empty handed," she said with a slight smile.

"Not the right paperwork?" Steve asked, leading the witness.

"I nearly blew it," she replied chagrined. "He gave me a song and dance about being the little kids' father. Told a cute little story about when the baby sister was first brought home from the hospital and how Clay was a doting big brother. It took me quite a while – we usually need at least twenty-four hours advance notice to pull the records – and he was huffing and puffing, but I finally found them. Clay Frederick Jamps.

Born 2008. Sophie Tweetie Jamps. Born 2011. Mother: Lisa Jean Jamps."

"And father?" Steve asked.

"Father unknown," she replied, with a shake of her head. "Both of them."

Steve drove away from the courthouse with a satisfied feeling. *This time I can bring Romyn and Earl some good news.* When he got to the Days Inn and had settled in at his computer, he took a break to call his lawyer friend. Their conversation was brief.

"Good job, Steve. Knew you'd be on it."

"Rather simple, actually. But I have a favor to ask. We can have a longer conversation about this when I get back home – I'll give you all the details then. But I have a proposal. Clay and Sophie's mom, Lisa Shapiro – her real name is Jamps – seems to have no living relatives. I found that her parents are dead and that she was an only child. I want to find the deed and will, if there is one, for her parents' house in Morrisville. She is the likely sole heir to it."

"I think they were poor people, weren't they, based on what Romyn has been able to get out of Clay?"

"Yes, true. The house is a shambles and it's likely their only asset. But the land is worth something."

"Really?"

"Yes, the old frame house and forty acres is listed for $500,000. That kind of money, even after paying for the nursing home expenses, will help pay for Lisa's care. And I'm sure that's what the old people would have wanted."

Steve wearily turned off his computer. He stood and stretched and then turned to the window and stared at the parking lot of the hotel which was now completely filled. It was after midnight and the night was dark but there were pools of light illuminating the perimeter of bougainvillea and hibiscus trees. Despite the late hour it was still warm.

Better close this window and turn on the air conditioning, he thought. *But, a good night's work. I think I struck the mother lode. I'll hit the Register of Deeds again in the morning.*

50

"Do you want to help out in the store today, Clay?" Romyn expected an enthusiastic "Yes!" and she was not disappointed.

"Can I help, too?" Sophie asked.

"You can help out next time. When I get in the next delivery of snacks and candy, I'll let you help, Sophie. I thought it was time to teach Clay how to identify and sort the minnows. Think he would do good at sorting out the hornyhead chubs from the jumpers and shiners. Aaron is helping out today and he's the real expert."

"Cool!" Clay exclaimed.

"I will come back and get you when Aaron comes in at ten o'clock. And then I can come and get you, Sophie, and we'll head over to McDonald's for lunch."

"Yay!"

The store was quiet. It was a glorious Minnesota summer day – cloudless, brilliant blue, a soft breeze. Romyn knew most of her customers would have gotten their bait at six-thirty this morning to get out on the lake while it was still cool and there were some shadows along the shoreline. Terry had opened up this morning and she pointed out the stack of mail and waved goodbye as she rushed out the door.

"Goin' waterskiing myself," she announced. Her brother, Aaron, came in just then and immediately grabbed the broom and began to sweep out the backroom.

He's a good boy, Romyn thought, not for the first time. *Both kids were. Raised right.*

The morning passed quickly and Clay was waiting anxiously at the door when Romyn returned to the house to get him.

"Will I get paid for my hours?" he asked as they rode the short distance back to Crossroads. They soon arrived at the store and walked into the pleasant coolness.

"We'll see. Let's see how long it takes you to learn about the minnows and then we might start you out at half the hourly rate in a little bit. Once you can be backfill for Aaron or Terry, we'll talk about something permanent. Cleaning the store is part of the work, too. Aaron does a good job of it, along with watering the flowers and helping out the occasional customer who needs help at the pumps."

"I'd like to help pump the gas," Clay said. "I like the smell. It…reminds me of something."

"Well, don't go smelling it too much. It's bad for you."

"No, I won't. It's just the smell of old cars, gas, oil, that kind of stuff. I like how it smells. It's almost as good as Dad's workshop."

"I know you want to learn woodworking, too, don't you, Clay?"

"Yes, but he says I have to be a little older.

"You can't work with the power equipment. It's too dangerous."

"I'm eleven. Other kids …"

"You're not other kids," Romyn said definitively. "You're our Clay and we're not going to let anything happen to you."

"It's already happened," he whispered, and looked away.

"What do you mean, Clay?" Romyn asked gently, kneeling down to the small boy and holding his arms.

"We lost our mom. We lost Lisa."

"Oh, my sweetie. You think that?"

"Yes. We left her on that street in St. Paul and then she was lost. And now she doesn't know how to find us." The last said with a pitiful wail. Romyn hugged him tight to herself. There

382

was the sound of a customer coming into the store and she caught Aaron's eyes, signaling to him to wait on the customer.

"Come over and sit at the table with me, Clay," she urged. She handed him the box of tissues and went to the cooler to get a bottle of chocolate milk.

"I think you're old enough to know this, Clay," she said. "Earl – Dad – and I have been trying to figure out the best way to tell you, but now I think it's best you know."

He rubbed his eyes and blew his nose, trying to stop the tears that continued to pour down his face.

"Clay, we have found your mother," she said simply.

"She's dead, isn't she?"

"No, she's not. But she is in a hospital."

"We have to go see her!" he entreated. "Can we go see her?"

"We can't go right away—she's in Kansas City. It's a long way away, nearly one thousand miles. We're working with her doctors to get her moved up here to Peace Ridge Village. So you and Sophie can see her when she's here. When The Jason House is finished."

"Can we talk to her on the phone?"

The plaintive request broke Romyn's heart.

"We can't talk to her right now. She has gotten hurt – we don't know how – and she's having a hard time remembering very much. The doctors and nurses are working with her every day to help her with that. Helping her to remember more about her life."

"Do you think she's forgotten Sophie and me?"

"No, I don't think so, Clay. The nurse told me that she has your picture under her pillow and she takes it out every day and looks at it." No use telling him that Lisa's expression was usually puzzled.

"I want to write to her," Clay said decisively. "Sophie and I need to write her a letter. Every day!" He snuffled and looked around the store. "You have paper here, don't you, Romyn?"

"That's a great idea, Clay. A great idea." Romyn tousled his head and brushed his fair blond hair away from his face. "We'll make sure that as soon as she is ready, we'll give you a chance to visit and love on her. We promise you that."

"If she's hurt and she can't remember, then she can't take care of us, can she?" His question spoke worlds.

She knew his desire for love and security was fighting with his loyalty to Lisa. For a brief moment she was angry with the woman who left these precious children in this awful quandary.

"No, I don't think she will be able to take care of you. Not right away anyway. She'll have her hands full trying to get better, to get healthy, Clay." Both Earl and Romyn had agreed that they wouldn't tell Clay and Sophie about their adoption until it was really finalized, but Romyn's heart was shattered, wanting to offer the best security she could to them. Life with Lisa and that uncertainty had been awful for the two little ones. Sophie never said much about it and Clay put on a brave front, but the hurt was there in both of them. "Oh, Jesus," Romyn prayed, "be with us now. Be with Lisa as she tries to get better. Amen."

"Amen," Clay echoed.

Her cell phone rang at just that moment. "Hi Romyn. Steve here. Got some interesting news. Do you want it now or when I get home?"

"Clay and I are working in the store now, Steve. When are you coming home? Why don't we talk then?"

"Have you seen Veronica lately?"

"She hasn't been in the store. Ed and Jill were in earlier and I know she's planning to go to the parsonage and have what she calls her 'forgiveness' session with our pastor."

"Great. That's what she told me too. I'm just so worried being so far away. Like if I am in Minnesota, even if it's the Twin Cities, I'll be able to protect her."

"Just pray, Steve, and hurry home. We'll keep the home fires burning. And Earl is faithful. He talks to her a lot every day. Finds any simple reason to call. She might be tired of his calling but they always find something to talk about."

"I'm jealous of Earl, Romyn. Is that possible? Jealous of an older, married man in a wheelchair?"

"You sound like a man in love, Steve!"

Little pitchers had big ears. "Steve is in North Carolina?" Clay asked Romyn innocently. At her nod, he said, "That's where we're from. That's where that bad man came from." At Romyn's questioning glance, he said, "Dirty shoes."

Jill stood at the stove making a delicious-smelling spaghetti sauce. Ed walked from the office into the kitchen and stood behind his wife, nestling his nose in her neck. "Mmmm, smells great. Can't wait," he said.

"Oh, Eddy," she laughed. "It's just my usual thrown-together sauce. What's in the 'fridge? As long as you have garlic, you have the world."

"It's always delicious, Jill. I sure missed your cooking." She didn't reply but turned around and gave him a big hug, a big promising hug. They lingered together at the stove for a moment and then she said, "Veronica coming over tonight?"

"Yes, she wants to keep on with her forgiveness sessions. For an hour or so. Steve is in North Carolina and I think she might just want—need— the human connection."

Jill turned the heat down under the spaghetti sauce and sat at the table. Ed joined her there, seeing her latent intention. They were getting used to reading different signals now. It wasn't seamless as before. Sometimes Jill was direct, but often she was very indirect and Ed was learning how to read his wife.

"Ed, we have to do something."

"Do something...about what?" Ed asked.

"We don't talk very much about Robby." She looked at him directly.

"I know, Jill. It's...painful."

"Tell me again what happened. I need to know." She seemed calm but she was twisting her hands convulsively and Ed felt a rising fear. This was a subject he'd wanted to bring up but didn't know when would be a good time, and truth be told, he was a coward about it. Robby felt like a failure.

He gave her the bare facts, ending with Robby's visit last winter to Peace Ridge Village.

"And he's never been back?" she asked.

"And he doesn't want to see me when I come to visit." Ed said, surprised at the sudden anger that welled within him.

"Eddy, I don't really remember him at all," she confessed. "I can remember a small boy, but you say he's a young man? I can't...I can't envision that," she said, as tears began to flow silently down her cheeks.

"He's twenty-six now, Jill." Ed said quietly. "He's been in the home for the blind for the last ten years."

"Ten years," she mused. "Tell me again..."

And Ed recounted the sad story which caused even more tears. He got up from his kitchen chair and bent over her shaking shoulders and cried with her. The two of them were immobile in their grief until the smell of the burning sauce began to penetrate their senses and Jill jumped up and frantically stirred the pot on the stove.

"Rescued it, I think," she said in a forlorn voice.

"And I think we need to try to talk to Robby, Jill. Don't you think? Should we plan a visit soon? Together? Maybe he'll see you and open up. He seems to have written me off." The last was said with a choking sob. The long-buried hurt.

"Let's go soon, Eddy. We must. He's our only child now. And I'm sure he's hurting, too."

Veronica came over after supper. She was calm but subdued. She had a notebook with her and gave Ed and Jill a brief nod in greeting. She seemed anxious to talk to Ed, so they walked quickly to the parsonage office and after serving tea, Jill closed the door softly.

"How are you, Veronica?" Ed asked.

"I'm finding myself. A little bit. It's slow going and I'm finding it very hard."

"It always is. Scraping one's mind and heart and uncovering bald truths is always hard. This is something that Christians who try to be more like Jesus discover pretty soon in the walk of truth. We think we are pretty good people until we decide to follow Christ. To be like Him. It doesn't take very long until we discover our truly depraved nature. Little things. Big things. One of the reasons we need a Savior."

"I know that I have to fully accept responsibility for the abortion and all the reasons for it," she replied softly.

"And," Ed responded, "accept that Jesus forgives that sin and forgives you. Completely. With grace. Without any exceptions. 'Deliver me from the guilt of bloodshed, O God, you who are God my Savior, and my tongue will sing of your righteousness.' Isaiah."

"When do I feel that in my heart, Pastor? I can accept it intellectually but I keep slipping back into guilt and shame."

"This is a poor analogy, Veronica, but I'll use it anyway. When you work with wood, trying to make a bookshelf or something, you take a piece of board. Just a rough board, coarsely planed. Like you'd find at Menards. Run your hand along it and you'll find slivers and your hand will catch. So, what you do is you take your planer and you begin to carefully scrape down the length of the board. You run your hand alongside it, brush off the shavings, and begin again. Pretty soon the piece of board becomes smooth. Really smooth like the soft skin of a baby. You brush off the shavings again, maybe take a damp rag to it to get rid of the dust, and the board is perfectly smooth. Perfect. You hold it up and look at it carefully and you realize that the imperfection is completely gone. As if it didn't exist. The piece is amazing, you can see the grain in its natural perfection. Just as God made it. You are amazed at the beauty and you study the board. Your work with the plane has made it perfect.

"So, we take our life—our sins, even the so-called unforgivable ones — and lay them at the feet of Jesus Christ. He planes them away with solace and encouragement from His word, the Bible, and the amazing love of His sacrifice for us on the cross. We become like perfect boards, Veronica. As perfect as He originally made us. With Jesus, our imperfections are as if they never existed. It's called expiation, but we don't need to use the theological terms because we feel clean in our hearts. Clean and free to worship Him.

"God takes us redeemed Christians and makes us the strong timber of His church so that through our redemption we can help others to find Him and find all the joy and peace that they are searching for. Most people in this world, Veronica, are searching for that peace."

"Just as I am. Though I think peace is far from me," she said, her gaze on her lap, "but with God's help, maybe I can grasp it."

"How is it going with Project Rachel?" he asked. Best to defuse the intensity. *I get carried away,* he thought.

"I am amazed. So many women, young and old. Suffering. Suicidal. Lost." Her face worked and she was close to breaking down, but she held it together to continue the conversation.

"I wish we had a ministry here in Peace Ridge that could help. I'm glad St. Cloud is close enough that people can get there, but I'm sure there are many young women suffering in our town," Ed said.

"You can be sure of it, Pastor. I can't share, but there are others considering abortion right here in Peace Ridge, and I want to shout at them 'Don't do it! Don't do it! A life of pain and regret!' but I can't." Veronica stared out the window at the perfect evening. "I don't feel worthy to advise others…"

"I can understand your reluctance…" Ed realized the pain and insights that compelled her conversation.

"It's just that I'm working through it myself, after all these years. I still haven't come to a place of complete release from the guilt. I'm getting closer, but…"

"Let's pray, Veronica." They bowed their heads. "Father God, most great high God, You gave us Jesus, Your only Son, to be the offering in our place. To stand before You in Your awesome holiness as an advocate for us fallen creatures, and You did not see our sin because You saw Your beloved Son in our place. We are humbled, grateful, in awe. Help Veronica to see that great gift today. Help her to see that, in Your love, no sin is too awful to forgive if we call on the name You sent to the world to redeem us. Our Savior, Jesus Christ. We love You, Lord Jesus. Forgive us, we pray, Amen," Ed said quietly.

Veronica sat quietly in her seat without moving. Ed leaned back in his office chair and looked out the window. There was a beautiful sunset to enjoy— he could see the bright summer sun sinking slowly into his garage. Soon the backyard would be in shadows, the time when Biep found his hunting most fruitful. *Oh, to be like the little creatures You made for our love, God. Our pets who show us how to live humbly and gratefully in this world. Accepting Your gracious gift. Life.* He turned back to Veronica.

She sat immobile in her chair and then spoke softly. "I have been so focused on my shame and guilt, Ed, that I couldn't process Gary and why he committed suicide. Last night, I lay in bed in that unique time between prayers and falling asleep when images fill my mind. I don't know where they come from. I thought then of Gary and his suicide. Maybe the reason he killed himself wasn't because the business was failing or because he was cheating on me. Maybe it was because he, too, felt the guilt and shame of killing our only child." Tears were falling down her cheeks. Ed walked over to her and put his hands on her shoulders.

"Veronica, I think you've found an insight that can help you with your forgiveness. Did you ever talk about it with him?"

"No, I just went to the Planned Parenthood clinic, had the procedure, came home, said nothing, drank until I was numb and passed out. The next morning Gary tried to talk to me about it but I shut him out. I felt awful, like I had cut out a part of myself. An arm or a leg. Certainly a part of my future. He would never be able to understand. I remember he tried to hug me and I pushed him away and then I went back to bed where I stayed for several days. Only getting up to go to the bathroom and get another drink. It was awful.

"Finally, I had to be among the living again and I tried to pull myself together and restore my relationship with Gary. But that was what had been severed. Along with the baby."

Ed squeezed her shoulders gently. "Father God, Holy Spirit. We lift Veronica to You now. You have given her the gift of empathy for the man she loved. A first step towards forgiveness. Help her now as she walks this journey to You, freed from guilt and shame. Free her to love You as You always intended. And in that love, find the freedom to live joyfully again. We love You, Lord Jesus. We pray this simple prayer in Your name, Amen."

Veronica got up from the chair slowly and turned to give Pastor Ed a chaste hug. "Thank you, Pastor. Thank you. You've saved my life in more ways than one. I am so grateful." She blotted her eyes with a tissue and looked around for a wastebasket. Ed took the tissue and dumped it in the wastebasket.

"How about a cup of tea before you leave?" he asked.

"No, you've given me too much to think about. I want to go home and think about it." She looked at him directly. "I am so grateful. I hope I will be able to think of myself as straight timber from now on," she added.

Ed closed the door behind Veronica and went and sat in his office chair. He spun it around to look out the window. There was the departing beauty of the sun and the violet night of the approaching evening, but his eyes were unseeing. He felt both hollow and agitated, hearing the scripture of Matthew 7:3-5 reverberate in his head, accompanied by a glimpse of the unhappy face of his son, Robby.

390

Forgiveness, Ed mused to himself. *Here I am talking to Veronica about forgiveness when I harbor ugly thoughts in my heart towards Robby. Talk about the plank in my eye making it impossible for me to see the splinter in another's eye.* He got up and walked over to his bookshelf and took down his standby Bible, the New International Version. *Jesus,* he breathed. *One of the great Jesus lectures.* "Why do you look at the speck of sawdust in your brother's eye and pay no attention to the plank in your own eye. How can you say to your brother, 'Let me take the speck out of your eye,' when all the time there is a plank in your own eye? You hypocrite..."

He sat heavily in his chair, his mind going over Robby's last visit, the times he'd gone to the Home for the Blind to visit him and returned empty, the sad last days of their family before Robby blinded himself, the anguish of rebuilding their lives after Emily's death, Jill's catatonia, Robby's placement in the home, his own move to this calling in Peace Ridge Village...

"Father God, please forgive me for my hard heart towards my own son. I need to face the fact that I blame him for the accident, for Emily's death, for destroying our family—and then for not wanting me—his father! Probably mostly that. I try to show Veronica how to forgive and I am the greatest hypocrite there is. If I am honest with myself, I harbor resentment towards Robby and I don't want to forgive him for...this mess."

He sat there immobile. Ed felt the tears well within him and he fell to his knees at the chair and laid his head down on the seat, his tears soaking the leather and making his cheek stick.

"Ten years! Father God, forgive me for my heart of stone. Give me a heart of flesh. Help me, myself, to forgive. It's the beginning of healing. I know that. Veronica knows that. Maybe even Robby knows that as he camouflages his guilt and shame through the mask of rejection and anger. Help me to remove my plank so I can help others with their splinters. Help Robby. It's not only hypocrisy – it's about being unable to help others unless we ourselves deal with our own planks. Oh, Father God, I am such a sinner..."

Ed placed his head in his arms on the chair and his words were anguished and known only to the Holy Spirit. He was drained when he finally rose and blew his nose and slowly opened the door to the office and walked into the kitchen. Jill was in the den and Ed grabbed a bottle of water from the refrigerator and walked into the den where his wife sat reading *World* magazine.

"Was it hard, Eddy?" she asked sympathetically, giving him a loving smile.

"Facing up to the evil and ugliness in one's own heart is always hard, Jill," he said bleakly. "This situation with Veronica has revealed to me my own need to forgive. We do need to see Robby, Jill. Let's go next Saturday." He sat down in the comfortable chair and put up his feet. Biep, always at the ready, jumped into his lap and stretched languidly under the indifferent hand.

"His promises are sufficient, Eddy," she said.

Lying awake next to a deeply slumbering Jill, Ed tried to calm his restless mind with brief whispered prayers and pleas to God for peace. Why did he feel such an overwhelming sense of his own guilt? His prayers for forgiveness of Robby were genuine and he'd felt the peace that came with repentance but he still felt ... dirty somehow. Unfinished.

He slipped out of bed and walked into the kitchen to make a cup of tea. He switched the light on over the sink and stared out the black opaque window to the backyard. It was still warm at eleven o'clock at night, one of those Minnesota days that never seemed to cool down. He took his cup of hot water and teabag and quietly opened the back door to the house, shooing Biep away from the door. *He'd be out all night if I let him.* There was a slight scent of flowers in the air and he breathed deeply as he sat in the Adirondack chair on the pavers. The peace of the night began to penetrate his thoughts and his mind emptied, feeling nature's solace. *Something undone.* He knew his own heart and mind well enough to know he still had unfinished work with God. *Show me, God. Help me.*

His mind drifted back to the earlier conversation he'd had with Jill at the kitchen table. Their plans to reach out to Robby. "He is our only child now," she'd said. "And I'm sure he's hurting, too." Ed slumped back into the chair as the stab to the heart came. *Hurting. Robby hurt Emily. All these years I've shied away from thinking about the sexual abuse. My mind has not been able to really confront it and I haven't forgiven him for it. I must admit that. We didn't raise him to become…a monster like that.*

"Forgive me, God, for even thinking that word." *What did I do? Where did I go wrong in raising Robby? What could I have done differently? I never saw any signs. Nor did Jill. And I can't ask her now. She'd fall apart. I don't think she even remembers that part of those days. She had withdrawn even then."*

What could I have done? I didn't see it. "Father God, forgive me!" It was nearly a wail. Suddenly a face flashed into his memory. A long-buried image of the neighbor man, a shop teacher at the school. Lived a few doors down and always took a special interest in Robby. Ed was glad at the time because he himself was swamped with studying, picking up pastoral jobs, trying to keep the household afloat with only a little money coming in. Robby was at the age when camping and fishing was a big passion and this man—*his name was Jim, I think –* Jim took him on trips to northern Minnesota.

There was a blackness about Ed's thoughts and he tried to clear his mind. A glimpse of the man's hand on Robby's shoulder. The diffidence of his son as he returned from a weekend trip to the North Shore. A sense of panic began to rise in Ed's chest and he stood up suddenly and lifted his hands to the skies.

"Father God, have I been blind all these years? I didn't see this? I failed Robby?" A sob rose in his throat and he choked out the words. "His guilt. My anger. My lack of understanding…

oh, God. Forgive! Forgive…" he said as he fell to his knees at the edge of the grass, the tears falling freely.

Jill and Ed slept in later that next morning. Ed had slipped back into bed well after midnight, grateful for his wife's warm body. The call from Bill woke them and Ed fumbled, reaching for the bedside phone.

"Pastor. Ed. It's Bill. I'd like to talk to you if you have some time today." His voice was barely audible and there was a strained note in his voice.

"Sure, Bill. You can come right over. We're just getting up now, so give us an hour or so. What's up?"

"Kellie just got back from her overnight in Minneapolis with her friend Eunie, Pastor." Bill's words were choked out as if through a sieve. "Pastor, she's gone and had an abortion. She and Eunie went to a Planned Parenthood clinic in St. Paul. She's killed the baby."

51

George walked into the Crossroads Convenience store with a jaunty step. "I see you have a full pie safe, Romyn," he said, sitting heavily at the table. Romyn predictably waited on him as he knew she would and he attacked his banana cream pie with gusto. "It gets better and better," he avowed. "Hope that little girl doesn't give up her pie making business with all the ideas she brought back from New York."

"What have you heard, George? As far as I know, she's back at the pie baking and figuring out how to do the herb business, too. Paul has got the pack house done and they're deep into the thick of drying herbs. Don't know how she does it. More energy than me, that's for sure."

"She doesn't have kids to raise," George said. "You and Earl have your hands full. I'll tell ya'. I watched Tom and Shiloh work that tiller in Eva's old garden and I was amazed at the strength in that girl. She was bossing him around."

"Yeah, they were in here earlier today. All tired out. She couldn't wait to tell me how she's planting the flower clock in Eva's old garden. She and Brian found an old book that shows flowers that bloom at different times of the day and nothing would do but that they'd plant the garden her way. Tom said they spent hours at the greenhouse place in Brainerd."

"Kids! Where do they get these ideas, anyway?" George scoffed.

"Well, Carl Linnaeus in 1751, I think," Romyn said drily.

"So...?" George asked.

"Morning glory and daylily at six in the morning. Before you get up, George! Sweet pea at eleven in the morning. Four o'clock at – you guessed it – four o'clock, evening primrose at five at night and then moonflower at six. There are a couple others for later at night, too. Tom was telling me that Shiloh was insistent that they have a sundial in the middle of the garden and they were picking that up, too."

"Brian with her?" George asked.

"No," she replied. "Why do you ask?"

"Wonder what he thinks about his mother selling her father's house?" George said slyly.

"You been listening to the police scanner again, George?"

"Nah. You don't get that kind of intelligence from the police. I was talkin' to Alan over at Peace Ridge Valley Realty. He was crowing – pretty happy – because Delaney texted him from London and told him to list the place."

"Really? I find that hard to believe. She's just over in England for a week or two. Trying to get herself sorted out."

"Yeah, sorted out. Leaving Brian here by himself. The little kid." George looked down sourly at his empty pie plate and slurped his coffee cup noisily. 'Week or two," he echoed.

"Well, perhaps she needs the money and goodness knows, she's not going to live in it. She has her own house here and Michael has his own place with Brian. Why does she need the big house anyway?"

"I would have thought she might have wanted to keep it for Brian. He's the only one with the name. End of the line. Maybe he'd like to have it someday."

"He's only a little boy. Probably not thinking about that kind of stuff now."

"Well, she's selfish anyway. Goin' off and leaving him."

"Michael wanted to find a way to get closer to Brian and he's been enjoying their time together. He has a girlfriend from Bloomington and they get together and do things. Brian likes her, I think."

"Well, I'll tell ya'. They don't make women like they used to. My Kathy, for example. She'd never go tramping off to London leaving a kid behind."

"George, for some women – and I think I'd put Delaney in this category – being a mother isn't completely fulfilling. They want to live their lives in a different way and though they love their kids, they want to explore other avenues for happiness."

"Yeah, and then there are women who really want kids. My Kathy and I..."

"And Jeremy and Tiff, too. And Titos and Maria. They had only the one child and he died in Afghanistan."

"By the way, speaking of the police blotter, d'ya' know what happened at Jeremy's place while he was out of town?"

"A no-good scum from out of state tried to attack Tiff, that's what happened." Romyn's face darkened when she thought of the panic and fear in Tafani's face when they arrived to comfort her. "They are tracking him down. Steve had a hunch that he might be from North Carolina and he called me to tell us that he 'has good news,' so I hope we'll be able to help Chief Baldwin with it. What a complete and utter loser! I can't tell you how much I detest this guy. Poor Tiff—she didn't deserve it."

"I suppose she'll think everyone in Peace Ridge is like that guy. Out to do bad stuff. That's not who we are here."

"I know, but things happen. Small towns in Minnesota are not immune to the stuff that goes on in big cities. It's just that it doesn't happen as often."

"Well, we don't need it, that's for sure. What's happening with your adoption, Romyn? That moving along?"

"We've had a glitch. The father wants them – I think I told you that? – but we're fighting that. Steve's working on that, too. He's back tomorrow." *And what if he's run into a dead end? What if Shapiro is legitimate? I can't bear to think about that.*

✿

Brian and Michael walked into the Petros Diner and were greeted by Titos. They could see Maria in the kitchen and she looked up with a brief smile and then turned back to her table covered with filo dough for baklava. Titos looked harried – there were many customers and it was strange to see Titos away from the kitchen.

"We'll seat ourselves, Titos," Michael smiled. "You look busy…"

"Thanks, Michael." He gestured to an empty booth and handed them the menus and dashed back to the kitchen. A young waitress soon took their orders and placed the coffee pot on the table.

"Where is the pretty lady, Dad?" Brian asked. "The one who is usually here?"

"I think she's sick today, Brian," Michael answered. "That's why they're so busy." No use telling him about the attack; that would only sicken him, as it had nearly everyone who'd heard the story.

"I wrote a poem for her, Dad," Brian said softly. "I wanted to give it to her today."

"When Titos has a moment, I'll ask him when she'll be back."

They enjoyed their pancakes and bacon in silence. Since Michael had moved to Peace Ridge from St. Cloud, he and Brian had their routine of an occasional breakfast together at Perkins or the Petros diner, and then a hike up the ridge. They'd stop at home and pick up Snow who would be over the moon with the excursion.

The door opened and Jeremy came in. Seeing Michael and Brian, he came over to their booth. Michael asked Brian to shift over and motioned him to sit.

He nodded to the waitress as she poured his coffee and then sat back with a sad sigh.

"All okay at home?" Michael asked.

"Yeah, she'll be okay. Just taking her a couple of days to adjust. She's fearful of meeting strangers now after…that."

"Totally understand. Any word?" Their conversation was deliberately opaque.

"The chief called and he has had a conversation with Steve Banfeld who was just in North Carolina. He'll be home later today and he asked me over to the station to hear his report. So perhaps..."

"I think she's really beautiful, Jeremy," Brian said softly, his eyes shining.

Jeremy patted Brian on the shoulder and said, "So do I, Brian. So does nearly everyone here in Peace Ridge."

"Tell her I'm sorry she's sick and that I hope she'll be back here soon."

"I will, Brian, and asking about her will cheer her up a lot."

"I wrote a poem for her, Jeremy. Would you like to see it?" At Jeremy's nod, he reached into his backpack and dug out his Moleskin notebook.

"This is a first," Michael said under his breath to Jeremy, nodding at Brian, who paged through his book to pause at a page with neat handwriting.

He looked up expectantly at Jeremy who smiled encouragingly.

Beautiful Stranger

Tall, an elegant tree, willowy,
Bare skin gossamer, silken.
Black eyes flash friendly and see
My confusion, senses awakened.

Exotic mountain to Midwest plains,
The Hindu Kush to simple village.
Your presence welcomed, our gain
Smiles and loving embraces pledged.

Thrive and be happy with us, we plea.
Tafani taproots sunk into warm friendly ground.

Remain here forever, your grace and your beauty
Enhances our lives, our circle of life found.

For Tafani
Brian Peterson, age 9

Jeremy sat silent at the table before clearing his throat and filling up his coffee cup again. "Brian, that's wonderful. Tiff will love it. I can't wait to give it to her."

"Maybe Titos has some paper. I will write it out for you here and you can give it to her."

Jeremy waved to catch Titos's attention and requested some paper. Titos found a placemat and handed it to Jeremy, who pulled out his own pen and handed it to Brian. "Be sure to sign it, Brian. I know Tiff will be really pleased to see it." He grabbed his iPhone and said, "And when you are writing it out, I want to take a picture of you, so she can look for you and thank you in person."

"How did you know about the Hindu Kush, Brian?" Michael asked.

"I have that old book—the old geography book, Dad, that's in the bookcase. I knew Tafani was from Afghanistan and so I looked up where it was. The Hindu Kush is a famous mountain range in Afghanistan…"

"Remember it well, Brian," Jeremy said. "Sometime maybe you and I could sit down over a map and I'd fill you in on all the places where I was there. A couple of years ago."

Brian's eyes were shining. "Did you ever see anything left from Alexander the Great, or Tamerlane, or Genghis Khan? They were all there!"

"I was near Herat, near the Western border. I have a lot of maps, but I can't remember how they played in the history of the place. I should show you my pictures from when I was there. We were in operations and on maneuvers all the time but when I had downtime I would take pictures. A lot of pictures. There's a part of the lowlands of the Hindu Kush where there are rolling fields – it reminds me of Minnesota – they called it the *pamir,* the grasslands. They were high in the mountains above the tree line We don't have something like it here because we're not high enough. Don't have enough mountains. But there was nothing like seeing the northern slopes of those mountains. You'd see goats. Sheep. Sometimes a few cows but they were rare. I'm not a farmer, but I'll tell you, I longed to be a simple Minnesota farmer when I saw that land.

"Of course, everything I saw was seen through the prism of a sniper scope. I was there to do a job. And I did it," he said definitively.

"We're glad you're home," Michael said compassionately.

"Me, too. Me and Tiff."

"Sometime I'd like to hear her story."

"She doesn't share much. And this business with the invasion – the scumbag bust into my house! Well, that will make her even more shy. And I have been trying to tell her we're all good folks here in Peace Ridge. She's not experienced that very much."

"I am sorry, so sorry, about that, Jeremy," Michael said. "I hope Brian's poem lets her know that there are more people loving her here than not. She *is* loved."

Jeremy sighed heavily. "She talks to Maria. Maria is still smarting from the attack on their car. I have a long way to go to convince her that we really *do* like foreigners. Neither of them really believes it. Titos and I try to help them along but they feel isolated and rejected." He looked out the window at the now-filled parking lot. "I do what I can, Michael. That's what I can do. But it's hard. I love my people here, but 'my people' need to show Tiff and Maria that they welcome people from other places."

"I think Tiff is really pretty," Brian said in a small voice, "and I would like to know her better. Do you think she'd visit me sometime? I know Shiloh would like to know her, too. She thinks she's fantastic. She told me."

Jeremy looked Brian squarely in the eyes and said. "Soldier to soldier, man to man, Brian. We will make this happen." He turned to Michael, and before he had a chance to say anything, Michael said, "I would love for Pam to come to Peace Ridge and meet you two, and we could have an afternoon together. Pam is my friend from Bloomington."

"Let's plan it. And soon. I've got to get Tiff out among people again. Or she'll just close up. I saw that in Afghanistan when she was so destroyed when her family and village disappeared. I promised her that Peace Ridge Village, Minnesota would become her new family. It hasn't happened exactly like I planned." Jeremy poured himself another cup of coffee. "It's just…we are finding it hard to fit in. Tiff is …a little too strange, exotic… for some of our people. I don't know what to do about it. Titos and Maria help. This helps," he said, gesturing around at the diner. "Maybe we can meet people here and we'll begin to fit in."

"We need to make more of an effort, Jeremy. I will spread the word. Sometimes all it takes is one person – Romyn is one – and the rest just follow behind. I think we are scared of her a little bit because she's so beautiful and so …different… from the apple pie and ice cream appearance of most of our ladies. Tiff can be threatening," he said, holding up a hand as Jeremy was about to object. "because she's so beautiful and because she doesn't look like any of us prairie folks. We are plain, build solidly so we don't blow away in the wind that sweeps across the prairies and stocky women folk are what we tend to like. Farm women. We know they'll do their part. Tiff represents a whole 'nother world to people here. And we're tired of the war in Afghanistan; we don't understand it. So there's that."

Brian had been listening to the talk. Some of it was over his head. In his mind he saw the brown woman in the brilliant, bright, colorful clothes with an entrancing smile. Deep inside himself he felt warm and comforted when he thought of her. Part of him was sad because she felt alone, but then, he himself felt alone sometimes. When Shiloh and Clay were laughing and talking about something he didn't care about.

"Jeremy," he said, catching the attention of the two men. "Tafani is *my* friend. She's my special friend. There is no one like her." He looked down at the table and rubbed his hand around in a circle on the laminate. "I would like to see her. Please tell her." A command from a nine-year-old.

"Aye, aye. Sir!" Jeremy responded.

52

"Bill, I'm coming up to Peace Ridge!" Pam exclaimed.

"Ah, you don't have to do that, Pam," Bill rejoined weakly.

"I have been worried about Kellie and this just makes me sad. And sick to my stomach," she added under her breath.

"Me, too. She didn't even talk to me about it, just went off and did it. And now she's hiding out in her bedroom crying all the time. She's locked the door and won't talk to me. I just don't know what to do."

"Have you talked to the pastor?"

"Yes, I'm headed over to see him. But he has his hands full…"

"Give me some time to make arrangements for Bradley. I may stop by in St. Cloud and leave him with Tory. She has the weekend off."

"Pam, I don't want to put you out," he said hesitantly.

"'That's what friends are for,'" she half-sang Dionne Warwick.

"What time do you think you might get here?" he asked.

"Around eight o'clock tonight? That okay?"

"Yeah, that's fine. I'll treat you to a fine dinner at the Tall Rigger."

"Looking forward to it, Bill."

Looking forward to it. That musical voice rang in his head.

❀

Paul ran to grab the phone that was ringing in the kitchen. He was just about to head out the door. Probably for Jennie, but she was moping around in the bedroom.

"Hello, Paul?" It was the lawyer for the class action lawsuit against the county and Dane Johnson. Paul groaned internally. Just what he wanted: a legal conversation when the fields were calling. Jennie usually ran interference for him with this stuff.

"I have some good news Paul, and I am calling all the plaintiffs in the case. You will be happy to hear that the county has agreed to an out-of-court settlement," he said, with a note of satisfaction in his voice. "They will, of course, restore all the land records to reflect the true ownership. That had to be done at a minimum, but they've done more. We insisted on it. They have changed their procedures at the courthouse so no one person has that much authority and they are building in new safeguards. Don Jenkins, of course, is facing felony theft charges for stealing the deeds and titles and that will proceed as a separate trial. Serious stuff.

"Dane Johnson is also facing felony theft and deception charges. Mark Prentiss, the lawyer, too. Their trials will be handled in Hennepin County as a violation of state law and they're facing quite lengthy sentences. Johnson has posted bail and is out on his own recognizance. Mark, too."

"Would expect someone like Dane to skip the country," Paul said.

"Yes, not too easy to do. He will violate his probation if he leaves Minnesota. So he'll likely stick around. Guy like that thinks he's smarter than everyone else, so he probably thinks he can beat the charge."

"What about the tribe? The Moc-a-Sioux?"

"Little more complicated. They have hired a lawyer who claims this is a sovereign nation case, not just land theft. It'll go to court and I don't think they'll win, but it will be dragged out. But the important thing is that they have no claim on any of your land. Or Bill's, or George's, Eva's...that has all been resolved with the county's plea."

"Well, I'm glad it's getting wrapped up. I knew you guys were working on it and I trusted you, but every time I thought about how close we came to losing our land, it made me sick to my stomach."

"One bad apple...well, two or three. Dane Johnson and his lawyer accomplice, Mark Prentiss, and Don Jenkins at the court house. Can create a pretty big mess. I'm sorry it's taken over a year to get this resolved, but I think you'll be happy with the outcome."

"Yes, I am, and I can't wait to tell Jennie."

"Yes, and here's something else you can tell her. The county has agreed to pay damages to all plaintiffs. We are in the phase of negotiating the amount right now, but you can tell your wife that she can go to Mall of America to do a little shopping if she wants."

"Great. Any idea...?"

"Somewhere between $75,000 and $100,000 for each of you. That should help out."

"Heck! Forget Mall of America. We're heading over to John Deere!"

Steve's step was jaunty as he strode into the Crossroads Convenience store, greeting Romyn with a big smile.

"Glad you're back, Steve," Romyn said. "We missed you."

"Well, I like North Carolina all right, but there's no place like Minnesota. Miss the mosquitoes!"

"No mosquitoes down south?"

"Oh, yeah. They have mega mosquitoes with all the floods they've had recently. They have everything – Asian beetles, cockroaches – I'm just happy to be back home."

"How is Veronica?" Romyn asked intuitively.

"She's good. She even told me she'd go on my next trip. I might have some time and we can take a quick trip to the Black Hills or somewhere. Take her away somewhere so she doesn't have to spend all her time thinking about stuff. Wears her down."

"I know. She's confided some of that to me. But she's making progress."

"Yes, she is." He smiled. "And so are we! Let me fill you in."

"Please do!"

"I just came from meeting with Chief Baldwin and filling him in on what I found in Hillsborough at the deed and registry office. Here's the good news: I have copies of both Sophie and Clay's birth certificates. Their last name is Jamps, not Shapiro."

"Was that—?"

"Yes, that was Lisa's maiden name. Lisa Jean Jamps of Morrisville, North Carolina. And the good news: the name Shapiro does not appear anywhere on the certificates. In fact, it says 'father unknown.'"

"Praise the Lord!" Romyn said, tears beginning to fill her eyes. "I have to call Earl. He's been so anxious. Praise the Lord!"

"It's weird. The ladies at the registry office told me that Richard Shapiro had been nosing around there a few weeks ago but they didn't give him anything. Here is the strange thing: He is married to a Lisa, but it's not our Lisa. She showed me the marriage record on the downlow—I think because I schmoozed her a bit. But because I'm not a relative, I don't have the rights to have a copy. I think she felt sorry for the whole situation, especially the kids. She knew the Jamps family, spent time with Lisa's parents in the nursing home in their final years. I was able to fill her in on Lisa and the kids. She was happy to learn that they are okay. In any event, Chief Baldwin will be able to get a copy of it if he needs it for his prosecution of Richard Shapiro."

"Prosecution? Won't we just get the paperwork to our lawyers and they'll take it from there? I suppose we could prosecute on the basis of adoption interference, but that seems weak..." Romyn looked confused.

"Prosecution of attempted rape of Tafani Hardin. Your Richard Shapiro is—"

"Dirty shoes! The same guy?"

"Yes, I was able to do a little bit more sleuthing while I was in North Carolina. I had the security camera picture which wasn't very good, but I was able to research the faculty records of the university and discovered the photos online of the adjunct faculty in the Sociology department. That's how I found out he was married though he doesn't live with his wife. From there it was a simple way to track him down on Ancestry.com. I pulled the two pictures and was able to compare them and they were a clear match.

"So that's when I decided to haunt a couple of the watering holes near the campus. I figured he was a drinker because Tiff told us that his breath smelt awful, like nail polish remover. As a Muslim she's not around alcohol very much and wouldn't recognize ketone breath. Anyway I got lucky. The first bar I visited, The Essex, is one that he and his buddies go to a lot. I showed the photo to the bartender and he recognized him right away. Comes in on Friday nights and drinks microbeers until he's stupefied. Happily I was there on a Friday night and did some undercover surveillance. The guy is an idiot. Bragging his visit to 'Nowhereville Minnesota' and his 'towering piece of tail' he got while there. Describing Tafani in the most unflattering terms."

"Let me guess: you also had a tape recorder?"

"Just happened to have a curious ballpoint pen handy." He smiled.

"Oh, that's a relief. I'm sure the chief was happy to talk to you."

"Yeah, all we had to do was restrain Jeremy from a quick trip to Chapel Hill. He was ready to get in his truck and drive 1,300 miles non-stop to murder the guy."

"I wouldn't want to mess with Jeremy."

"The chief calmed him down. Told him to let justice work its way. The best news for Tiff and Jeremy is that he's not from here. She was beginning to lose faith in Peace Ridge Village people."

"Steve, you are a marvel. I can't tell you how relieved and happy we have what we need to get the adoption underway again. Clay has been asking about Lisa and the sooner we get it finalized, the better."

"Yes, well, he's in trouble. We have quite a good case against him with the attempted rape and you or the State of Minnesota could probably press fraud charges, too."

"So he came to Peace Ridge Village to scope us out and to also do some awful dirty work," she said. "I called him a scumbag. I stand by that description."

"Chief told me the kids, Clay and Shiloh, had gotten his number when they spotted him at the grand opening for the Petros Greek Diner. That they thought he was bad news right away. The big clue for me was when Clay told us that he 'sorta recognized' the guy, that he gave him a creepy feeling, and he thought he'd been with his mom, Lisa. That tied your Richard Shapiro, erstwhile husband to Lisa, to Tiff's attacker."

"Needs to get a reward, I think," Romyn said fondly.

"Well, actually, there is a reward. Titos and Maria have put up $5,000 for information leading to the arrest of Tiff's attacker. I think a case could be made that Clay and Shiloh deserve it."

"Hmmm. Something to think about. They're both too young to get that kind of money, but it could be saved for college." Romyn was thoughtful.

"Here's something else I discovered. Lisa's parents' farm— house and land— is for sale, and once they deduct the cost of the nursing home care for her parents who both died in the last year, the proceeds should go to Lisa. I talked to a lawyer friend of mine who's working with the Ramsey County police force to track down Lisa's attacker and get her back to Minnesota. He will work with the Hillsborough County and State of North Carolina people to make sure the net proceeds go to Lisa. It can go to her care and possibly to Clay and Sophie."

"I think Clay would like the fact that he had some connection to the family farm. Did you see it, Steve?"

"Yes, it's rather forlorn, but I have pictures to show to Clay someday."

"I'd love to see them, too, Steve," Romyn said. A barely formulated thought came to her mind. *Farm for sale in North Carolina.*

Romyn walked around the end of the counter and embraced Steve. "You're a true friend, Steve," she said with a tearful smile. "Could you and Veronica come over tonight to have dinner with us? I'd like Earl to hear the good news from you directly. And maybe it would be a chance to show Clay the pictures; he needs a little cheering up these days."

George came into the store with a big smile on his face. "Romyn, sit down and let me give you the good news, if you haven't already heard it?"

"This is a day full of good news," she replied. "You have more?"

"Just talked to the lawyer for the Dane Johnson mess. It's going to be settled out of court by the county, and a bunch of us are going to get a pile of cash."

"Oh, George! That's a blessing. Praise the Lord!"

"Yes, praise the Lord! I tell you, it was weighing on my mind. I knew the lawyers were working it but until it got to this point I was afraid he'd get away with it. Takes off a big burden."

"What are you going to do with your riches, George?"

"I don't know. I'm too old to spend the cash on myself. What do you think I need? Nothing—that's what I need! I'll tell you what I've been thinking, Romyn. I would like to set up a scholarship fund for the kids in Peace Ridge. The Kathy Govitch Scholarship Fund. It would go to the kids that want to stay here and farm or build a business or whatever. Just so's they stay away from the big cities. That's where they get corrupted."

"That's a great idea, George," Romyn said. "But I would call it the George and Kathy Govitch Scholarship Fund. You're a big part of this community. Kathy was, too, but don't sell yourself short. People love you here."

George smiled at that. He didn't get many compliments and he'd take them when he could.

"I'll take that into consideration, Romyn. I've been thinking. There's a new teacher at the high school – one who replaced that scoundrel drama teacher – this guy teaches the kids about social media and digital communications. All the new stuff. Wouldn't it be great to give a scholarship to a couple of Peace Ridge kids in that field? Would bring us into the 21st century. I'm too old to catch up, but these young'uns like Clay, or Brian and Shiloh. It's right up their alley. Anyway, I just know that I want to put that money to good use. Like you and Earl are doing with The Jason House."

"Yes, well, it's a blessing to be able to do it. I just have to tell you, George. I'm bursting with news that I have to share but you dare not tell anyone. I haven't told Earl yet – I will tonight. Please, please! Keep this a secret: the adoption will go through. The father that was fighting it doesn't have a claim. Steve found that out when he got Clay and Sophie's birth certificates in North Carolina this last week."

"Ah, I knew it would work out. He's something else, that Steve."

"Yes, if you are up to no good, you don't want him nosing around." Romyn smiled and thought about how hard he'd worked to find Jason. But now he'd restored Clay and Sophie to them and that was blessing enough. That was enough. *Praise God from whom all blessings flow!*

"George, how about a home-cooked meal at my house tonight? Steve and Veronica will come and we can have a little happy party. What do you think?

"Do I ever turn down a home-cooked meal, Romyn?" he asked with a broad smile. *And to be there when Earl hears the good news. Well, that's icing on the cake.*

Romyn walked around the store after George left, checking that there was enough water and food for the guard cat, Millie. Time to celebrate a little tonight. She grabbed several Heggie's pizzas from the freezer, a gallon of vanilla ice cream, and a couple of liters of root beer. It might be an adult party, but they'd eat like children. *And I feel like a kid again,* she thought. To finally set aside the worry about Clay and Sophie and just feel that they all had a future together. *Well, God is good.*

"You are great and greatly to be praised," she said to the peaceful, quiet store as she clicked on the "Closed" neon sign and closed the door. "Greatly to be praised. Thank You, Lord Jesus. For blessings received."

About the Author

M arilyn Hayes Phillips lives with her husband, Lem, in rural Minnesota. She is the author of "A Wild Olive Shoot", an autobiography of her spiritual journey, and "Shattered Peace", Book One of the Peace Ridge Village series and Book Two "Jason's Gift" which continues the Peace Ridge Village Series. She has also penned a memoir of her family history with a cookbook entitled "How About a Little Lunch?" with a significant family history tracing back to 1749 and over 650 "keeper recipes" from the family.

CPSIA information can be obtained
at www.ICGtesting.com
Printed in the USA
FSHW011533230719
60313FS

9 781545 666111